Edna A. Barnard

Maple Range

Edna A. Barnard

Maple Range

ISBN/EAN: 9783337878849

Printed in Europe, USA, Canada, Australia, Japan

Cover: Foto ©Andreas Hilbeck / pixelio.de

More available books at **www.hansebooks.com**

A FRONTIER ROMANCE.

MAPLE RANGE.

BY

EDNA A. BARNARD.

"That we may lift from out of dust,
A voice as unto him that hears,
A cry above the conquered years."

CHICAGO:
HENRY A. SUMNER & CO., PUBLISHERS.
1882.

CONTENTS.

MAPLE RANGE.

CHAPTER I.

THE MAPLES.

"The liberal board for welcome stranger spread."

"WHOA! Hold on, Nellie! Don't you see here is the winning tree, and you are past it ever so much?"

"Yes, Robbie, but we came so suddenly upon the tree, galloping round that old Indian mound, that I could not stop my pony at once. Yonder is home, too, and allow me to quote from my old text-book, 'At the right hand I descry the dark blue waters of an inland sea.' I was ahead at the tree. I won the race!"

"Yes, you are the winner, and I am as ready to meet the consequences and pay up, as I would be exacting if old Deacon had been more fleet. Let's see! I was to row you across Lake Loui, Nellie, and so I will tie the horses, and leave them here in the shade till we come back. Whoa, Sampson! you savage! A girl's pony ought to be less ready to show bite. Whoa! I say."

"Now, don't be cross with my pony; he thinks it time for something to eat after that race."

"He can't dine off me if he is hungry; I need

9

my own shoulder to carry my gun, and if divided
with him, we should all fare poorly for game, I think.
He likes post meat, and he may eat this tree, bark
and all, and welcome.

> ' Come and glide along the tide,
>   And sing to tuning oar.' "

" There's not an oar here, brother, and the boat
is half full of water. How about our afternoon
sail ? "

" Oh, that is certain enough. I shall bail out the
boat with my old straw hat, and show you how old
Mock-ane-sah propels a dug-out independently of oars.
I can take you over the lake in a jiffy, and make you
just as proud of me, as if I was really an Indian,
instead of being only an Indian's pupil in the art of
boating."

"And whose pupil in the art of bragging, eh ? "

"Nobody's ; that is not an acquisition. Blowing
is just as natural as winking."

" I know it is, with big things, such as whales and
the wind, but somehow I never thought you—"

" There, now the water is out ! Nellie, jump in
and take a seat well forward, so as to give plenty
space for the shifting of my birchen propeller. Away
we go ! "

"O goodness me ! we shall surely roll over. See
how the awful thing tips ! We shall be drowned, I
know we shall ! Stop and let me jump out ! I *will*
get out—right here ! "

" How much better is it to jump into water than
to tip in, I should like to ask ? When you get a little
more placid, tell me. In any case you are sure of a

good ducking. But don't be scared, little sister; we are not going over. If you sit still and keep cool, you are all right in my boat. There, is n't that nice, now?"

"Splendid! But why don't you sing, my brave poler?"

"Sing! Yes, that 's appropriate; but what shall I sing? 'Swiftly glides my bonny boat?'"

"Not that song, in a dug-out! Let 's sing together something more in keeping with the style of our craft."

"Will you sing, too?"

"Gladly. I feel just like singing."

A sweet, thin, girlish pipe and a youth's fresh voice, something between a woman's treble and a man's falsetto, bear up the boatman's well-known air.

> "'Push along, boys, push along, boys.
> Merrily, cheerily, push along!
> And whilst our prow makes merry music,
> We 'll, too, raise the song.
> Each to his pole, boys, bend to each pole, boys,
> And whilst the waters ripple round us.
> We 'll, too, raise the song.'"

"How clear the water is, Robbie! I believe I could reach the bottom, and get a handful of pebbles, if you would not shove along at such a rate."

"Don't try that, Nell! Those pebbles, that look now so near, are many feet below the surface. 'T is refraction makes them seem so near. This boat requires an equilibrium of ballast. You are safe enough, if you sit still; but if you lean over the side, we shall capsize. It is necessary to keep your per-

pendicular while navigating this inland sea, in an outlandish craft."

" Why don't you post that caution in some con-
spicuous place in your cabin? The safety of the
traveling public demands it."

"Oh, I prefer repeating it to my passengers, and
getting up a reputation as a sociable, attentive and
jolly sea-captain, who looks to the safety and comfort
of those who sail with him, while he spins yarns and
sings for their entertainment."

" But do you ever transport mermaids in your
old canoe ? "

"Both out of date."

"Both what ? "

" Why, transportation as a penalty, and the queer
water-women you mention—that makes two, don't it ? "

" I s'pose ; but say, are those mounds, so thick
upon the shore, the graves of the obsolete mermen
and maidens ? "

" Oh, those are not graves of the dead ; they are
homes of the living. They are muskrat houses, with
hollow runways beneath the shore. There are some
of my traps which I'll take along, and bring out
again when fur is prime."

" What a lovely cove at our right. I wish we
could explore it—so sheltered, dark and cool ! "

" I'll just cut a pigeon wing with the dug-out and we
will go clear up that arm of the lake. Here is where
we killed the doe, last week, and captured her fawn.
'T was a mistake. Father did not mean to kill a deer
this time of year—was fire-hunting for other game.
I wish you could, or would come with us some night.

I know you would be charmed with lamp-lit views of green trees and still waters, the night sending back the rays of light, and perhaps, of a great antlered buck, standing out bold and beautiful on the margin of the bay, his eyes blinded by the unaccustomed brilliancy, turning toward strange sounds. I will push to deeper water over there, and show you where I caught the curiously mustached pout, armed with his dangerous dagger, the other night. I told you how mournfully the loon cried, and you thought fishing at night must be dismal work ; but I like it."

"Oh, show me where you find trout. "

" Directly. Let's sing again."

Over the waves and among the interlacing trees, leaps and creeps the batteau man's song, " Push along, boys," while rapidly is ascended the long watery avenue. Suddenly Robert cries : " Bend low now ! This vicious willow took hold of me, Absalom-fashion, once. It guards the mouth of Willow Run, a little brook that has no self-assertion, or importance. But here, a little more demonstrative," he added a moment later, " is Dimple Run. Bend while we pass the pikes of defense ; now we are in the deepest, though narrowest, channel of the stream— my favorite haunt, where I decoy the speckled trout."

" What makes the water look so green ? Don't dip your hat in it !"

" I want to show you how mistaken you are. The water is as clear as crystal. See ! In my hat, it is not green, but clear and pure and cool as in our own spring at home. The appearance of deep green is caused by the water-cress that covers the bottom, and affords a lurking-place for the most delicate and dainty fish that is beguiled by the angler, which in turn beguiles the epicure."

"This place is growing really dark and lonesome, Robert. If you would only go back now! I am afraid, it is so still here, with the rushes and alders so thick and high upon the bank. I shudder as I fancy some huge, wild creature, man or beast, crouched low in that tangled growth, ready to pick me out of the canoe. Most terrible now comes the thought, we can't turn round, the brook is so narrow. What will we do with this great long unwieldy log, our only method of escape, and that useless to return."

"Don't go distracted over nothing, you foolish little puss! There is nothing to be afraid of. Every bush and willow on the bank are friends of mine, and consequently yours. I will go back with you certainly, you look so scared and white; but as to turning the boat round, that is not necessary. Our barge is like a craw-fish; will go as well one way as the other. The propeller only has to change ends."

"Oh, I comprehend. You stand on your head, going back!"

"That laughing relieves me, Nell! I am sure your fright is past, and I grant you license to make the woods ring with your fun, though I generally caution my passengers not to poke fun at, or 'sass' the commander, while they still have to cross the high seas with him."

"Thanks, for the courteous exception in my favor. Still, I think I will defer all indecorum of spirits till we have crossed the 'still and silent lake.'"

" Now we are once more on the bosom of Lake Loui, I will sit down and rest my pole while enjoying with you a tranquil float on this enchanted wave. Look up, Nellie, and look again below. See how, at rest, we seem to hang between two equally distant and curving skies. I have floated this way alone hundreds of times. This spot, which makes me seem an atom with no visible relation, has a peculiar attraction for me. I am always so happy here, I could muse and sing and float forever! I sometimes think, by a little study, I could learn to read marvelous things. Looking down into the lower sky, where the white clouds glide, one from below another, are the slow-sliding leaves of a great manuscript. Look closely, Nellie. They unfold for us either a poem, a revelation, or a prophecy."

"We had better consult the sun, which lays a command upon us to hunt up our horses and hurry home."

" A very sensible command, too! My inner conscience enjoins absolute obedience, as I believe it's a commandment, with promise of supper, and—true as I live, a long walk for me. Old Deacon has slipped his bridle and gone home without me!"

"Well, what of that? Sampson carried off the gates of Gaza, and his namesake ought to be able to carry double.

"All right! I will ride with you, Nellie, and we won't be long going home."

The speaker was, perhaps, fifteen years old, large of his age, and of bright intellect. Well-trained thought lent a luster to his eyes, and spread its grace over his handsome face.

His companion was a lovely girl, many years his junior; fair of face, so pearly in tint and delicate in outline that, but for a gaiety of manner amounting to playfulness, you would have called her spirituelle. She was a fragile, wavering, half-timid vine, clinging to sturdier natures. But fragile as she was, her very clinging strengthened and ennobled her brother, who, adventurous and daring to a fault, became gentle and thoughtful as a girl, in her companionship. Looking with his clear blue eyes into her own as blue, he would talk of her flowers, or listen to the curious dreams she had a charming way of relating, forgetful that other companionship would be desirable. These two, all in all to each other, were the only children of the only white settler in a new, uncultivated region, the then frontier of Minnesota. Their father, Mr. James Maynard, an English gentleman of means, had settled recently in plain sight of Lake Loui, though a goodly two miles away. Look you directly north from the lake, across the green, billowy prairie, whose grasses sweep to the foot of an upland that rises abruptly, and then spreads out to a table, broad and magnificent. This table was originally heavily timbered; but the larger trees have been cut down, leaving a fine grove as great protection against the furious snows and winds that often threaten to overwhelm the traveler. North of this table another rises, and another of less depth and more inclination, which retains also much of the forest growth of maples, and presents a beautiful outline as it stretches back. At the distance of half a mile, the timber grows more dense, forming a right royal crown to this commanding eminence, and is the commencement of a maple forest of many miles extent. A double log house stands (or did, at the time our story commences) on the first-mentioned, or lowest table-land, midway in the maple grove. Its new shining roof was a land-mark by day, and its lighted windows beacons by night, to the chance pilgrim along the territorial road. This road followed Lake Loui's western shore, a mile or more perhaps, then, keeping due north across its outlet turned east at the foot of the first plateau, continuing at its base, and following its contour to the entrance of a ravine, which led up to the high land of the maple forest ; then stretched away on through the wood to an old stockade, built long ago for Indian defense, but now in decay.

In the vicinity of the lake, nature has been particularly lavish of noble views. The one from the lake of the twin plateaus, the new home in the grove nestled up to the bosom of a high forest. Looking eastward over an immense prairie under certain atmospheric conditions you will see the blue waves of a lake, fifteen miles away. Nearer, your eye may trace the sinuous course, and in some places you may even see the waters, of Dimple Run, as it comes down from its forest source, threading the prairie and contributing its liquid wealth to the picturesque Lake Loui.

When this eastern view palls the senses, bend your gaze upon that smooth prairie directly south,

and thank heaven for the blessedness of vision that
embraces not only the prairie but the lake and
forest beyond, as an emerald frame, reflected in the
deep crystal mirror.

A sunset mist often hangs over the outlet of Lake
Loui, as it creeps down toward the west, and the
delicious languor of the vine-clad hills of Italy is repeated in the atmosphere of this broad valley. The
Waubece river comes silently around the heights of
the northwest, and, meeting the outlet, grows noisy
as it dashes down in numberless cascades. Your
eye may follow this broad valley by its northern
bluffy battlements, hoary and gray and scarred with
time, or its southern line, sooner lost to view, of green
hills and shady vales.

The home of Mr. Maynard, builded in this grove
of marvelous beauty, was christened THE MAPLES.
It was one of Minnesota's new and lone homes, but had
already become known afar for the "rest and guid-
ance, food and fire," insured those who crossed its
friendly threshold. Its owner had found this part of
Minnesota wild and sparsely settled, but beautiful
beyond all his most extravagant fancies; containing
the elements of commercial and agricultural grandeur. He believed its settlement hazardous only as
it was remote from white neighborhood and protection, as the Indians would certainly manifest hostility, and guard with jealous eye all the inroads of
civilization upon their rich hunting-grounds. He
was so captivated by these lovely surroundings that
he resolved to hazard even savage ire in their lawful
possession. He had much hope in establishing

friendly relations by the Christian conciliation, which he believed not only possible, but imperative, in dealing with a savage race. He purchased largely of the government, and his place had wide fame for the comfort of its appointments, the urbanity of its master and the generosity of its mistress. A long distance in any direction would weary the traveler who sought a white man's roof; so, first of necessity, later of preference, many were warmed by the huge fire-place and brake bread at the well-ordered table. The extra chair at one, and plate at the other, bespoke an expected, though a stranger, guest, to a friendly welcome. The two buildings that composed the house were connected by one roof, with a large space between. The eastern part contained two sleeping-rooms and the family sitting-room. The western apartment, large and convenient, was devoted to cooking, eating and general housework. It was a warm, comfortable and pleasant home, considered quite fine by the frontiersmen. The large, well-built out-buildings and shelters told their own story of the thrifty farmer, and the merciful man considerate of his beast.

Mrs. Maynard was of good Scottish birth, the daughter of a gentleman with some wealth who had the misfortune to inherit a suit in chancery and a hope of winning it. Consequently, a great portion of his money passed early in life into the possession of greedy Barnacles. At his death, he had little to bequeath his daughter, save what she valued most, his blessing. She had received at his hands a treasure more enduring than gold, a

thorough education, which he had personally super-
vised. Her social advantages had been of the most
ennobling character, from which her ingenuous soul
had easily taken impressions. Truth's moulding is so
much more exquisite where there are no thwarting
influences to overcome. Her own and her husband's
early history, interesting as the narration might be, is
not essential to my story. I present them to you,
gentle reader—a gentleman of sterling qualities, rare
culture and deep piety, striving to redeem from
the wilderness a home whose foundation should
have permanence ; a lady who would grace any
home, however elevated, and blessing particularly this
one upon the frontier, herself the mirror of her
husband's and children's happiness, as well the most
efficient agent in its creation. Husband and wife,
together toiling earnestly for the good of all within
their reach.

Here, even on the frontier, Mrs. Maynard
proved the value of education, for her children were
as well-taught as she had been. In the forest of
Minnesota, far from civilized habitation, the winter
evenings were employed by her children with books,
charts and scholastic instruments, as the evenings
of her early life had been, away on the banks
of the rippling Tweed. It was one of those wintry
evenings, following the summer of our first introduc-
tion to Robert and Nellie. The skating on Lake Loui
had been spoiled by a recent heavy fall of snow.
The gallant officer of the " outlandish craft," and his
timid passenger were engrossed with books and reci-
tations, while their mother seemed a girl again, as

she helped them through the mist that often obscures
the young scholar. Thoughtfully, she had drawn back
the curtains from the south window, saying, "The
snow is so deep, progress would be painfully slow
to him whose way is clear, but God pity the bewildered wayfarer on such a night as this!" Her husband looked up from his paper, his pipe and his
pippins, into his wife's face, smiled approval of her
thought, and as if to supplement the small charity
expressed, heaped the dry sticks of maple upon
the fire, already sputtering and roaring up the great-
throated chimney, till the room was one blaze of light
and warmth; and chairs drew instinctively nearer
the fire.

Nellie said: "It's too cold to comprehend a lesson to-night! Will you excuse me, mother? Father,
please pass the apples?" But father was dozing
in his arm-chair, with feet on a decorous rest.
Robert came forward, helped his mother and Nellie,
finally himself, to the golden fruit, and was seating
himself to enjoy it, when they were all startled by a
stentorian "Hullo, the house, thar!"

Mr. Maynard, his wife, children, Cloe the domestic, and Hall the hired man, were speedily at open
doors, peering out into the gloom of the stormy night.

A nondescript vehicle on runners had anchored
near the steps, and was rapidly discharging its freight
of shivering children. In obedience to some silent
unseen agency, the living parcels rolled out, utterly
regardless of the precaution, "This side up;" but
fast as they rolled out, Mrs. Maynard, Cloe and

Nellie, bore them into the warm sitting-room, and disposed them comfortably.

Mrs. Maynard again stood upon the porch, waiting for more parcels, while her husband stepped out into the deeper gloom, where he heard muffled and peculiar sounds, as if some overworked engine was striving to recover its breathing ; sure enough, a snorting human locomotive labored into view from near the horse's head, and, with much slapping of chilled hands, delivered himself satisfactorily in having "got thar at last." He was grizzled and grim and frosty, as he made his way toward Mr. Maynard, and extending his hand, in a voice pitched to the key which came into use with railroad crossings and deaf switch-tenders, shouted :

"How d' ye du, squar ! My name's Wilson— William H. Wilson, if you want the whole figger. I 'm movin' my gang and plunder up country, and I reckoned ye 'd give us a bunk and some provender here, t' night. Leastways, I telled my woman, that's Betsey, that 't would be playin' powerful low down on us, ef ye didn't, for it 'pears like we are enamost done out, her and me, ain't we Betsey ? Say, Betsey ! What ails ye, woman ? Come, get out o' that thar concern, now ! The lady has got the children in by the fire, and says we are all welcome. Betsey ! "

"Oh, go long, William ! It 'pears like you 're worse than Balaam's critter ! The young ones are all out, but Theoph, and I am so stiff and cold I can't get him out of the twilts and wrappin's. He is fast asleep, ye see, an' ef ye don't move lively and fetch

him out o' that kiver, I won't answer but he will be
froze stiffer 'n a mackerel."

Mrs. Maynard had now got hold of the poor
woman's arm, and, while the husband disappeared
under the " kiver," in search of Theophilus, led her
into the house, where the children were already showing signs of warmth and returning life. Wilson,
soon after, came in with Mr. Maynard, bearing the
sleeping child, who was not frozen, or even cold, the
mother had so comfortably disposed him in the
sleigh. Robert had gone with the hired man to attend
the one horse which drew this load of humanity ; that
is, was supposed to have drawn them ; but when
the fire had done its work, and Wilson had thoroughly
thawed out, some light was thrown on this.

"Stranger," said Wilson, addressing Mr. Maynard, "one of my hosses caved in teetotally, a spell
below here, by the lake ; fell down dead at the 'half
breed tract,' and t'other one pulled the load, with
me a-pushin' behind, till we got foreninst the pitchin'
off place of your bench, thar. I had onhitched the
dead hoss and drug him out into the snow by the
road-bed—as I was sayin', the other hoss drew the
load till jest below here—when I see he was in a fair
way to give out too. Well, I jest took hold beside him,
and old gray and me done some of the peartest pullin'
outside of a dentist's shop. I hain't got the most
powerful purchase on the ground, nor old gray so
much meat on his bones that butchers spot his stall;
but say, now, you can hitch us up together, and,
stranger, I lay we will pull even and move anything
that is cut loose at both ends. Why, my woman will

tell ye we made better time than the two hosses, didn't we, Betsey ? "

Betsey had fallen· asleep in her chair in the midst of her eight roguish, rosy, rustic children, ranging in regular order, a half head difference between them. They might have been likened to stairs, commencing with little toothless Tad and topping off with the buxom Ruth Ann. Supper was soon in readiness, and they all filed into the kitchen, the children given high seats, the parents made to feel that even larger families could be accommodated. Wilson discoursed less of his mishaps during the meal; but his wife seemed more talkative, over her cup of tea. She said :

"It seems almost a impersition to crowd in so late at night ; but what with the poor slippin' and the dead beast, we got belated a heap. I did feel powerful feared we would perish, when it grew dark, but then we seed your light, and oh, ef you only could know the courage that came into our hearts ! I was on my knees, rubbin' the children's feet to keep the frost out, and, though my teeth chattered and my hands shook like the fever 'n' ager, yet I told 'em funny stories to make 'em laugh, for I thought a good ha-haw would 'liven 'em and set the blood to circula-tin'. When we fust cum out of the woods round the lake shore, William said, 'Thar is the north star ; ' and, sure enough, it looked like it, only a million times brighter, and we knew ef we could only stand it across the prairie, we would bring up, in the eend, at a warm coop ; and we did, thanks to our Heavenly Father."

This was the first meal, as paterfamilias affirmed, that had been partaken "square" in a week; the apparent relish confirmed his statement, if there had seemed any doubt of its truthfulness. But honesty of purpose was written all over his homely face, and rung in the accentuation of every syllable that dropped from his lips. Mrs. Maynard assisted in waiting upon them, supplying the particular dish for which each showed a preference. She also discovered the existence of a family tooth for the unctuous sweet which accompanies the hominy and bacon bill of fare, prized by the class the Wilsons represented, called "low-downers." It was noticeable that Ruth Ann was the "big eater" of the family; that when the general appetite seemed to falter, hers was still up to the mark. Another piece of bread was preparing for sacrifice on her plate; had received its modicum of butter, and she was absorbed in the action of pouring syrup over it, watching with pleased abstraction the curves and lines that formed mouth-watering intersections. The door opened, Robert entered the room, advancing to the stove, with some boyish and pungent remarks upon the weather. The girl's eyes were transferred from her plate to his face, and fixed there by its promise rather than the fulfilment of masculine beauty. Her ideas had been formed from observation of ruder specimens of humanity, and though she could not trace to its source or name the peculiar charm which refined influences lend, she recognized its presence.

While she sat staring with wonder and admiration, her employment all forgotten, the syrup still flowed,

2

drowning the bread, filling the plate, then, slowly
swelling over the circling rim, it fell a golden river
on the table, thence to the floor. At this juncture,
her mother discovered her unfortunate predicament.
Rising quickly, with Tad in her arms, she leaned,
with detriment to the yielding cream pitcher,
clear over the table, administering a rousing box on
the poor girl's ear, shrieking :

"Wha'! thar, *you!* Are ye goin' to keep on
pourin' them molasses till ye can see the nigger grin-
nin' at the bottom of the jug? Take that! and
that!" boxing her, "and jest toddle out and scour
up a little, for, see! ye have jest gone and stuck yer
two hands in the mess, and thar's a powerful chance
ye'll get a good lickin' to top off with. Mind!"

Mortified and abashed, the girl had reached the
door before her mother's sharp words had ceased.
Great persuasion from Mrs. Maynard was necessary
before she would return to the sitting-room after
supper. Robert and Nellie were missing, but their
mother found them in the bed-room, with pillows
stuffed tightly to their mouths, their eyes full of tears
of suppressed laughter. She cautioned them against
the possibility of wounding the feelings of their
guests, by indulgence of this kind over their peculiarities.

"But, mother," said Nellie, with words hurried
by merriment, "I *shall die*, they are all so queer!"

"Yes, mother, I shall, too! One grave and one
monument for Nellie and Robert ; one inscription—
'Laughed themselves to death!' How pitiful!"

Perfect mistress of herself, as she was, even the

self-possessed Mrs. Maynard laughed at the ludicrous
picture, and left her children to recover from these par-
oxysms in their own way and time. The little people
were all glad of a suggestion to get up stairs to bed.
The kind hands of Cloe, who had a good memory of
childhood, helped them to get under the warm wool
sheets, and tucked them in. Her own bed-room Mrs.
Maynard assigned to Wilson and his wife. Nellie
and Ruth Ann occupied the other, while, on a bed
used only when company made it necessary, occupying
one corner of the large sitting-room, she would herself sleep, when the loquacious Wilson should conclude to strike in for the night. This, even at near
midnight, seemed a remote probability, for he grew,
in the quiet after the children had been sent to bed,
more voluble and communicative than before. After
awhile even "Tad" was asleep, and the hostess led
the way to the room where the Wilsons, *père et mère*,
were to repose; Mrs. Wilson returned, and seating
herself near Mrs. Maynard, said:

"I calculate that you and yer old man will sleep
in this yere bed."

"Yes," was the reply. Mrs. Maynard won-
dered at the remark, but did not have to wait long
for its explanation, as the visitor continued:

"Wall, now, you look tired-like, and delicate to
boot, though you do carry a good bit o' meat. You
needn't mind us a picayune, but turn in whenever
ye git ready. William won't never know when to
pinch off his gab, as long as yer husband shows a
shadder for him to shoot at; besides, we always have
a season of prayer, before we go to bed, no matter

where we are. You see, we 've belonged to the meetin'
nigh on to ten year; and William, as he grows in
grace, gets powerfuller and powerfuller in prayer.
He has got some very sot ways, and one is, holdin'
on to the horns of the altar a good spell. You will
git sleepy a right smart before he is through. I know
you will feel pimpin' all day, to-morrow, and may jest
as well undress and git into bed, for, bless yer heart,
William *won't look*."

But William did look at that very instant, turned
round, bestrode his chair, took another hunk of
cavendish, and stared at them while he manipulated
the sweet morsel, preparatory to new utterance. He
had not heard his wife's words—oh, no! That was
not his way. His own voice was too charming;
when it got a chance of a good run, as to-night, it
went "without let or hindrance." He only paused
to fit the tobacco well to his cheek—a good cheek—
and proceeded to square himself with his host and hostess, as it just occurred to him, might be advisable and
timely, late as it was.

"I calculate you 'ns take me to be the father of
all the childer we brung here to-night. Now, that is a
little mistake, but a harmly one, as a good pile of 'em
are mine; but my woman, thar, the fust time I ever
seed her, was leadin' Ruth Ann, and carried Peter in
her arms. It was on a steamboat; and the capting told
me she was a inconsolable widder."

"Yes," the woman interrupted; "I 'll tell ye
how 't was."

"Now, Betsey, that ain't fair! I started this explanation myself; commenced tellin' how 't was—"

"I don't care ef you did! I guess I know the story a heap better 'n you do, an' I 'm going to tell it, ef anybody does!"

"Well, go on, then!" said Wilson, evidently resigning himself to what he had reason to know was inevitable.

"In the first place," she said, "you must know me and my first man lived on the Mississippi bottoms, in old Tennessee. We emost always, one or 't other of us, had the chills—sometimes both, and the children too. Of course, we was always poor, and lived, as they say, 'from hand to mouth.' Hearin' a good bit about how much healthier it was in Illinois, we concluded to go thar somehow. Just as soon as you make up yer mind you *will* do a thing, the way is always clear. My husband found a chance and dickered with the capting of a Orleans steamboat, goin' up, to take us and our plunder, for him lendin' a hand, takin' truck off an' on the boat, at the different landin's. Well, at St. Louis, they put off a large cargo of sugar, and tuck on railroad iron, for a point above thar. When we shoved off from the levee, the good-natured mate, knowin' the hands were all tired, treated 'em to the drinks, and my man, not ever havin' been used to it, and being weak besides from the chills, felt the effects of the whisky more than the rest, and more than the mate expected he would. I was sittin' in among bales and boxes, forward, with the steerage passengers. Ruth Ann, about three years old, was standing by my knee—Peter, the baby, asleep in my arms—when, all to onct, I seed my man start to come toward us—seed him

stagger and stumble, and then disappear. A few
minutes afterwards, they brought him to me, dead.
Yes, he had fallen, in his first drunken fit, clean
through the hatchet. His neck was broken, but he
looked as natural as of he was asleep, and I s'pose I
took on powerful. It was awful lonesome, sittin'
there, day after day, on that noisy, puffin' old steamboat, with only the freight and strange people and
niggers about me, and I cried as of my heart was all
goin' to pieces. Him, that was dead and left behind,
had been a good, kind husband, though middlin' close-
mouthed—not so talkative as William, to be sure ;
but then we didn't have half so many jaws. One
of the cabin passengers, a purty creter of a girl
that had been to Orleans with her pap, come down
thar to me, in my grief, and give me a purse of
forty dollars, collected among the passengers. She
was terrible sorry for me, and put her white, dimpled
arms around my neck, which, I reckon, must a looked
a good bit browner, and begged me not to grieve so.
Stooping low to kiss the baby, while tears fell upon
his dress, she whispered of One who had promised to
be a father to the fatherless, and the widow's God. I
had been sort o' unbelievin' in sech things, but then
I had never heard the word from any one but these
loud-voiced circuit riders, who proclaimed a shriekin'
gospil, and seemed bent on scarin' folks to glory.
When she, with her low sweet voice, told me of His
tenderness and care, His mercy, His death for me—
even me, so poor and no account—my heart was
softened. I fell on my knees and prayed. I knelt a
sinner, but rose a rejoicin' Christian."

Her humble story was told in a monotonous, sing-song tone that, toward the last, sometimes was almost a wail, and then a whisper, while her face lost all its rudeness and took on an expression of peculiar gentleness—so much so that Mrs. Maynard, commenting mentally then, but afterward to her husband, declared that "Child-like faith transforms the plainest features, and the Creator's image is clearly impressed upon the brow of the believing creature." In the lull, she laid the family Bible in her husband's hands. He read a chapter, followed the reading with a brief prayer, after which a longer, boisterous prayer, exhaustive of words and lungs and listeners' patience, was made by Wilson. Mrs. Wilson, also, but in low, earnest tones, prayed, then retired at once, so that Wilson had no opportunity, in his own words, to tell "how 't was."

It was a long breakfast table in the kitchen next morning ; and, as Johnny Wilson said to his sister, "Nobody don't have to wait for nobody else to get done eating." Each chubby little stranger had a place at the table, and an appetite as well, that compared satisfactorily with those of larger growth. Here let me say, lest I forget it, that unfortunate indeed is the individual who, after a few weeks residence in this beautiful State, breathing its pure, invigorating air, fails to experience the pleasurable sensations of real Minnesota hunger.

Successive cups of coffee served to unloosen Wilson's tongue, which seemed to find no end of material upon which to comment. But for the wife, who could shut off the member at short range, his tongue might have furnished anew the suggestion of perpetual motion.

At last, however, he made some inquiry about the country "above," and received a very full and evidently satisfactory description from Mr. Maynard, and the promise to accompany him in search of a location. A courtesy which a rich speculator need never expect from such men as James Maynard, whose whole soul was devoted to the settlement of the country of his adoption, particularly this wooded, watered and productive belt of promise. He made, too, the thoughtful and generous provision that Wilson's family should remain at The Maples, until he could look around and decide if he would locate there, or go on. Both Wilson and his wife were moved to expressions of gratitude at this unexpected offer. The former, clearing his throat, said :

"It's a big offer, neighbor. My family is not used to such kindness and such quarters ; but we 'ns will accept it, bein' that I hain't got the rhino, jest at the present winkin', to do anything else but accept. But I will hope to get quits with ye somehow, in the long run of our three score years and ten ; and it 'pears like "—his eyes moistened suspiciously, here— "I can't a-bear to question too closely and put from me too independently the first streak of light that has come across my cloud for ever so long. I have, one time and another, shoved round a power, livin' now at the pillow and now at the post, with all sorts of luck, makin' moves in all sorts, too, of jumnibusses ; but I declare," he said, laughing again, "last night was the fust time I ever had to turn locomotive." Turning suddenly around, as if a new, large idea was born in his brain and struggled for expression, he looked with intentness of gaze and parted lips into his wife's face a moment, then, "D' ye mind, Betsey," he said, "the time, last winter, when I tuck young school-master Thompson to Gelena, and went with him that night to a lecture on 'Stronemy?"

"Yes; what of it?" said the wife.

"Why, I thought about that lecture, last night, when I was tuggin' along by the side of old gray, up the pitch. Ye see the man told us about a critter, put in the sky by shepherds, down there at Chaldea; though ef he had jest said Yankees, I would a-took more stock in the yarn, as they might manage to boost the thing up somehow. Anyhow, he said the thing was half hoss and half human. I done forgot the name precisely. Let me—Sent—Senter—'

"Century! I have seen the word a hundred times in readin' books. I know it's Century," said Mrs. Wilson, warmly.

Robert looked up at his mother, receiving her signal of approval, turned to Wilson, and inquiringly suggested: "Was it not Centaur, sir?"

"Yes, yes, boy; that's the very it!"

"Oh, I thought it must be Century," said Mrs. Wilson.

"That was a queer lecture, any how," continued Wilson, "got up, I warrant, by some college chap that knew so much he did n't know anything, and thought he could stuff any nonsense down a Westerner. He undertook to prove by some kind of a

C

jimcrack, I forgot the name of it, that the earth goes round the sun every so often, and turns a complete summersault itself every day ; showed just how 't was done ; and a lot of other stuff about the planits and their orbs and consolutions, and what not ; but I can't remember the name of the machine he used."

"I wonder if in this upper region," said Mr. Maynard, "we shall ever listen to such lectures upon the revolutions of the earth and other planets—ever have our perceptions quickened and benefited by scientific illustrations ? "

"Illustrations ! that was the name of the feller's machine that he handled, to show up the whole hum. bug. He told it often enough for any fool to remember, even if it 's a long word. No question about it, though ; that was the name that he called that machine of his 'n—*Illustrations !* "

Nellie and Robert were missing again ! Breakfast was over. Mr. Maynard was examining his gun, and Mrs. Maynard was putting up a lunch of biscuit and boiled ham ; but there was a perceptible quiver about the corners of their mouths as they exchanged glances, which would have comforted Rob and Nellie.

The two men were soon off on a long, tiresome tramp through the deep snow of the woods and across the drifted prairies, circling round at last to the choice timbered land, north of The Maples. A location a few miles distant was decided upon, and trees blazed to define its boundary. Mrs. Wilson and her children were made entirely at home, feeling the sweet privilege after having for so many days known only the cramped covered sleigh. Nellie and Robert, upon "hospitable thoughts intent," took care that time should not hang heavily, nor the days seem long to their young visitors, whom they liked in spite of their peculiarities of manner and speech. Evening came down almost unawares upon their enjoyable games. There was a stampede of youngsters though, when Wilson's face was discovered at the small opening of the door, and the hearty "Ho, ho, ho!" which rolled in like the tide of the sea, lifting the children it challenged, by its heartsome buoyancy. By the time he had reached the center of the room, he was literally enwreathed with his olive branches. Johnny, his own, and Pete, his foster or step-son, strove together for a seat on his shoulders. Luke and Matthew sat, one on each knee, while two little red-faced fellows tugged away in the attempt to climb up by his legs. Then his wife, with a beaming look that belied all the sharpness of her speech, came forward and laid little Tad in his bosom, her own head resting there, as it were to hold the child, but really to express her gladness at his return.

"I had no idea, Wilson, you could carry such a 'oad," said Mr. Maynard, "or I would have accepted your offer to bring in the elk we shot to day."

"Oh," was the reply, "a man can carry a big load of his own flesh and blood, kase he has so much of heart help."

"But Wilson would carry your elk, I'll be bound, Mr. Maynard, if you would just brag him up now and then. He will work harder any day for praise, than he will for pay," said Mrs. Wilson, good-naturedly.

At supper the plan was laid, and the morrow witnessed the first step towards building a house on the farm chosen in the deep woods. This farm lay on either side of the road that passed The Maples. Several succeeding days were employed in getting together logs and material for the building. In two weeks time, by the assistance of Mr. Maynard, Robert and the hired man, Wilson had built a comfortable cabin, and it waited only the occupancy of the family to constitute a veritable "lodge in the vast wilderness." Wilson looked with pride and satisfaction upon its rough-hewn walls. Hitherto, he had lived in mean, often comfortless, rented tenements; and now to call this warm, cosy cabin and one hundred and sixty acres his own, made him feel kingly. The tears stood in his eyes, but there was no weight at his heart. The floors were made of puncheons, the chimneys of mud and sticks, the roof of shakes, and the window panes were oiled paper; but a palace was never completed with more genuine satisfaction than swelled his heart, as, when after boring a gimlet hole through the rude door and slipping a narrow strip of buckskin through, he attached the wooden latch on the inside, straightening himself proudly up, thanked his neighbor that his house was done. That night was the last of the sojourn of the new comers at The Maples. They had all retired, and, with the exception of Mrs. Maynard, were asleep. The fire still burned brightly on the hearth, though it was late, when the door opened softly and the tall form of an Indian entered.

"Welcome, friend," said Mrs. Maynard.

"Ugh!" was the impressive response, as he advanced, squatting on the hearth, lit his pipe, and in a moment was smoking as if he had never done anything else.

"Are you hungry, Mock-ane-sah?"

"No; me eat venison plenty."

"Well, get a pillow from the lounge, and lie down by the fire," she added.

"Ugh! Me no want pillow. Me have no sore head afraid of stones. It is tough from lying on the ground in rain and tempest. Me no woman!"

This dusky addition to her family, sprawled full length in Mrs. Maynard's view, wrapped in his blanket on the hearth, slept as soundly as she in her feather bed. If the hired man, grown accustomed to such visits, exhibited surprise when he came in at daybreak to make the fire, what must have been that of the Wilsons, big and little, when they assembled in the breakfast room and encountered the stolid look of the big Indian. Mr. Maynard met him then, and extending his hand in welcome, said:

"What is the matter? Why do you come this long distance to see us now, when it's cold and snow is deep?"

"Mock-ane-sah don't feel cold. His heart is burning. He has trouble deeper than the snow!" With poor English, he managed to tell his story and object of his visit.

A party of his braves had, for some slight provocation, attacked a lumbering crew of white men, killing one man and fatally wounding another. The party guilty of murder, Tonewah by name, had been

arrested, and was now lying in jail at St. Paul, awaiting his trial. Mock-ane-sah, though heartily disap-
proving the course of the Indians implicated, was still
intent upon the release of Tonewah, and had come to
beg Mr. Maynard to use his influence to prevent conviction.

"My friend," Mr. Maynard said, "I can scarcely
tell you how much I regret this occurrence; but if it
is as you say, it's plain the law justly demands the
punishment of the murderer."

"Ugh! the white man's law," was the significant
reply.

"Yes; but a just law—'an eye for an eye, a life
for a life.' We feed and shelter our criminals; give
them a fair trial; but if found guilty, they must
suffer the penalty of crime."

"You think Tonewah must hang."

"Most assuredly, if he is guilty of murder. You,
too, think that he should be punished. He is a bad
Indian."

"Yes; I have great trouble with Tonewah; but
my people will not have him hung; they will make
war then."

"Well, come and eat breakfast with us, and we
will talk farther."

Full as the table had been, room was found for
him, and he had evidently eaten there many times before; he showed preference for Cloe's nice buckwheat
cakes and coffee, well sugared; also a preference
of fingers to forks. After a long talk with Mr.
Maynard, he turned his face sadly again toward the
homes of his people, far northward.

Later, Mr. Maynard's sleigh was driven round to the door by Robert. Nellie was one of the merry youngsters that went out in it to the new cabin in the wood. Wilson, with his wife, baby and "plunder," followed in the old pung, with old gray "goin' it alone," Wilson chuckled.

They had spent a happy time together and neither of the families would ever forget the mutual pleasure. The new home, so humble, was destined to become the nucleus about which a thrifty settlement would ere long cluster; and for the present, we leave it, knowing its owner, with industry and thorough farming, aided by his fish-rod and gun, will supply it with all the comforts of life.

Some time passed. Settlers multiplied, and the Indians fraternized, more than at first with the settlements — venturing more and receiving more their confidence.

After a year's incarceration, Tonewah. who had not been tried, was not only discharged from custody, but armed and equipped with a new "blanket and the accessories of Indian garb," and sent rejoicing home. As he was undoubtedly deserving of punishment, this act of judicial clemency, indicating the pacific policy of the government, naturally gave boldness to the Indians. Their encroachments upon the rights of whites became frequent and grievous. They had been pampered by indulgence and generously kept, notwithstanding their indolence. In open defiance, they insolently spat in the face of the hard-working settler, the sweat of whose brow aided to swell the revenue that

clothed and fed them. No wonder that growing dis-
content resulted from the petty impositions of those
thieving, non-producing neighbors who held large
tracts of the very best land in the State—lands coveted by enterprising pioneers, who could have turned
them into national benefices. Those reservations were
a real detriment to civilization; for there was nothing to induce individual effort. There was no provision made for an Indian who possessed the requisite
ability, to acquire individual estate, the right to transfer his title, or independently to engage in the tillage
of the soil, as white men did, inspired by the home
and labor spirit that conduces to good society.
There was a public demand, though smothered in
its incipiency because it would cripple the interest of
demagogues and political leaders, that this system
of wholesale pauperism should be discontinued; that
Indians should be placed on a par with other men ;
given the prerogative of living through toil, or dying
through indolence ; rising to affluence, as had been
proven in Minnesota even an Indian might, or wasting away by merited starvation; that they should
be made separate land-holders, vested with property that was transferable ; that the Indian titles,
which public sympathy was strongly against, should
be made perfect by destroying their common character and casting them on the individual. This
would parcel reservations and make separate owners.
Each man of a tribe would thus become the sovereign
of his own estate, to have, to hold, or to sell.

Some, in defining the most feasible Indian policy,
recommended a revolution that would make reserva-

tions a memory only. Annuities, like other public charities, applicable only to helpless age and infirmity. Through processes known to humanity, make toil the condition of comfort, and let the Indian understand that, without aid farther than the gift of a farm, his bread should be the fruit of his own labor. Let him once understand positively, that no longer would cattle and ponies be given to him, a certain district assigned to him. a blanket, rifle and ammunition, food and money, annually awarded to him as prizes for his indolence and insolence, and it was believed that "The poor Indian," would follow the leading of even his untutored mind, and learn the meaning of the terms, manhood, home and law. Not at once, perhaps. Persuasions might be necessary, and of different kinds—some wearing even the semblance of coercion. There would be no doubt a time of suffering—a time when they would be neither Indians nor men; but the transition period from one state of existence to another is necessary, though void of loveliness.

Latterly, as the settlements increased in numbers, the Indians took umbrage, and depredations became too frequent to be borne. Complaints were made to the authorities and arbitrations held, without recourse to open war. Mr. Maynard seemed to hold the confidence of both whites and Indians, and was the peaceful go-between. It came to be understood, in high places of power. that he was the natural mediator, and transactions were frequently submitted to him. His coolness and courage enabled him to surmount difficulties that would have appalled other men, and gained for him the respect even of the sav-

2*

age he reprimanded. His every act bore the impress of the lofty Christian charity which marks the noble man, who attributes success not to his own personal wisdom, but to the blessing of higher wisdom, and gives to that wisdom all the glory.

A number of murders had been committed by the Indians in different localities. Most unprovoked that of two white women, on the upper Mississippi. The first was shot while walking beside her husband, who carried their child in his arms. The reason given by the murderer for his atrocious deed, was, "She did not carry the papoose herself, as a squaw should, and must be made to do." The second was a missionary lady, shot through the uncurtained window of her room, while attending upon a sick child. The murderers in both cases escaped their merited punishment; but public indignation was so aroused by these crimes, that the most trifling indiscretions on the part of Indians were magnified to grave offenses. Some difficulties had cropped out between the settlers in the vicinity of Maple Range and Mock-ane-sah's band. Mr. Maynard, as usual acted as mediator, had with Robert visited their reservation, and with success. Home was doubly enjoyable after the roughing and camping, the fire of early autumn delightful, and the faces of his wife and daughter fair to him. Is it any wonder his spirits were high, and that the incidents of their journey wore a soft coloring, and were related in a graphic charming way, so that the inmates of his home, with him did not suspect the treacherous red man. After supper the evening sped rapidly.

"I was very glad, mother," said he, "that Robert was with me. He made agreeable acquaintance with the ladies. with the result. I think, of obtaining sympathy : I think his acquaintance led to the immediate and pacific adjustment of my commission."

"O mother," said Robert, hurriedly ; then, recollecting himself, " Pardon me, father, for interrupting you."

"No matter! Proceed, my son," the father replied kindly.

" In the woods I met a woman, unlike an Indian, save in some portions of her dress. She was not fair, still she was no darker than Mrs. Wilson is, but more graceful and lovely than any woman I ever saw."

" Take care ! take care, my boy ! " said Mr. Maynard, with a gesture toward Robert as if threatening chastisement, while his whole face beamed only love and merriment. "I say, take care ! Mother is the handsomest woman in the world ! You must except her—indeed, you must."

" Certainly, father ! It will take longer journeys I hope to obliterate the instincts of good training. My mother taught me never to involve present company in praise or censure. Her lessons are indelible," he replied, looking proudly at her of whom he spoke, and upon whose lashes lay the suspicion of a tear, as, slightly bowing in acknowledgment of his tribute, she said :

" We all believe in your loyalty, Robbie ! but see how impatient Nellie is getting for your wonderful story."

"I was in the woods one day," he continued,
"with some young Indians, shooting at a target, and
rushed with them to examine the mark, knowing,
however, that the indenture was central, though the
marksman did not braid his hair or wear a blanket.
Just as we reached the tree, a woman stepped out of
the undergrowth, took hold of my arm, and with a
voice thrillingly sweet, spoke to me both in French
and good English, asking my name, residence and
age. I took off my hat, mother, as I would have
done to the queen, and answered her as reverently.
After which, she said : 'I have a son just a few years
yonger than you, home. He must be very handsome, as I know him to be good and true ; but oh, I
can never see him—never press him to my hungry
heart, as your mother may you ; can even never know
if always I must bear this exile. It is long since I
have heard your accent, or seen a white face, and it
really does me good to speak with you. I am only
the Indian woman, Miannetta ; but my children,
whom your voice seems to bring nearer to me—the
best beloved of my sad heart—are not Indians in
name or resemblance.' She sank on the ground and
wept bitterly, while I stood there and pitied from my
inmost soul, yet feeling that no word of mine could
comfort her in her mysterious affliction."

"But she had told you your voice brought her
comfort ; that her children were nearer, in seeming.
I think you had great inducements to converse with
her ; yet I do not at all wonder, my child, when you
stood as dumb in the presence of sorrow you could
not fathom. I should doubtless have been had I such

an adventure—to listen to such an avowal of woe,"
said Mrs. Maynard.

"I hope she did not wear a real Indian blanket,"
said Nellie; "or, if she did wear one, that it showed
the aristocratic number of points." Robert continued:

"I felt no farther interest in the target shooting. I
assure you, but sat long and talked with her of ourselves, of the settlement of Maple Range, and the
discouragements father encountered in his diplomatic
matters, to all which she listened intently, and
answered intelligently; but said nothing more of
herself and her pale-faced kindred. I saw her but
once again. It was the morning we left—the one that
followed the final settlement of difficulties. She
bade me a friendly good-by, and promised to visit us.
What do you think of that, Nellie?"

"Think? I can not stop to think, I am so impatient to see her! Did you make her acquaintance,
father?"

"No, daughter; but am greatly interested in her
mysterious history. 'Who can she be?' I ask over
and over again."

"I am thinking, too," said Mrs. Maynard, "how
she may have suffered—how she must ever suffer—
poor child of woe."

"How have you got along, reciting alone, Nell,"
said Robert, after a little silence.

"Nicely," was the reply. "I have finished the
grammar, philosophical notes and all, and parted forever with my old aversion, fusty, musty Mr. Kirk-
ham."

"You never liked grammar, I remember, and I am glad for your sake the work of acquisition is done."

"Grammar was tiresome, and, I used to think, very useless, until Mrs. Wilson came, and I compared her manner of speaking with mother's. I shall never forget how my face crimsoned once, when she said something to me, which I thought would mortify her when she discovered her blunder."

"She has never discovered it, I dare say; but what was it?" said Robert.

"I was saying to Ruth Ann, the night they came here, 'How I wish I had a sister,' Mrs. Wilson, overhearing me, which I did not intend she should, turned round to me and said: 'You hain't never had none, eh?' Incorrect as the whole sentence was, in a minute I had repeated the rule: 'Two negatives are equivalent to an affirmative,' adding, 'I know now the application of that rule.' A few minutes later, when she asked, 'Be you very lonesome without no sister?' my ears tingled as Ruth Ann's must have, when she boxed them to cure her wool-gathering."

The remembrance caused a general laugh, and, waiting a minute for composure, Mrs. Maynard said:

"You are behind, Robert, in consequence of this trip with father."

"Yes, ma'am; but I will study harder to catch up. Let me recall my latest achievements — translations, I believe. Oh, yes; I have them — a German proverb, 'Den Muthigen gehört die Welt,' 'The world belongs to the courageous;' and this rendering of the Latin: 'Opportunity has hair in front; behind, she is bald. If you seize her by the forelock, you may hold her; but if suffered to escape, not Jupiter himself can catch her again.'"

"In the spirit of the first, I will profit by the letter of your last translation," said Mr. Maynard, with a merry twinkle in his eye, "and 'seize the present opportunity' to propose preparations for bed."

Together they all sang:

> "The day is past and gone;
>   The evening shades appear;
> Oh, may we all remember well,
>   The night of death draws near.
>
> "We lay our garments by,
>   Upon our beds to rest;
> So death will soon disrobe us all
>   Of what we here possess.
>
> "Lord! keep us safe this night —
>   Secure from every fear!
> Let angels guard us while we sleep,
>   Till morning light appear!
>
> "And, when we early rise
>   And view the unwearied sun,
> May we set out to win the prize,
>   And, after glory, run!
>
> "And, when our days are past,
>   And we from time remove,
> Oh, may we in Thy bosom rest—
>   The bosom of Thy love!"

Good-nights were affectionately exchanged, and ere long the sweet angel of sleep poised watchfully over The Maples.

CHAPTER II.

FOREST DAYS.

"The early days—the days when we were pioneers."

SINCE the events recorded in the preceding chapter, Springs and Autumns have come and gone. Minnesota's face is fairer and her children more numerous and exacting of her favors. Having thrown off Territorial trammels, she has taken a proud position in the procession of States. The financial crisis of 1857, the year before she was admitted into the Union, proved to be "the birth moon of her agricultural greatness." Speculation in Western lands was suddenly checked—one happy result of the stupendous collapse which proved the old saw, "It's an ill wind that blows nobody good."

In many of the Western States, the speculator, ever on the alert—quick to scent marketable property, even when it has no appreciable value—managed to distance the immigrant in his slow-moving ox-train, and, before his arrival, had bought up the most desirable lands at government price—a fact to which large tracts, in their native wildness, in the most beautiful section of the Mississippi Valley, bear melancholy testimony.

In Minnesota, fortuitous circumstances had placed most of the public lands beyond reach, except under

the provisions of the pre-emption law. Through the
bursting of the bubble in 1857, speculation met with
a sudden revulsion. Money disappeared, and property
depreciated with a rapidity equal to its former infla-
tion. Immigration almost ceased, and upon immigration the Territory depended for the rapid growth on
which was based the enhanced value of property.
The rates of interest, paid by sanguine speculators,
were fabulous. When property suddenly fell, speculators, ruined, went their way. Here let me say,
the passage of the homestead act, years afterward,
saved forever from their blighting grasp our beautiful
and productive State. To the poor man's children
to-day, it is a heritage inalienable, except through
their voluntary act.

While portions of contiguous States lie idle, held
by non-residents at prices above the reach of immi-
grants, the fertile lands of Minnesota—one of the
healthiest States in the Union—are reserved by legis-
lation for the homes of those who, through toil, may
become veritable monarchs.

Many of the victims of the great commercial
reverse turned, sad and depressed, to the hitherto
despised occupation of farming, and sought by unaccustomed labor to avert the doom that seemed to hang
over themselves and families. Like the fabled Antæus,
many of them were invigorated and refreshed by
touching their mother earth and mingling freely with
that ancient peerage whose coat of arms an eminent
statesman has called "a pair of shirt-sleeves." This
sensible method of meeting disaster was not only a
domestic blessing, in bringing plenty home, but a

D   3

public good, since it greatly augmented the area of
cultivated acres, which, in 1857, was estimated at
forty-eight thousand, and, in 1860, had reached the
grand total of four hundred and thirty-three thousand
two hundred and sixty-seven acres. Thus you see
how that which is baneful to one becomes another's
wholesome meat. Princely fortunes were swallowed
up in a disastrous wave, but the wave rolled on,
proving itself a blessing to this remote garden.
Many whom the remorseless sea had torn from their
anchorage and thrown, penniless, upon the virgin soil,
had the wisdom to realize the significance of labor,
with its present necessity and its prospective reward,
and, with a cheerful spirit, had put strong hands to
the plow, employing skill and patience where force
was not available, thus becoming thrifty and wealthy.
Others, however, became impatient of fortune, because she was tardy. Of this latter class was Charles
Center. He had once been a successful and well-to-
do merchant in Chicago, until tempted by the treacherous yet delicious promise that has lured to ruin
thousands who were not content with well-doing. The
fever of speculation in Western lands seized him,
notwithstanding his natural shrewdness and business
qualities ; yet, those heavy ventures are often made
by men even shrewder and more far-seeing than he.
That speculation is hazardous and its consequent failures common, does not detract from the marvelous
charm of stocks and shares and real estate, and did
not prevent Charles Center from yielding to the
peculiar hallucination. But misfortune came. The
alluring yet false hopes vanished, and he was plunged

in ruin. Taking his young wife and money (the gift
of her father, a lawyer of Chicago) enough to purchase a team, a cow and a generous supply of farming
utensils, he pre-empted a farm adjoining Wilson's,
and sought to bury himself—" the world forgetting,"
and, save by his creditors, " by the world forgot."
His was not a happy soul, gathering to itself love by
loving. He was a sour-tempered, fault-finding man,
who, if a woman, would have been termed a shrew.
Clearing off heavy timber and putting in a crop, even
of a few acres, involves hard work ; but this done, a
mine, rich in recompense, awaits generous culture,
producing in proportion to the investment of seed
and muscle. The young merchant - farmer worked
hard, but always at a disadvantage. He would plant
this crop too early, that too late ; he plowed this soil
too shallow, that too deep ; and if admirably adapted
to the growth of vegetables, ten chances to one he
would sow it to grain, and *vice versa*. Failure came
partly through lack of recognizing the " sublime
fitness of things ;" partly through agricultural antag-
onisms — unpropitious skies, destructive animalculæ
and early or later frosts. A sour temper seldom loses
its acidity during the prevalence of thick weather,
and every adverse event served to make him more
bitter and irritable. He knew he was inexperienced ;
but he would not see that failure came often because
he refused to advise with farmers, who, by a life-long
practice, had been educated to their vocation. Instead
of seeking information and by a change of tactics
achieving ultimate success, he was many times on the
point of yielding to despair, and declaring all further

effort useless. He attributed all to his particular
demon, *luck*, half believing his patient, quiet wife
was in league with that much abused author of men's
misfortunes, inasmuch as now and then she was roused
from her reticence and, woman-like, would say exas-
peratingly, "I knew it would be so!" Late in the
Autumn of his second year, his grain harvest, all
told, afforded but one load of wheat, and with this
and his cow (which he proposed selling) tied behind
his wagon, he started for market—quite a long journey. His team was the envy of many a richer man
—noble bays. They stood at the door a short time
before starting, while he secured some bolt beneath
the wagon box. His wife came out with her baby,
and held him up to caress them. As Center got onto
the wagon and gathered up the reins, she spoke with
an apparent effort at cheerfulness, that could not disguise her apprehension that her words would call out
some unkind retort :

" Charlie, dear! I put my watch into your luncheon basket. Will you be kind enough to exchange
it in town for some flannel and shoes for little Carlos?
He's so delicate, I think he needs thicker clothing,
and warm shoes and stockings—and my watch is so
useless! Will you take the trouble to make this
exchange?

"No ; I am no lacquey to run errands ! I hate
paltry bargains, and you know it ! It would save
appearances if you were willing to wait till you have
the money to buy flannel and shoes; but you could n't
be satisfied to let me start for town without some disagreeable commission ! "

"Well, I will take the watch out, Charlie, if you don't want to sell it for me," she said; and sitting the child down, she climbed up over the wheel. She was standing with one foot on the hub, reaching over to get hold of the basket, when he, with brutal impatience, though well aware that he was imperiling her life, started up the spirited horses, saying:

"I have no time to wait. You seem to think that the machinery of the universe must stop while you recover your breath, lost in running after some tomfoolery! It's enough to make a man swear!"

"O Charlie! don't be so cross," she said, as by a dexterous spring she avoided the revolving wheel and lifted her pleading eyes up to his, that were flashing with anger: "If you leave me in anger, I shall cry myself to death."

"Cry and be damned, then! I wish I was going away forever! You do nothing but cry and complain! Get up, Selim!"

He was gone, this man for whose love she had left an affectionate father's house—gone without a word of farewell to herself, or a smile to her boy. She turned into the house, and wept long and bitterly as she recalled the many evidences of his coldness and the unkind words that had taken the place of the honeyed expressions which once made her blessed mother's love seem tame and common-place. As she sat, thus absorbed in her own miserable thoughts, she heard not the light step of a bare foot upon the floor. A brown, toil-hardened hand was laid kindly on her shoulder, honest gray eyes looked down into hers, swimming in tears, and the voice of Mrs. Wilson, subdued by real feeling, said :

"Now, du tell what's been and happened, to put ye out so ! I mind the time (the wust time ever put over my head), when you, a sweet, young thing, unselfish of your sweetness as the blossom that ye looked like, hunted out a poor, no-account cretur, on the bow of a steamboat, takin' on jest that ar fashion, and yer words, full of comfort and hope, brought that poor cretur to the light of the truth and the joy of believin'. Though I never wished ye to have sorrer like that of mine that day, yet I have always wished I could prove my gratitude, and comfort ye. Come, tell me all yer grief, for two can tote a sorrer better than a lone body, an' I take it fortnit I came over to-day."

Yes, it was fortunate, for there was a special need of her. Unconsciously, she had a mission, and she performed it faithfully, to her own infinite advantage as well. There are anointings for coronation less illustrious than Hebron knew. Her humble words were as balm to the sorrow of her friend. Mrs. Center's tears were dried. Cheerfulness came back to her—came back, but not through revealing the cause of her sorrow. On her marriage morning, her mother, who was a very discreet woman and a noble wife, had presented her with a little volume, in which she had marked with pencil one passage : "Have no confidant. O wife, save thy husband?" Ah, if wives would obey this recommendation, how much domestic scandal would be avoided, and how many clouds would fail to reach the zenith of gossip and notoriety.

Mrs. Wilson spent the day—and it proved to be a profitable one to both. Mrs. Center gleaned lessons of economy, needed in the every-day housekeeping of those who "are obliged to live short," as Mrs. Wilson said, while the pure, untutored soul of the latter gathered sweetness and richness from a more refined intelligence.

"Come, Mrs. Wilson, please tell me what ails my soap. I can not coax it to thicken as yours does."

They went down cellar, and removing a board from the window, Mrs. Center indicated the location of the barrel which her friend peered into, and then said:

"Did ye taste of yer ley before ye biled it with yer fat?"

"Taste it! of course, not; why?"

"Why, ye would a knowed that 't was too weak to make soap. Now, next time mind and tech yer tongue to the ley, an' if it bites right smart, use it; but if it don't, it ain't strong enough, that's cl'ar. Now, if you will git a box of this yere penetrated ley, and put it into yer bar'l, I'll go a purty on it, ye'll have soap in tu days that 'll b'ar up a cat."

She discovered that the brine on the pork failed to cover it, and directed Mrs. Center, in adding to it, to pour off the original, scalding and adding both water and salt, boiling all together, and when cool, pouring it on again, and keeping the brine higher than the pork and clear as a crystal, "or yer bacon will be rusty in spite o' yer teeth."

When told that the one window was kept tightly closed in Winter, she gave expression to an emphatic

"Du tell! Now, I remember yer taters an' cabbage all rotted last Winter, an' no wonder, if they got no more air than they would with that shet."

"Why," said Mrs. Center, "I thought them safe enough, if frost was excluded."

"La, honey!" was the rejoinder, "you can't live without breath; no more can garding truck."

After leaving the cellar, they had a nice cup of tea—light biscuit and butter. While eating, Mrs. Wilson watched the child opposite her very closely, and said:

"Ain't yer baby ailin'? He looks dreadful white livered!"

"I can't say that he is really ill," was the reply; "but he is never thoroughly well, and seems petulant as if in pain, at night, when most children sleep soundly."

"Well, the poor thing is enamost eat up with wums."

"But I am giving him vermifuge all the time! what more can I do?"

"Sling the bottle into the middle of next week—so fur that no dog you have any respect for can find it! Make yer butter tol'able salt, an' whenever he frets at night, git up an' coax him to eat a piece of bread and butter, an', if ye can git it down him, a raw onion. I've pulled quite a gang of young 'ns through the whooping cough an' wums, and never used any other medicine than I jest telled ye of."

After tea, they chatted long and pleasantly. The afternoon sun shimmered through the vines at the window, and the shadows lengthened in the yard before the door.

"Cur'us things is shadders, and kinder speakin' too," said Mrs. Wilson; "but they are the most deceivin' things in the world—always seemin' to be standin' still, and yet always movin'; invitin' ye to sit down an' be sociable, and yet slidin' away from ye. Did ye ever think about it? Shadders is always the longest in the mornin' when it's cool an' ye don't need 'em; but when at noon the sun pours down upon yer head, where is the shadder that looked as if it never could grow less?"

"In some respects not unlike worldly friendships, always most generous when there is no *need*," said Mrs. Center. "If sudden misfortune deprive you of wealth and real assistance is needed, ah, then you inquire for your friend as you just did for your morning shadow at noon—Where is he!"

"But there is a shelter for them as are weary in the heat of the day—the shadder of 'the Rock that is higher than I,'" Mrs. Wilson said.

"As there is an unfailing friendship," added Mrs. Center. "He who glorified the manger, left upon the earth this comforting assurance of His unchanging love: 'Lo, I am with you always, even to the end.'"

Just as the sun was going down, Mrs. Wilson took her departure, for, as she remarked,

"It's chore time, and the children never air thoughtful, even when I'm to hum; but when I'm gone, la, they are as triflin' as pasteboard jumpin' jacks, not even takin' a hint when the cows come bawlin' home."

A little way from the gate, she met a neighbor, and saluted him with

"How d'ye du, Mr. Cross? I hope yer woman is purty smart?"

"Well, I can't brag as to Polly Ann's smartness; but she's main well, an' judgin' from your gait, you are, too, Betsey."

"Oh, yes," she replied, "peart as a nightingale. William got a letter from old Mr. Sutton to-day. He has been superanimated by the Illinoy conference, an' says if we will all on us agree to help him a little, he will move up to Maple Range, take a claim and settle down among us."

"Bless the Lord! He is still on our side, isn't He? My woman was jist a sayin', this arternoon— 'Cross,' says she, 'we shall all backslide if we don't stir ourselves up to new engagedness.' Now, Brother Sutton is a good Christian man, and, as to preachin', ye know, Betsey, he's zealous as a bear."

"Won't it seem like old Illinoy though, when the new lot come from there, an' Brother Sutton among 'em? William is goin' right around among ye, to see what ye will do for the poor old man, an', Cross, ye mustn't be backward about this! It's only 'lendin' to the Lord,' an' not money either; it's only yer hands out of yer pocket a little while."

The two parted. Mr. Cross, going on, entered the house and found Mrs. Center in a terrible fright, holding her child and sobbing pitifully over it, while its wide, staring eyes were fixed in convulsions. He

felt himself utterly useless, and telling her he would
send his "woman over," he set out rapidly for home.
Just then a shadow flitted past the window. A dark-
browed woman entered the house, and Mrs. Center
exclaimed:

"O Miannetta, I am so glad you have come!
Look at my poor dying child!"

"Not dying, I hope! We will soon have him
better. It's fortunate your tea-kettle is full and hot.
A warm bath will bring him out of the spasm."

Skillful hands ministered to the little sufferer all
night, and the morning saw him smiling again; but
Miannetta remained with the alarmed mother all day,
and even longer, until the child was fully restored to
his usual health.

Now let us follow Mr. Center and his *mis*-fortune.
He reached the river which lay between him and his
destination near nightfall, the third day after his
departure from home, and drove at once onto the
ferry boat. The ferryman, preparing to start off,
said:

"You had better stand pretty close to your horses'
heads, if they are not accustomed to the river."

"They are too well trained to make that necessary," he replied—so decidedly as to awaken a little
choler in the mercurial boatman, who retorted:

"Very well, sir! You must take all the responsibility of accidents, if any occur. I make the suggestion only in the way of duty. Shall we tie
them?"

"No; my voice will suffice to keep them quiet?"

Just as they had about gained the middle of the

river, a steamer rounded a curve and puffed down toward them, while a band on board struck up "Yankee Doodle." A shrill whistle completed the fright of the poor horses that in the country had lost all memory of navigation and its unearthly signals. They reared and plunged in a manner that showed how useless was any human authority. Finally overcoming all effort to restrain them, they plunged frantically through the frail guard into the river, dragging the loaded wagon and the cow after them, and the deep, remorseless waves closed over them forever. Charles Center stood like one petrified, regarding the spot where they had disappeared; and ye who have never sorrowed because of a like disposition, will scarcely credit the fact, that in that moment he blamed his wife more than himself; that the greater loss of horses, wagon, grain and cow, was less bitterly considered than the trifling one of the "watch in the luncheon basket;" that after plodding the long, homeward way on foot, and recounting the circumstances to her, he had said impatiently:

"I can't understand, Clara, what on earth ever induced you to send that watch. It was worth fifty dollars, and would have purchased for us another cow, which now we are likely to be without long enough. It does seem as if you and the fates were against me! Work hard as I may, there is always some contemptible hitch in the machinery — some infernal lock to the wheel!"

"Why, Charlie! one would suppose from the way you talk, I expected and really wished to lose that watch! How could I anticipate that terrible misfortune on the boat?"

"How could you? You might have guessed something or other would happen! There always does! Any other woman would have been more prudent than to risk the last valuable article she had! Any other woman would have thought more of her husband's interests; but you did n't care! Everything we had must be tucked into *that* load and sold *that* minute!"

"Do n't be so unreasonable, Charles! You know how few opportunities we have for sending to town, and the things I wished to get by selling the watch are really so much needed! Poor little Carlos!"

"'Poor little Carlos!' Clara, it is one eternal whine about your needs and his! I'm sick of it! Your bread is sour! I wish you could see some Mrs. Bacon had for dinner to-day—white as snow—and such sweet, nice butter, and coffee—ah, genuine amber colored—no such stuff as this, I can tell you."

"Well, I suppose Mrs. Bacon has good flour (this, you know, is made of grown wheat), several cows to make butter from, and a nice, cool place to set her milk—a very essential thing in making butter, I assure you; and, Charlie, this coffee is made of rye —I am out of the Rio."

"I'll warrant ye! never knew it to fail! get clear out of an article before you ever say a word! Why in thunder did n't you tell me the coffee was gone, when I went away, so that I could get some?"

"Because you peremptorily refused to undertake

the sale of my watch, and I knew you would have no money, if you did not sell it."

"Did n't I take wheat to sell?"

"Yes; but the whole load would scarcely pay your debts in town."

"Did n't I take the cow to sell?"

"Yes—with the avowed intention of buying another with what you got for her."

Seeing she had the advantage of him, he concluded to return to his "best hold," the subject of the bread. He again made a home thrust:

"Clara, I notice you have poor bread oftener than good!"

"Say, rather, that you oftener notice the poor, but are silent about the good."

"Well, one thing I can say! I never saw a slice of poor bread on Bacon's table!"

"Most likely you would, if you were there oftener. All cooks have their failures."

"I do n't believe Mrs. Bacon ever had a failure. She is a splendid woman—far too intelligent for Sam Bacon."

"She did come a little short of success, it seems, in selecting her husband."

"Yes, indeed; and I do wonder how it is these particularly fine women are always mated with just such contemptible fellows!"

"By your rule then, Charlie, whoever compliments your wife must disparage you."

"No danger of compliments, if they stay to dinner."

"Perhaps not, unless they have the sagacity to

attribute the poverty of the dinner to the resources of the cook; but come, it is high time we changed the subject! Let me tell you some pleasant news. We are to have some new neighbors. A Methodist preacher, his family and several other families are expected, this Fall, to settle in Maple Range. They are old acquaintances of both Cross and Wilson."

"More Hoosiers!"

"Humans, I hope. There is not a woman in all my acquaintance, of finer sensibility than Mrs. Wilson. No matter if her speech is rude; a good heart, with homely utterance, is preferable, I'm sure, to polished speech and a soul corrupt."

"I should think it would have been more to your taste, then, to have married an idiot with a hare-lip."

"The hare-lip might be an advantage. Don't you think one could be cultivated, Charlie?"

She knew by his countenance her thrust had gone home, for he was painfully sensitive. One moment she dallied with the "old Adam" of revenge, for the many personal wounds he had given her; the next, the sweetness of revenge had palled upon her. Rising, she stepped round the table to him, with that readiness to right a wrong characteristic of noble natures. Stealing her arm about his neck and putting her forehead close to his, now purpling with anger, she said:

"Forgive me, my husband! I was rude, to say what I could not mean. I am so sorry, my darling!"

Pushing her impatiently away and laughing a peculiar laugh, more devilish than human, utterly devoid of merriment, he replied:

"Even the epithet implied in your pleasantry is

more agreeable than the sickish finale with which you
adorn the scene. It would do credit to a gushing
schoolgirl, in her love quarrels! Faugh, get away!"

She sat down, humbled and subdued—less by his
words than her own—by which she had fallen in her
own estimation. In the silent half hour that followed,
she was purchasing a scholarship in the lofty school
of self-denial. Upon retort she would set an inexor-
able seal, and to herself she said :

"God helping me, I will bear all that is in store
for me—will bear it and be still."

About two months later, one still, cold Winter morning, just as the sun showed his disk at the verge of the
sky, and his two Winter satellites (termed sun-dogs
by the woodsman) established themselves on either
side—an unmistakable indication of extreme cold—
old Mock-ane-sah paused on the outskirt of the big
clearing. He watched the wreaths of smoke emerg-
ing gray from the chimneys, growing white and
voluminous in the sunlight, and then thinning out
to threads of blue, till, victims of an inordinate
desire to rise in the world, they lost all outline and
were dissolved in ether. Mentally calculating the
strength of the late reinforcement of whites to the
settlement; with great gravity and deliberation,
counting off the curling columns upon his fingers, his
only arithmetic, he found that his ten tawny digits
"just filled the bill." The ten hardy, heartsome
families were a welcome addition to the Maple Range
settlement, giving new courage to the active forest
band, and the frosty air was resonant of busy life. The
sound of many industrious axes rang through the

echoing woodland. Ungainly oxen, with slow gait, plowed innumerable cross roads in the deep snow, and drew the great logs away to Watkin's new mill, on the Waubece, in Clipnockum Hollow, where, with shining saw, it stood ready to adjust its gates and hum a utilitarian lay, when Spring should unfetter the winding river. There was a holiday inaugural at Wilson's, and, more momentous still, a wedding on Christmas day. Benjamin Palmer had brought a load of household goods for his uncle, Carce Smith, one of the new settlers, intending to return to "Illinoy;" but he had changed his mind and taken a farm on the western lake-shore, south of Mr. Maynard's. It was a beautiful selection, and valuable as well—half prairie and half timber—and had fallen into hands that would develop its inherent wealth. Ben was an industrious, well-informed man, who believed in the union of thought and toil. He had already built a plain, but neat, substantial frame house—white, with green blinds—which promised to look very pretty when the grove, in which it would be half hidden, was green again and the lake lighted with flash of Summer sun. His barn was in process of erection—a roomy and convenient structure, adapted to the needs of a good farmer. He tightened the reins over a pair of chestnut six-year-olds: was said to have a comfortable fund at interest, and, what is rare at his age, the good judgment to draw from it only for the purpose of more discreet investment. Add to these solid recommendations the fact that he was both good looking and agreeable, and you will be prepared to take an interest in him, as well as the girls (who these

E   3*

were, we shall not now inquire) that admired and angled for him. However this may be, Ben had fallen in love with our old acquaintance, Ruth Ann. Wait a minute, reader! She is so improved that, although I credit you with the best memory in the world, I am certain you would not know her. The past two years she has lived at The Maples, and her hoydenish manners are much toned down. Her rather coarse features have assumed a pleasing regularity. Her teeth (of which she is so careful) and complexion are faultless. She is rather fleshy, but dresses neatly and in good taste. Altogether, she is really a nice-looking girl, and being sweet-tempered and obliging is very much loved. When Ben, who had taken her sleigh-riding, told her one starry night, a few weeks ago, how happy he would be to call her wife, next Christmas day, she could not find it in her gentle heart to thwart his happiness. She could not say him " Nay."

So, now come the guests to witness his happiness, and judging by the smile that now and then irradiates her features—hers as well. Nearly all have arrived, except Robert and Nellie Maynard ; and there are ill-natured ones who wish something would prevent their coming : who, if not jealous, yet feel a prejudice, not infrequent with ignorant folk, against those more popular and wealthy. A little knot of women is seated near a window—among them, Mrs. Center and Mrs. Cross, a sharp-featured woman, with small, keen, coal-black eyes and a rasping voice that recalls one of my childhood's memories—an old hunchback meat-man, playfully placing his ponderous steel beside my ear, and drawing his huge butcher-knife across it.

Mrs. Ellis, the third one of this group, is a handsome, rosy little body, all life, all animation, never finding anything in this world but enjoyment. Of course, she does nothing to add to this world's misery ; but, on the contrary, is largely instrumental in adding to the sum of human happiness. One look at her round, eloquent face, her bright hazel eyes—to once hear her speak—were always enough to unite the neighbors in social harmony, for, though quite unconscious, the rich flow of her simple good nature was irresistibly contagious. There was a murmur of subdued conversation running through the room. Mrs. Cross nudged her right-hand neighbor, and, leaning over, confidentially, said :

"I am thinkin', Miss Center, that 'twould be a heap better for we 'uns, if them thar big bugs would stay away : like as any way if they come, we shall be poked at as no account by them all, for ye know a Guinea hen is no show in the same yard with a peacock.

"She has the compensation of a marvelous voice, at least," said Mrs. Center, smiling.

"Quantity if not quality," said Mrs. Ellis, striving to look innocent, but the fun cropping out all over her pleasant face.

Mrs. Cross was not to be diverted from her purpose, and continued—

"They do say as how that thar girl of Maynard's couldn't as much as wash her pocket handkercher. If her mother had good sense she'd try to larn her a little housework.

"Why," said Mrs. Ellis, "I should as soon think

of making pavements of thistle-down, or of utilizing
the milky way, of cooking my breakfast by the sun's
rays, of accomplishing *any* impracticable thing in
fact, as of setting that delicious little thing to do
housework. Why you can almost fancy her with
wings, dropped from the skies, to win hearts to
purity by winning them to herself."

"O—" said Mrs. Cross, while her eyes took on a
beryl hue, and the turned up nose was elevated still
higher, "If she was a poor man's child, I reckon she
would lose all that folderol deliciousness, drop her
wings, and be showed the use of her hands. I allus
hated pets anyhow, an' it makes me out of patience
to see you uns, run stark, starin' mad about the Maynards. I never seed any of 'em but Robert, but
Cross has worked for 'em, and he says they are as
stuck up as Lucifer. Why at every meal they eat off
real cheeny ware, with these 'ere narrer silver spoons
with slits in 'em, and, as if they was the greatest of
strangers, they palaver and nod over their 'thank
you's' an' 'if you pleases,' an' as though they was
goin' across the ocean, instead of into the next room,
they bid each other good-night, when they go to bed,
and good-mornin' when they get up, as if they'd
been gone a year. And Miss Maynard, only think, a
putting a cap on her head when she sweeps her own
room. And one day Cross said the great fat thing
put on gloves to go out to the garding and pick a
bowl of raspberries. Now I'd like to know if there's
any sense in sich kind of ornerry doin's. Hadn't
they better put on sackcloth and ashes, and think
about their soul's salvation, instead of continually

running after the follys of the world. I wonder why
the Almighty is so long sufferin' with some folks, an'
if He raly will have another purification like Sodom
an' Gommorroh. How are you growing in grace,
Miss Center? Do you feel the indwellin' of the
Holy Sperrit, or do ye git worldly minded and lukewarm—"

Mrs. Wilson came along just then, and supposing
the last remark was addressed to herself, she replied
unctuously and very sincerely, as she sat down.

"No, Mrs. Cross, I ain't a lukewarm Christian.
I never allow myself to neglect to replenish the faith
that keeps me warm. It is our blessed privilege to
live so near the throne, that we may feel every hour
of our lives its peace and glory. Come here, Tad."

"I am glad to hear you speak so, Betsy," said
Mrs. Cross, and as Tad was lifted upon his mother's
lap, a throne none younger had ever disputed with
him, she asked of the mother, though really addressing the child with her eyes, "Does Taddy know 'I
want to be an angel.'"

"Well what hinders ye. Pap says ye boss the
loft," was the childish rejoinder, cut short by a sudden pinch administered by his mother. But this admonition was lost on Mrs. Cross, who had not even
noticed Tad's remark, so intent was she on pressing
the original theme.

"I was enquirin' as to the spirtual state of Miss
Center, Betsy, but I do think she is a kind of stillborn Christian, don't you?"

"No, indeed, I think she is one of the Father's

elect, a beautiful witness to His love, a minister at
the holy altar," whispered Betsy.

"I should like to see the effect of the holy fire
then ; sanctification will show itself. God's love will
find expression sometimes, an' it's a duty to speak if
a soul is raley converted, an' if they don't speak, can
we believe the conversion is genuine," said Mrs.
Cross, in a low tone.

Now if she really were genuinely converted, no
one would have questioned if Mrs. Cross had the love
of God continually in her heart. But there was a
question as to the good of parading the subject of
religion, or as another has said, "wearing the soul's
jewel in the nose," and making it on all occasions the
subject of conversation. While 'tis for our continual
peace that religion be the spirit of our thoughts, it is
neither possible nor profitable to make it our perpetual theme. Mrs. Cross, however, had a zeal not
according to knowledge, and showed it in ill-timed
inquiries regarding the state of other people's souls.

Suddenly turning from Mrs. Wilson, she fired directly into the enemy's camp. Ben Palmer was known to
be a little skeptical, and Ruth Ann had never had
any convictions. Sitting there, side by side "the
observed of all observers," it was very startling to
the blushing girl who sat waiting her nuptial crown,
when in a voice of strained solemnity, Mrs. Cross,
addressing her across the room, said, "I hope Ruth
Ann, that you have a conscience void of offence to-
day, that you take this important step with an eye
single to the glory of God, prayin' continually for
grace to help you to perform the duty of a wife.

And you, Ben, I hope are thinkin' of your new relation, and promising God to erect an altar in your house, for you will find it sweet to commune together, not only as husband and wife, but as God's children. Don't you think so?"

The silence was truly painful, and the embarrassment of all complete at this untimely question, when Grandma Smith, out of sympathy for the young couple, sprang to her feet, crying,

"Come girls and boys, don't sit here like owls. We may as well have a game of something. Hold fast all I give you, hold fast all I give you."

Round the room she went in the old-fashioned game, and after completing the circuit, cried—

"Button! button! Who's got the button? Let the culprit rise."

The persistent old lady never gave up till, what with accusing wrongfully, choosing judges and paying forfeits, the house was in a perfect hurly-burly. The roof was in danger of being raised by the explosions of laughter, when some of the odd sentences were enforced; for instance, when Jehial Smith was sent to Rome, and Mrs. Cross (who regarded the wild scene with feigned horror) refused to show him hospitality on his journey, and positively declined to be kissed, declaring it "all a contrivance of the adversary of souls, to draw our thoughts from heavenly things."

"You mean the wedding supper, I suppose, Mrs. Cross? It does smell splendid, no mistake; and this is an appetizer. I don't believe in it a bit more than you do; but in Rome we must be Romans, and if pickles are eaten before meat, we must take ours *à la mode.*"

With all of his mother's playfulness and his father's strength, he drew the thin, emaciated form into his arms, and in spite of her resistance, kissed her cheeks, alternately, until they looked like hickory nuts rubbed with red chalk, while the old men and women laughed at her wrath and discomfiture as immoderately as the young people. This sensation was followed by another equally ludicrous. Mr. Cross was compelled, much against his will, to execute an Irish hohum with the prettiest girl in the room, which by general acclamation was Belinda Porter, and the look of martyrdom he assumed called forth general applause. Then long Dave Persons drew the attention of the merry-makers by his awkward attempts to turn a double and twisted "laud o' massie," with Mrs. Ellis, whose arms were too short, as his were too long. The chairs in which they stood suddenly parted company, and brought down the laughing couple and the house together. Just then Johnny Wilson rushed in, with the announcement:

"Here come Maynard's bells!"

All was decorum in an instant. People got to their seats, and found their pocket handkerchiefs, in which they must have deposited their merriment, for every face assumed its most becoming company look. All was still within doors; but without, the air was fairly jubilant with musical bells, as the elegant sleigh and pair dashed up to the door. A handsome, gentlemanly young man assisted a frail-looking girl from the sleigh. Together they entered the house and were warmly welcomed. Johnny Wilson proudly drove the horses round to the stable, ample and warm, log though it was.

"Angels paint, eh?" whispered Mrs. Cross, spitefully, to Mrs. Center.

"Wait a little," was the reply. "Nellie has been riding in the cold."

"Must suffer awfully in all them there shawls and wraps and feather blows (furbelows)!"

And now the young couple advanced to the center of the room, and were united in holy matrimony by the white-haired minister. The words that made them one were spoken, the benediction solemnly pronounced, and silence fell a space upon the crowd; then there was a sudden flutter, a tumult of impetuous feet, which accompanied the customary rushing of rustics to kiss the bride, and the laughable presentation of a cotton night-cap to the newly married man, by the successful competitor. Then followed the usual congratulations and the merriment occasioned by the abundant *bon mots*, which, though lacking a little in delicacy and elegance, had still the merit of heartiness and good will; after this, the crowning announcement, "supper;" and in William Wilson's log cabin, away upon the frontier, they sat down to a table whereat a king might have supped, with no wish ungratified. The eating of those hard-working, healthy, backwoods men and women would have been a caution to dyspeptics, only that dyspeptics do not get so far into the interior of dear Minnesota. Conversation hung fire while the savory viands were being discussed. Long Dave, however, ventured to observe:

4

"We all fall to as if it was a log-rollin' and each one on us claimed to own the logs, and was bound to get all the work out of the others by settin' a lively example."

"Eat all ye can, Dave," said Mrs. Wilson, who, with vulgar pertinacity, insisted upon the compliment to her pudding, implied in the eating.

"Christmas don't come but once a year, an' weddin's, to most folks, but once in a life time; an' they ain't no sign of any comin' to you, as I see; so, now, eat! Betsy Wilson has a right smart o' failin's, I allow; but you all know she ain't stingy.".

"Stingy!" said her spouse, with an emphasis intensified by the enormous tart he had just closed his teeth upon; "Well, thar! that's the best joke I've hearn to-day. Pass it round: 'Stingy!'"

A fresh invoice of dainties put an extinguisher upon his brilliancy, and he was compelled to address himself to the inner man, while uncle Carce Smith, addressing him good-naturedly, said:

"There, William, you are whipped for once—what with the long—draws from the metheglin—keg—in the—kitchen corner, an'—Betsy's—pies-an'-cakes."

"It is possible the "metheglin keg" had something to do with the liquid condition of uncle Carce's words. All things terrestrial must end, and this supper was no exception. One by one, the seats were vacated, guests saying facetiously:

"I'm not hungry; thank you, Mrs. Wilson."

When all had risen, grandma stepped with a busy, bustling air back to the table, saying:

"Come, girls, turn to here, and red up this table,

if you want the wish bones! and here, you boys, lay
hold of them dish towels, and wipe the plates you 've
eaten your supper off. You must try to be useful!
So much *bone* and *sinner* can't be wanted for ornament
here in the woods, now! Never mind your meetin'
clothes! The girls will find some aprons for ye.
Girls glory in makin' aprons. Ye need n't be afeared
of gittin' siled! A man that 's afraid of a grease spot
will never be famous, except he is a Sepoy."

In the city, far from his home, a country boy may
blush, stammer and appear awkward enough; but
bring him back to his own element, the backwoods;
turn him loose among a playful, saucy lot of country
girls; pin an apron, improvised for the occasion—a
white flour sack, lettered as usual—about his waist to
preserve his " Sunday suit ; put a calico sun-bonnet
on him, and give him a cup-towel, and, in spite of
your dignity, or the remembrance of your grandfather's funeral, you will laugh at his pranks and pro-
nounce him clever, handsome and even graceful.

The elderly people smiled in memory of their own
hilarious youth, for that memory gave them the clue
to the scene enacting in the kitchen, whence came
sounds of unmistakable mirth.

" How old is grandma, uncle Carce?" said Mrs.
Cross, with a pious pucker.

" She was sixteen, and I believe a little past, when
I first saw her, and she is a little past sixteen yet,"
was the quiet reply.

" Now that's a mean dodgin' of a plain question,
uncle Carce, her hair is as white as snow."

" So is her heart, Mrs. Cross, pure and young

and full of all sweet charity," said the old man with
such earnestness, that none could doubt the love that
prompted that simple eulogy of her, once the choice
of his youth, now the comfort of his old age.

At that moment a sharp wail brought the revelers
from the kitchen, and ere long the dancers had the
floor.

> "Bright eyes looked love to eyes that looked again,
> And all went merry as a marriage bell."

But the dancing, its time, and expenditure of
pedal energy, demands a cleverer pen than mine. In
fact it beggars description. Robert Maynard joined
heartily in the terpsichorean exercise, though at first
a trifle slow. Once he led Nellie through a cotillion,
and was observed to bespeak for the occasion, music
in moderate time. Directly afterwards the impatience of other lads and damsels found vent in the
old Irish jig, "Cover the Buckle."

Again Mrs. Cross, who was as malicious as
Mephistopheles, vented her spite ; as Nellie took her
seat after her one dance, she said,

" Well one thing is certain, that girl is too lazy to
enjoy herself. Ef my Lizbith was to drag through a
dance that ar way I wouldn't own her. Lookee, not
a bit of color."

"Are you convinced now that Nellie doesn't
paint ?" asked Mrs. Center.

"Why, I thought you was opposed to dancing,
Mrs. Cross," said Mrs. Ellis.

" So I be," was the reply, "and to stealin', jumpin' claims, and—"

"Envy, backbiting—indeed the whole catalogue

indicated in the service, no doubt," interrupted Mrs.
Ellis with mock seriousness.

Mrs. Cross raised her head like a serpent whose
evil plans have been thwarted, and fastening her
bead-like eyes upon Mrs. Ellis, she continued.

"I be opposed to dancing, for dancing cost one
man his head."

"Ah, made him giddy most likely. Some late
occurrence I presume. But you have the advantage
of late news, which shows the wisdom of taking a
paper published the night beforehand. Now I mean
to coax Mr. Ellis to subscribe for the 'Midnight Cry,'
and then I can hope to keep up with the times."

Utterly regardless of Mrs. Ellis and her irony,
Mrs. Cross, with persistence, which rightly directed
might have been praiseworthy, but had no purpose
save to injure Nellie, continued :

"As I was a sayin', I be opposed to dancin' and all
sin, but if a person will dance, will commit sin, I like
to see 'em do it thoroughly."

"No doubt of it," said Mrs. Ellis, now almost
brimming over with merriment. "I notice your
example is always consistent with your expressed
belief. Whatever you do, you do thoroughly."

Mrs. Center, who felt a desire that Mrs. Ellis
should bestow the pearls of her wit more worthily, if
at all, said :

"I am strangely apprehensive sometimes, when I
think how delicate and frail Nellie Maynard is. Compare 'her little spiritual figure and waxen face with
the bride's, as they sit talking so animatedly. I am
thinking how an ardent blast that would annihilate

Nellie, would only deepen the healthy glow on Ruth's cheek. Yet in my heart there is a presentiment connecting these two in one terrible calamity."

"O Mrs. Center, do not indulge in such mournful fancies. Think how much of human strength surrounds and protects them, to say nothing of Him who holds them and us in the hollow of His hand. You remember how the old mythological deities were guarded by their worshippers—with like care will we guard our little deity Nellie."

Mrs. Center smiled at her friend's enthusiasm, and as Mrs. Wilson, from across the room, saw the smile, she wished smiles were not so rare upon that face, which she remembered so radiant in her girlhood's loveliness, but which was now fast taking on the lines of sorrow, which only heaven's music could charm away.

The night had waned, and there had been "no sleep till morn." Stars knowingly blinking, one by one had disappeared. The wedding party took the hint, and, in imitation of the stars, one by one disappeared into great coats and mantles.

"Mr. Center," said Robert. "If you and your wife will ride with me, I will take you home, while Nellie is getting on her dry goods."

"Thank you, I accept with pleasure for my wife, but I prefer to walk, the distance is nothing."

Mrs. Cross was at the window looking at the handsome turn-out, side by side with her own equipage (a yoke of white-faced muley oxen and a bobsled with loose boards to answer for box). The comparison proved too much for her Christian equanimity.

She fired a parting shot, as Mrs. Center, assisted by her husband took her seat in the sleigh.

" Some women is satisfied to ride with their own honest husbands, on their own honest bob-sleds, behind their own honest oxen, and some women ain't."

" Some women happen to have honest husbands, honest oxen, and honest bob-sleds, and some women haven't." said Mrs. Ellis in comic mimicry.

This excited no little fun among the guests waiting to take their leave and exchange neighborly good-bys, as it was well-known that Cross was none too scrupulous in his acquisition of property. His oxen were both "bulky and breechy," while the very bob sled had come into his possession under circumstances decidedly suspicious.

Mrs. Cross, however, instead of taking the implication home to herself, generously applied it to Mrs. Center, looking a whole sermon from the text, " I am holier than thou," and turning to Mrs. Ellis, fervently ejaculated, "That's so!"

As the rising sun tipped the crowns of the forest trees with gold, a curious procession moved down the narrow lane leading from Wilson's house to the high road. The sleigh bells jingled gladly in the crisp morning air, as some steeds, impatient of curb, reared and danced, picking their feet daintily out of the powdery snow with a rapidity their progress in no wise seemed to justify—a step altogether unsuited to the gait of the oxen just ahead, for they were reined in without regard to comeliness or speed, behind sleepy, plodding, old "break up" teams. Every sleigh, that morning, whether drawn by oxen or horses, was laden with children, parents and boisterous youth, girls and boys, bent on frolic, who, heedless of danger, expressed only satisfaction at the impossibility for once of the good teams passing the poor ones.

Now, I am not justifying, but only relating the facts. You must settle the question of cruelty and mercy for yourselves — but there was an artillery practice of bright eyes going on that morning. Handsome girls, in those slow-moving sleds, shot saucy glances over their shoulders to helpless drivers —young men—for the old ones dared not pull the reins over those fleet, fractious horses. Oh, they were merciless—these girls—and cared not if every glance found fatal mark. What business had a young man out without his armor on? Theirs to speed the shafts! Let those parry that could. As a result of one of these last looks, there was another wedding only a few weeks later. One of those very Jehus thus confessed to a bantering crowd:

"Well, if you must know, you must know I suppose; but the first time I ever thought of marrying Belinda Porter,"—

"Belinda Smith!" cried a voice. "You can't dodge that now, Jehial Smith!"

"Dodge it? I don't want to; I say 'Belinda Smith.'" I never thought of her, save as a good-looking girl, till that morning after Ben Palmer was married. I was right behind her father's sleigh, trying my best to hold in father's five year olds. I couldn't do it with mittens on, if I had a clear title

to the road. You know that, boys! I had all I could
do, to keep them from dashing right over the sleigh
load in front of me. I got mad as the mischief at
the girls, who kept throwing up their handkerchiefs
and laughing, to scare my horses. I had just about
made up my mind that I would let the critters go,
and kill every last one of the darned girls, and called
to 'em to say their prayers *quick*. I should have gone
over 'em, sure ; but Belinda, she looked back at me,
with a ' Do, if you dare ! ' in her eyes—"

"Well, that beats me ! I never thought you 'd
take a dare, Jehial ! "

"I did, though ; at least, I changed my plan. I
concluded to marry her and kill her by inches, as
other men do."

CHAPTER III.

SHADOWS.

"O MOTHER! what do you think? Miannetta has just come all the way on foot from Ben Palmer's, and she says Ruth has the sweetest little boy in the world," cried Nellie Maynard, to her mother.

"Nellie, you hear with your imagination! I said she had a nice baby boy," said Miannetta. She had followed Nellie into the breakfast room, where Mrs. Maynard and Robert still lingered over their English breakfast tea. Nellie had been down to the gate to meet her, and learned from her the news which she, in turn, announced, with a pardonable exaggeration and all the enthusiasm such events have awakened since the first man-child was laid in the arms of Eve.

"What makes you think the new baby 'the *sweetest* in the world,' Nellie?" said Robert.

"Because it's Ruth's baby, and therefore mine. I shall name it 'Freddie,' teach it all a little boy should know, and, if any thing happens to dear Ruth, while I have life, no harm shall ever come to her child. What a grand Christmas gift!"

"While you are 'taking on,' Miannetta sits there with her wraps on. Don't you think a little present work is sometimes worth more than so much prospective usefulness?" said Mrs. Maynard.

" Forgive my thoughtlessness, Miannetta ! Take off your wraps, and come close to the fire while I remove that horrid head-gear. I should be tired to death 'totin'' that on the top of my head, to say nothing of the walk of two or three miles—and, *child !* your moccasins are full of snow ! Let me take 'em off. Now, if it is not a shame ? your hair has not been touched since I put it up, day before yesterday. I will take it down and brush out the braids, while you are drinking that cup of tea mother has poured for you. Please, let me," she insisted, as Miannetta offered objection. " Never mind Rob ; he is reading on the other side of the room."

A moment afterward, all forgetful of Miannetta's objection on his account and her own words of re-assurance, she cried :

" O Robert ! do look at Miannetta's hair ! Is it not perfectly magnificent ? "

The young man looked over from his newspaper, carelessly at first, and then with some surprise and more attention, admired the luxuriance of the raven hair that rippled down and swept the floor, though its owner sat on an ordinarily high chair. Miannetta might have been forty ; but, if so, she had so conciliated time that she looked still young and beautiful. Some care, unusual to Indian women, had preserved her complexion from their bronze, though darker than the average brunette of the Anglo-Saxon race. She was reticent, an universal favorite in the settlement, and considered indispensable in cases of illness or accident, much to the discomfiture of poor, spiteful Mrs. Cross—her one enemy, who had medical preten-

sions and was wont to ascribe to the "pet squaw " the
languishing condition of her own finances, as her own
employment not infrequently resulted in the employment of her husband also.

Her success in his interest was certainly great,
though not very inspiring to her patrons.　In short,
she practiced medicine, and, to eke out the revenue
of his farm, Mr. Cross dug graves.

But to our story.

Nellie brushed, plaited and pinned up the long
shining braid, while Robert, forgetful of his paper,
watched the proceeding thoughtfully, nor seemed to
hear his mother, though she had thrice repeated his
name.　Nellie at last roused him from his apparent
reverie, as she said :

"Robert is getting wonderfully given to day
dreaming, mother ; I believe he has, as they say, fallen in love with some fairy nymph in that saintly city,
where he tarried awhile on his way to college.　'T is
said the immortals love at first sight.　He has a
picture that causes me some suspicion, for he won't
let me see it, which you know is neither flattering
to me nor to the picture."

Mrs. Maynard smiled at Nellie's nonsense, and
said :

"Is it your purpose, my son, to show us the
original of that cherished picture some day."

"Yes, mother ; and to you the picture now.
Nellie shall wait as a punishment for her inquisitive-
ness."

"I pray you be merciful, Mr. Autocrat, and place
the period of my punishment within the limits of

feminine endurance," said Nellie, with hands uplifted
in mimic entreaty. Miannetta, who had fallen asleep
under magnetic hands, awakened at the voice, elevated above its usual gentle tone, and bewildered at
the appealing attitude and pitiful expression, said
quickly,

"Why Nellie, what's the matter?"

"Nothing at all the matter with me, but Robbie
has just been and gone and fallen in love."

"One would think from your look of anguish, he
had been and gone and broken his neck," said Miannetta, with, for her, unusual playfulness.

"It's just as bad, I suppose, for we shall lose
him, and who knows but a broken heart lies at the
bottom. I have read somewhere, 'whoever plunges
deepest into love, will soonest find the boulders and
surface hidden cliffs upon which lives are wrecked.'
I know my brother's true heart so well, that I know
if he loves at all he will love with all his soul."

"It is sad to think then," said Miannetta, with
some warmth, "how he might suffer should the
object of his love prove unworthy; but even the
anguish of a broken heart seems to me preferable to
having a heart, so light and vain, it can neither love
nor break. Such hearts are many, and sometimes
inspire a devotion they never can experience or
reciprocate."

She had spoken so intelligently and with such
evident feeling, that they sat astonished for some
moments after she had hurriedly risen and glided
from the room.

"Poor Miannetta," said Nellie, "knows what it

is to find the hidden rocks where hearts are broken."
And with tears in her soft blue eyes she followed
the Indian woman.

Robert crossing the room, laid the picture of a
young girl in his mother's hand, and putting his arm
affectionately around her neck, said in a voice not
devoid of emotion :

"Mother, this is Miss La Moore. The original of
this picture I hope to bring to you before this time
next year—a daughter that you must love, for she
will be my wife."

"Your wife, my son ! Is this indeed true? I
did not credit Nellie for cleverness to discover such a
secret, before I had even suspected it. I thought it
was all her mischief."

"But mother, what do you think of my Annette ? "

"That her lovely face explains my boy's precipi-
tancy," was the reply.

After examining the features critically, she said:

"She is not simply lovely; she has one of those
rare faces, upon which there is no shadow of guile or
deception. Ah, Robbie, with this woman's love you
will be blessed ; for I believe if she loves once she
will love forever. Whatever may arise to mar your
happiness, or to separate you, do not doubt the faith
that is the beauty of these eyes. Though now looking at her for the first time, I yet seem to have known
her long. Acquaintance with her is not a thing of
growth. 'T is a beautiful picture, Robbie, and the
original must be a sweet girl and a refined lady."

" Indeed, mother, those are tame expressions; she is an angel."

" Well, dear, I am but the lover's mother, dealing in practical terms ; the lover himself must supply the poetical. I am looking at Miss La Moore without her wings."

" Capital, mother," said Robert laughing, and with just a tinge of color mantling his handsome brow.

" Now sit down and tell me all about this romantic affair, my son, which promises to increase our little household band, and to give Nellie what she has always wished for—a sister," said Mrs. Maynard.

Robert drawing a stool to her feet, and laying his arm across her knee, told her the history of his love, which I will give you in his own words.

" You remember, mother, last Spring, when I went away to finish my last half year at the academy, father desired me to stop in the city of St. P——, and deliver a message to Mr. La Moore, some business matter requiring a verbal explanation, which—"

" I remember it well, Robbie. Some transaction in real estate, but I had not till this moment asso-ciated the names of the young lady and your father's business acquaintance of St. P——."

" She is, however, his daughter. They have a fine residence on the heights, overlooking the city, to which I was invited by Mr. La Moore, when I called at his office. I had formerly met Eugene, the eldest son, a pleasant acquaintance, which was renewed and deepened at once into friendship, when I became at their earnest wish a few days' visitor at their home.

Mr. La Moore, a most affable man, desired me to
wait, as he and Eugene were going to Europe, and
they would accompany me as far as New York.

"Of course, I waited, for I knew Annette would be
of the party going East, as she was to be left in Montreal, Canada, to finish her studies there. You smile,
mother! That smile tells me that I need not extend
my story. Suffice it to say, I loved her from the
moment of our meeting, and I obtained her father's
full and cordial consent to address her. Eugene is to
remain in France some time. Mr. La Moore will
return the coming Spring. At Autumn, if you and
father approve, I hope to bring Annette home to the
dear old Maples. I think—indeed, I know—she is not
entirely happy in her father's house, though much
beloved by him as well as by Eugene and the rest of
the children. She said nothing of this to me ; but I
readily divined it. Her own mother is long since
dead. Her step-mother appears to be a proud, unfeeling woman, and frigid as an iceberg."

"Bring her to us, Robbie ; we have sunshine
enough, and to spare. Blessed with the love we will
all give her, she shall forget there is any coldness or
want of feeling in the world ; and God grant you
both happy and useful lives."

While she was speaking, Mr. Maynard entered,
and noticing the tremulous tone in which she spoke
these last words, he inquired very tenderly the cause.
With a smile, she said :

"Robbie has been telling me a love story of which
he is the hero, and the daughter of your acquaintance,
Mr. Pierre La Moore, the 'bright, particular star.'"

"Ah! and when is this star to dawn upon us?"

"He proposes to bring it to us in cheerless November—I suppose, to quicken our appreciation of its brightness."

"Well, Robert," said his father, cordially, "I was just about your age when I had a similar experience. There arose in my firmament a star which has brightened my path ever since. I wish your happiness, my son, may equal mine, for a greater it were impossible to conceive on earth. I am glad that, in the spring-time of your life, you have won a good woman's love. It will steady you all through life."

Mr. Maynard's feelings overcame him for a few minutes, when he continued:

"In view of such an event, I have recently drawn up some plans that we will talk over this afternoon. I need only say now, your proposed marriage has my approval, Rob, and I shall be ready to give you the proper outfit, and put you in the way to prove your own accumulative abilities."

"Let me here say a few words," interposed Mrs. Maynard. "Robbie, I want to caution you against making *gain* paramount in your plans. Remember the 'golden mean of Agur's prayer: 'Give me neither poverty nor riches. Feed me with food convenient for me.' Too often, alas, we fail to appreciate the beauty of this humble petition; yet we have ourselves seen souls narrowed by the recognition of no logic save that of money. Men, arrayed in the purple, have dazzled the eyes that looked only on the magnificence of their personal appointments. Thousands have knelt in fawning servility at their feet until

4*

something has revealed the fact that their souls were
closed to every generous impulse and noble thought;
that, in reality, they were pitiably poor. One of Sir
Walter Scott's characters declares that 'The penny
siller slew mair souls than the naked sword slew
bodies.'"

"I believe it does," said Robert, "when money
is loved for itself alone, rather than for its uses.
Scott, however, recommends money,

> 'Not for to hide it in a hedge,
> Nor for a train attendant,
> But for the glorious privilege
> Of being independent.'"

"May I venture to come in, or will I interrupt
your discussions?" asked Nellie, peeping in at the door.

"Why, Nell," said Robert, rising and leading her
to the seat he had just occupied, "I was very near
forgetting you."

"Well," said she, with assumed resignation, "I
suppose I must get used to it. Wise people say it is
a bad sign when a young man gets absent-minded,
to say nothing of forgetting his sister!"

"The wheel revolves, daughter!" said Mr.
Maynard, gayly. "I remember very well when you
appeared on the scene and broke Robbie's nose, and
now, as if to avenge him, a Circean divinity has
arisen and broken yours."

"Well, I've no further use for mine any way!
The frost killed all my fragrant plants last night.
My chrysanthemum and heliotrope look like unsightly
rags dangling about their ornamental supports. Not

a tint of loveliness—not a breath of sweetness answered my good-morning to my flowers."

"What a pity, my pet," said Mr. Maynard, sympathetically. "It froze very hard last night. The mercury fell to thirty-four below zero—the lowest it has been since we have been in Minnesota."

"Well, but yesterday was not cold! Flies and actually a mosquito were on the same window with my plants, at noon. As it continued mild, I thought last night there was no necessity of removing the pots; and who would have imagined the change? But 'alas, alas!' as Cloe says, there is no placing dependence in men or Minnesota weather."

Mrs. Maynard here signified a wish to go over and visit the young mother, at Ben Palmer's, and the sleigh was soon at the door, and a basket of delicacies stowed away under the seat. Robert assisted his mother in, with as much gallantry as if she had been eighteen instead of forty-eight; but a beloved mother never grows old to us. In twenty minutes she had been left at Palmer's, and Robert was returning home. When there, he persuaded Nellie to take a ride and call on Mrs. Center. Controlled by cool, masterly hands, the horses flew rapidly over the snow "to the music of the bells, bells, bells." Mrs. Center was all alone with her little boy. Her husband had gone in pursuit of work, which he might have found at Mr. Maynard's; but his pride prevented him from accepting any so near home. They were very needy now. Fortune had not fallen to him from the clouds. No marvelous discovery of mineral wealth had been made on his quarter section; and, though he would

not acknowledge that he expected and waited for
these things to turn up, yet there was evidently a
cause for his waiting till starvation actually stared
his family in the face. There must have been a bright
dream of some fabulous release from his difficulties,
or he could never have borne the gradual restriction
which had reduced their meals, first to bread and
potatoes, and now even bread was gone. Nellie
noticed how more than usually despondent Mrs.
Center seemed, but could not have guessed the whole
truth of her want, till at last the poor woman ventured to be frank with them.

"I can not give you a cup of tea after your ride in
the cold," she said, "nor will I offer you my only
food—potatoes."

"That was not surely your only breakfast this
morning," said Nellie.

"Yes," she replied sadly, "Carlos and I have
eaten nothing else for the last fortnight. Mr. Center
has been gone a week, I hope he will find the work
he seeks."

Robert, always clever to devise a way out of any
unpleasantness, so that even his motive was scarcely
mistrusted, said quickly,

"We had no thought of staying, Mrs. Center, to-
day. We came for you to go home with us and
share our Christmas dinner. Mother and father will
be delighted to have you, while Nellie and I want to
have some fun with Carlos."

So saying, he caught the little fellow and throwing him over his shoulder, trotted up and down the
room, singing, "won't you buy a bag of beans, shake,

shake, shake." The child was soon shouting with laughter, and even his mother smiled at the queer spectacle of this young man, who was the beau of that part of the country, playing nursery horse.

"Come get ready, Mrs. Center, while I stir up your boy," he said.

"I shall have to boil a kettle of potatoes first, to feed my chickens," getting up to put the kettle on.

"No, I'll fix them," Robert answered, as putting Carlos into Nellie's lap, he went out and took from the sleigh a bag of oats, which he emptied into the hen house, his generosity being greeted by a great flutter of wings.

Mrs. Center was soon ready, and with happy little Carlos, really enjoyed the ride behind the fleet horses.

As they drove up to the door, Mr. Maynard came out bareheaded, the wind gently raising his silvery locks. He reached out both hands to take Carlos, saying heartily. "A very merry Christmas to you. Mrs. Center, you are indeed most welcome. I have been deserted for two mortal hours by Mrs. Maynard and the children ; have read my newspaper and eaten my apples, and am heartily glad to see you. Come in, come in."

He seated himself by the glowing fire with the child on his knees, and bravely sought to undo the mysterious strings and buckles that fastened on his infantile wraps. till completely baffled, he good-naturedly handed him over to Nellie.

"There." he said, as looking through the window he saw Robert driving towards Ben Palmer's, "what a piece of thoughtlessness; I ought to have made Robert come in and warm himself, while I drove over for mother."

However it was not long before the spanking bays, fresh as when first they left the stable, dashed up through the long grove, and stood with arched necks and tremulous ears before the door. Mrs. Maynard exchanged warm greetings with her friend, and soon the appetizing aroma of well-cooked food penetrated from the dining room, and in a moment, divested of mantle and furs, she was ready, as Robert said, "to put a substantial enclosure around Cloe's roast turkey and plum pudding."

How kind they all were; how sweet the home atmosphere. Mrs. Center's heart swelled as she took in all the affection of this home, contrasting it with her own—chilled and blighted by indifference. How she wished, at one moment, that her husband could share with her the pleasures of this day, yet the next, thought with a sigh, how sure he would have been to mar the harmony of the conversation, by crabbed opposition, maintained to the verge of rudeness.

He was one of those characters Nature sometimes seems to create out of the scraps of humanity, and in this case, unfortunately, the scraps were all poor.

Mrs. Center was grave, she was never otherwise now, but she was social and at home; had seen enough of better days to know what was required of her, as well as to appreciate the compliment of a seat at her host's right hand.

Though she could not forget the empty flour barrel at home, nor the limp purse in her pocket,

yet she conversed happily and profitably, as became
one who was a lady independently of all externals,
proving that soul wealth is, after all, the only true
independence.

Miannetta was not at dinner. She was weary and
preferred sleep in her room.

Carlos was given a high chair beside Nellie, who
helped him to separate the fruit from the pudding and
mince pies, and broke wish bones with him, while
Robert, who sat opposite him, pared the skin off his
big red apple into one long spiral piece, with which he
made a fanciful decoration for the castor. Then,
with using his napkin ring as an eyeglass to discover
the cause of the brightness of the little boy's eyes,
tasting the little fellow's wine under the pretence of
keeping it from Nellie, Carlos was kept highly
amused.

So the day passed pleasantly away, a day set
down in Mrs. Center's record as one of the pleasant-
est of her life. Poor woman, she had so few pleasant
days in these later years, this one stood out very
clear in her calender.

Two days afterward she spent the day at Ben
Palmer's with Mrs. Maynard, and when they returned
to The Maples toward night, she said, "I must
surely go home to-morrow."

In the morning Robert drove round to the door
with a larger sleigh and she got in with a grateful
heart, for she knew she was not going back to the old
regimen of potatoes and salt. Under the robes were
stored a bag of flour, meat, jars of lard, butter, and
groceries, not forgetting meal for the chicks. Last,

but in size not least, was a box of mellow apples,
with " Carlos " painted on the cover in big red letters.
All of these things Mr. Maynard had stipulated,
should be paid for when his century plant blossomed.

" With interest," Mrs Center had said.

" Yes, if you insist," was the reply.

The plant had blossomed only five years before.

After leaving her at her own house, Robert drove
over with the intention of offering Mrs. Wilson a
ride back with him, on the way to visit her daughter.
She had been at Ruth's only every other day for the
last week, and this was her day off. He only
intended it as a bit of fun, as he enjoyed greatly
these little friendly tilts with Mrs. Wilson, who not
unfrequently, could pay him back in his own coin.
But when she came to the door the expression of her
face, not only forbade the nonsense, but drove it from
his thoughts. With alarmed earnestness, he cried:

" What can be the matter with you ? Speak, Mrs.
Wilson."

She could not tell him intelligently, but hurriedly
directed him to the residence of Mr. Cross, where all
the men of the settlement were assembling, and
where, in a few moments, he heard an explanation of
fears, not confined to Mrs. Wilson alone. Fears
based upon these facts : Two Indians, Mock-ane-sah's
braves, had lately committed a murder in the pineries,
killing in cold blood a lumberman of high connections
and good standing. The Sheriff of Blakeley, a town
on the Waubece River, several miles below, was con-
veying them in irons to that place for confinement in
jail. He had stopped the previous evening at Pierre

Scott's tavern in Clipnockum Hollow, had ordered supper for himself and prisoners, when suddenly a tall heavily-built man entered and accosted him :

"My name, sir, is Jerome Hyche, the life-long friend of the man these miscreants murdered. If they are taken below for trial, some legal technicality will furnish a loop-hole for their acquittal. I am determined to secure their punishment—you understand ?"

The Sheriff, who was determination personified, calmly replied :

"If you intend to use strength, let me tell you these men shall not be taken from me without a struggle," significantly tapping his revolvers.

Opening the door and revealing a crowd of sturdy looking men, about thirty strong, Hyche said quietly, "It is folly to offer resistance."

"I am sorry your words belie your looks," said the Sheriff. "I should have taken you to be a law abiding man."

"So I am," was the reply, "but human laws are not for the benefit of these devils !"

"They are my prisoners," said the Sheriff. "I shall defend them to the last."

His coolness re-assured the prisoners, who sat down to supper and ate heartily, even lighting their pipes afterward.

The sleigh was brought to the door, and as the Sheriff appeared with his prisoners, the crowd closed round them. As the Indians were getting into the sleigh, two men stepped forward as if to seize them. The officer quickly drew a revolver, saying:

"Touch them at your peril,"

G   5

Convinced that he so acted only to screen himself from all censure, they each caught hold of an Indian, and in less time than it takes to tell it, both men lay weltering in their life blood. Their companions immediately seized the Sheriff, and secured him. The redskins were seized in a twinkling, hustled into another sleigh, driven rapidly up the road under a large oak tree. Two ropes were thrown over a limb, and in a few seconds, as the sleigh drove away, two lifeless forms were left dangling between the white cold earth and an unpitying sky. At midnight a tall figure stood near them, and regarded them long and silently. It was old Mock-ane-sah, looking upon the faces of the dead, one of which was indeed his own—his only son. Long he gazed upon that distorted face, then climbing the bluff, by which stood the fatal tree, he gained its summit, commanding a near view of the homes in the valley, and the settlement of Maple Range. He was not unlike the forest trees upon the bluff, as he stood there for a while, immovable, his towering form clearly defined in the moonlight that shone brightly on the snow. Nor was he conscious that he was observed. The wakeful spirit of Gus Harkness had impelled him forth to watch the Hollow, and he followed at a safe distance, noting Mock-ane-sah's every action. Saw him look upward to the moon and counting on his fingers, as once before he had calculated the force of the settlement. A low murmur issued from his lips. Was it a prophecy of the time when vengeance would be fulfilled? None would ever know. But the thought of his sweeping down with his merciless band upon them, caused the spectator's heart to quail. Of course so large a force as had attended Jerome Hyche had not been recruited without some drafts upon Maple Range, and though that had been almost accidental, it was felt to involve the whole settlement in peril. It mattered little how they came to be there, or whether they were there. White men had killed the Indians and white men would have to answer for it, and not alone white men, but women and children too. An Indian's vengeance is not discriminating. The new-born child and its mother are slain with as much satisfaction as the man for whose deed, fancied or otherwise, they suffer. The Indians had been hung at the Hollow and the settlers in the Hollow should make atonement, and Maple Range must suffer with them.

In this conviction, the male portion of the settlement had met to devise some plan of defense. From Smith's they had moved to Wilson's; from Wilson's, with added numbers, to Porter's, and thence, still gaining in number, to "old man Cross'." At each place there had been angry declamation, some sensible discussion, and much purposeless talk. They all dwelt more upon the demerits of their treacherous foe, than upon sensible measures for deliverance. Though discussion was vehement and backwoods oratory original, yet they had so far been unable to settle anything definitely. It was while in this state of disorder that Robert arrived. He soon learned the facts we have just narrated, and realized their gravity to the fullest extent.

"They need some one to *talk 'em down!* Go in

and do it. I will hold your coat, Robert," said Gus
Harkness.

Robert entered the room unperceived. The men
were all standing—all talking at once; but he could
gather enough to discover that they were discussing
the expediency of sending his father as an envoy
extraordinary to the Indians. There was, however,
a strong opposition to this, for, as yet undiscovered,
both those friendly and averse to the proposition
expressed their views freely, unembarrassed by the
knowledge of his presence. He was astonished to
find how the leaven of envy and jealousy had worked
in a few short weeks—yes, you might say hours;
but he was rejoiced to find that his father's real friends
were the better—the more intelligent of the settlers.
The first voice distinguishable was that of Charles
Center, who, having returned that morning, and finding his wife away, had followed the tide of excitement and was evidently working for some personal
end. He opposed strenuously Mr. Maynard's intervention.

"Uncle Smith," he said, "proposes to send Maynard to the Indians. Now, look here! if his mediation
had been the correct thing heretofore, the necessity of
mediation would not now exist. What assurance have
you that he has kept faith with you, or that he will
keep faith with you, if you send him again? I believe
he has been treacherous to you; that the very intelligence you esteem in him, he has used against you,
with the Indians."

Cries of "No, no!" and "Maynard is true blue!"
met this assertion.

"When old Mock-anc-sah comes down from the woods, whom does he visit?" asked Center.

This was a damaging question, and was answered by several with cries of "That's so, boys!" "He stops at Maynard's every time!"

This suggestion, though of little weight with the more sensible, who knew old Mock-anc-sah was not to blame for the deeds of his warriors, took readily with a certain class. Comparative silence prevailed for a moment, and a peculiar sound issued from one corner of the room. With his usual sniffling, Cross rose to his feet, laboring from head to foot with a big thought striving for utterance. His hands worked nervously and his eyes rolled spasmodically. With a wrinkling of his forehead that brought down the stiff black shock of hair till it almost met the shaggy eyebrows, Mr. Cross delivered himself as follows:

"Center is dead set ag'in' Maynard; my woman is too. She hain't got the l'arnin', may be, and couldn't talk as well as he can, but she aims at the same idee. Center speaks her sentiments, and them's my sentiments coractly."

On the delivery of this speech, a merry little fellow was seen fussily making his way through the crowd to the door.

"What's up? Whar you goin', Birdsell?"

"Home, to get my woman's 'idee.' I want to get it in close to that of Mrs. Cross, for, next to me, she has always said she liked Maynard; but I'm goin' to find out if she has changed her mind, like some of the rest here! Back, in a minute."

This sally elicited some laughter, which, however,

gave way to close attention when long Dave Persons took the floor.

"Neighbors and friends," he said, "I think you are all more scared than hurt, to-day! If you will insist upon mediation, Maynard's your winning card; but, for heaven's sake, emphasize the *die*, in your instruction; all other logic is just so much powder wasted and time thrown away. Why don't you go and cut down them red cusses and send their cold car- casses home to their smoky wigwams? Tell their howlin' kindred to come down here and you will settle their hash by servin' them the same way! The tree is strong, and there's enough of ye to hang every infernal Sioux that ever clutched a scalp lock ; and as for rope, there is no want—"

"Don't waste the rope, Dave! Remember 'Char- ity begins at home,'" cried Jehial Smith.

"Yes!" said Gus Harkness, "and supposing you undertake the execution of the nice little plan you propose, will *you* take those two bodies home, eh?"

Uncle Carce Smith here cleared his throat, and they knew something was to be said worth listen- ing to.

"Boys! boys! the Bible says 'There is a time to be grave, and a time to be mirthful.' Whoever doubts the time has now come to be serious, must be an infidel indeed. To waste it with idle nonsense or impractic- able suggestions, is to deprive us perhaps of a chance to secure our imperiled homes and even our lives. While you are here joking, Mock-ane-sah may be massing his dusky warriors in some cover dangerously near, awaiting only the advent of night to swoop down upon us and light up the forest with our burning homes, and mercilessly slay or torture all we hold most dear! Let us cease discussion, and agree upon immediate measures to avert this horror. Send someone, known to us and to the Indians as a true friend of both, and having influence enough with them, to urge conciliation; otherwise, I tell you, we are doomed as surely as the sun shines on the corpses of these human beings, hurried out of this world without regard to mercy, law, or justice! Once more I urge upon your serious consideration the need of the hour, and I propose, as a man of undoubted integrity and influence, Mr. Maynard."

Before anyone could second the proposition, Mr. Center threw in a counter motion to send Pierre Scott, the half-breed.

"His personal relations bind him to the Indians while his pecuniary interests bind him to us. Let another be sent to the commandant at the nearest military post. We pay heavy taxes for the support of idle garrisons within short marching distance, and yet we stand here quaking with fear. We have the right to demand protection from the troops we uphold. Should pacific measures fail, we shall have the satisfaction of getting back the value of our taxes in the defense of our homes."

As he stopped speaking, Robert stepped forward and said:

"Fellow-citizens: Let me say at once that my father's physical health will not admit of his taking the long journey some of you propose for him in connection with this unhappy affair. The situation to-day seems to be one full of danger. The impending peril can only be averted by immediate and concerted action. The exigencies of the hour forbid our lingering over the dark features of yesterday's horror. Its sickening details have ere this been recited with passionate vehemence by hundreds of tepee fires, while, doubtless, the pipe of war was circulating. Pardon me a hurried repetition of some of the grave complaints by which to-day the red man will justify the use of his final argument—the tomahawk. It will serve to remind you of what must now be going on among the Indians, while we are engaged in fruitless discussion. This latest deed of violence will serve to awaken older grievances. White men stealing the affections of Indian women, and under forms of marriage by them considered neither sacred or binding, broken at will, after possessing themselves of the estate which is often an Indian woman's goodly dower. Many a repudiated squaw, who has thus been stripped of her heritage, deprived of her children, and sent home to her kindred, will add the story of her bitter wrongs to the great burthen of the white man's sins. These heart-broken mothers, wailing for the children God gave them and of which man has robbed them, have become desperate in their desire for vengeance, ready to aid and forward any work of cruelty against those to whom they attribute their wrongs. Again think of the fraud and extortion practiced by the legalized Indian traders. We all know this. Has it not been a standing joke for years? The paltry trinkets bartered for Indian gold have marked among dealers' supplies the worthlessness of Indian goods. Have we not ourselves watched the wily miller, and perhaps smiled—a smile by no means creditable to our principles of honor and integrity—when, after other custom work was done, he has swept the refuse from the floor and placed it in the hopper to manufacture the villainous Indian flour, for which the consumer would have to pay the price charged for the best. These are hurried glances at the evils which, among many other wrongs, fancied or real, grown by constant nursing and recital to colossal proportions, have given the red man grave cause to hate us. These, exaggerated and dwelt upon, without considering the offenses on their own side, make them feel their cause a just one, which is said to be equal to being 'thrice armed.' In meeting this emergency, success depends on our acting wisely, promptly and unanimously. I cordially second Mr. Center's motions to send Pierre Scott to the reservation, and also the call for military protection "

Robert's name was immediately proposed, and he was duly chosen to represent their claim at the fort.

There was no opposition to Pierre Scott and he received his commission with dignity and readiness, feeling sure he could serve his neighbors satisfactorily. I must, however, qualify that statement of no opposition, for Paddy O'Shannon, before the decision had been taken, sprang into the middle of the room, depositing an enormous quid of tobacco on the floor, and with the richest brogue imaginable, cried :

"An' is it Pierre Scott, the craythur, ye'd be

sindin' till the woods. A dirthy half-breed himself, an' the two-facedest cuss that iver run on two legs. Sure now, if the crowd goes in for the loikes o' that, ye 'll see me lavin' Clipnockum with niver a look behind, for the Lord himself could n't save us! Sind a bastely Injun to thrate with bastelier ones! Why, it is like sindin' an Oirishman with a bottle of whisky to quill a whisky row. Pierre Scott, indade! Why, gintlemin, ye better now jest turn the same boot and kick yerselves clean to Bedlam."

"Hold on, Paddy," said Gus Harkness; "what's your plan? What would you do supposing we send you to the Injuns?"

"I 'd take the pay loike a man."

"But what would you do with the Injuns?"

"Make 'em show thir paipers, bedad."

"But they are natives; have no papers to show, Paddy."

"No paipers! O begorra, thin, I 'll niver thrate or bodder wid 'em at all, at all."

And he thrust his hands into the waistband of his blue overalls, stumping ferociously out of the room, while Gus called after him:

"Where ye goin', Paddy?"

"Out o' this counthry, be jabers, where the biggest half o' the people have no paipers."

This little episode had not interrupted the real business of the convention. Instructions had been prepared and were now given to the delegates, who departed at once upon their respective missions, each earnestly desirous of averting the gloomy cloud.

Robert was unaccompanied, but *Miannetta went with Scott.*

Peace was for the moment secured, and, though built upon a volcano, was considered satisfactory by the too confiding settlers, who buried their fears away, cleared and put in larger fields of crops, tore down their old buildings and raised better ones, inviting with the arm of labor the prosperity and capital which is its reward. In the light of later events we know that beneath the outward peace smouldered a fire, unsuspected by those who, above it, went on their way, busy with the common things of life.

The Indians were now seldom seen, but appeared friendly and some acts of real kindness were exchanged with the whites. It was believed they were not brooding over the outrage in the Hollow, but had come to set off that awful punishment on the part of the whites, against the awful crime on the part of the Indians. Jerome Hyche was not a resident of that section, and though he was never seen, had never been dealt with for his part in the lynching, yet to his death he must carry the gangrene of remorse in his soul. It was no palliation of his crime that the victims were guilty, and of a cruel and dangerous race. Obedience to the commandment, "Thou shalt not kill," is especially required of the race enlightened by the word of God.

CHAPTER IV.

THE LOVER'S STRATEGY.

"He looked at her as a lover can ;
She looked at him, as one who wakes,
The past was a sleep, and her life began."
—MRS. BROWNING.

"COME in, girls ! You can not stay out in the moonlight and dew, without some danger to your health, or your complexion, or your dresses, and pray what can be of more importance ? " It was Robert Maynard who spoke, addressing his sister and her friend 'Lisbeth Cross. They were sitting or reclining on the branch of a tree that jutted out from its trunk ; Nellie at her friend's feet, leaning languidly over, with elbows on her knees looking intently into her face.

The day had begun with a joyous gallop at sunrise, lazy and cool mid-day floating in the shadowy coves of Lake Loui, and was now ending in quiet happy moonlight talk out in the old trees.

Nellie is still slight but a lovely creature, fully matured as to years, but she would always seem much younger owing to her extreme delicacy of frame and feature. Her companion was a graceful beautiful woman of perhaps twenty-three . or four, with pale olive complexion, dark eyes, and a mouth in which lurked a smile of mischief, though some-

times almost haughty in its expression. It was the
school teacher of Maple Range, making one of her
occasional visits at the Maples. Little has been
said, if indeed anything, of Elizabeth Cross, or, as
her mother and consequently everybody else called
her, 'Lizbeth. Till within the last year she was only
occasionally at the home of her father, as she earned
her own living teaching district schools, and many
thought, found living more agreeable, as well as
more generous, anywhere than at home. Her schools
were generally too far away to admit of her coming
home excepting at the Spring and Fall vacations, yet
those periods were eagerly looked forward to by all
the young people, who, with few exceptions, liked
her. Her vivacious manner added greatly to the
zest and enjoyment of life in this rather out of the
way spot. The girls were mostly buxom, good
natured and hearty, and feeling it in no way detri-
mental to them when brought in social contact with a
young woman decidedly handsome and cultivated,
provided she were sociable and full of fun. So 'Lizbeth had the friendship of the girls to begin with,
and, I need hardly say, that of all the boys, little and
big. She was never quite so gracious and good to
the "men folks," as she proved by her behaviour
towards the girls that it was in her power to be, and
was forever tantalizing them with a regard half given,
half withheld. Her good manners, piquancy and
wit inspired general admiration, yet that wit was
often directed to the great discomfort of her admirers.
No matter, she was all the same—the desire, as well
as the dread of the sensitive masculine hearts at

Maple Range. They loved to be near her, like moths about the candle ; regarded even the wounds, which were the cost of her society, as preferable to her inattention, or their banishment from any gathering of young people graced by her presence. When she was in the settlement there was always something going on, and they were ready with all homage to wait upon and fulfil her behests, and when she was away, uncle Smith said, "they all seemed to hanker after her." She taught the Winter school in Clipnockum Hollow the Winter before, and was now teaching at Maple Range. It was wonderful how she came to be on such intimate terms at the Maples, since her mother, and therefore her father, were so "dead set agin the Maynards." But there is nothing so stubborn as facts. She read, sang, and entered with her whole soul into whatever of gaiety or gravity Robert and Nellie were engaged in. Many a picnic party given under the trees, owed its life and blytheness to the gay spirits, let loose in unconventional fun and nonsense, of Nellie and 'Lizbeth. The morning had now come for her return to duty, and Robert was waiting at the gate with the horses to take her, as she and Nellie walked slowly down towards him.

"Are n't you glad your school is most out," said Nellie.

"Why should I be, the Summer will be gone then, and Autumn days fly fast. I have only to commence another term for the Winter then at Clipnockum."

"Are you really going to brave another term at

Clipnockum, after all you suffered there with fear last Winter at the time of the lynching."

"O yes, there is no danger now, everything is peaceful, and really, though the school is smaller, they pay better wages at the Hollow than anywhere else."

"Do n't hurry girls, I had just as soon sit here in the buggy all day as not. Take your time, tell all the long stories, and pick all the late roses you want to. You can rely upon my patience," said Robert.

"How long?" asked 'Lizbeth.

"Till I could hit upon some expedient to cut short those last words girls are sure to exchange when the horses are impatient."

"Hereafter we will intrench ourselves behind a vocabulary of monosyllables, won't we Nell."

"Why yes, if Rob will be equally brief."

They were off so soon when 'Lizbeth was seated, that her good by floated back on a gust of wind.

By the time her Winter school was half through, it began to be evident that some of her admirers considered it best to let sour grapes alone, and settle down to enjoy her simple friendship. There was, however, one noticeable exception to this philosophical course, and a noble one too, for Gus Harkness was a whole-hearted fellow, as every-body admitted. Gus loved 'Lizbeth, and had told her so a hundred times or more; had told her in his own impetuous way, that he not only loved her, but he worshiped the very ground she walked on, every inch of the earth beneath her, and the air above, clear through from purgatory to paradise; and she, she took the longer walks, as she merrily told him, to give him more territory to worship. No doubt she loved Gus, but she would never give him the comfort of saying so ; that was not her way. All that he could gather from her actions he was welcome to ; but she had never, unless her silence implied it, said "yes" when he had asked her to marry him. On the strength of this tacit consent, he had built a snug little house in the valley, not far from the school-house, the first Winter she taught there ; the Summer following, had set out shrubbery generously and tastefully improved the grounds about his house ; had realized a large crop from his farm, for Gus was a good farmer. When he pressed his suit and asked her to name an "early day" in the Fall, she, for all answer, placed her school contract in his hands; then he was mad and broke a commandment ; said amongst other things, not nice to repeat, that he would see her further, and he did. There was never more persistence and devotion than he manifested, calling at her father's door for her every morning with his big, strong team of iron-grays, and bringing her home after school at night ; often exhausting all his ingenuity to wring a promise from her before she could get a chance to take another school, and getting almost frantic in his attempts to keep his temper over her cruel reserve. One morning she was riding to school beside him, on an enormous saw-log he was hauling to the Waubeee mill. It was very cold, but she was closely wrapped ; besides, he had carefully drawn about her the soft large buffalo robe he had taken from its original owner, slain by himself the previous

Fall, and they rode rapidly, talking gayly in spite of the cold. They were near the bottom of the long hill that flanked one side of the valley—a lovely solitary place—and Gus, in his attempts to make her more comfortable, had been rewarded with a peremptory "Hands off, sir," which rather tended to strengthen his determination, than otherwise. May be every body would not, but Gus did swear to himself he would know one of two things now.

"I'm going to be married next month," said he, with a laugh.

"I congratulate you," was the reply, without a smile.

"Congratulate yourself too, then, and kiss me for my unselfish consideration of your happiness, in setting the time so early. Kiss me, I say."

"I won't do it."

There followed a desperate struggle, without any satisfactory result to Gus, however, whose gallantry caused him to stop first, saying:

"Well, the fourth of March is to be our wedding day then, or never, by hokey!"

"Why, that's inauguration day," said 'Lizbeth, looking rosy and sweet.

"Of course, it is. I am to take the chair and govern ye till you dare n't say your soul 's your own."

"Well, you can 't do it, sir! My tongue belongs to me forever."

"May be you think I can 't, but you 'll see; and I 'm goin' to kiss you and break your spirit to begin with, now!'

He held the lines in one hand and 'Lizbeth tightly

H 5*

in his left arm, when the struggle recommenced. She
reminded him that he had always claimed he never
could do two things at once, adding :

"You had better attend to your driving."

"The horses know the way," he replied, and
redoubled his efforts to pave the way to nuptial discipline. In the struggle the horses were reined out
of the track onto a large but low stump, at the wayside. Left to themselves, they made the attempt to
elude it by going each side ; but that would bring the
off horse into a deep drift of snow, which, when
abreast of the stump, he concluded to avoid by jump-
ing over it. This brought the runner directly onto it.
Gus was thus suddenly recalled to another line of
duty and responsibility. With a loud command that
stopped the horses, he sprang clear off the careening
load, at the same time attempting to rescue 'Lizbeth,
but too late. She had been thrown by the impulse
of the load, downward into a narrow gully formed by
heavy rains, but now filled with light snow—the log
in some miraculous way passing clear over her, went
with a crunching swash into the snow beyond. Though
it had not harmed her, yet, so narrow was the escape,
that it held fast the corners of the robe and even her
own mantle and skirts—worn, as was then the fashion,
long and full—and thus, fairly imprisoned, she lay,
unable to move a limb, her face covered with snow.
She lay there paralyzed and speechless for an instant,
which seemed an age ; then Gus was clearing the snow
from her face and calling her name with tender, agonized accents. He really feared she was dead—death
had been so near, so imminent ; yet, when with living

voice and eyes she assured him she was not hurt, but
only very uncomfortable, he shouted aloud with joy and
laughed away the tears that apprehension had brought
to his eyes. He stood there beside her, making no
effort to release her—this devoted man who for two
years had gone at her beck and call, ready to perish
for her, if she had so willed it—laughing like one
demented over her plight. A thought had struck him,
which, with her there for once at his mercy, he proceeded to act upon.

"Say you love me, 'Lizbeth, just once before you
die!"

"Die, Gus? I tell you I am not hurt—am not
going to die, unless you let me suffocate! Oh, do
hurry and get me out!"

"You love me, do you? will marry me the fourth
of March?"

"Why, Gus, do help me out! How much value
would you place upon the ratification of a promise
made under duress?"

"Of eleven hundred feet of clear lumber?" he
interrupted.

"I'll tear my clothes all to pieces and get out of
this myself, before I will make any promise to one
who could demand it at such a time! and then, I fear,
I might not present a very edifying appearance!"

"And you might take cold! You are comfortably wrapped now; have a nice view—at your back!
I will leave you. Some good Samaritan — a bear,
likely — will come along and relieve you of your
clothing, and astonish you with the embrace you
have long denied me! Good by, 'Lizbeth!"

He strove to get away, but she cried :

"In heaven's name, Gus, don't leave me here alone! I am sure I can't stand it much longer! My blood is congealing! My limbs are cramping painfully!"

The tears were gushing from her eyes, and Gus was ready to fall down and kiss them away; but he held out steadily, determined to conquer.

"'Lizbeth, in five minutes I can effect your emancipation; but I have danced attendance upon you with no assurance of reward just as long as I am going to. Now, I can help you out, but with the understanding that you will tell me if you love me, and me alone, and that you will marry me the day I have named, and occupy with me the little home that has waited so long for its chosen mistress. Shall I help you?" he asked, looking down earnestly into her eyes.

"I don't deserve it, Gus! First, put your face down here, let me kiss you, then help me out. As your wife, I will make amends for all I have caused you to suffer."

He did not wait for the kiss, but with strong hands and a stronger will soon effected her release. Taking the loved burden up in his arms, their lips met for the first time, and their hearts melted together in mutual words of love.

She was late that morning to school, but she was not wretched. A bird sang in her heart all day, and all the days of the remaining term. At last, one night, she called the roll, and tearful children answered, knowing it was the last time. The little ones had learned to love her too. The door swung to, the key turned in the lock, and now emancipated from school contracts, she stepped into the new, stylish sleigh, and was driven home to the music of silvery bells. The house was furnished, the dresses made, and a wedding at Cross' gladdened young and old. It was the fourth of March, and Lincoln, that very same day took his seat at Washington.

There was happiness and peace in the home of 'Lizbeth and Gus, for neither of them desired to be first, and they therefore secured the perfect harmony resulting from mutual concessions. Soon after their marriage, Mr. Sutton opened a series of revival meetings in the meeting-house of the settlement, which proved a season of great and gracious outpourings. Many were turned from paths of wickedness into the ways of truth. 'Lizbeth, who had been very thoughtful upon the subject ever since her near and appalling view of death, was among the first to manifest a desire for a change of heart, the first to go forward for prayers, and hers was among the first of the many professions of conversion to God. Her experience was pronounced very bright and clear, and she was welcomed by the little band of believers with great rejoicing. After her conversion, it was but natural that she should desire that of Gus as well. Gus, poor fellow desired it too. In his new-found joy of communion with her, he could not bear a separation, even of interest or thought, from his wife, and admitted to himself that he feared he would be jealous of the very God she worshipped, if he were to be shut out. He knew, of course, she would unite with

the church, and having all his life known only veneration for the church, he had no earthly objections ; but
he told her, when she pleaded with him to "renounce
the devil and all his works," that he would gladly do
so—gladly become a Christian, only that he had no
religious emotions, no particular hatred of what was
termed the follies of the world, beyond what he had
always entertained. All he wanted of the world was
just what was honestly his. Of that, he was willing
to give a portion for the support of the church, the
spread of the gospel ; only he did not want 'Lizbeth
included in that bequest, unless he could give himself
too. Comparing his emotions with the extravagant
expressions of some under conviction of sin, he had
grave doubts as to whether he really was convicted,
though he knew " something was the matter of him."
Mrs. Wilson, at 'Lizbeth's request, talked and prayed
with him ; Mr. Sutton, also ; and while the former
was in doubt as to his real state, the latter declared to
Mrs. Cross, that " he was not far from the kingdom."
Mrs. Cross felt that he must be labored with. There
was a woe upon those "unequally yoked together
with unbelievers," and 'Lizbeth's perseverance would
depend greatly upon him. She wrestled with him
energetically ; told him his backwardness and want
of emotion was a device of the adversary of souls to
keep him from accepting the offers of mercy now
extended to him. She with half a dozen others, as
zealous, got around him and almost dragged him to
the anxious seat ; and there, under the excitement of
the hour, when a peculiar exaltation had possession of
him, he really believed it was as they represented.

In the midst of praise and prayer and exhortation, lifted, as it were, out of himself, he confessed aloud his sins and prayed for mercy. It was the last night of the meetings. He went home to begin a new life of service and devotion to his Maker; but he could not bring his soul into that subjection to God that he believed was the result of true conversion ; could not possess the joy which was expressed in every line of 'Lizbeth's face, and rang in every tone of her voice. He questioned his soul deeply, and that examination convinced him he was deceived. In the broad, garish day, he grew ashamed of the part he had been persuaded to act; ashamed that he had prayed. The mortification attending this peculiar experience, or rather want of experience, was great ; not that Gus would have been ashamed to acknowledge his God by a public profession of his acceptance with him, had he felt that to be genuine. He respected Christians, in whom he had confidence, as much as he despised hypocrites. He expressed his mortification to 'Lizbeth, who had the good sense to comfort him in quite a different way from what her mother would have done ; told him it was only a mistaken emotion, and proved nothing against him or the religion she hoped he would some day enjoy. Her sensible way of looking at the matter had the effect to reconcile him. On town meeting day, he ventured out timorously, expecting somebody would rally him upon this one sore point.

He fell in with Center on the way and learned that he was cherishing ambitions that Gus believed were fruitless. He knew the man was and had been figuring for some time to build himself up by the over-throw of another ; knew that he had been trying to undermine Maynard, and, moreover, Gus knew well that Charles Center was powerless to do so. Though he had worked early and late with that object in view, he had really overdone the matter, and instead of weakening, had strengthened his adversary's position. Mr. Maynard would be ever gratefully remembered as one whose unselfish efforts had always been for the good of Maple Range. Center, it will be remembered, had secured the final appointment of Pierre Scott at the time of the panic over a year ago, and though astonished then to find he was so influential, it had decided him to venture into political life since he had signally failed in everything else. He had caused the suggestion of his name in connection with the office of magistrate, and confidently believed he would get the nomination, and nomination in that town was equivalent to election.

He had modestly remained away until after the caucus, and entered the school-house with Gus just as the polls were opening. Gus was too good-natured to inquire who were the nominees in Center's hearing, but Dave Persons told them off, snapping his pocket-handkerchief at each name, and watching Center's face as he lingered over that of "Ben Palmer, Justice of the Peace," adding :

"It's a pity, Gus, that you was in such a deuce of a hurry to get married, for Ben is bound to marry the first couple for nothing, just to get the hang of the business, and they do say you paid old man Sutton ten dollars for that job of yours, eh ? "

Jehial Smith had been through the mill, and knew that Gus would wince at this public allusion to his recently assumed matrimonial responsibilities, and so came to the rescue with a bit of history that would turn the tables on Dave.

"I say, Gus," said he, "it's an awful pity Ben was n't Justice once at least, during the eight years that Dave was sparkin' the widder down in Illinois. They do say he would have married her sure, if he could ha' raised the money to pay the Justice, so scared was he that she would sue him for breach of promise."

Dave vanished. Poor Dave! No one was liked better, no friend more true than he; yet he had a knack of running against snags. When he returned it was late in the afternoon; he deposited his vote and just then caught sight of uncle Carce Smith on his knees away in one corner of the room, changing a ballot for some one. Here was another chance. Dave directed attention to that corner and the room grew so still the jabs of the old blunt pencil could be heard distinctly, then in a solemn voice said:

"Let us unite in prayer for uncle Smith's candidate."

Uncle Smith got on to his feet during the applause that followed, then, with long, thin finger pointing to Dave, he prepared to send that shaft of ridicule back, and he did.

"You are the man, Dave, and no one needs prayers more. But if ever I scratch another ticket and substitute your name, I will get down in dust and ashes and pray to be forgiven."

6

At the close of the polls, nearly all those that had been there in the morning were there still. That was the way to maintain the proper dignity of the town. If men were to vote and run away, there would be no crowd, no gossip worthy the name of town meeting. They might live to vote another day, but to all appearance no one believed they would. No use of going home either till after the counting of votes; without a crowd, where would the cheering of successful candidates come from ?

The votes· were counted at last, but the only announcement of interest to us was this one, and it was received in silence—"Charles Center, *constable.*"

The next day, obedient to invitation, there was a big gathering in the "sap bush" of uncle Carce Smith. It was a magnificent Spring morning; the snow had disappeared and left the brown patches of leaves which the last Autumn spread, but which the winds had gathered and piled to their own liking, and from which the warm sun brought delicious exhalations, steaming pure and fragrant, mingled with whiffs of balsamic odors from the evergreens that skirted the Waubece just over the high divide. Sunlight lay in patches also under the trees that looked stark and uncomfortable, denuded of their leafy garments. Of just such it was the poet discoursed for childhood's benefit :

> The colder it blows, they fling off their clothes,
> And in Winter quite naked appear.

The sounds of the camp were discernible a long way off in the Spring atmosphere, through the bare trees. Men were shouting to one another and to the oxen that were slowly bringing in the great tanks of sap. Some were chopping wood; some were hewing out troughs, while some were manufacturing the same of birch bark. Others were busy building and attending to fires under the kettles, little and big, and the cauldrons of boiling syrup. Another was busy about the huge evaporators.

The fires over which the multiform utensils hung, suspended by curious devices, were in front of a three-sided shelter or cabin, where, upon clean straw and a goodly supply of bedding, the more feeble of the visitors and the babies were deposited. In the cabin the watchmen of the camp were wont to sleep, "turn about," as they boiled the sap night and day during the season.

Women were busy here now, unpacking dishes and arranging them on the long table improvised of rough boards and covered with white table linen. There was a great deal of work on hand, and willing, if sometimes "fussy," hands to do it, and bits of choice gossip were exchanged during its execution. Check aprons were in demand, and hither, thither and everywhere their wearers appeared, like jack-o'-lanterns in the twilight mist.

The talk that rose and fell upon the distant ear was not unlike the perpetual music of the sociable little peepers on the borders of a pool. A perpetual flow of words and a burden of "What's the news? tell the news, all the news," piped in treble voices which sank to a low diminuendo at the recital of some choice tid-bit of gossip. The women were all so

intent upon their employment, wordwise and otherwise, that Ben Palmer had driven right in among
them, the sound of the wheels deadened by the leafy
carpet, unnoticed till he came to a standstill and
called to Mrs. Wilson :

"Have you women folks no eyes for the 'Squire
and his family."

There was a sudden lull and then a swell of voices
as they rushed to the wagon, to shake hands and
welcome the new arrival, and Ben, with satisfied
looks, said :

"That looks a little more like now, when your important citizens honor your sugar bees you want to
fly around and make a big fuss over 'em."

"Why the la sus ! Ruth you will catch your
death out here, and Freddie too. Ben orto hed more
sense than to bring ye out, even if ye did tease to
come, as I'll warrent you did," said Mrs. Wilson.
"There's Ruth been pimpin' all Winter, and a drinking yarb tea all Spring, with Miannetta there, week
in and week out, trying to cure her up, and now to
come right out into these damp woods, seems like
tempting Providence, it does."

"Mother, I feel so much better to get out and
away from home a little; I will be real careful, see
how I'm bundled up."

"Well we must make the best of a poor idee,"
said Mrs. Wilson, putting the fortieth great biscuit on
the table, while as many as could get hold of her,
hauled Ruth off to the little cabin near the great fires,
where Freddie was taken in hand by Nellie Maynard,

and, led by her hand, knew and asked for no other attention all that long delightful day.

Ben having disposed his team safely, came back to the merry party, and leaning with folded arms against a tree, commenced a good humored complaint against the ills of life generally.

"Why," said he, "I've been up ever since four o'clock this morning, hard at work to get up an appetite for all the good things here. After doing up all my own work at the barn, I went into the house, and just pulled off my coat and rolled up my sleeves, and washed, and churned, and baked, and brewed, and made a cheese."

"That was nothing," said Jehial Smith. "A man can *work*, but I tell ye it's hard to *starve*. Now I got up with a tolerable appetite this morning. I hadn't had a single mouthful since yesterday, and to-morrow, you know, would be the third day. Well, when I asked Belinda for my breakfast, she told me we was 'jest out.' Think of that Ben, and now, though I took a good deal of comfort for once in hurrying, I've got here right in sight of all these nick-nacks, just in time to wait nobody knows how long for my dinner. There is no hard work like starving."

"Here's my hat," said Ben, stooping to take up Freddie, whom Nellie had led to his father, and carrying him to see the curious baby in the cabin, "without no hair on its head." It was Belinda's baby and evidently better fed than Jehial.

"The very image of Belinda," said one, while another declared it looked exactly like Jehial. Another saw in it a perfect likeness of grandma

Smith, while she suggested a resemblance to Paddy O'Shannon, who just then was lumbering into view.

"How blue his eyes are," said Nellie, and Mrs. Ellis said :

"Yes, his eyes are blue, but in this fresh atmosphere his nose I notice is getting a little reddish."

"Be sure I like horse-radish wonderful well," said old Mrs. Porter, who was not quite as deaf as a post, for she caught now and then a whole word, and always used it as a text on which to expatiate, to the great amusement of all listeners.

"I think the baby would be right pretty," said grandma Smith, "if he was not so extravagantly bald."

"O, so you heard about that did ye. I knew Jehial would tell on 't, it was so funny," said Mrs. Porter, who had struck another word, and they were all in for a good one now. "I told father that it would be in everybody's mouth, and the neighbors would all be sayin' to one another, 'O, have you hearn about that scrape?' I dropped my patchin', thimble and all, and run out directly the cow bawled, and there she was a goin' it, lickerty brindle, through the garding, with her head stuck clean through a old baskit that I had been strainin' soap through, and the bottom had fell out down inter the bar'l ; but bless ye 't want no loss." The last sentence was added in a soothing consolatory manner, and she joined in the good humor, laughing with the rest till the tears came into her dim old eyes.

"Mamma," said Carlos Center, who was regarding the baby as curiously as if it was a mummy just from the catacombs, "It hain't got no eyes nor no mouf in its face round here," and he went behind the baby and put his hand on the back of its head, and looked up into his mother's face with puzzled look, adding, "nor no teeth, but it wants to bite all the time."

"It has a very wise look," was uncle Carce's observation, "as though it had been engaged in profound thought ever since the dawn of the Christian era."

"Era! Why that's the very railroad my Samantha's man got killed on," chimed in Mrs. Porter. "Marcy to us, but wasn't that a smash up, though. Took the kink all out of Samantha, for ye see they never could find hide nor hair of the chists, and she hadn't the fust blessed rag nor ribbin to put onto her children, nothin' but a little old bake kittle that I gin her with her sett'n' out."

"No, no, mother, that was the New York and Erie," said her husband, "not the Christian."

"Well, I can't say that he was raly a Christian, though he had a good many wak'nin's and backslid ag'in. But he was under a powerful consarn of mind, I remember, that Winter that the Millerites was round. But that was a good while ago, and he might a gone back to the beggarly elements, for all I know." Here the old dame heaved a sigh that seemed to come from clear down below her apron strings.

"Good day, O'Shannon," said uncle Carce, advancing to take the hand of the Irishman, who claimed he had "papers," and was, therefore, a man and a brother. At any rate he was a welcome personage at all gatherings. "Why where's the wife and babies, you promised to bring with you to-day?"

"Oh, they'll be afther comin' next time, Misther Smith."

"Next time! Why, man, do you think we make sugar all Summer?" said grandma Smith.

"Well, but, Mrs. Smith," was the deliberate explanation, "the wather in the Waubece is so high that I was fareful it wusn't safe to bring me wagin across the dam, an' me woman, you know, is too low on the ground to wade."

"What's that, O'Shannon? Is the water running over the dam already?"

"Sure, an' it is; in some places half the height o' me boot now."

"Well, friends, we will have to look out for our logs over there. When the water gets that high, it's time to wake up, and nearly every man of us has logs in jeopardy."

"Jeopardy! Why, I thought you hauled yer. logs down to Watkins' mill," said Mrs. Porter, looking mystified.

"Yes marm, that's just what we did."

"Well, what d'ye mean by sayin' yer logs are in jeopardy?"

"Oh, ye see, mother, that is the old Indian name," said Mr. Porter.

"Well, I never hearn it called that before. Jeopardy! what a name! Them Injuns beat everything in naming places. I du declare to man."

And the old lady addressed herself again to her

knitting, counting each stitch with a jerk of her head that flapped her wide cap border back and forth with great effect.

"It'll be hard for us to lose them logs, but nothing to Watkins' loss, if he should have a break in his dam, just as he might begin to saw."

"Wall, now, I do n't know, Mr. Smith, as Samanther reely thinks he is damned. She do n't say so, but she is kinder flighty and wanderin' in her mind, and has been ever since the smash-up. It puts a body out a good deal, ye know, when they lose all their chists and things," broke in the old lady.

Uncle Carce got up with a terrible frown on his face, and set to work punching the fire energetically. Grandma knew the frown was only the effect of sup pressing the smile that he feared would hurt the deaf old lady's feelings, and he never was known to willfully hurt any one's feelings in all his long, simple and pure life. Those who knew him well respected him all the more that, as they knew, he possessed a wonderfully quick appreciation of the ludicrous, and frowned away many a time the laughter which was almost irresistible, but whose indulgence might have wounded some simple heart.

He examined the kettle of syrup "sugaring off" for the occasion and pronounced it done. The boys had been at work some time preparing little dainty wooden ladles or spoons, and now each one was helped to a generous saucer of warm maple sugar.

"Boys, can't you find some ice somewhere?" uncle Carce said, and lo, in a few moments his dutiful son, with Gus, was seen bringing in a great basket

I

full of solid crystals they had found, sheltered by a ledge of rock just at the source of Dimple Run Creek. Delicious wax was manufactured that had a marked effect in suspending conversation, the ejaculatory attempts·at which by the wax-eaters induced great amusement. Then a shout rent the air when Wilson, thinking to improve upon the manufactured article, scraped a huge mouthful of the adhering sugar from the side of the kettle, and put it in his mouth.

"It waxeth hot," said Ben Palmer, laughing with an irreverence that was scarcely relished by his suffering father-in-law. Just then dinner was announced, and they gathered about the table, hats, hoods, scarfs and sunbonnets on, these being humorously declared to be "full dress." What tea and coffee, with *real* cream! what bread and biscuit, with such delicious butter, eaten with a crisp water-cress for a relish. Home-cured and smoked ham with a handsome garnishing of parsley and boiled eggs held the place of honor, surrounded by a numberless array of good and toothsome food of every description. Last of all came dried-pumpkin pie, a pie that originated with the Pilgrim mothers, and has been handed down, with due credit to them, as delicious, economical and always to be had. Upon the frontier, after the first crop, this pie is as common on the settler's table as the universal bread and butter and coffee.

"All mankind, in spite of color and caste and estate, occupy a common level three times a day, through and amid all the commotions of life, when the universal stomach, the foundation of trade and brotherhood, is satisfying its importunities. How few reflect, as they eat the nicely prepared food, that they thus replenish an irrepressible principle of life and growth," said Mr. Sutton, after grace at the close of the meal, while still all lingered at the table in that pleasing after-dinner communion, where there are good talkers and good listeners.

"An irrepressible principle, truly," said Herbert Gray, a young man from Ohio, now visiting his sister, Mrs. Ellis. "A principle that, in spite of all obstacles, still pushes on. The foot of a Chinese woman may be encased in an iron shoe, but the growing force of nature is simply thwarted, and produces an uncouth ankle above the dwarfed and useless foot, like that unsightly gnarl upon the tree."

"The peculiar taste of the Flathead Indians is another instance which shows the omnipotence of this force. By the application of powerful pressure, a malformation of the head changes features not otherwise repulsive until the human face resembles that of goblins," said Mr. Sutton.

"And to come nearer home," interposed Mrs. Ellis, "if not convinced that symmetry demands the freedom of this force, we have its evidence right among ourselves; health is outraged, proportion set aside by the use of restraints, which produce an unnatural slenderness of waist, and an equally unnatural breadth of shoulder. We women folks have two masters, fashion and appetite."

"We have submitted very willingly and agreeably to one of 'em to-day, I'm sure," said Mrs. Wilson. "But if there isn't Tad Wilson in the very tipmost top of the trees."

"What are you doing *there*, Tad?" shouted Wilson.

"I want to get the other side of the table," said Tad.

"Well, why in the name of wonder did n't you crawl under then," said Mrs. Wilson, exhibiting some excitement.

"Or go round?" asked several.

"Cause 'Lizbeth Harkness told me never to go round anything I could get over," explained Tad.

"Why, Tad!" cried 'Lizbeth, "I'll forgive the misapplication; but come down now, that's a dear boy! and I will try and make my meaning more clear to you. Oh, dear! I am so afraid the child will fall!"

"He fall? Never!" was Wilson's cheerful assurance. "Why, thar's none o' my gang that can climb with that boy! He lives in tree-tops."

This expedient of the boy's drew out some good remarks which at last brought them around to the theme of the hour, and an earnest discussion ensued on passing events (that reached them but tardily compared with their importance and their own impatience for news). Perfect unanimity of sentiment apparently prevailed, till uncle Caree made some reproachful allusion to the "Southern chivalry." Mr. Center undertook its defense in sharp words that astonished that loyal, Union-loving company.

"You have great contempt of the chivalry now, Mr. Smith; but wait a few months and your contempt will change to respect and fear. When the North crosses swords with them, and that is a certain event, disparagement of their power and courage will end. They are too spirited to submit to Lincoln's or any other mud-sill's administration. It is the revolt of noble natures against the rule of the ignoble, the *parvenu.*"

"Men are not blind! They can see that this objection to Lincoln's administration is only the pretense! Through it old fires break out. This matter has been brewing for years—and ever so many years. Capital has striven to get its heel upon the neck of labor; to alter the constitution so that it should conform to this end; to rend in pieces the United States. Why, secession was the midnight dream and the noonday cry of Southern statesmen, when I was a boy. The dark plans incipient then are maturing now; and it would be the same if the angel Gabriel himself had been chosen President," said uncle Carce.

"Where is your freedom?" inquired Center. "What is the liberty worth which denies the right to withdraw from a compact that cripples your interest? It is an Old-world despotism, which issues passports and places restraints upon subjects guilty of no crime."

"What! Is it no crime to plan treason; to arm and fortify, using public material to do so? It is a design to overthrow free institutions; to perpetuate slavery and introduce a reign of aristocracy, with strong monarchical tendencies!" continued uncle Carce.

"Those institutions were based upon the assumption of the equality of human rights. The government the South will establish when victorious, will have another—an opposite foundation—of real benefit

to all, for the negro will be brought into healthy subjection, and, denied a Northern asylum, he will once
more have a value," said Center, pompously.

"You say those institutions *were* based upon the
assumption of the equality of races; now, I say they
are based upon the equal rights of all men ; that we
have that government still, and it *will* be sustained
without the withdrawal of a single State," said uncle
Carce, fervently.

"If you were an Hibernian, you could not in one
breath have uttered a more glaring contradiction,"
laughed Center. "You boast of the assured liberty
of action, and then declare that South Carolina,
though she came into it voluntarily, can not as voluntarily leave the Union! Like the Roman Catholic's
religion, than which there is no blacker despotism
under the sun, which invites with all the blandish-
ments of unscrupulous hypocrisy the unsuspecting
nun, and then denies her enlightened desire to withdraw, you would say to South Carolina, You can
come but you can not go ! "

"I do not say that, which is untrue of equal rights
and equal rewards. Your claims and mine to respect
and protection are equal, as our efforts to earn them
are equal. None can deny these assurances of our
government. As to South Carolina, she came into
the Union with her slaves, and might have retained
them perhaps ; but she was not satisfied with this ;
now demands, as a condition of her loyalty, a consti-
tutional protection of slavery in the Territories ; even
proposes to chastise the North into acquiescence with
her demand ! Oh, sir, terms *will* be dictated and

she forced to remain in the Union, and very likely deprived of her slaves," said uncle Carce, warning.

"That's all bosh, now, uncle Smith! The South never will submit to Northern coercion," cried Center, losing his temper.

"It's more cussedness than anything else that ails the South," said Gus, losing patience and indignant that a secessionist should suddenly be discovered among them. "You say the South will not submit to coercion; I say they will; they *shall;* and secession principle will have to keep pretty close too. The North will not submit to an alteration of the constitution; neither will she submit to secession — the breaking up and destruction of the Union, as that is in opposition to the constitution."

"Why, ye do n't say, Gus!" chimed in Mrs. Porter. "Ye do n't say that your constitution is breaking now, at your time o' life? but then, there was our Emeline, you know; she was as young and chipper as you be; but she jest went and broke her constitution all to flinders, working up there in them piney woods; worked! of course she did, and never any pay either, for ye see the boss, he ran off. and then the company failed; and Emeline, she never got what would buy an ounce of nutmegs. Nutmegs is dreadful good now in this new-fangled dope that they call 'mange'—yes, that's it—the same that ailed our dog. They make it out o' corn starch, Belinda says; and another thing, nutmegs is good for babies when they are troubled with colic. You must steep it in tea, and put in a little sugar and cream, though if you hain't got sugar, molasses 'll do, and if ye hain't any milk—"

"O thunder, mother ! hold on ! or, if you know of anything in the world good for wind, take some ; take a lot of it ; and then see if you can't catch the boss," roared Mr. Porter, rubbing his bald head and laughing immoderately, as did everybody else.

The old lady laughed too ; she always did laugh, if she saw others laughing, and cried if they cried. She did not dream they were laughing at her remarks ; had even now forgotten what she had been saying. She was so deaf and so innocent, living much in the past ; as regarded the present, except that she could see, and sight is a blessing, with ten thousand around her, she would be, "poor soul, all alone."

While the dinner was in progress, Nellie, whose appetite had been ruined by too much sugar, had volunteered to take care of and amuse the children. So with Freddie and Carlos Center on each side of her, she was comfortably disposed upon the blankets and hay in the cabin, with Belinda's baby in her lap. An invoice of small fry about her.

"Tell us a story, Nellie, about some other baby. I'm tired of this one," said Carlos, and Nellie responded :

"Well, once upon a time there was a king—"

"O, Nellie, you need n't try to fool us, that was Mr. Sutton's dog, his name is King, tell us a *real* story now."

"This story is not about a dog."

"Honest injun ! Ain't it a dog ?"

"No, it was a wise man; and one day two women

came to him, and between them carried a baby, each one saying it was her baby."

"And could n't the baby tell by crying which was its own mother. Why did n't it reach out its hands, this way?"

"It was too little. One woman said, ' It is my child, O king,' and the other woman said, ' Nay—' "

"I know how she did that. Our horses neigh," said Freddie, giving her an imitation.

"She did not talk that way, but said, ' No, no— the baby is mine.' The king was perplexed. so he said to his servant, ' Bring me a sword.' "

"What is a sword, Nellie."

"A long sharp knife."

"Was he going to feed the baby ?"

"No, he wanted to see which was the real mother, and, taking the knife in one hand and the baby in the other, he said, ' Now I will cut the baby in two."

"Oh! Oh! What a awful man he was."

"Well, one woman screamed, and said, ' Oh ! do n't harm the baby, let the other woman have it, rather than to have it killed.' But the other woman never cried or said a single word against his cutting it in two. So the king gave it to the woman that cried, because he then knew that she was the real mother, and loved the baby ; and she went home very glad."

"Was n't he good, Freddie. What did you say he was ? "

"A king, a great monarch."

And Carlos cried :

"Would n't he make a splendid *constable.*"

The dinner was over, the party was breaking up.

6*

Mrs. Porter had refused Ben Palmer's invitation
to a seat in his wagon, on account of her fear of his
" skittish horses," preferring the more slow but sure
locomotion of oxen. She had with some difficulty,
been boosted, and shoved, and pulled into the hind
end of the wagon, when Mr. Cross had called out,
" all aboard." Her width secured to her the entire
seat, which was nothing but a board, held in its place
across the wagon box by the stakes in front and her
immense weight, which forbade the possibility of its
moving either forward or back. Her loading was
always a ceremonious affair, calling for general assistance and eliciting humorous remarks, which latter she
was too deaf, and her husband too busy, to hear; but
there was universal satisfaction when once it was accomplished, and she finally settled into position. Sitting there alone awaiting the other passengers, who
were striving bravely to get in the last word, she
looked not unlike " Patience on the monument," excepting that she seldom smiled at grief. Like nearly
all deaf people she labored under the delusion that
other people, too, were "hard o' hearin'," and her
voice was always pitched above the ordinary tone.
Her husband stood by the wagon. Bending over
towards him, she made a simple request, but in a tone
of voice, such as an irate sea captain would employ in
a gale, shouting:

" Hizabee Porter, git my knittin' bag from that
stump, and reach it here."

That scream was too much for Spark and Bally,
to whose honesty and steadiness there were some
bounds. They started like frightened deer out into

the pathless wood. The fleshy old lady keeled over at the first jump they made, falling backward like a pillow, and where her comfortable form had been a moment before, nothing was now visible but her two slippered feet and ankles, encased in striped crimson and white hose. There was very little taper to her ankles, yet they reminded one of barbers' poles, as they helplessly whipped the edge of the seat or swayed right and left as the wagon bounced on over logs, and dashed against stumps in the wake of the demoralized oxen.

Men followed, shouting the customary command of "whoa! whoa!" as unavailingly as if they merely added to the excitement of the chase.

Fortunately the animals soon undertook to pass a tree on either side, and were brought to a sudden standstill by the yoke. All out of breath with fright and rapid running, Mr. Porter, first to reach the vehicle, climbed in and removed the seat, so as to let the two helpless feet down on a level with the rest of the old lady's body. He raised her up with the assistance of the others, who now arrived, and affectionately inquired as to her hurts, expecting a harrowing recital, but instead was met with the question:

"Did you git my knittin' work?"

"No, mother. I didn't suppose you would want it right away. I thought you had got started after the 'Boss.'"

A loud hurrah had gone up when it was found she was unhurt, and the welkin rang again with laughter and merriment. She was brought back to the road where the rest of the company waited to congratulate her and exchange comments upon her peculiar and oft-recurring misfortunes. There was no accounting for the seeming contradiction, but the settlers universally liked the old lady, pitied her, and yet "everlastingly made fun of her."

This was the memorable month of April, 1861, memorable for the commencement of the war undertaken to conquer the great conspiracy of this century, perhaps the greatest known to the world; and in the history of revolution, famous not only for the grandeur of its conception, but for the audacity and boldness of the measures adopted for its execution. The conspirators had maneuvered to fill all the important posts in the government, at their leisure had stripped of their available defenses all its forts and arsenals, and when the crisis came, there was a temporary paralysis because of the discovery.

Secretary Floyd had treacherously transmitted much of the arms and munitions of war to the Southern strongholds, and then, placing them in the hands of the insurgents, resigned his position, uniting his fortunes with the South, which now took up the cry of the aggrieved, "Let us alone, Northern mudsills. It is cowardly to invade the rights of a chivalrous and unoffending people."

"The Star of the West," a Northern war steamer, had failed to communicate with the garrison that lay beleaguered on the wave, and the thrill was felt even in Maple Range when the stars and stripes at its masthead were assailed. The retaliating flash from Sumter enkindled their devotion, warming the blood of

the settlers, who had felt the warning of later events
in that first thrill. They rose at the flash to the
height of inspiration, which they did not know was
so universal,— that resolve to daring deed, in sympathy with which "the common pulse kept time."
Throughout the land was felt the jar when Sumter
fell, and there awakened a patriotism as noble as that
of '76. Lincoln's proclamation reached the remotest
vale that had slumbered beneath the protecting arm
and the peaceful banner of the United States. Sev-
enty-five thousand men responded. The student's
midnight lamp was extinguished as he buckled on the
sword ; the counting-room was exchanged for the
camp ; the plow stood idle in the furrow ; both plow-
man and horse had donned the trappings of Mars, and
sought the field where was budding, so soon to burst
into crimson, the blossom of strife. Down from the
sacred desk, even, came men whose religion comprehended resistance to the arm that dared to threaten
the dismemberment of States.

Herbert Gray, like others of his profession, heard
the clarion call, "To arms !" It meant him as truly
as though he had been called by name. His mother
country had need of his young arm. She had nourished him, and like a grateful child he would defend
her. Not only would he dedicate his person, his fortune and his sword to her, but all his influence and
talents were thrown into the cause. His sister and
her husband accompanied him home to Ohio, where,
after enlisting in a regiment then forming, and receiving the commission of captain, Herbert had turned
his persuasive talents in the same channel, and his

brother-in-law, with his sister's consent and encouragement, was the recipient of a lieutenant's badge.
George Langmere, an acquaintance from Blakely,
who chanced to be in Sandusky on business, was persuaded also to volunteer, and was gratified with the
position of first sergeant in the same company. After
a few weeks of drill, they were all three permitted to
return to Minnesota to make final preparations to
leave with their regiment, then awaiting orders. Mrs.
Ellis returned home with them.

There had, in their absence, been industrious re-
cruiting, in which Robert Maynard had taken an
active part, until stricken down by a fever which left
him near the threshold of Eternity. The lingering
sickness that followed prevented his joining the army
that Summer. In accordance with his ardent desire,
David Sears took his place in the ranks, with many
more of our friends at Maple Range and Clipnockum.
Just before the return from Ohio of the three who
had, without intending it, "deserted their country"
and joined an Ohio regiment, there had occurred one
of those unpleasant circumstances that serve to
shadow a whole neighborhood in gloom. A new flag
had been procured for the school-house in the Hollow,
the only public building excepting the church, and
where all the war meetings were held. The staff was
already awaiting it. One evening, just as the sun
was setting, and its shadows were gathering over the
valley, they assembled to raise the flag. A lonely
whippoorwill was piping his sad lay. Mr. Center, as
usual at all war gatherings, put in an appearance that
night, and as usual had disagreeable things to say.

He had openly avowed his sympathy with the foe his neighbors were going out to meet; had served that foe by placing every possible obstruction in the way of enlistment; yet, because he was a neighbor, and more especially because his wife was respected and beloved by them, he had met only silent reproof. Often unrebuked, he had declared the Southern rebellion a righteous one; had mocked their enthusiasm, whenever they had given to it patriotic expression. Now, when the beloved banner slowly unfurled amid the cheers, when manly eyes were wet with manly tears, and sobs were stifled in manly breasts, Charles Center stood unmoved, and with folded arms and scornful lip watched their emotion. When they cheered he groaned; three times through the twilight the cheering rang; three times the miserable groan that followed exasperated them, till at length all eyes turned upon him, as Gus Harkness asked,

"Are you sick, Mr. Center?"

"Yes. It's enough to make any man sick, to see folks make such fools of themselves over a contemptible dish-rag, that in two months will have no meaning under the sun, save as it is associated with ignominy and defeat. The very men denounced as rebels in some of your spread eagle harangues, will bring it from the clouds and trample it in the dust—and for my part, I say most earnestly, God speed the hour."

"There, that will do, Center," said Gus, "you have made the last speech on that platform that will go down with this crowd. We have borne that kind of talk a good while, not because we liked *you*, mind

you, but because we respected your wife, and hoped
that for her sake, if not for inborn principle, you
would desist. There are times when forbearance
ceases to be a virtue. While you confined your insults to us, we did not molest you. But, sir, you
can not insult that flag," lifting his eyes and pointing
upward, "without rendering an account to us, who
have sworn solemnly to defend it from insult."

" *That's so*," said a heavy voice in the crowd, "we
all think well o' yer woman, an' becos ye know it, ye
think ye can say what ye like safe enough ; an' ye've
jest be'n yowpin' treason an' sech all the Spring,
right under our very noses. Naow ye say ye're
s-i-c-k—an' ye have only to tell us yer symptoms,
while a few on us feel yer pulse—we're reckoned
very skillful in the cold water treatment."

"Yaas, an' we'll larn ye a new ditty, 'kase we
think 'tain't healthy for ye to harp on one eternal
string, an' the new music ye can dance tew."

"Now you must promise to shet pate, Center,"
called another voice, " or ye'll have a blarsted fuss,
that belike will end in introducin' ye to the buz-
zards."

"Yis, indade, we'll sind ye a throttin' on a long
road that's got no turns, nor guide board, be jabers,"
cried another.

"And knock all the steam out o' yer locomotive,
to boot," yelled still another.

"You'd better commence pretty soon ; you are
spinning out a pretty long programme ; the audience
will be tired before the curtain rises," said Center.

" We are going to give you time. to frame that promise, not to spout treason any more."

" You need n't wait. I shall never make promises to men, scoundrels rather, only fit, it seems, to murder the queen's English."

" You must be careful of your nicknames, Center; we are not scoundrels, but we intend to have your promise, in less than twenty minutes, never to open your head in favor of secession again," said Dave Persons.

"Sorry to disappoint men when they set their hearts on anything. Desperate times these, when miserable vagabonds, who never saw the inside of a spelling-book, talk of extorting promises from free, intelligent citizens. It's a God-forsaken cause that employs such agents and resorts to such measures. But now, see here, I shall express my sentiments, and no thanks to anybody in this crowd. The rebellion, I say, is just. The South is disgusted with a union that brings them into contact with just such men, aye knaves, as you are.

"Not a word more, sir," said Dave Persons, stepping up, but uncle Caree drew him back.

" Do n't forget that you are a man, Dave ; these proceedings are disgraceful," said he, "and not in accordance with law, peace or good neighborhood."

" Do n't talk of law, Mr. Smith," said Center, "to men who assisted in hanging two helpless beings on yonder tree " (Dave was not present when the Indians were hung), " nor of peace to men who have just enlisted in the wickedest war the world shall ever know."

" We intend to finish your treason first, an' ef ye

K   7

do n't shet yer mouth, what 's left of *you*, won't make much of a grease spot, Center," said a voice ; while uncle Carce drew Mr. Center back a little from the crowd, and tried to persuade him to retire with him at once.

"For your own sake and that of your wife, and for ours, who are ready to assist you, and yet may not have the power soon, come. Do you not consider the danger you incur, in thus exasperating men whose blood is already up? A remote insult to that flag is about to take them from home and all they hold dear—to exposure, danger, and very likely to death. Let me entreat of you to withdraw now, without further allusion to your sentiments."

"No use coaxing me, uncle Carce, my rights here are just as good as any other man's, and I shall say what I d——n please, if every red-mouthed cur in the settlement snarls."

Raising his voice, he continued :

"I say once again, what I have said many times, that it is an unholy harvest of blood that you are going to gather, the fruit of years of Northern tyranny and Northern oppression. A quiet, noble, high-minded people desire to be left unmolested in the possession of their God-given rights, and when their prayer is denied, they wish to retire, to withdraw themselves, their property, and their State; and ye, *such as ye*, protest, and prepare to swoop down upon, and lay waste their sunny land. You have recruited your impious horde from the very dens of pollution. Under that very rag," pointing scornfully to the banner, "will march the vile spawn of Satan ! "

"There now," said uncle Carce, in a trembling undertone, "I am afraid he has hit the buck in the eye, and you can't mad the animal more."

Rough, strong hands were laid upon Center, while the excitement grew intense. Old men were tugging at the coat-skirts of young men, begging them to desist from violence, while voices mewed like cats, barked like dogs, crowed like a cock, and made noises like the flapping of wings. Curses and threats mingled with piteous pleadings.

A tremendous bully, who maintained a safe distance, was vociferating, "Pitch in to him, boys, give him ——!"

During a lull, Center was heard to say : "I reckoned without my host, in expecting civility from my own neighbors, and my wife's friends."

"O you can't come any of your civility dodges— we don't swaller insults in this neighborhood any longer ; caliker won't save ye now."

"No, old cock ! Ye can't cackle that chune any longer on this roost."

"Nothin' b-b-b-but a clean j-j-j-jacket will save C-c-c-center !"

Gus Harkness caught him by one arm, while Dave Persons took the other, saying :

"We want that promise now, Center! or by the great Jehovah, we will chuck ye into the Waubeco quicker 'n ye can spit !"

Away they started down the steep bank, dragging their victim despite his desperate struggles, despite the cries of "Hold, boys, for heaven's sake," "Stop, boys, stop," and the like useless counsel ; for a crowd, on the double-quick down an incline, is in truth beyond recall, and irresistible. In less time than I am relating, they had reached the water and plunged Center in, while some voice on the bank, in solemn, camp-meeting tones, lined a hymn :

> "' Plunged in a gulf of dark despair,'

sing ! "

In slow measure the crowd obeyed, after which the pale, shivering man was drawn up and given time to breathe. His promise being demanded and refused, he was again plunged in, while the same voice lined the same measure :

> "' A wretched traitor lies ; '

sing ! "

The slow, solemn meter rolled out over the water, and again Center was drawn out ; again, after breathing pace, interrogated, and upon giving a firm "No," he was again sent struggling into the water.

> "' His clothes seem very damp to wear,'

sing ! "

As they drew Center out again, another line was added with exaggerated bass :

> "' He 'll change them if he 's wise.' "

"Now, Mr. Center," said Dave Persons, "we have drawn you out the third time and the last, for as sure as there is a hereafter we will neither draw you out nor permit you to be drawn out again. You shall promise now, never to open your mouth in the interest of traitors again, or—*die !* "

"I promise you ! " said he, who knew what man

he dealt with, and that he stood on the last plank offered him.

He was instantly released, and, climbing the bank, disappeared in the darkness ere the sounds of exultation had died away on bluff and in forest recess, whence they had been echoed and re-echoed as they rolled up from the crowd on the banks of the winding Waubeee.

Mr. Center reached home to find his wife absent, she having accepted Nellie Maynard's invitation to spend the night at The Maples, leaving a note of explanation, containing a promise of return to-morrow, upon the table. But oh! ere to-morrow he was far from her in person, and farther still in criminal designs, having left behind a detailed account of his humiliating treatment, glossing over his own conduct so as to make the abuse seem undeserved.

"I leave you and my child," he wrote, "because I am a man too independent to submit to ignoble terms. I will send you money as soon as I can raise it, that you may go to Chicago to your father, if it is your wish to leave these people who have laid an indebtedness upon me which I will not fail to pay."

The wife returning next day found this beside her own note, caught it up, read it swiftly and fell to the floor insensible. Nellie who accompanied her, ignorant of the terrible transactions in the Hollow, sprang to her and tried, with the aid of cold water, to restore her to consciousness, but in vain.

Sometimes, when otherwise the heart would break, it is preserved from the full pressure of its misery by those kind opiates of nature, insensibility

and disease. Days of prostration and delirium merci-
fully ward off the crushing weight of despair.

Miannetta, on hearing of the events of the night
and guessing the unhappiness of Mrs. Center when
she should know all, had hastened to her aid ; and
most opportune was her arrival.

Mrs. Center was still upon the floor, a pillow
beneath her head, and Nellie, whose strength was not
sufficient to place her upon the bed, was making every
effort to restore her.

With Miannetta's help, she was raised and placed
upon a couch where for many weeks she remained,
stricken by a fearful fever. Kind-hearted neighbors
gathered round her with a sympathy that was more
than sympathy—a sorrow mingled with reproach to
their own flesh and blood, whose unrestrained passion
was thought to have caused the suffering of this
fragile woman. All that love and kindness could
prompt was done for her.

Once, just as the day was dawning upon the earth
now clad in its mantle of green, she opened her eyes
—in them no glare or wildness ; in her speech no
sharpness or incoherence. Looking into the face of
Mrs. Maynard who was holding her wasted hand, in
a voice so faint, and yet so sweet as to bring tears
to the eyes of the faithful watcher, she said :

"I will wait patiently, praying God in his own
time to bring light out of this darkness, order out of
this confusion."

CHAPTER V.

MARTIAL STRAINS.

THAT the wing of an eagle is not so gentle as the pinion of a dove, was in a measure realized by the volunteers as soon as they were sworn into service, and were henceforth subject to another will than their own. They began to think how delightful was the old free life ; how hard to break the chains of habit. It was sweet to think of being one's own master after all, if it was in the backwoods ; to plan out one's own work ; rise early or sleep late as the mood came on. To plow, plant, or hunt ; or, better still, when indolence favored the occupation. to loaf at Watkins' store, where all was spick and span new, shiny and fragrant ; where some of the pretty girls were almost sure to drop in, mayhap the very one loved best in all the world, mischievously inquiring for odd wares, such as "extract of pocket-handkerchief," "aggregate buttons" and the like. Then the walks home with the saucy little minxes, through the bird-blessed woods, while down deep in each breast a rhythmic measure was beating in unison. O those loves unspoken, those loves avowed, those loves already ratified by heaven ! how sweetly now they drew their tendrils round the heart ; how hard to wrench from their fastenings, and hie away—to what ? The question checked the breath, and manly dignity was often summoned to arrest the coming tear.

Perhaps, of all the sad hearts, none was heavier than that which beat under the vest of Gus Harkness, for a true lover is not cured of love by the possession of its object. The difficulties of his wooing had increased the importance of his winning. Though he had been bluffed, cajoled and tyrannized over to the end of the chapter, yet the chapter had ended in his being loved, and the very traits which some would have deemed unpardonable faults were charms dwelt upon and recalled again and again with delight. Every peculiarity of 'Lizbeth's, no matter how hard to endure at first, now increased her value, and he declared he should always admire a downright wicked coquet more than any other woman. Often a mother who dotes upon her deformed child, does it the more because of that which to others is repulsive. Just so Gus loved 'Lizbeth for traits which had caused him much pain, and which others deemed reprehensible. Now he must leave her and the love she so freely gave him. He must leave 'Lizbeth at her father's, and the little home in the valley, where were rose and vine and song, must be closed and silent, how long or if forever, God alone knew. Mrs. Cross gave him much good-advice and many cautions against exposing himself to night air lest he should contract "malarian fever;" against sleeping on hard straw beds in "open housen with the chinks all knocked out;" against "eatin' unhullsom and irregler meals," which advice often recurred to him as he lay on his blanket beneath the stars or less merciful clouds, on an unfenced field, having fallen there, too weary to prepare the meal of hardtack and coffee.

The dreaded morning came all too soon, and the line of march, augmented at each house, moved through the woods to the inspiring strains of martial music, till it reached the last house, that of Jehial Smith, where the scene became agonizing to witness. Mothers wrung their hands and wept, while fathers' farewells were choked by emotion ; wives clung frantically to necks of agitated husbands ; maidens coyly hid their tear-stained faces, while little ones begged their fathers not to leave them.

"Fall in !" Hands loosed their clasping as the order was obeyed, while mothers, wives and maidens knelt beside the way.

"Forward, march !" With one mighty voice rose the thrice-repeated hurrah, and with it from the kneeling, sorrowing ones, mingled the wailing "God bless yous" and "good byes."

Capt. Herbert Gray and Mr. Ellis went with this company when it joined the regiment, thence continuing their journey to join their own, which received marching orders at the same time.

"I thought I had nothing to be thankful for," said Mr. Ellis to Herbert ; "but indeed I am thankful that my Kitty is not here with these. I am sure I could not bear it if she knelt there crying so pitifully as many of these women do, who can not realize the hardship they impose upon those who must march away, poor fellows. God pity and help them—ay, as Tiny Tim would say, 'God help us every one !'"

As there is a gladness too intense for laughter, so

there is a sadness too deep for tears. The latter Mr. Ellis had felt. While life should last, his memory a certain picture would retain—himself led away by Herbert's friendly arm ; a sweet woman, tearless, but white as though touched by the hand of death, although illness had never robbed her of her bloom, standing in the door of his home ; a little child smiles his farewell with graceful gesture, shouting " bye-bye " from the step at her feet, while by the open gate, prostrate in grief, lies a beautiful boy, crying,

" Kiss your Herbie again, papa."

Will he kiss him again? Does the sky at which the father appealingly gazes in his agony hang out among its fleecy clouds a signal of promise ?

The company marched to the rendezvous of the regiment, and with arduous drill wore away the long Spring days, till their complement was full and marching orders came. Embarking upon a Mississippi packet, behold them gliding swiftly down the river, away from the homes they have builded and can not defend, from all whom they love and cherish. Troops were now rapidly massing upon the Potomac from North, East and West, all inspired with untried valor, and, to a great extent, with contempt of the foe they came out to *look at and conquer!*

There was yet little bloodshed, no warrant for the carnage that followed and the scenes so fearful that even Europe, from her thousand battle-fields, looked amazed across the waves upon the conflict of brothers. There was so much to be hoped from the old method of suasion, that the better-disposed on both sides still had recourse to argument, each giving the other time to reflect before using the weapons they grasped. So the great belligerents stood, each with a half-defined hope that reason or concession might arrest the carnival of blood, yet both preparing for that dire extremity.

Our Minnesota regiment is still on its way to Virginia. Leaving the river, it is drawn by the fiery iron steed, linked to the huge train, now the charger and chariot of war, following through the hills and valleys the winding and curving of the glinting iron track. Still on they dash, across the prairies of Illinois, through that farming country which challenges and the world, through the peach-orchards of Michigan, on through the beautiful gardens, past the fruit trees and rich fields of Ohio. From city, town and hamlet; from wood-station, field and farm-house, arise the cheers of an excited populace, as though seeking a vent for their enthusiasm. Even the solitary tramp by the wayside greets them with the same noisy demonstration. Women and children fling flowers, trinkets and handkerchiefs to the astonished volunteers, and ladies, gently born and tenderly reared, wait for the train that they may look upon and encourage the " Nation's hope, the boys in blue." Everywhere the air is ringing with sturdy yeomen's shouts ; elegantly-worded " God-speeds," from gentlemen with uncovered heads and moist eyes ; sweet words from women who throw spring garlands on the iron track, hang them upon the locomotive, or cast them dexterously into car windows, to be eagerly appropriated.

At one little village, as the train moved slowly up to the platform, it was greeted by a band of seminary girls, laden with flowers, choice and fresh as their own beauty. Each car window framed a living picture of at least two faces; and where humanity was more densely packed, in some instances a half dozen crowded down to the small out-look. One only of these windows now concerns us. There are two heads; the first, Herbert Gray's—his high, intellectual forehead crowned with wavy, raven hair; brows finely arched, and the large eyes matching the hair in color; a soldierly, black moustache, shadowing but not concealing the lips now slightly parted in a smile at some gay remark of his companion, George Langmere. *His* head has a covering, coarse, wiry, and so intensely red that each hair seems to glow with its own blaze. Small eyes shine out from beneath jutting sandy brows, and great freckles spread over the spare, bony cheeks and pug nose, even to the chin, innocent of beard. Merriment, irresistible, but coarse, is stamped on every feature of the face. He noticed the figure of a beautiful girl, remarking not too delicately upon its outlines, when she turned and advanced toward them, grace in her every movement, dignity on her brow.

"Look there, Herbert! Our window takes, you perceive. It draws, by Jove!"

"Medusa's charm, possibly," was the low, unheeded rejoinder.

The young lady stood now just beneath the window, her eloquent blue eyes resting upon the face of Herbert, her musical voice floating up to his ears as she spoke words designed to inspire courage, and expressed the hope "that these dark days and heavy skies would burst at noon into radiant light ; that soon might return these brave men, now moving on to danger — to death, perhaps, for your country and mine," she added, and held up to him, earnestly begging his acceptance, a delicate bouquet.

"If ever in suffering or want through the cruelty of war, as you would those of a sister, command the services of her whose name and address accompany these flowers."

She saw not the face of George Langmere, nor that it was his hand took the flowers—so intent was she addressing Herbert Gray, whose absorption equaled her own. The last glance, as the train moved on, was each for the other a wordless prayer. Her "God protect you" seemed to him an angel whisper, and he buried his face in his hands to hush the cry of his soul against a fate that bore him from that sweet other self. There fluttered from the window a card, which she supposed dropped from his hand. Eagerly seizing it, while the rich carmine mantled on either cheek, she read :

SERGEANT GEORGE LANGMERE,
—— *Regiment, Ohio Volunteers.*

That personage was busy in discovering and concealing the slip of paper deftly hidden in the bouquet, whereon was delicately traced :

ALICE MEADE,
Xenia, Ohio.

Some time elapsed before Herbert raised his head. When he did, he turned toward Langmere, and reaching out his hand for the bouquet, said :

"Mine."

"Oh, no !" was the rejoinder ; "there is no personal application of these things. They are but the vehicle of a great patriotic idea, and this happened to come through lovely hands to *us*, boy. 'T is *ours*." See ! The other boys have divided bouquets—flowers as sweet—but by the gods, they can not boast that they were given by girls as beautiful, or that when culled they were kissed by such delicious lips as—"

"George Langmere !"

The tone was almost savage, the eyes aflame, the face deadly pale, as Herbert took the bouquet in his own hand, saying :

"This can never be a theme of conversation between us."

And if possible, his face grew paler when his search for the name among the flowers was found to be in vain. He knew that farther and farther he was speeding from her, his newly found, heaven-designed bride, and he had no clue even to her name. He again covered his face and dwelt rapturously upon the strange event that had changed forever the color of his day dreams. Should he ever look again into those eyes that had so suddenly claimed the tribute of his love? Should he ever know that name close beside his own on the great record above? Although he had never pronounced it, he felt that its owner, should he fall in battle, would be surely widowed. The angel face, with an appropriate syllable of his own fond coining, was then and there enshrined in his warm, true heart. The inward verdict of his fun-loving, somewhat unprincipled companion-in-arms, was :

"Smitten and done for by an unknown beauty ! I hold the key to the mystery," was his further reflection, "and she has my card (that was a good one and does me credit), though she thinks it's Herbert's. It is a rather taking name though, and it shall win for me what my face never would, an avowal from the loveliest woman I ever saw, except the wife of Gus Harkness. *She* leads in beauty, to my notion. This woman is next though, and will do ; must do—*shall* do ! "

The regiment sped on its way, passed the crouched lions in Baltimore, and lost its individuality at Arlington Heights, as in the camp routine the soldiers lost their spirits. Langmere, especially, wearied of the "All quiet on the Potomac," and determining to try the key to adventure, which he believed he held, wrote to Miss Meade. He was an accomplished penman. With a view to some position which proved a disappointment, he had once made correspondence a special study. His first letter was a wary, guarded note— the cultivated gentleman presuming upon her forbearance and the permission to write, acknowledging her gift of flowers and its inspiration to deeds of lofty import, begging her to write, if she deemed the stranger soldier worthy of attention, adding :

" My audacity in asking this favor perhaps deserves and will receive its merited punishment—silence ; but if otherwise fate shall favor me, I shall begin to think that even war with all its grimness has something for which we may be glad."

Alice Meade, the accomplished daughter of a worthy and patriotic banker, in the quiet of her father's house, blessed with a brother's cherishing love, had little experience to discipline a romantic, yet pure-minded disposition. Men were all judged by her father's and brother's standard, and they were both exceptionally high-minded. Unsuspicious of man's duplicity, except in the general knowledge of the world's sinning.

When Alice read the delicately-worded and elegantly written letter, signed with the name she associated with the handsome open face of Herbert Gray, the interest that face had inspired grew to a warmer feeling. Her reply was immediate, sincere, reserved, containing well expressed thoughts pertinent to the hour, and the vocation of him she addressed. One after another, letters came to her from the same source, very gems of composition, to each of which she responded, so simply, so womanly, that had he not been sold to depravity, George Langmere would have felt their unintentional rebuke.

But instead of remorse, he grew eager to look deeper into her pure soul. Wrote again as a suitor, who woos hoping to win, yet deserving nothing, and is prepared to die willingly in the battle-field, if his suit is not prosperous. He declared it was his only desire to possess her promise to be his wife, when from the war he should come, as that promise would ensure his coming, and begged to exchange pictures with her, sending with the letter Herbert's photo-

graph. We, who know her susceptible heart, untutored in the world's follies, can guess the reply—
indeed know it. It came—the promise to be his wife,
accompanied by her picture—a beautiful response,
and worthier a better destination. The river of a
woman's noble thoughts flowing sweetly to its ocean.
O what sacrilege was that, when that picture and that
sweet letter, designed for other and nobler eyes, were
placed exultingly near the hollow heart of him who
had dared to invoke them; while day after day he
shared the friendship of the unsuspecting man for
whom they were intended. He had a vague plan in
his head. The enemy should move on and make
possible, by the concurrence of fortunate circumstances, some means by which he would secure some
of her wealth, even if, in so doing, he should lose
Miss Meade. She, after all, was to him far the less
desirable acquisition of the two.

Spring had gone with little gain to the great
cause, although the time had been industriously employed in drilling and equipping the army. Excitement had been intense all over the North, as well as in
camp. The "On to Richmond" cry promised at
last to be a reality, and the whole country held its
breath. In balmy summer time, just past the noon of
night, orders were received to pack knapsacks and
prepare breakfast. The whole army was astir with
unwonted excitement.

Herbert and Langmere were seated at breakfast
in the tent, before which Lieut. Ellis was pacing
slowly. His thoughts we can easily divine.

Herbert scarcely knew what prevented his feeling
L   7*

cordial regard for Langmere. He was repulsed by the man's coarseness sometimes, and if he accidentally touched his hand, he recoiled with a shudder, as if he had felt the slimy fin of a monster.

Suddenly Langmere addressed him :

"Will you do me a favor, Gray ?"

"Certainly; mention it."

"If I fall to-day, will you take from my left breast pocket a package, and transmit it to the address (a lady's), you will find within it. I do not wish it to fall into a stranger's hands."

"You are too gloomy, Langmere. I am as likely to fall as you."

"O no, you are not engaged to be married, while I am. It is always your disengaged chaps that seem to be bullet proof, simply because there seems nothing in particular for them to live for, I suppose. This may explain, perhaps, my desire to come off without any eyelet holes in my cuticle."

So, lightly speaking, he handed Alice Mead's picture to Herbert, drummed idly on the table, sang catches of a ribald air, yet watched keenly the face of his companion.

Herbert took the picture from its envelope, his face slowly blanching, in a hollow voice he said :

"Pardon me. Did I understand you to intimate— Have you ever met this lady, since—"

"This letter will explain. You may read it."

He handed him Alice's latest letter, in answer to one alluding to the probability of an engagement, and expressing apprehension and foreboding. It was her great anxiety, tenderly expressed, and closing with

endearing terms. There could be no doubt of its
genuineness. Herbert handed it back with no word.
From that moment he resolved to think of her no
more in the old tender way. It is easy to resolve.
'T was all a mystery, but no act of his would un-
fathom it. How could he guess of the villainy that
accomplished it? How could he detect the trail, who
had no suspicion of the serpent?

They were soon summoned to head-quarters, and
ere long the columns of infantry were marching away,
having crossed the Potomac, towards Manassas. How
sanguine and expectant! The morning elation of that
host, that looked invincible upon its winding way
under the starlit sky, and the evening despair that
settled upon the scattered rank and file as it fled,
panic-stricken, from Bull Run, are strongly contrasting pictures, upon the American heart. They are
engraven by an artist whose sketches are as lasting as
time. Hark! Hearts beat with one mighty throb,

"It is—it is the cannon's opening roar!"

and they are marshaled on the battle-field. A moment
that seems an age, they tremble and shrink and desire
to rush away. Although later in the campaign abject
skulkers were developed in great numbers—a proportion to every regiment—yet faces that came to be
associated with daring deeds turned pale at that first
deafening scream of shot and shell, with hasty look
for succor and safety. From front to rear, aloft, on
every side was terrific thunder. It was not the
slaughter, perhaps, that caused men fresh from the
still forests and quiet places of the Union to quail, but

the stupendous clamor of the fierce cannonade. The sickening view of ghastly wounds came later. It required education, a great deal of education in bloody scenes, to bring men to perfect coolness. Yet the terror gradually gave way, and upon the Bull Run battle-field, no doubt, there were as cool heads as were carried through the Wilderness when the war was old. Sterling characters grow firmer by trial.

What hopes they had, how they pressed on toward the rebel guns over hidden obstructions. The sun had passed meridian, McDowell had achieved a stupendous gain! The news was wired, the land rejoiced inasmuch as the great Army of the Potomac was slowly beating back rebellious squadrons, who fought feebly as they retired. The war was virtually over! Non-combatants at home took an afternoon nap. Still the cloud of hostility hung over the hot July battle-field, where the dead and dying lay.

"Guide right! charge the batteries!"

"Jehial Smith, of the First Minnesota, was just carried to the rear, Captain."

"Are you sure 't was he?"

"Yes; I spoke to Dave Persons, one of the bearers."

"Poor fellow! charge!"

Again the war shout, again the impetuous rush of men in earnest obedience to command. They meet a counter current, are borne back by its overwhelming force.

"There is Dave Persons again!"

Yes, it was Dave on a slight mound of earth, drawn up to his greatest height, stretching and craning his long neck to its utmost to distinguish something. The smoke baffles him, yet he peers eagerly in every direction.

"What do you see, Dave, the battle?"

"No, worse than that; a hellish smoke, and through it men flingin' knapsacks, guns and everything. Jehoshaphat, see 'em run!"

They could not see the retreat, but felt its impulse, and the drear rebound of hope, a moment before so buoyant. They can not understand, but before them lies impassable ground; behind, in flight, possible safety. Over the slope, dread and terrible, unseen because of the blinding haze, they come, they come,— Johnson's forces. The impatient question, "Where, in God's name, is Patterson?" can not now effect the desired result. The day is lost! Drifting back are disordered infantry, mixed pell-mell with grimy artillery and riderless horses, a long confused line of hurrying objects, dimly defined through clouds of smoke and dust.

"Halt!"

A wild stare gives evidence that the order is heard, but wilder haste shows it to have been vain.

It was unmistakable retreat, confused and universal. All night the straggling remnants of broken, demoralized regiments poured into Georgetown. Next morning, Langmore and Ellis met in the streets.

"Have you seen Gray?" asked the latter.

"No; not since the retreat. Possibly he is still advancing, determined to see Richmond," was the unfeeling retort.

And Herbert was advancing, a prisoner, toward

Richmond. Many of the boys of his company were cut off from the main body by rebel cavalry and lost in the woods and open country in their attempts to get back to headquarters. It was rainy and they could not get their bearings. The sun, as if in league with the foe, refused to enlighten them, and they dared not inquire the way or even ask for food. After three days of fasting, some straggled, nearly famished, into camp, while some, alas, are even yet among the "missing."

The whole army, lately so exultant and impatient of restraint, were disgusted with war. They had *seen* the rebels! The North was pulseless with dismay. Defeat had not for a moment been taken into consideration as among the possibilities of the advance.

"On! on!" had graced the columns of newspapers in huge head-lines; and the cry was taken up impatiently by the people. The careful generals who protested that plans were not yet matured, different branches of the army still too far apart, too immature in their development for concerted action, that advance would result disastrously, had been decried as traitors and disgraced before the applauding public. Why disastrously? Could not our army show greater numerical force, was it not better equipped and more generous in its commissariat than our crippled adversary? Our common soldiery had been recruited among the learned professions, gentlemen of philosophical habits. Favorites of fortune and many known to fame marched in the ranks; they would not recoil, but serve to cement weaker material, for the great thought nerved them all. Indeed, it was not want of merit, it was not want of numbers and weight; it was not for want of treasure, nor yet want of devotion to the cause, that we lost Bull Run and languished through the fruitless Summer that followed, when victory seemed to incline to the rebel army. Our failure lay in the want of system, without which even stupendous force is impotent, "borne to earth by its own weight." It was not until that want was remedied, and General Grant empowered to impose thorough system and subordination, that the great machinery of war began to move toward success. The rebel army was smaller, but to a man they had reverence for their commanding general, and that general was a thorough military genius, scrupulously exacting of discipline, insisting upon obedience to the letter as well as the spirit of his orders. He did not confide in himself, but in the perfect subjection of the immense machinery entrusted to his manipulation. A late writer says of Napoleon's expedition to Russia: "The component parts of his vast force were not perfect in themselves. His marshals were not to be trusted beyond the supervision of his own eye. His numerous orders were neglected, and the disorder of the advance on Moscow brought forth the bitter fruit of retreat."

In contrasting accounts of the march to and from Moscow with the narratives of the more recent advance of the Germans from the Rhine to Paris, it will be apparent that while one army depended on a man, the other rested upon a system, the system organized by a man of genius.

Lieut. Ellis spent the day and part of the night in earnest search among the soldiers and in the hospitals for Herbert. Then, hoping he had been detailed upon some service and was safe, he dashed off a letter to his wife, then betook himself to his blanket and the pavement for the rest which his wearied nature required ; yet mortification and solicitude for Herbert kept him long awake. He knew his entire company would have fought on against fearful odds even, had there been generalship to command them. There was no want of devotion and bravery manifested in the army, and the mortifying result of their first engagement he attributed to delinquency in high places ; still he knew that the disgrace would for long attach itself to the common soldier. No doubt it was the result of official blundering, but the blunderer would be screened, while the soldiers would feel the disgrace forever. But he was mistaken as to the endurance of the stigma. By later events that disgrace was wiped out effectually. For the present they plunged deeper into tactics, and prepared themselves, by the most rigorous drill and observance of discipline, to participate in the battles to come,—battles that should have a two-fold office, subjugation of the armed insurgents and reparation of their lost ground at Bull Run, for they would wash out all memory of it. Beauregard had not yet occupied Washington. The country again breathed freely, and when more troops were called for how thrillingly pealed the chorus,

> We are coming, father Abraham,
> Three hundred thousand more.

Personal efforts to maintain the Union were as popular as ever and her cause no more despaired of than though Bull Run had never been heard of. This devotion and loyalty had been thought to be cooled by defeat. Like the proverbial new broom, it had suffered from the friction of use and adversity. We had been nourished in the arms and at the bosom of peace ; our infantile cradle had been rocked by her. Our education had been conducted under the shadow of her wing. Could then the enthusiasm for this ferocious war be more than temporary? for did it not require stern logic and adamantine resolution to sympathize with it to the bloody, cruel end? A story is told in the following camp scene, told in soldiers' own words, a story of their hopes and sentiments, and fears, and illustrative of the feeling of the hour.

"What's the news, Gus?" said "Long Dave," as he was now always called, as he stretched and sprawled on the hard floor of the tent, regarding with wistful eyes the letter Gus was reading. Dave never knew the pleasure of correspondence. In all the world he had of kith or kindred none. He watched and respectfully waited for Gus to go through his letter two or three times and then repeated his question.

"They are all well at home, Dave, excepting Robert Maynard and Mrs. Center ; the latter it is thought can not live many days.

"They have been enlisting there again, taken ten men more from the settlement and the Hollow, and the draft took ———," naming them.

"Wal I snum, if they keep on at that gait it will

8

take the last man, even to Paddie O'Shannon," interrupted Dave.

" It did; 'Lizbeth says the fun of it was, he claimed he was not naturalized."

" Had no papers ! Gosh, I'd gi'n a hundred dollars to a been there."

" They proved he had the papers and made him ' show 'em, be jabers,' and then drafted him into the army, but there was a hulabalo of a time with him."

." Well they had another, I'll warrant, afore they got his hair cut and his uniform fitted to him. Gracious, how he must a kicked when for the first time in his life he ' got a fit,' and felt cloth. O Moses ! "

" 'Lizbeth says it's lonesome enough there and they, the women folks, begin to feel as if a good deal of responsibility will fall upon them if the war continues two or three years."

" What's that ! Who says the war is going to continue two or three years ? Show me the feller and we will have it out in five minutes. Good gracious, I calculate we can finish it all up snug this Fall."

" Not unless you can read a better account of us than that of Bull Run, Dave."

" O, that was a failure, I allow. What a fizzle, though. I say there never was a scareder set o' fellows than we 'uns, except the other fellers, the Rebs."

" No wonder there was fright on both sides, there was lots of us that had never heard a gun fired in earnest in our lives—had smelt powder to be sure, but only at shooting matches and hunting."

" That's so ! Two green armies met at Bull Run

face to face for the first time and which ever had its line turned was sure to git like the devil. There was no other way to escape annihilation."

"Of course not, and

> He who fights and runs away,
> Will live to fight another day.' "

"If we had been the successful party we thought we were at noon that day, if Patterson the old fraud had held his ground and done his duty we would a got no end of praise though. Printin' ink would have been all exhausted markin' us up like this: HEROES."

Dave had written the last word in immense characters on the side of the white tent with a coal, then flinging himself down again continued: "Our fightin' would a been considered the most wonderful action under the sun, for I notice it's the result that gives color to any undertakin'."

"Of course, Dave, nothing succeeds like success," said Gus.

"Well it ain't fair, a fellow wins a race because his opponent who is ahead and the best runner, stubs his toe near the end of the race, the victory almost won, and this poor snail of a chap who ought to count it honor to be allowed to walk the same course in his tracks, is hailed as the victor and gets all the honors."

"Save your breath to cool your porridge, Dave; let's talk about something interesting, Patterson for instance, what have they done with him?"

"Pronounced him a cursed fool; an old woman not responsible for the imbecile inactivity that—

"He ought to be *hung*. He has caused more heads to hang than any man in the army. I felt so dog on'shamed, I did n't look up for a week after that 'ere retreat."

"You did n't go fer enough. One feller, they say, retreated clear to the State of Maine."

"Good soldier. Heard the order to retire and nobody halted him, I s'pose."

"Langmere is in the same list, and Gray's going on, I s'pose, like old John Brown's body."

"Langmere; why he was here yesterday, I saw him."

"Well, I'll bet nobody has seen him to-day, for I heard the Colonel tell him to go to hell, and he is powerful good to obey orders."

"We shall meet him again then, the most of us."

"The Colonel knew it would be for the good of the country for him to go."

"Langmere has got a black heart; anyone could read that."

"He has been figuring for furlough a long back; they say he is going to marry a girl up in Ohio. He told of it when he was drunk."

"Well, I would advise that girl to get insured; that's an awful red head of hissen."

"I've a red head mesel'," chimed in a rich voice from under a blanket in one corner, "but it never kindled a fire yit."

"Why, Mike!" said Gus, "I thought that last

whisky fixed your music to-night. You have been snorin' like the seven sleepers."

"Seven sleepers, is it. I'll bet you a cow, Gus,' there is more nor seven hundred under this same blanket wid me, and ivery one of 'em wide awake. They kape up such a divil of a thrampin', gittin' up an' settin' down on me, so unaisy loike. They are a dale worse than me ould woman at home, or me stip-in-mother, that used to lick me, till me legs would tingle a wake."

"What was the complaint about your 'ould woman,' though?"

"Och! She would peck away at me head all day, and thin she would peck at me back all night wid her sharp elbeys, an' snappin' at me in me dthrame, hollerin' 'Lay along, Mike!' an' me loike a lamb, hangin' jist on the bed rail, holdin' on wid me teeth an' toe nails, and the whole len'th of me body all night a swayin' clear of it."

"I's powerful sorry for yer back, Mike, but I spec's I could show yer blacker scars, an' more of 'em, though I was never rightly married, an' never had a mother or a step-in-mother to lick me."

"Och! ye are one o' yer aunt's childhren, are ye, Pomp. Well now, if the scars on yer back are blacker than yer face, do ye be after tellin' us how ye coom by 'em. I can't a bear mysthery at all."

"Spit it out, Pomp, tell us who branded you. Don't be afraid, you are in Uncle Sam's pasture now, you know," said Dave.

"Wal," said the negro, "I used to belong to ole massa Wilbur, down in Norf Carlina. I done the

fid'lin' an' preachin' on the plantation, an' ef I did n't
go right for'ed in the way of duty, why my missus
would scole an' tear an' stop my 'lowance of meal and
bacon. But laws, I did n't mind it at all. It was a
kind o' means o' grace,"

"Made ye shoin, Pomp."

"The cullud people never tole of my short cum-
mins, 'kase the Lord bein' on my side, I allus had
more meal an' bacon than I needed, anyhow, an' if
they got short, they could get it of me instead of
stealin', which was a great help to 'em moonlight
nights. Besides, I was in c'mand of the chicken
militia, you know; boss of the fowl brigade, and
managed the capture of a comfortable number of
hens every night. All went on swimmin' and according to gospel, till massa brought home a mulatto boy.
Yes, sah, his name was Tom, and I knew the minute
I sot eyes onto him, I could never make a Christian
on him. An' so I hated him. He was allus a sneak-
in' and courtin' the gals, and finally got to shinin'
around Dinah, the housemaid, that was promised to
me. One night there was a little fuss at the hen
roost, and missus, who was purtickular about her
pullets sleepin' sound, run out and kotched Tom jest
comin' round the cornah of the v'randah. She licked
him smart for it, an' he up an' tole her it was me
made the fuss at the roost. She did n't believe it at
fust, sah, but watched out, and suah as you live she
kotched me. O but she was mad tho'. You nevah
seed such a devil as she was then, and she tole the
overseah to stake me down to the ground flat on my
face, and then she stood by an' laughed, O, ye ought to

hearn her, while he drew a big half-starved barn cat
by its tail down my naked back, so many times I
forgot to count, and besides, I was busy talkin'."

"What was ye afther sayin', Pomp?"

"My prayers, honey. I was one of the Lord's
'tickler chilluns, and went by the lightnin' of his
spirit."

"And the cat, he went by lightnin' I 'spose," said
Dave.

"He clawed toleble."

"Ye shud a been a Oirishmon, sure thin, Pomp."

"O I was raw enough, Mike ; the days I lay and
'fleeted how I'd git even with that overseah, sah. At
last a plan. O yaw, yaw ! Gorry that was a plan,"
and Pomp rolled in convulsions on the ground at the
bare recollection.

"Let's hear it. I hope ye polished 'im."

"Yes, sah ! Ye see he had been all along hanker-
in' arter Dinah. Gorry mighty, but she hated him !
and was mad ca'se he hed humiliated me. I tole her
to fool 'im along till I got ready for him, un' I'd
finish up the amoosment. So one moonlight night
she was pertendin' to a little likenin' of him, and
'lowed his soft sodder a good bit while they lem-
onaded down to the cotton-gin, where she knew I was
hid, waitin' for 'em. She came a teterin' in un' whis-
perin' to him that "niggahs might hear 'em un' he
better take off his boots." When he sot down to take
'em off, I raised up still as death an' slipped a noose
over his neck, an' jerked it tight to a beam afore he
could help himself. Then I tied his hands behind him,
pulled his feet straight down to a ring in the floah so

that the leastest stir would choke him. Then, sah, I took a big cat that I had n't fed for a week, and put it in a bag and drew the eend of the bag up an' tied it so that thar was jest room enough for the cat and the overseah's feet. Oh, I tied it tight, sah, squeezin' the cat till it growl'd like satan, an' then I stirr'd that cat, sah, an' I punched that cat, sah, till it was a match for a tiger and took hold o' them feet for keeps, sah ; then I said good evenin', sah! Leavin' a boy to punch and keep up the cat's grit. I took my Dinah by the waist and left 'em. But, lo'd sakes, sah, I could heah that ole cat a swearin' after we got clean up to the niggah quarters, the rations was so tough !"

"An' yer yar-rn is loike the rations, Pomp, an' makes me incloin' to swear with the cat, only the pair of us would be loikly to overdo the matther of swearin', so that the officers would be out o' bisness althegedder," said Mike, good-humoredly.

"Swear away then, Mike," said the soldier, who had just dropped in and heard only Mike's comments, "swear away. If the officers would give a little of that kind of work out to supernumeraries and attend closer to the real business of war, it would n't last till snow flies.

"You have got a level head, comrade," said Long Dave. "If every officer, from Scott clear down to Langmere, the poorest of the lot, were obliged to keep their mouths shut and work without pay, and it was agreed to leave politics and the Presidential question to Providence till the job was done, there is nothing surer than that we would whip the Rebs."

" Yes, an' get home to Christmas," cried a voice outside.

" But Pomp — what would become of 'Pomp?'" asked another.

"Pomp could celebrate Christmas wherever he pleased, for when this war is over he will be a free man; free to marry Dinah; free to prosecute the *overseah* if there is anything left of him, or administer the cat to him again."

Just then a raw recruit who had been detailed upon picket duty that night, rushed into the tent, smiling and rubbing his hands, saying :

"I—goll, now, this looks·a little more like ! "

He looked dirty and self-neglected. His new uniform was too big for him. His hair, for want of combing, had matted on top of his head and hung in little stumpy twists clear down into his eyes and refused to acknowledge the hat that had slid off down over his left ear. His brogans sounded rattley, as if they were tied by strings about his ankles and dragged along behind him when he walked. He took his hat in his hand, and shaking the rain drops from it said :

" It rains like the mischief. I 'm wet as sop."

An officer had slipped in behind him, and touching him on the shoulder, with a look more humorous than severe, said :

" You must go back at once to your post of duty."

"What ! to-night, cap'n? It 's too durned fur ! I jist got here."

" Can 't help it ! You *must* go back."

" Why, cap'n," he said, crawling up to the officer

M

and smiling as if it was a good joke, "it's dark as thunder."

"No more words, sir. Come right along!" spoken more sternly.

"Oh, gosh darn, cap'n, 'tain't safe out there; a feller might git shot!"

CHAPTER VI.

A FAREWELL VISIT.

"What avails this wond'rous waste of wealth?"

THE stately residence of Mr. Pierre La Moore stood upon the side of a bluff, overlooking the city and the river. The owner was still abroad, "detained," his wife said, "by intricate suits at law, entailed by the settlement of an estate that he claimed for his elder children—property that should rightfully have gone to his first wife at the decease of her father, many years ago."

As she was the sole and undisputed heir, it would seem that the recovery of this property for her heirs should have been simple enough; but Mr. La Moore found French lawyers very exacting in regard to details concerning individual demise, and those details very numerous, and months passed away until another year came round and he was apparently as far from the accomplishment of his object as when he first introduced himself to the punctilious legal gentlemen who had custody of the valuable documents he wished to obtain.

It is a hard thing to say of a man who has enjoyed the protection of a government, that he will shirk the responsibility of defending it in its hour of direst need. But truth compels me to regretfully admit my conviction, that the war and the repeated calls for men and money had something to do with Mr. La Moore's long absence in France. Eugene expressed great desire to return and enter the Federal army, and his father feared his authority could not prevent his enlisting, besides he himself was not past the age of military duty. Conscription was just then the demon that disturbed the slumbers of many men with a like faith and political creed, and Pierre La Moore believed that he was safer, and his son as well, upon a neutral shore. There, for the present, he determined to remain, while his family were still in St. P——.

Mrs. La Moore was an American lady—handsome, haughty and high-tempered, according to Dame Rumor—exacting punctilious deference from all the children ; and to the judicious training of their own mother she was indebted for the sweetness with which it was rendered by the elder ones, who rarely asserted their own preferences.

Some peculiar, but mysterious influence prevented the degeneration of their noble, though proud spirits, and that influence was not Mrs. La Moore's, nor yet her husband's. Their obedience was, indeed, wonderful, when it was considered that instead of loving their step-mother, in their hearts they almost loathed her.

Annette had been long engaged to marry Robert Maynard. Yet her mother's caprice had so far interfered. Once in the Autumn, when his health was feeble, she declared it unwise, and caused a postponement until Spring ; and when Spring came and the day was appointed, she again laid the blight of hope deferred upon their love, under the plea that, in the absence of her husband, she had no authority to permit the marriage of his daughter, who was under age. She said also that she believed Robert's purpose was to enter the army, as soon as his health would permit. To this he could offer no sincere denial, and the former he was too proud spirited to combat, though it grieved him sorely, as well as the dear girl, whom he wished to rescue from her tyranny.

The war had reached its second Summer of blood and carnage—many histories have recorded with what sacrifices. Regiment succeeded regiment in the winding way that led from Minnesota to the theater of strife, and now still another awaited marching orders. In this one Robert Maynard is enrolled. They have been some weeks at Fort Snelling, and he has permission to visit home once more before the final move.

The sun is approaching the Summer solstice, and the twilight hour is grateful to weary nature.

Robert and Annette gratefully improve this hour by a long promenade in the shrubbery. The evening star beams bright and solitary just above the purple line of clouds that lately screened the sun. A gentle wind refreshes the lovers as they walk, keeping step together. They are a noble pair, with something suggestive of resemblance, yet not at all alike. Both are above the average height but the lady is a rich brunette, while Robert is fair-haired, and with a fine white forehead, blue eyes, and good English complexion.

The grass was moist with dew, and observing this

they entered an arbor covered with climbing roses, and sat down. Robert's arm encircled the slender waist, his face was close to hers, his breath upon her cheek ; his voice musically earnest as he said :

"Annette, I could not stay, now I am well enough to bear arms. My country, mine at least by adoption, needs me. It is not an easy task to leave such a mother and sister as mine," here the bright blue eyes grew dim, his voice sank almost to a whisper, "to tear myself from such a love as yours, my darling."

"Hush, Robert," she replied; "you do not tear yourself from my love, for to whatever fate you go, my love goes with you. It is more emphatically yours than before your enlistment. It deepens, grows graver and holier, because of the danger which threatens you, and I confess it grows prouder too. I have high hopes of your military career, and believe that, although this is not your native country, your brave loyal arm will purchase a kin-ship as noble as nativity."

"God bless you, my Annette, for lifting the weight from my spirits. I feared your remonstrances which, though they could not deter me from my duty, would greatly sadden its performance. Instead of reproaches and remonstrances I have your encouragement, and I am impatient to meet and conquer all difficulties that lie between me and the undisputed possession of such love. Promise me only this, that when all other obstacles are removed your mother shall be powerless to place a barrier between us again."

"I promise you. Robert, her will shall be naught.

Ah, surely my obedience need not extend to the wrecking of my own happiness and yours."

Enfolding her resistless form with his strong arms he drew her to his breast and laid long, lingering, passionate kisses upon her brow, cheek, and lips; then rising together they moved towards the house. The parlor was not lighted, but the moon shone full into the room, and made every article visible as they seated themselves upon a sofa in a spacious bay window. Upon a table near, stood an exquisite vase filled with rare flowers, Annette took it in her hand and held the flowers close to her lover's face, saying:

"Their beauty is not all of form or color ; here, press this rose a moment in your hand and behold how fragrant. Even as this flower when crushed emits a sweeter odor, so, crushed by life's cruel reverses, the soul is chastened and purified.   .

"Do you not think," he replied, "that many are embittered by sorrow. That all the soul's antagonism is roused to resist inflictions that seem undeserved, and though the infinite design may be to chasten and to purify, the result is coldness to man, infidelity to God."

"There may be," she answered, "examples of that kind. I have not met them. I know but one of life's martyrs, one who has bathed for many years in suffering, who has been ruthlessly stripped of all comfort and blessedness, but I know the sweetness of that soul rises heavenward with new fragrance each morning."

She had risen from her seat while speaking and stood before him. The waving wealth of long raven

ringlets thrown back from her forehead, her dark
eyes humid with emotion ; her cheeks, now flushed,
now pallid, and her heart beating perceptibly.

Robert, wondering he had never realized before her
transcendent loveliness so far excelling the beauty of
other women, drew her gently down beside him, saying :

"Annette, I have seen in all my life but one such
face as yours, and that one lacked more than half
your present beauty, the charm of soul ennobling
physical perfection."

Thinking to soothe her excitement, which was
almost painful to him, he took the vase she still
held in her hand, and smiling, said:

"Why, my sister Nellie has just such a vase as
this.   I wonder if yours was as costly.   I must tell
you the story.

"Many years ago in England, our family
was preparing to come to America, and a few days
before we embarked, father sold a valuable colt we
had raised, and which I had always called my own.
He gave me its price, a ten pound note, which I very
carelessly put in my pocket.   In the morning, wearing another suit of clothes, I went with him to Liver-
pool, a few miles distant.   While we were absent an
itinerant vendor of glassware, a persuasive Bohe-
mian, induced Nellie to invest in his merchandise to
the extent of all her available cast-off clothing.   This
proved insufficient to meet the price he set on the
vase.

"To obtain it she was obliged to make a draft upon
my wardrobe and when I came home, talking with

some boyish boastfulness of my trip and trifling acquisitions, she triumphantly brought forward her new purchase, claiming our praises for her sagacity in palming off for so lovely a vase, many worthless old garments among which had been the identical one that held my ten pound note." Annette laughed gaily.

"Well now as a partial reward for the suffering poor Nellie must have endured through your raillery, I shall send her my vase. I have no recollection of how we came by it, but who knows, some day, perhaps this one and Nellie's may have been twins."

It was growing late but the lovers still lingered and the wish to stay grew stronger the faster time sped. He rose to go at last, saying:

"I will come again next week and our parting then will be for a longer time."

Annette went with him, hanging on his arm and saying many last words half playfully, half sorrowfully—down the first flight of steps that led to another terrace and past a fountain, whose cooling spray reflected the moonbeams. They paused, and watched the goldfish playing with sparkling fin in the marble basin beneath. Then they walked to the next stairway where he took her hand and tenderly pressing it to his lips, whispered :

"Our separation will not be long, darling; good night," and with a lover's kiss the parting ended.

He went down the stairs gaily waving his hand to her, and when he was lost to view, with a sinking heart she returned to the house. Mounting leisurely the piazza steps she met at the top her step-mother

8*

and with a pleasant " good night, ma'am " would have
passed on to her own room but Mrs. La Moore peremptorily bade her remain, and haughtily addressing
her, said :

" Let your folly end to-night, Annette. I forbid,
positively forbid, your meeting this young person
again during your father's absence. Since your own
self-respect seems to have abandoned you, I shall not
allow it to be said that I forget what is due to propriety. I will not allow you to sit till this hour in a
room, without other than the moon's light, with a
young man, who is nothing, and can be nothing to
you."

" Indeed, mother, you know he is every thing to
me ; his image has the truest place in my heart, his
ring is on my hand, and his kiss lies yet warm upon
my lips. If life is spared us I will be his wife as
surely as the stars shine."

" Spare me your heroics and this nonsense about
being his wife, for you will be no such thing. I tell
you I will see that you do not disgrace us by these
improper interviews at least until your father returns,
when his authority will, I trust, put an end altogether
to your foolish dreams of an union with this young
farmer."

At the sneer with which the last word was spoken
the passion which lay dormant, kept down by Annette's
firm will, flamed up into the wild eyes that looked into
Mrs. La Moore's, and in a voice trembling with suppressed anger, she replied:

" Be careful, madam, how you exasperate me.
Who are you that you talk of propriety to me. Who

but yourself prevented the lighting up of the parlor this evening. The question you have raised as to my union with Robert Maynard is not within your province, and I will not discuss it with you.

"I warn you that your continued interference will be absolutely disregarded. Down deep in my heart there is the memory of wrongs, that you never can obliterate, and which you shall not forget, so long as my features retain their likeness ; you must not dare to encroach upon the sacred ground of my love."

Grand and queenly, she swept past the woman who had insulted her, through the open door, and, mounting the stairs, was soon alone in her own room, where, kneeling before her own mother's picture, she wept and talked to it, as though indeed the canvas were a thing of life.

"O mamma," she cried, "what a hard duty you imposed upon me, when you bade me treat with consideration the canker worm that has sapped the happiness of our home. O give me back my promise, sweet mamma, give it back or bend on me to-night the quiet beams of your forgiving eyes. Why am I so selfish, whose sufferings are as naught compared with your long anguish. O mamma, darling, forgive me, I will not again forget the promise that grew out of your great woe."

Below through the two midnight hours, the last of the evening, the first of the morning, an infuriated woman paced the moonlit porch of her regal home and angels had no part in dictating her thoughts.

At breakfast table next morning all traces of her passions or of last night's collision were gone. An-

nette's bow and polite "good morning" were as politely returned by the proud woman who sat behind
the shining coffee urn.

Plate and cut glass enhance the relish of a good
breakfast, and a good breakfast it was, for the cuisine
of Mr. La Moore's establishment was professionally
perfect. Yet with plate and cut glass and good cooking Mrs. La Moore was denied the relish which is indispensable to gastric enjoyment, for though she occupied the seat of honor at the table, yet a silent, unseen
presence claimed co-partnership.

Wherever she moved she was inwardly conscious
of and recoiled from it. Involuntarily it shared her
chair, her pillow, and her path, as from her footsteps
she seemed to hear the double echoes ring.

If for a moment she joined in the family merriment, laughter, gentle, sad and low, seemed to accompany her own.

If to her babe she sang a lullaby, another voice in
the same key responded with a mocking symphony—
and when she wept she felt upon her hands the warm
rain of another's tears.

This dual existence had form only in her fancy;
none others guessed its presence, but it followed her,
ever taking one half of all her comforts.

The aristocratic wife of the rich man walked,
talked, ate, laughed, sang and wept, yet all the while,
with furtive glance around—shuddering and shrink-
ing away.

CHAPTER VII.

IN THE NET.

Thou art not dead, the narrow grave
Is not for me thy resting place;
There's something in me that can save
Thee from Mortality's embrace.

As when the dying sun sinks low
A line of crimson tints the west,
Thy beauty from my path may go,
But leaves the charm that made me blest.
—ALEXANDER.

ON the 14th March, 1862, Gen. McClellan had issued an address to the army of the Potomac, announcing the reasons why, since the battle of Bull Run, they had remained inactive save for the daily drilling behind entrenchments. The infamous stars and bars of the Confederacy were flaunting in full sight, Washington was literally in a state of siege, and every Federal craft that ascended the river, challenged the frowning batteries of an irate foe.

Marching orders were once more issued, the sick sent back, camps broken up, and all prepared to encounter the dragon of Rebellion. The bitter remembrance of Bull Run rankled in many a heart, and the army was anxious to retaliate upon the enemy and win back the laurels so ingloriously trampled down

on that disastrous day of July, 1861. Various prophecies were current regarding their destination.

From the dock they crowded on board the trans-
ports till a whole fleet lay anchored upon the heaving
flood—a hundred thousand throbbing human hearts,
all eager for a hostile encounter with those who had pro-
voked a wrath that hourly grew and intensified; hearts
that had been thrilled by the successive victories of Ro-
anoke, Pea Ridge, Newburn, Winchester and Donelson
—victories in which they had not shared, but the ring
of which had reached their inactive camp and fired
their soldier hearts. At a given signal the whole grand
fleet swept down the noble stream—the stars and
stripes streaming at every mast-head, and national
music waking the slumberous air that brooded over
the scene. They ride the elements, each ship "a
thing of life," cutting with queenly prow the sparkling wave and dashing from each side the foaming
spray. As they glide past its anchorage a hundred
thousand voices respond to the salutation of the floating battery—the triumph of sea warfare, the pride
of the Northern wave, though an unpretentious raft
—the Monitor.

The troops disembarked at Fortress Monroe in a
drenching rain, marching through mud and discomfort to Hampton, where they encamped, made forlorn
fires and prepared as best they might their coffee,
cooked their bacon, and gratefully partook of the nice
fresh bread brought from the Fort. Here, Pomp, who
had been installed cook and " *valet* " to the person of
Lieut____ant Langmere (whose self-importance grew in
propo____ion as his worthlessness became apparent to his

comrades), met many old friends of the "colored persuasion" among the crowds of contrabands who occupied a long row of board buildings. They were employed
—the men, about the Government vessels and trans-
ports at anchor ; the women, in cooking, washing and,
as Mike facetiously remarked, "repairin' the breaches
made by the b'ys in the bothersome flank movements
that has come to be as common as sunrise, bedad."

They were exceedingly pious, those contrabands,
just tasting of freedom ! What, though their zeal was
of the kind written of as "not according to knowledge?" The prayer meetings of the "bredren," a
source of amusement to some, were edifying to others
who recognized the image of our Lord, though the
mirror may be common, the frame ebony. There
were many of fairer complexion than is sometimes
believed to exist on the bitter side of the line that dis-
tinguishes the bond and free. One of these proved
to be the heroine of Pomp's story. The day after
this meeting she acceded to his renewed entreaties,
and he was for once "rightfully married."

The officer of the picket guard was nightly
besieged by these people who were passed through
the line to protection and food. Their joy to know
themselves liberated from bondage was touching to
witness. They regarded the advent of the army as a
sign of the promise of deliverence that had cheered
the gloom of their servitude for many years. In their
benighted ignorance they had not learned of him who
later promised to be their leader to Beulah, *the Moses
of Tennessee.*

"On to Richmond" again resounded through the

camp, and the army, with two days' rations, was in motion toward Yorktown, through such mud as the Minnesota boys had never dreamed of. The distance was only twenty-five miles, but it required diligence to march half that distance in a day. Yet the mud was alternately plunged into, crawled out of, amid curses and laughter by soldiers in different moods, till at last they bivouacked in front of Yorktown, on ground over which the water was actually running. There they remained for three days before the supply trains could by any possibility struggle through the mud to the relief of soldiers who had never as such known want of food. Many times it had been said, "Our army waste daily what would feed two in Europe."

Many Minnesota boys drooped and grew despondent before Yorktown. Lieut. Langmere became really ill and was removed to the hospital, where Pomp and his yellow wife proved efficient nurses, and the former, that he was not above a bribe. An apt disciple of an artful man, he proved also that a clean white heart and a coal black face were not always possessed by the same individual.

"Tired of campaigning on the peninsula" said master, said man, and when the army advanced in pursuit of the rebels after the evacuation of Yorktown they were left behind with the sick. Let us here leave that armed host sweeping on to victory and fame, to watch the working of a scheme that would have done justice to the father of fraud himself.

Langmere's ambition had always been to live without exertion. Too indolent to work and too cowardly

for a good soldier, he bethought himself of a plan
whereby he might insure independence without effort.
He had satisfied himself of the unquestioned wealth
of Alice Meade — wealth which might be his if he
could secure the fulfilment of her promise to be his
wife. But the obstacle in the way of this consummation, so ardently desired for mercenary ends, was the
difficulty of securing it without revealing the deception which had made him an accepted suitor. How
could this marriage be brought about without her
discovering the fact that the face she loved and the
name of Langmere were not identical? He could
not visit her; that step would be a fatal one. Finally
he wrote thus:

BEFORE YORKTOWN, March —, 1862.

MY ADORED ALICE:

While I address you, my heart stands still with very anguish,
and only justice to you could make it possible for my pen to per.
form so sad a duty. I have been fearfully wounded; the harrowing particulars I will not give. The face you remember is hopelessly disfigured; it is only a chance that I preserve my eye-sight.
I will not claim the fulfilment of the engagement which has
blessed the last few months, and the memory of which will make
my future life a weary blank. I am going now to a private hospital — that of Dr. Bartholt, in Washington — for treatment, yet
with only a faint hope of physical restoration, still less of recovery from the horror my mirror reveals. I will not deprive myself
of that which shall be my only solace, your picture, unless you
insist upon its return to you. I am now but a physical wreck,
and as an honorable man I release you, my best beloved, from an
engagement which now would doubtless be as repulsive to you as
it would be contemptible in me to insist upon it. Your name will
be the last my mortal breath shall utter, but I beg *you*, darling, to
forget *forever* that of   GEORGE LANGMERE,

By B.

His correspondence with her had revealed to him Alice's true character, and, as he expected, his letter only fired her heart with greater love. With an ardor and enthusiasm she had never permitted herself to reveal in any former letter, she wrote :

MY LOVE:

I will not accept your release from an engagement which was not lightly considered. That love would indeed be worthless, if it could wane when a blight is laid upon its object. True, your face first inspired in my heart a sentiment that has grown into affection, into love that will cling to you so long as rebel guns leave enough of your body to hold your generous soul.

I am, as ever, your own   ALICE.

Would she sit now with folded hands and wait, who had so long prayed to be shown her work in this great struggle. Were repose and idleness for her while lives as precious as her own were being daily sacrificed for the welfare of her country ? No ; she would go to him and bring her soldier lover back to health and happiness. She had health and strength, and the command of generous coffers, for her father had grown to be controlled almost entirely by her. Her brother was now in the army. She laid the whole matter before the old gentleman, who had conceived an enthusiasm for those who wore the Federal blue almost equal to her own. He entered into the spirit of her plan at once, taking every measure to hasten its execution. The old housekeeper, Mrs. Garret, was taken into the council, and the result was immediate preparation and speedy departure of the three for Washington, to seek Langmere.

Arrived in that city, they ascertained the retreat

of Dr. Bartholt, and were soon on their way thither. It was eight o'clock in the evening when they were set down at the door, worn out with rapid travel ; but Alice had no thought but for her suffering lover, and to her eager questions Dr. Bartholt replied :

"Lieut. Langmere is hopelessly injured, and indeed it is not possible for any lady, except she be mother, sister or wife, to see him."

Love will not recognize defeat. Alice proudly, and yet with maidenly blush, replied :

"I am his intended wife, sir, and as such I claim the right to go to him."

The doctor bowed respectfully and led the way to the room, followed by Alice, Mr. Meade and Mrs. Garret, but turning, he stopped them at the door and said :

"Is this other lady a relative of the lieutenant ?"

"No."

"Then I must positively forbid her entering," he said. "Pomp, conduct the lady to the sitting-room."

A look of intelligence passed between the doctor and Pomp, and Mrs. Garret descended with the latter, while Mr. Meade followed his daughter into a dimly-lighted room. Alice dropped like a snowflake beside the bed whereon this deep-dyed villain lay. She was denied a look upon his face, but she took his hand in both hers and instinctively felt the same loathing that always affected Herbert at the touch of that hand. How she took herself to task for it, ascribing her repugnance to her love and regret for the face, so brilliantly handsome as it existed in her memory, and now disfigured beyond recognition.

"Is this my heroism?" she said to herself. "Is
this the self-sacrifice I came here to make? Nay; I
have come up to the mountain to slay my Isaac, and
now I will neither shudder nor go back." Kneeling
there she poured into his ear her loving sympathy,
and, as he had dared to hope she would, proposed
an immediate marriage, that her care of him might
be entirely devoted and unembarrassed. The circumstances must excuse the haste; but whatever
the world might say, she was resolved to marry
him at once, and thus immediately set at rest all con-
siderations of delicacy and propriety. To her inex-
perience he seemed to require the most devoted
nursing, and Mrs. Garret, who would have *known
better*, had been prudently excluded from the sick
room. Dr. Bartholt's complicity had been secured by
the promise of a large reward, if the plan succeeded.
He had taken the precaution to send for a clergyman,
who was then in the parlor, it being understood that
if the plan failed, he would be taken to visit the
patient, as though that were the real object of his
being summoned.

Pomp, who stood without, was sent to request the
clergymen's attendance. When he came in he was
informed in a hurried whisper of the request of the
lady, still weeping and pleading with her lover, who
seemed so loath to grant her wish, for reasons, apparently most noble. Afterwards she remembered that
his consent at last was sudden, saying:

"As you will, my darling."

The clergyman took her to a window in the dim
lit room and questioned her closely, she thought

almost impertinently, regarding her knowledge of the person she wished him to unite her with.

"Pardon me, madam," he said, "but you are about to convey to another the supreme right to yourself as well as your estate, and should be very sure that his principles are worthy and pure ; for most surely your happiness will be forever wrecked, should you discover when his wife, that they are not such as you desire to find in your husband. The world, dear madam, is full of deceit, and your personal acquaintance, I understand, is very limited."

"I have long corresponded with him," she said, "and have had many evidences of his worth and truthfulness. His release of me after a long engagement, owing to his terrible misfortune, would be sufficient to indicate a noble heart. Oh, sir, if you could have seen his face before this happened, you would not so question me now. A more perfect mirror of manly truth could not exist. He does not want me to marry him, but I will. It is *my* proposal, for only the strictest care will save his life, and I must be able to nurse him as only a wife can. Surely there is no shame, nothing unmaidenly, in this devotion to one who loves me, and has been nearly slain in the defense of my country. My faith in him is implicit; please do not keep me longer from my purpose to become his wife, for Lieut. Langmere is very low indeed."

They returned to the bedside, where she again took his hand, and the ceremony proceeded, she making the usual responses, which, she supposed, he was too feeble to utter, without a faltering voice.

Never were marriage vows spoken more freely and joyfully than by this woman—so strangely mated. Was it to wreck and ruin or even death? Her countenance beamed with a glorious light. Even as martyrs may look, so looked Alice Meade, standing by that bed. A lovely bride for any man to worship. Her eyes were full of tender love. The feeble lamp-light was reflected in her beautifully glossy hair, as she bowed her head to receive the clerical benediction. It was pitiful to see such youth and grace and sweetness united to the woe and misery represented by that man, now, to all appearances, a shapeless horror. The clergyman felt it.

Langmere's face was entirely covered, as well as the close shaven head, with the patches of black court plaster; the shapeless nose being cunningly disguised, and the whole shape of head and face rendered quite irrecognizable by bandages, judiciously disposed. He did not speak much, and only in whispers, lest she should detect his voice. Her father stood beside them, thus giving his solemn sanction, during the ceremony; and when the final words were pronounced, "What God has joined together let no man put asunder," he earnestly responded, "Amen."

Mr. Meade was very weary, and after being shown to a room, where supper was served for himself, Alice and Mrs. Garret, there he remained to rest, his daughter returning to the sick room, and Mrs. Garret retiring for the night. All night the bride sat there, beside him who had deceived her more basely than had Eden's serpent, the first of her sex.

All night, as devotees of old guarded the shrine of their idols, heeding neither weariness nor pain.

Then followed days of watching, reading, ministering to him she could not even touch without an indescribable repugnance, a something within her which she could not name, but which she had not been able to overcome. So it was that his polluting lips never even touched her own. How thankfully afterwards did she recall this fact, which had preserved her as pure as if still unwedded. Her devotion rendered the task of deception doubly difficult, the doctor and Pomp using the greatest care and precaution, to prevent the outcropping of red hair, or the displacement of the false bridge on the nose, which was adjusted every time the young wife could be induced to give the operators a clear coast. Pomp's wife was helpful, too, in the conspiracy, not that she was ever trusted with all the details of the case, for Langmere had said:

"Give a woman a secret to keep, and she will make such an extraordinary effort to do so, that she will be all the more sure to reveal it. She don't take the matter free and easy as a man does, but looks so mysterious and knowing, that she soon reveals her knowledge by the very efforts she makes to show her ignorance."

Dinah, however, did know more than had been confided her, for she possessed the rare gift of weaving long discourses out of short texts. When she saw Langmere's disguise she feigned to accept the simple reason given her by Pomp, but silently drew her own conclusions, which sundry peeps at the keyhole had confirmed.

She was touched with pity for the lovely bride, sitting there in that darkened room, watching for very love the man, who, for some unexplained purpose, was practising a wicked deception ; and she resolved to enlighten his victim.

Her purpose to acquaint Alice with the disguise worn by Langmere, was sooner executed than she at first supposed possible. She accidentally encountered Mrs. Garret, who, hearing that she was one of the servants of Lieut. Langmere, at once plied her with many questions in reference to the man in whom she now, naturally, felt additional interest, heightened by the fact of being still excluded from his room, and told she could not see him.

It happened early in the morning of the day set for the return to Ohio of Mr. Meade and Mrs. Garret, it having been arranged that Alice should follow with her invalid husband as soon as he could be moved, the doctor and Pomp to accompany them. Mrs. Garret had come up into the hall that led to the sick room, for the first time since the night of her repulse. She felt lonely in view of leaving Alice, who had been her charge many, many years—ever since her mother slept the sleep that knows no waking. A kind, faithful heart beat in the bosom of the old English housekeeper, and clung to the young girl tenderly, and with tears in her eyes she told Dinah how sorry she was to go home and leave her.

" Even with her own 'usband ; who after hall might 'ave a temper, and be 'arsh to Miss Hallice."

"Not till he gets a good hold of her money, I reckon," said Dinah.

"Why, 'as n't 'e plenty o' money 'isself."

"O, I don't know, but I most guess he is playin' some game, along of wearin' them patches on a well face. Can't tell ye what, but I'm powerful 'fraid of men that put on sickness, and do n't even stand up to git married."

"Do n't you think 'e is sick."

"No, I don't now, he was before we left Yorktown, but he can eat as hearty a meal as me, gets up when Miss Alice is gone and jumps and exercises to kill."

"Well, I want to see this dangerously sick man. Is the doctor in?"

"No, he has gone down town."

"Good! You open that door and let me in, Dinah, or I shall burst it."

Dinah opened the door and the old lady passed into the room. Alice and her father were discussing some details concerning their departure. She walked around to the head of the bed by the window, whose heavy brocatelle hangings she dexterously looped up to one side, letting the sunlight fall full upon the bed, saying:

"Sick folks and flowers oughter to 'ave plenty o' sunshine, and deary me 'ow they do bundle you up. W'at's the use of wearing all them patches on yer face? O, I can tell by yer pulse w'at's best for ye. Fresh air for 'ippocrits, I say," and as she spoke these words and before any one could interpose, she tore off the carefully arranged disguise, leaving bare the red head, the freckled face, and the miserable pug nose!

Cold as ice, immobile as a statue, Alice stood gaz-ing at that face, without a scar and a stranger's.

Natures such as hers do not give way to violent emotions. For some time she looked at him, then with unfaltering voice she said:

"Who are you?"

"The husband you would marry despite his wishes to the contrary, madam."

"Where is the man you have personated?"

"Dead."

"At your hand?"

"Do men usually plead guilty to the charge of murder?"

"Whatever your object may have been in devising the scheme by which you have deceived me, I warn you never to venture to approach me."

"You are my wife and as such I will proclaim you before the world."

"You *dare* not! A wife only through your forgery of another's name and through your base deceit, I will meet proclamation with proclamation," said Alice.

"Who most loves notoriety will suffer least," said Langmere, coolly.

That was true! She felt its truth, as did her father. Yes, Langmere, villain as he was, what would he care for notoriety?

"Will money be any object to you?" said Mr. Meade.

"If handsomely counted out I might consider the blight upon my affections less," said Langmere, with a mocking laugh. "I have some expenses to meet, growing out of my recent confinement, as well as a doctor's bill."

His tone throughout was a jesting one, even as he

heaped insults upon the venerable head that had gathered nearly all its portion of honor and of years. Mr. Meade now saw plainly the kind of adventurer he had to deal with, and said :

"I will give you one thousand dollars a year, the first installment to-day, and the same on each anniversary of this day, to secure *your silence and separation from my daughter.* A word from you or an attempt to visit her will stop your annuity and I will risk every dollar I have in the world to place you in your most suitable home, a dungeon."

"I accept your terms, sir, for the present, reserving to myself the knowledge of the moment when I may risk the alternative. Alice—"

"Not one word to her!" said the old man, sternly. "She is now as far removed from you as the stars." He took his daughter's hand, and followed by Mrs. Garret, left the room and almost immediately the house. In a few hours' time Mr. Meade had returned, paid the doctor's exorbitant demands, made arrangements at the bank, interviewed the clergyman who had so reluctantly performed his part in the miserable drama, and then the trio turned their faces homeward.

It was in the leafy, luxuriant month of June, when nature is at her gladdest that they returned to their rose-bowered home, situated on the green bank that slopes gently down to the river, sparkling in the light and heavenly blue. Beautiful river, thou shalt never tell the secret confided thee, the tears and prayers, and the long vigil of renunciation upon thy mossy bank. How many times at eve a lovely woman sought thy

shores, there to weep and moan, and to lovingly dwell
upon the memory of him whose image was ever in her
heart, but who seemed lost to her forever.

After her tears and grief had in part subsided
there would steal into her soul a strange comfort, a
soothing thought of God and His tender mercies and
she whispered, "Though He slay me yet will I trust
in Him."

> As shines the moon o'er distant hills,
>   And breezes fan with gentle wing,
>   hisper oft her spirit thrills,
>   Still fraught with earthly comforting.

CHAPTER VIII.

THE MASSACRE.

"Also when they shall be afraid of that which is high, and fear shall be in the way, and the almond tree shall flourish, and the grasshopper shall be a burden, and desire shall fail, because man goeth to his long home and the mourners go about the streets."—ECCLESIASTES.

MORE than a year has passed away—more than a year of sorrow, pain and death, and here we meet again on the woody banks of the Waubece. Change, the twin brother of Time, has reveled here in the *interim*. Though every scene is still familiar, the faces of our old friends are not as much so. Look through this cottage window! See this one bent over her work! Yes—lines new-graven mark the brow of dear, chatty little Mrs. Ellis. Her face has lost some of its fulness, yet she is still very pretty. Let us drop in and hear her good-natured accounts of people and things, for we know that she will give us all the news and that free from the slightest taint of ill-natured gossip. Pause a moment. Listen to her low, sweet song,as she rocks the cradle where her fine rosy boy is sleeping. She speaks sadly of Herbert who has never been heard of since the battle of Bull Run, though from Lieutenant Langmere, now home on a furlough, she hopes to hear tidings of that brother so loved and regretted.

Of her husband, she speaks proudly, lovingly, for

he has been the deserving recipient of honor and pro-
motion. His soldierly bearing and gallant conduct
have secured him the command of the company, yet
mingled with her joy is the sad thought that he now
wears the epaulets which once graced Herbert's shoulder. His last letter was brighter for the promise it
contained : "Perhaps this month, perhaps next, my
Kitty, I will fold you to my heart, and take my boys
again upon my knee."

The house is literally hidden in rose bushes and
vines, and with its snowy curtains, bright carpets and
tasteful furniture, one can imagine how grateful 't will
be to him who so long has known no dwelling save
the tented field.

Mrs. Ellis drops a tear upon her sewing as she tells
of the patient sufferings and peaceful falling asleep of
saintly Mrs. Center. How her affectionate spirit lingered long in the hope of tidings from her wandering
husband, or his possible return from his mysterious
mission ; how at last her drooping head was supported
tenderly upon her father's breast. He had heard in Chicago of her illness, and came on, hoping to take her back
with him. He carried back only the clay that had
held the imperishable soul which, chastened and purified by sorrow, had now gone up for ever to its eternal
home beyond the skies. The last months of her life
had been spent at Mr. Maynard's, where she was made
as welcome as though in her father's house ; where
loving sympathy had been lavished upon her and she
was made to feel that the ties of relationship were not
needed to ensure the care which her waning life
demanded. So it was with many another who, having

left home and kindred in the East, found on the Western frontier friends as true and loving, though oft bearing strange names and hailing from distant lands. Little Carlos had gone with his grandfather and the silent remains of his mother to Chicago, leaving Nellie, who had been so good a friend, with a sad heart. Nothing had ever been heard of Charles Center. Some believed he had committed suicide; others that he had entered the Confederate army. Somewhere, perhaps, a stern, cold man was wandering, in whose inmost soul there was a longing to behold her once more, who had ever manifested such pitying love for him in his wayward moods. Sometimes, perhaps, those eyes grew dim with moisture, when remorse for his unkindness to her forced him to remember, or when a chance bird-note recalled the tones of the childish voice that called him "papa." Ah! had not some kind angel borne to him his wife's expiring sigh, which was a prayer for her erring husband. The men, old and young, are nearly all away. Some have enlisted very recently, among them Wilson and his two sons. "The draft" is the nightmare of the whole country, in spite of the three hundred dollar clause, from Maine to the Pacific. Mr. and Mrs. Cross have accepted it as a personal grievance, in that they have not the amount about them in loose change, and their Tommy has been compelled to enlist in order to escape conscription. 'Lizbeth is not happy in the absence of her young husband. Last Autumn she accepted attentions from Langmere, who was a short time at home, which gave not a little scandal. Marriage and grass-widowhood

had not entirely destroyed the germ of coquetry in
her nature, but it was a satisfaction to know that Gus
—trusting and worshipful Gus—would never hear of
it. In all the settlement there was not one who
would enlighten him, for, excepting her own mother,
malice had no disciple, and for once she had no desire
to air her knowledge.

Jehial Smith's wife had not remained a widow
long. Two weeks after the news of his death was
received, with her stillborn babe upon her bosom, she
was buried near the pleasant new log house, whose
doors and windows are now boarded up. The path
is overgrown with long grass. In the midst of the
desolation that hangs about the place, we can recall
the morning when the soldiers halted here to speak
their final farewell, and we hear Belinda's cheerful
voice saying :

"Keep up good spirits, Hie, our parting will not
be long."

Mr. Maynard's old log residence has given place
to a handsome, substantial frame house. Through
the aspiring maples that shade the croquet grounds
and guard the house like giant sentinels, the afternoon
wind sobs with a low wail, while the setting sun stains
the clouds a deep red. Are these prophetic? these
crimson clouds, this wailing wind. The farmhouse
has settled down into a peaceful after-tea quiet. The
blinds of the western windows in the long dining room
are closed, and the room is refreshingly cool after the
hot glare. Mr. Maynard and his wife sit beside the
vine-covered window that reaches nearly to the floor.
They are now looked upon as elderly people, yet the

lady's brown hair half dares to curl out of its staid confinement of long comb and matronly cap, and the fair, full face is rosy and beautiful yet, in spite of ungallant years. In her plump white hand she holds an open letter, at which she glances, though at the same time listening to her husband who is still "a fine old English gentleman." Now he takes the letter from her hand, and glancing through it himself, says:

"This is Saturday. Robbie will be here to-night. Do n't you think, mother, I had better go with him on Monday when he returns to his regiment? We have such efficient help now. I want to keep sight of the dear boy as long as possible, and if money will make the stormy military road easier for his following, money shall be used. Of his courage there is no doubt; it has been measured by too many tests in our frontier life. His trials will now be of physical endurance and military discipline. I am very anxious to procure him a commission."

"You seem to forget, father," said Mrs. Maynard, "that he is now essentially American. Let him work his way up, in the democratic manner, if he wishes. All his life we have sought to impress upon him the duty of self-dependence, and we must not let our overweening tenderness and solicitude *now* induce us to belie our teaching. Go with him, certainly, if you can; provide whatever will add to his comfort, but let him win his commission himself. I am so glad he comes to-night. My heart has been heavy all day, realizing more and more, as I do, that though our life here is so peaceful, at this very moment a

O   9*

cruel war is waging, homes are desolated and hearts are breaking."

While she spoke, Nellie had come softly into the room, and seating herself on a low stool at Mrs. Maynard's feet and laying her arm upon her knee, now looked fondly up into her face. A light caressing hand was laid upon her snowy shoulder and the mother continued,

" By the way, father, I wish to go over to Mr. Palmer's to-night. Can you take me now ? "

" I 'll drive you over there at once."

" I won't be driven," replied his wife, smiling. " Moral suasion is vastly more agreeable to me."

" Very well ; you shall have moral suasion, and the horse shall be driven," he says, leaving the room to order out the carriage.

The mother bends over the sweet girl seated at her knee, and placing both hands lovingly about her neck, says :

" Nellie, Cloe has made everything ready in brother's room. If Mrs. Palmer's baby is no better I may remain all night, and you must welcome him when he comes, and then go to rest early. To-morrow is Robbie's last Sabbath at home. It will be to him and us both a memorable day. We must prepare ourselves to live much in those few hours, the last we will spend together for so long—perhaps forever."

" O mother, that is such a sad thought ! To-day I noticed the purple wild flowers that Robbie and I have cultivated where they grew on the prairie, are all in bloom. When you leave I will get some to put

in his room in the little vase he teases me so about.
I will place them near his bedside on the stand by the
lamp, so he will not fail to see them. But there is
father at the gate with old Deacon and the buggy."

Mother and daughter walk down through the
grove to where Mr. Maynard stands, whip in hand.

"Going, too, Pet?" he says, so tenderly that you
discern "tears in his voice," as was said of Rubina.

"No, father, I came down to kiss you good-night."

The kisses of both father and mother are fervently
bestowed upon that pale, sweet face, and Nellie is going back to the house, but turning suddenly she cries:
"Wait a minute," and tripping down swiftly to the
gate she climbs upon the carriage step like a child,
woman though she now is, saying:

"I must kiss you both again, one kiss was not
enough, the nights are so long."

Mr. Maynard lays his hand upon the rich golden
curls, while a tear unbidden rolls down his cheek as he
gives his child the coveted kiss. A feeling of apprehension fills her mother's heart; Nellie's face is held
in both her hands, and fond kisses are pressed upon
her lips and brow as she falters through her tears:

"Good-night, my child. God keep you."

As they drive away she says:

"Father, I think Robbie's enlisting has made us
all a little nervous."

"Yes," he replies. "But I am always nervous
about my little Nell; she seems so frail, so in need of
constant protection, still a child in spite of her
years!"

Nellie, now evidently satisfied, goes slowly toward the house, watching the carriage till it is lost to view by a dip in the road at the foot of the grove. Then she says to herself, regretfully :

"There, why did I look so long? My old English nurse used to say that bad luck was sure to overtake people if you watch them out of sight. But old Deacon is steady. Father is strong, mother watchful and, well, and all of them so good. I am sure nothing can happen them."

She stops now beside the graveled walk to tie back a recreant bunch of roses that caught in her dress, stooping to inhale the delicious fragrance with long-drawn inspirations, then she steps upon the porch where lies old Hector, superannuated and lame. Him she fondles and pets while he wags his great black shaggy tail so earnestly as to move his whole body at every wag. One earnest thoughtful look she turns upon the sun, just setting in gorgeous clouds, shading her eyes with her hand. Then passing into the hall and on to her own room, she lifts a vase from the table regarding it a moment with a smile. With it in her hand she passes through the house again and out through the kitchen door, taking a path that leads to the open prairie, her favorite walk.

By the side of the dairy house bubbles up a beautiful spring, whose waters are conducted by a pipe into the building where they spread a cool running carpet over the smooth stone floor. There is a rich gurgling sound where they collect again in a little cascade at the south end and fall in a rivulet that threads its melodious way through the clover and short lawn grass down toward Dimple Run. Placing the vase in the bushes, and dipping her hand in the waters, she scatters pearls of moisture over the grass, singing meanwhile in her low sweet voice, an old fashioned hymn. Hark! "I love to steal a while away—"

A heavy blow breaks off the melody and fells her to the earth. A tall painted savage stands over her, brandishing his hatchet, a hideous ghoul-like form.

Now from the ambush starts a hidden foe, while there rings out upon the air a succession of unearthly yells. It seems as if mother earth had suddenly, without premonitory moan, brought forth a demoniac legion, and pandemonium greets their birth with shrieks. From grass and bush and sheltering tree, a wild swarm teems forth. A mad impetuous horde of savages, each wielding a deadly weapon. The sun has dropped from view, leaving in the heavens a trail of blood-stained clouds and amid the scene of peaceful happiness tipped by its last rays, real blood now flows. Every human being that breathed so recently beneath the friendly maples is numbered now with the silent dead. Two farm hands as they sat at the kitchen door, another bringing in either hand a pail of foaming milk. Faithful Cloe lies in the pantry scalped. The dairy maid, Mary, fell while placing a glass of milk in a pan of ice for Nellie. And just where a little white hand lay ten minutes ago the brutal hatchet has cleft the brain of poor old Hector.

Not a moment has been wasted in the fiendish butchery, every stroke has counted, every thrust has told. In their haste to follow the carriage the Indians have seen depart, they neglect the mutilation of their victims, the wanton destruction of property which usually marks the closing scene of their murderous visits on the frontier.

Mr. and Mrs. Maynard chatted pleasantly as they rode along, till within a few yards of the dwelling of the neighbor they came to serve. their noble career of usefulness was ruthlessly ended. Like a furious tempest the whole mad troop swept down upon them, as steady old Deacon jogged along. Mock-ane-sah, the long-time friend, whose ear had been poisoned by untruthful reports, stepped up beside the buggy and placing his piece by Mr. Maynard's ear, as he walked along. said:

"Mock-ane-sah has seen that the white man whom he trusted, has two tongues. His young men hanged the only son, the staff of one who hurries to the grave, and said: ' Our ravens shall feed upon the carcass of the Indian dog.' But the lying white man shall *die*, and his squaw shall ride with him, *so*."

Discharging his gun, he stepped back, giving the command not to harm Mrs. Maynard, but another bullet had sped simultaneously with his own, and thus hand in hand they crossed the eternal threshold, still united even in death. The lifeless forms mutually supporting each other were thus borne over the road which old Deacon knew well. Ben sat with his wife beside the cradle of their sick child watching the heavy slumber, from which they knew it would awaken with the promise of returning health or immediate death. The strong man took the soft hand of the weeping woman in his own, stroking it as he said :

"Poor wife, this is very hard for you, to see your child suffer so ; you are worn out with long care and watching. Go, dear, and try to get some rest while Freddie sleeps. Miannetta and I will watch his breathing, and if the slightest change occurs, we will call you."

"I know, Ben, you say this with the kindest feeling, but it would be cruel to urge me to leave him for a moment. I do not doubt Miannetta's skill, and if Freddie lives, her hand will have saved him. But oh, Ben, I can not think of rest ; I can not leave the cradle of my precious little one now."

The sobs that burst from her bosom were drowned by a savage yell. The fiends had crept to the very door, and the dark throng instantly filled the room. One moment and a tomahawk was buried in Ben Palmer's brain ; the next, his struggling, shrieking wife is borne out to a fate than which death would be more merciful.

The savages at once saw the condition of the child. With the refinement of cruelty only to be found in an American Indian, they carried it out in its cradle and set it down beyond the enclosure by the roadside—there in loneliness to wail, and pine, and die.

The torch was applied, and the tasteful home of Ruth and Ben Palmer was consumed with its kind-hearted master.

An awful stillness then fell upon the twilight hour, of which the silence after a storm is but a feeble meta-

phor.   Over the glowing flames, and wreathing
smoke, and utter desolation, there hung now the
pall of night.

The Indians had come through the woods from
the west.   The first blood had been spilled at the
Maples, and very likely Palmer's residence would
have been spared, but for Mr. and Mrs. Maynard's
proximity to it when overtaken and killed.

Their destination proper was the settlement five
miles above Mr. Maynard's, and setting their faces
toward it, they rushed on to a new feast of slaughter
and rapine.

The thick wood and the darkness of night favored
them.   Upon many a sleeping family they crept
silent as the death angel, yet more dread ; the first
intimation of their presence being the shrill whoop
and crashing doors.

Ah ! few shall rise, where many lay down in
peace at eve.   Our whilom friends have fallen under
merciless hands ; the cruel thirsty hatchet is drunken
with their blood.

But the recitation of the revolting scenes of outrage and murder is too harrowing.   The soul sickens,
the pen recoils from it.   Till late in the night, the
Indians wrought in savage frenzy, spreading despair
on every hand.   Toward dawn their rage culminated,
and they laid waste the dwellings, tortured the men,
women and children in Clipnockum Hollow ; some
they bound and burned under the same tree that had
served as an instrument of more merciful death to
two of their own race.   Then they hurried back with

several prisoners to the fastness of distant forests; leaving behind them ruined altars, smouldering homes, and mutilated corpses. The eye of God alone was bent upon that ghastly trail of savage ferocity. He had spoken all unheeded:

"Vengeance is mine, and I will repay."

As the tides of the sea arise in the month of September,
Flooding some silver stream till it spreads to a lake in the meadow;
So Death flooded Life, overflowing its natural margin.

—LONGFELLOW

CHAPTER IX.

TO WIN OR LOSE.

WHEN Mr. Meade and his daughter had left the room, after Mrs. Garret's discovery and peremptory disclosure of Lieut. Langmere's hypocrisy, that distinguished officer almost immediately found the use of his limbs. Encasing the nether in top boots, and thrusting his arms into regulation broadcloth he turned full rigged to his sable attendant, and with perfect coolness, said:

Well, Pomp. Concert's over, the song is sung. What do you think of the performance?"

" Purty good, massa ; 'specially that chorus, ' Ten hundred a year.' "

" He shall double it next twelve month. A gentleman can't live elegantly upon that sum. Now, I am told that I am disgraced in the army, stripped of my epaulets, of course the pay will be proportionately lessened if I go into the ranks a private soldier, which I do n't intend to do. Richard is himself again, and proposes to tread the boards of some more congenial stage. However, I will walk down to the bank, and draw the first instalment of the old fossil's allowance. Pomp, my boy, you get your traps all ready to go when I come back."

" No ye do n't now, massa," grinned Pomp.

" 'T ain't no ways safe to 'low a gemmen what 's
been so oncommon low to go out alone. I 'll go long,
honey, and witness the cashing of the old man's
paper, 'kase I have a little claim ag'in the pile, and
think I may as well make sure of it while it 's kinder
loose and movin'. You 're powerful weak, and might
sorter forget what share you promised me, if I
would -help you through this business of matri-
money."

" But you did n't help me through. You did not
prevent that infernal old woman coming in here and
spoiling the whole kettle of fish; you failed to keep
her hands off me, and that ruined all my plans.
When you fail in one particular, you fail in all, and
thus wipe out the remunerative consideration. Do n't
you see ? "

" Now, massa, dat won't go down wid dis chile.
I 'se got a black hide, but dere is some cunnin' inside
ob it. You must pay me pretty smart, or I will jes'
inform on ye, and ye 'll get locked up for obtainin'
money under false pretences. Massa Bartholt told
me to watch out for ye, 'kase he reckoned ye 'd gib
us the slip, may be."

" Inform, you black ape ! but that 's all the good
it will do you ! What is nigger testimony worth, do
you think ? Take that, sir ! 'T is all you will ever get
from me, unless you oblige me to repeat the dose."

He caught the unguarded negro by the throat,
and with a lion's grip held him till his eyes stood out
like two great frightful balls, and his face grew more
intensely black and shiny, while his limbs hung loose
at the joints and refused their support. Then with a

frightful oath he flung the repulsive mass upon the
floor, and left it gasping faintly while he passed out
the door, which he locked. Flinging the key through
an open window into an area, he passed through the
long hall, down the stairs to the street door. He was
soon at liberty on the pavement, and on his way to
the bank. In less than twenty minutes he was in possession of the one thousand dollars—Mr. Meade having
just left the bank as Langmere entered.

He knew that he was disgraced forever in the
regiment, as well as deprived of his rank, for reasons not essential to relate, but which every reader
will readily surmise.

Hundreds of unworthy officers, about these days,
went with shamed faces into the ranks, realizing how
much more disagreeable is the experience—though
attended with less exertion—of going down than up.

Langmere left Washington in the shortest possible
time, forgetting in his haste to call for his servants
or settle the bill of his medical adviser and confederate. Dr. Bartholt had sown, as he hoped to reap,
largely confiding in his own sagacity and Pomp's
watchfulness to make certain that Langmere should
not escape when the harvest was gathered.

Langmere was a passenger—in another coach—on
the same train which bore her he proposed, sometime (not very remote, perhaps—that would depend
upon the length of the war and his freedom to assume
citizenship again) to claim as his wife, or force her
father to increase the significant figure of his yearly
allowance.

"After all," he said to himself, as he coolly

smoothed out the pile of crisp new bills on his knee,
" it 's not so bad having a rich wife, when a fellow
do n't want to work, especially. What if she is a
wife under protest. That protest is good capital."

Yes, her very aversion to him was cash in hand.
A feint of his to publish their relation would surely
result in the augmentation of his finances, for her
father would count out his last dollar to screen his
daughter. He knew her simplicity was coupled with
no ordinary pride, and coarsely calculating the extent
to which he could turn both her simplicity and pride
to his own mercenary uses, he chuckled to himself as
he folded the bills lovingly away. In the midst of
these amiable reflections he saw the victim of his late
artifice step from the train ; saw her many acquaintances press about her and her father, for they were
much loved in their own circle of friends. The
wretch laughed outright as he saw her lovely face
crimson at the inquiry of some friend, whom she
could not enlighten, as to the health of "her soldier."

Much as I love the truth, I can not feel it would have
been better for her to have braved all criticism and
told the story of his treachery and her mortification.

Alice Langmere's was a *very* human heart indeed,
with some of the passions and perhaps more of the
weaknesses that make us kin. She thought bitterly
how Langmere himself had taunted her with unmaidenly persistence when he hypocritically objected to
immediate marriage, and would the world be more
merciful? If any of my readers blame her for folding her secret away, I beg him or her to take the case
home.

Langmore's mother lived at Blakely where he had conducted, under the rose, a contraband traffic with the Sioux or Dakota Indians, and having considerable of the stock in trade on hand when he enlisted, he had buried it, thinking it possible he might sometime resume business on a more extensive scale. His mother only knew of the whereabouts of the liquid treasure and she kept faithful ward, for what was treasure to him was precious to her, poor old doting body. She was an illiterate English woman, bearing still her maiden name, for she never wore the ring that sanctifies motherhood, and was reaping one of the penalties of her early sin, in the tyrannical treatment of her heartless offspring. She had wrought hard in his youth to clothe and "heducate" him. The latter, indeed, was her hobby.

"Oh, 'is father was a clever mon, wi' plenty o' money and plenty o' words for 'is smooth tongue. Larnin' set 'im up in t' warld, and what if 't chucked me in t' mire, my boy and 'is boy s'all 'ave it if I work my nails off—the nails that mony times 'as ached to scratch 'is eyes out wi'."

And she had worked many a long year through heat and cold, "scrubbing at 'ouse or grubbing at field," with hunger that would have weakened others, but which gave a desperate strength to the forsaken woman. All her earnings, save enough to purchase "a pretty suit and dainty bit and sup" for her George, were hoarded with a view of giving him an education like his father's. The excellent opportunities her energy secured for him, his quick intelligence had improved, and his scholarship at an early age was very creditable. The one cherished bud of the desolate heart had his father's grace of speech, with, a proportionate villainy of soul and no gratitude for her who had literally hungered for his advancement. When he was thirteen, his father furnished means through an agent to take mother and son to America. The shrewd woman took steerage passage across the ocean, and thus saved enough to set up a fruit-stand in New York. The same self-denial was shown when her trade netted a hundred each half year as when, for a paltry "tuppence" a day, she wrought as a scullery maid in Yorkshire. She would have remained in the little seven by nine stall under the awning, grand enough to suit her simple ideas, but a wish to rove took possession of her son and sovereign. She sold out her stand, and they departed with the cry "Westward, ho." At the different cities they stopped, that her industrious hand might replenish the purse. The boy always went to school, for which, strangely enough, he manifested a marked predilection. The year they tarried in Chicago finished his education, and then they went to Minnesota where he assumed the head of affairs. With fifty dollars of her saving, he embarked in trade in a small way, investing carefully (for he had the maternal shrewdness) and realizing marvelously, with always a leaning toward something not exactly correct. If two roads led to a goal—one light and straight, the other dark and crooked — he was sure to choose the latter.

The trade in bad whisky with the Indians, all the more tempting because unlawful, yielded more than

double the ordinary profits of business. Just before
the war broke out, however, the Indians withdrew
suddenly from the hamlets where they had been wont
to loiter and imbibe. His trade collapsed and he had
enlisted, disposing of his stock in the manner already
indicated. His old mother had been his "clark"
while she was well enough to work, but her strength
had given way at last, and she lingered on, a burden
who had given her own life-blood to her ungrateful
son. She strove with painful effort to add to the
meager purse he provided, making rude willow ware
that she sold among the neighbors. To others she
was indebted for news from the "army," which was
but another name for her boy, inasmuch as she gave
him credit for every military movement, no matter
where or in what division of the army it was made.
One day a lady, pitying her loneliness, gave her some
illustrated newspapers. At that time soldiers figured
extensively in all the pictorial journals, and her dim
eyes readily detected the form and features of George
in many of them. Looking at one picture and then
at another, she exclaimed:

"Well now, I swan t' man, I never thought 'e
could get rount lively enow to do all 't seems t' coom
t' 'im. Bless ye, 'ow henthusiastic 'e seem 'ere, blow-
in' away on t' hinstrument! Wonder if 'e 's playin'
'God save t' queen.'"

"Oh," said the lady, "that is a soldier drinking
from his canteen."

"Nor summat good to drink, neither; by t' name
I guess soom nasty stuff. Why, if 'e can't get good
whisky, why do n't t' lout dhrink wather?"

"Do you get letters from him often?" was the kindly inquiry.

"No; 'e writ only but onct. 'Lizbeth 'Arkness, t' little war widder, 't teached school 'ere last Summer gone, read it for me and writ t' answer."

"How is your lameness? Did Mrs. Cross help you with her new discovery?"

"No; t' old thing got mad as fire wi' me, 'cause I sed Miannetta cured old Barnes' missus of t' same pains and swellings. Sed I coom fra the barbarous counthry where t' had kings and queens and ships, and might 's well roob t' 'intment on basswood trees 's on me. I 's frightened of pisen and threw t' bottle and all outen doors. S' now I think on 't, will you write a letter to my George for me? Ye can keep shet pate for what I tell ye, that I knows well enoo. Will ye write now, eh?"

"Certainly, while you dictate for me."

The letter was soon written, and read as follows:

DEAR GEORGE:

A white man in the woods sent old Jim John down here to see if you would take greenbacks for the liquor on hand. The Indians are all paid off in paper *this time* and have no gold. I told him I thought you would sell for paper money. Write if you will and tell me how to get the stuff to the upper agency, where the purchaser wishes it to be delivered. He is a man, it seems, that do n't want to be recognized by the whites, and of course the Indians can not be trusted to carry it. Who can I trust it with? I hope you will let me have enough of the money to get a little tea, a petticoat and a pair of strong shoes.

Your affectionate mother,
SALLY HOPKINS.

P

This letter, received at the same time he was apprised of his disgrace in the army, a day or two before
the final denouement at Dr. Bartholt's, had decided
him to return to Minnesota, and himself take his
liquors up to the Indian country. Where could he
hide from the Federal eye more entirely than in the
tangled and interminable forest of the North-west.
He well knew the worthlessness of paper currency
to an Indian, and soon concluded that there was nowhere in the world a more promising opening for a
young deserter. With a mental " I'll see *you* again,"
as Alice, unconscious of his gaze or proximity,
stood on the platform, he had gone on with as little
delay as possible. He was in danger of apprehension,
and, no doubt, but for the shoulder-straps he still
boldly wore, would have been arrested, for Uncle
Sam was lynx-eyed in the discovery of deserters. He
had reached home a day or two previous to the
occurrences which are related in the last chapter, and
had hurriedly unearthed his treasures and sent them
by secret means into the country whither his safety
called him.

The day before the massacre, he drove in a buggy
over to Mr. Cross'. 'Lizbeth met and welcomed him
at the low doorway, inviting him to partake of the
evening meal, which invitation he very politely accepted, and afterward asked her to ride with him.
She went, poor shorted-sighted girl, short-sighted
through vanity and loneliness. She felt an exultation
in winding men about her finger. George Langmere
had not only admired but had once, in her girlhood,
made her an offer of marriage which she had declined

with something akin to contempt. Now he was an officer and his attentions therefore very flattering in spite of his ugliness, to her who had been so long a wife and war widow. She returned a sharp reply to her mother's caution against "riding fur." They had followed the new road many miles and the sunset lighted up the pale ferns, tree tops and patches of sky visible now and then through the green roof under which they rode. Suddenly the bushes flanking their way were transformed into hideous forms with their savage ornaments of paint, feathers and beads. Ere her surprise had deepened into terror, she and her companion were the prisoners of a band of Sioux.

In the moment of supremest fear, she marveled at the feebleness of Langmere's resistance, and the ease with which the capture was made. Ere a half hour had elapsed, she tremblingly comprehended the truth. She saw plainly it was a ruse of Langmere's to get her in his power. That the one savage who walked ahead of the horse, and the two who loped along behind the buggy, as rear guard, were really his *confederates*. Her quick wit now realized that the admiration of this man meant her ruin. Her heart sank within her, as she reflected how absolutely she was at his mercy. What that mercy amounted to could be easily computed, from the mere fact that he was hand in glove with the painted wretches who had pretended to capture them. Few words had been spoken, there had been little brandishing of their favorite weapon, but enough Langmere thought to deceive her. Three had accompanied them, while the rest, a small war party on the way to the rendezvous near Mr. Maynard's, had gone on, and 'Lizbeth had felt a momentary apprehension for the settlement toward which they were hurrying. Langmere played his cards artfully, really hoping to impress the heart of his kidnapped victim, so that there would be no necessity of downright compulsion to effect the intimate relations which he had fully resolved should brighten his sojourn in the upper country. Artfully as he had planned and dealt he saw that still greater art would be necessary to conquer the regard of the quick-witted woman who had been surprised into his power. He knew that even now her spirit was arming itself against him in the discovery, too late to avail her, that she had committed an unpardonable error in going to ride with him. She really loved her husband. Yet she had ever felt a coquettish thrill of satisfaction at the admiration of other men, though once on her guard, and suspicious of the honesty of that admiration, and 'Lizbeth Harkness was as indignant as any other true woman and faithful wife.

Night fell early on their solitary way. They encamped near a brook that went singing on its way through the gloom. 'Lizbeth sat upon its bank, bathing her face and hands and tasting its cool water. No fruitless ambition for notice caused a deviation from its own course or disturbed its loyalty to its belongings as little by little it absorbed its natural tributaries and with new strength went on. A deep rebuke of her foolish acceptance of Langmere's attentions was voiced by the stream. Had she but taken counsel with her loftier nature she would now be safely at home a contented wife, and to-morrow would arise to sing at her humble task instead of buckling on the armor that might not avail to resist the attentions that she now dreaded.

It was quite dark when 'Lizbeth went reluctantly up the bank to the place where the sheltering tent was stretched. Provisions for a comfortable supper and night's encampment, that she knew must have come from under the buggy seat, argued forethought remarkable for an evening's drive. She remarked, "You seem well prepared for this adventure."

" Yes, I am too old, and have been caught out too many times, to ever start from home without the needful things to make night comfortable, if it happens to overtake me. We will some day laugh over this journey," he replied.

" On the contrary, I shall every day of my life grow graver in consequence of it. Though too late for regret, I shall never cease to reproach myself for coming with you to-night. It was not right; it was a wrong against my absent husband, my faithful Gus," she cried, burying her face in her hands.

"Now, 'Lizbeth, don't go to reproaching yourself for the most harmless and most natural thing in the world for a pretty woman to do. You only started out for a short ride with your own and husband's friend. We were taken prisoners, and now must make the best of it. We'll soon have some supper, and a good talk over old times," rejoined Langmere turning, to assist the Indians in preparations for the promised meal. He boiled the kettle, frizzled the pork in the blaze, cut the bread, and

made coffee, over the same fire that afforded a smoke
to quiet the mosquitoes.

'Lizbeth had an appetite that seldom suffered
through the wear and tear of the sensibilities, and
grave as her position was, she thought it best to eat ;
so partook of the clear strong coffee, sweet bread and
butter, pork, and dried venison.   She slept soundly
on a rude couch of leaves, covered with a blanket,
while Langmere and the intoxicated Indians slept on
the ground near the fire.   Once in the night she
awakened suddenly with intense terror, her eyes met
the small wicked ones of Langmere close to her face.
Starting wildly up, she thrust him back, and hissed in
his ear ·

"George Langmere, if you attempt to come near
me, if Gus does not kill you, I will."

"You will have to then, for Gus has n't time.
The yellow girl, and her brat that resembles him,
require all his spare efforts.   When the mother is
washing soiled regimentals, he brings water and
tends baby.   He has no ambition to shine as the
avenger of a woman he has nearly forgotten, 'Lizbeth," he said.

He drew closer, and holding her hands a moment,
kissed one of the curls that had strayed from under
the handkerchief bound about her head.   She
wrenched her hands away from his clasp, and drawing down the curl, bit it off, and flung it in his face.

"Take it villain, liar !" she cried.

Again taking a stronger hold of her hands, and
speaking persuasively:

"No, no, do n't, 'Lizbeth.   You shall see how I

·admire and love you ; and how much more faithful I will be, than he who prefers a woolly scalp to such luxuriant hair.''

For the first time in her life, 'Lizbeth felt the iron of jealousy tear through her soul, as she saw for a moment, in fancy, her husband—she had felt that he was indisputably hers—gather to his bosom the head of another women. She saw him, meanly as she fancied, interesting himself in the ignoble employment of a negress—the negress whose child was his. She remembered having smiled at his pain, when, before their marriage, she had caused him the pangs of jealousy, as severe as those she now felt, perhaps ; and she had then, unheeding the suffering he endured, augmented them by her trifling and insincerity. She now was the tormented. The words of Langmere had gone with fatal directness to her soul, and her faith in her husband was shattered. Even the most sensible people will lose all power to exercise ordinary reason, when their jealousy is aroused. Langmere withdrew, and she wept passionately over her forlorn and hopeless lot, even feeling a tolerance of Langmere's friendship, in her entire separation from her husband, and, indeed, all the world.

Morning came, breakfast was eaten, and at sun·rise they again set out. The path was obstructed and rough, and a breakdown of the light vehicle delayed them some time.

As they again took their seats and started, Langmere remarked:

''If I had come voluntarily here, I should have

taken the precaution of procuring pack-mules instead of this buggy."

'Lizbeth as quickly added, while her black eyes flashed—

"And, perhaps, left behind the big black bottle, from which you and our escorts imbibe alternately. No wonder it gets mixed who planned this expedition."

He looked wonderingly into her face. Could it be possible she had read through him so readily, and he boldly asked :

"Did you from the first, credit me with planning this adventure."

"No, not until you attempted to destroy the beautiful illusion of my belief in Gus. What could induce you to tell me of that woman—of that child? Ah, I know you. George Langmore."

"And are we friends or enemies?" he asked, as coolly as though inquiring the time of day.

"I will not tell you now. *Wait till we are out of the woods.*"

"O, you are a logician, and like myself inclined to take the matter philosophically. I believe such people get along the easiest, no bruising of impatient hands, no bleeding of impulsive feet, a simple drifting with the current, a patient waiting for the tide."

"No, you mistake me. I am none of your meek ones waiting the flight of the bird of fate. I have a fair amount of determination, or pluck as they call it. I may purr while the sun shines, but like other cats, I have my nails, and woe to those who provoke me to use them."

"I will not take your warning. I have no fear of
cats. Their rage is not lasting, nor their bite fatal. I
have done a little planning, 'tis true, but the righteousness of the object wipes out the transgression."

"I do not recollect that any special reward is offered to those who do evil that good may come."

"You quote scripture aptly but I never took you
for a saint," he said, looking so boldly into her face,
that she blushed with indignation and replied,

"No, I am not a saint; if I were I should not be
here to-day with you, a miserable captive with no ran-
som in prospect. Alas! George Langmere, you are
less culpable than you seem to be, perhaps."

"O, then you think it sad I am not worse, eh?"

"No, I mean alas for me, but for the vanity that
made your attentions agreeable, I would not have
accepted your invitation, the attentions which at last
have brought me here, an alien from home, with society's ban upon me. Ere this our elopement has been
reported, and worse than all, the nature of your esteem
embitters every look you give, every tone you address
to me, now when I regret my thoughtlessness, my love
of the admiration no married woman has a right to
accept, now when sadly needed, you can not afford me
the protection of respect."

"Hold hard, as the roughs say, wait before you
make any further confession, that dodge won't work
this time. It will take more than that to convince me,
that even religion can revolutionize your whole nature.
When you and I started three days ago, we each understood the other. Human nature is human nature,
in spite of custom and usage. You are a very pretty

10*

woman, impressionable as ether, and though cunning
as a serpent, and changeable as April weather, you
are not going to slip through any sanctimonious gap.
Listen: Gus is lost to you forever; you could not
take him back to your heart, even though repentant,
after this colored girl affair.   The world we have left
has already sat in judgment upon you, and pronounced
an irrevocable verdict.   I have money; you know its
worth to a handsome woman.   Wives are unknown
in the forest and you shall have whatever name best
suits you, mistress or queen.   My plan, let me tell
you, saved your life, for the Sioux were upon the path
of vengeance and would have killed you, if my hand
had not interposed.   Do not decide now; I will wait
and prove my love.   But mine you shall be, by flow-
ery chains if you will, or by force if you prefer.   I
warn you there is no escape, every Indian is my
sworn ally."

They were now looking in each other's eyes, and
she saw how certainly he meant to enforce his power.
In that gross face she read no hope.   With a sickening dread of him she buried her face in her hands and
cried aloud.   Gradually sob by sob her grief grew
less violent.   She settled to the soft raining of still
tears, in which he read acquiescence to his shameful
proposal.   Placing his arm behind her upon the back
of the seat, he said to himself, with a smile of satisfaction,

"She cries who boasted of her fangs.   This is her
determination and pluck.   When a woman weeps all
wooing is prosperous, for tears come as naturally of
love, as blood comes of war."

This conversation occurred the third afternoon of their journey. Many times they had come upon passable thoroughfares, and as often plunged again into blind by-roads or followed Indian trails. Ever avoiding the public highway, the Indians and Langmere seeming both to prefer obscure ways, the more tiresome and monotonous the better. It was evident they shrank from possible encounters with white men, while of Indians they were fearless. 'Lizbeth wept long and refreshingly. With dry eyes she looked up at an exclamation of surprise and admiration from Langmere, and following the direction of his gaze she beheld a novel scene. They had been gradually ascending a high wooded ridge, and came now almost abruptly out of the dense forest upon the brow of a precipitous promontory, where a pebble might fall straight into the waters of a river that glinted in the sun's declining rays. Upon this river many a birch canoe was moored, and others glided up and down and athwart the glittering stream, obedient to the dextrous paddle stroke of dusky women, erect in their sharp-pointed bows. The river here described a graceful curve, as though a great flashing sickle of steel had been laid upon the fair bosom of the earth, the lofty promontory forming the eastern bank and lying in the center of the arch. Following the outer curve or the western bank, with indifferent regularity, straggled the white tepees, and birchen wigwams of an Indian town. Tall linwood trees grew among and beyond the wigwams, and lent a wondrous charm to the scene, their broad, delicate-hued leaves, breeze-shaken, drinking in the sunlight till they seemed veritable censers

of gold, "held quivering to the gods." Women, in
all ages and stages of grace and uncouthness (for
among squaws are found exponents of both types),
were scattered about upon the green grass in front of
the wigwams or under the trees, engaged in work,
either manufacturing moccasins of deer skin, or the
various bead ornaments so highly prized by their
people. Children sported and laughed near their el-
ders with happy abandon.

The warriors were all away, and the old grayhaired
men were wisely seated under cover where they could
smoke, fearless of falling dew. The striplings,
yet too young to "beat the war-post" (a ceremony
that ushers the young Indian into a warrior's rank),
were mustered on the village green, engaged in their
familiar and favorite game of ball-playing, with rack-
ets similar to the battledore in use with white people.
The women, especially the younger ones, manifested
great amusement and interest in the game, and mingled with boys' hoarse shouts were peals of women's
laughter. In the background, scrubby-looking cows
and frowsy Indian ponies were quietly grazing. The
soft tinkling of their many bells filled the clear air
with pastoral music. The smoke of tepee fires went
lazily up, in rings of blue and gray, or in great white
feathery masses floated high over the river banks
that held a mirror to the evening sky, and lay upon
the unrippled air like wingless spirits.

> " Harsh sights and sounds with melting day
> Had from the lovely scene been driven.
> Nature seemed kneeling down to pray,
> In praise and gratitude to heaven."

CHAPTER X.

A FORTUNATE MEETING.

"We are well met; our mutual needs are great."

'TWAS the afternoon of a warm Summer day ; the air was oppressive, the thermometer standing well up in the nineties, as the stage-coach bowled along a dusty road. The passengers wiped their streaming foreheads as they commented upon the weather, the crops, the war, the late naval triumph at Hampton Roads, etc. One of them, a gentleman brimful of that humor which is the birthright of Erin's sons, as he aired his pocket-handkerchief out of the window, exclaimed :

"Hot ! hot as—well, as a place that rhymes with glory."

"Purgatory ?" suggested another, with a smile by which we recognize Robert Maynard.

"Good at guessin', ain't ye ?" chimed in a tall, cadaverous fellow in soiled Federal uniform. "A soldier goin' hum on furlow to 'cruit up," as he had several times informed his fellow-passengers. He was just about to tell them a story relating to some of his hospital experience which the word purgatory seemed to have suggested, when the stage drew up at an inn, the last station on the road below the Maples, where Robert's two companions got out.

Robert felt no loneliness at the prospect of having the inside of the stage-coach to himself, yet he expressed regret that his agreeable traveling acquaintance, the Irish gentleman, went no farther. As they entered the inn, the landlord was haranging a dejected-looking, powerfully built man, who sat with arms upon the table and his face bent down so as to hide his features. Robert stood in the doorway, unperceived, while mine host continued in a loud, harsh voice :

"That's a pretty, whining story! After eating my bread for four days, and making all the trouble you have here, to tell me you have no money. Why did n't you tell me so when you came ? "

"My wife and child were too ill to travel further, and this was the only house which afforded the shelter they required. My child's danger drove out every other thought, sir."

Here the speaker paused a moment, overcome with emotion, then continued :

"Since God, in his providence, has taken him away from us, we will go on now and obtain employment, which will enable us soon to pay you for the trouble we have made and the bread we have eaten. My money failed because we have been so many times detained by illness, but I will soon earn more than enough to pay all I owe you."

"Pay me ! " shouted the landlord. "Pay me ! I shall never hear from you again, or a word about my pay, after you leave here. I've been bit by just such as you before, and the only way is to hold on to your baggage. An' I'll do it; yes sir, *every dud!* Now take your wife, you whining pauper, and get out of here. There's work enough for them as want it, al-l'us, but I can't feed them as do n't. Them's my square sentiments, by Moses!"

Veering round suddenly, he ran bolt against Robert, who was regarding the seated figure with evident compassion.

But what a sudden metamorphosis. The bully in a moment was a toady. The freedom of the house was tendered "Mr. Maynard." Wine, cigars, supper were offered, and gravely declined.

The young man simply saying: "No, thank you," advanced to the table, laid his hand kindly upon the bowed shoulder, saying:

"You are a stranger, and in trouble; as I hope for assistance in my day of need, I beg you to command me in yours."

Dashing a tear from his large blue eye, the man arose, and bowing with a grateful politeness not acquired, and an accent that betrayed his nativity, replied:

"My name is McDougal, sir. Two months ago, I left Scotland hoping to find a home in this beautiful State. My purse was full, my wife was radiant with health and hope; my rosy, blue-eyed boy cheered us with his childish talk and merry laugh. The way is long. We were subjected to numerous delays and my purse gave out here. My wife is sick and des-pondent, for yest'reen we laid our boy in the grave, the song on his young lips hushed, and his bright eyes closed for ever. My bill here is not large, but I can not pay it, and, sir, I will accept gratefully your unexpected courtesy as freely as it is generously offered. I have heard of a gentleman, a wealthy farmer, a few miles from here; I will go to him and seek work in harvest. By your assistance I may be able to reach The Maples to-night."

"That is my home, and I promise you a warm welcome," said Robert.

The packing boxes and trunks were soon transferred from the hotel porch to the boot and roof of the stage coach. The Scotchman lifted in a pale comely woman, and, taking a seat beside her, gravely watched the pompous bustling landlord seized with a sudden desire to be useful to his late unwelcome guests. Robert paid the bill, sprang into the coach, and took a front seat, facing McDougal.

"You have become acquainted with our young State at a time when she is seen to a great disadvantage," he said. "Our enterprises are all at present military. Everything has had to give way to the necessary equipment and sustenance of a great army. Legitimate business is stagnant. The whole nation is absorbed in establishing beyond question, a principle, which has unfortunately been brought to a bloody test. Commerce, agriculture, and scholarship are subservient to the needs of the hour."

"I find," said the Scotchman, "my pre-conceived idea incorrect. This is a war with broader basis than I supposed. Before coming to America, I had the impression it was sectional—a border warfare between the free and slave owning States ; but I confess, however, that in American politics, I very soon get bewildered."

"And no wonder," said Robert. "The great question, 'What is it all about?' is imperfectly understood by many of our own soldiers. Even those who are fairly observant and intelligent, and have for a long time watched the boiling of the political chaldron, might answer the question differently. Its merits are very much obscured by rhetoric and bluster on both sides. But the simple fact is this : Two systems, aristocratic privilege and democratic equality, have at last come to an issue. The idea of the South is the perpetuation of their peculiar institution, an idea which has been too indifferently considered by the North. Though the question of slavery has been agitated many years, it has never assumed direct national importance, only once, I think, having been made an issue in a Presidential campaign, and then by a third and insignificant party. Abolitionism was unpopular even in the North, but secession has changed the public sentiment, and the war cry now is, 'Emancipation.' The South overreached itself, counting upon the Northern pro-slavery sympathizers. That sentiment was found to be insignificant when the Union was threatened, and died when the first hostile missive whistled through the rigging of the 'Star of the West,' flying the United States flag. An educated, religious and determined people, rose to defend those colors, and the unanimity of all parties is an augury of ultimate victory."

Mrs. McDougal listened, evidently with an intelligent appreciation of the subject. She said:

Q   11

"And your clergy are all, as I heard one say, 'baptized with a new, a military fire.' We attended church in Chicago: the clergyman was certainly eloquent, and said to be a very excellent divine. One part of his discourse impressed me particularly at the time; at the close of an impassioned period, he said. 'We will take our glorious flag and nail it just below the Cross, that is high enough. There let it wave as it waved of old; around it we will gather, first Christ's, then our country's.' Those are pure Church and State principles, though I believe in this country such a union is not recognized."

"My wife is a high church woman, Mr. Maynard," said Mr. McDougal.

"And," said Robert, "will not be less welcome at the Maples. My mother is a Scotch lady, and, like my father, a member of the Church of England."

A jolt and lurch of the coach interrupted the conversation, and startled them all, as, for a moment, they were in imminent danger of upsetting. As their equilibrium was restored, and the passengers breathed freely once more, Robert undid a paper parcel, of which he seemed to be very careful, and said:

"I hope I have not broken a present I am taking to my sister. O no, it is all right yet."

He was surprised by an exclamation, sudden and vehement, from Mrs. McDougal. On looking up, he saw her all aglow with interest; half rising, she caught his arm, and with great earnestness, said:

"O, Mr. Maynard, do not let the sunlight fall upon that vase, I beg of you; and pray tell me, where did you get it, and where is its counterpart?"

"This one, madam, is the gift of a young lady to my sister Nellie, who already possesses its counterpart."

"May I inquire, if upon the bottom is engraved the word 'York.'"

"Yes, madam."

"And your sister's bears upon it, in similar lettering, the word 'Lancaster.'"

"Yes."

"How very strange! Those vases must once have belonged to my mother!"

"Heirlooms?" inquired Robert.

"No; she once befriended a gypsy woman who, on her death-bed, gave her those vases, saying they would exert an influence on her fortune, or that of any possessor, prosperity and happiness being assured so long as they were kept from the sun's rays. They were manufactured by sun-worshipers, and possess the power of attracting its angry rays. They were dedicated to the roses of York and Lancaster, and a warning accompanied the gift against their misuse : York *must* be true to York, and Lancaster to Lancaster. Mother, not a little superstitious, as many of my countrywomen are, took the precaution of having them engraved, and valued them despite their weird power for their antique design and transparent beauty."

"How came she to lose them?"

"Most mysteriously ; and my father's financial ruin, my poor mother's sudden death, following almost immediately upon their loss, I can but regard them with something akin to fear—at least, I would want to make sure the sun would never light upon them if I possessed them."

The sun in the mean time had set, and as the twilight cast her misty veil o'er the earth. the conversation had drifted to other themes, and the vases seemed for the moment to be forgotten. Night fell, and for sometime they rode in darkness through a piece of heavy timber. Later, the moon rose. red and round, as they emerged from the wood, and the horses quickened their pace on the smooth road that followed a long, high ridge, a few miles from The Maples. Suddenly the neighing of a horse ahead and the sound of wheels aroused them ; then came a loud, startled "Whoa" from the driver. The rocking of the coach and a heavy thud upon the ground told them he had dismounted. Robert thrust his head out of the window, and with an exclamation of surprise opened the door and sprang out quickly. He affectionately patted the horse's flank as he passed him to reach the carriage, saying : "Why, Deacon, old fellow !—mother, father—O God !"

CHAPTER XI.

THE RETURN HOME.

"No voice in the chamber; no sound in the hall."

ROBERT got into the carriage, and the lifeless heads were strained to his breast, while he knelt before them, crying, "Mother! father! Oh, it can not—can not be! What hand so cruel as to deal thus with you? and Nellie—poor little Nellie!"

He seemed to be losing all self-command, now whispering his mother's name, then calling "Nellie." After a few hurried words with the driver, Mr. McDougal approached him, and disengaging his arms from the embrace of his dead parents, he drew him gently but firmly away, and leading him to the coach, bade him "Get in, and hasten on! We must be active, to save your sister from the fiends who have done this cruel deed; and you must lose no time! It is impossible for me to drive that vehicle as fast as you ought to travel now! My friend, for that sister's sake, be firm and faithful to yourself! It looks dark, but God has not forsaken you!"

The driver resumed his seat, but his horses were weary, and their progress was not much greater than McDougal's. Ben Palmer's house was still smouldering when they reached it—a blaze flaring up now and then where some heavy timber was longer being consumed. All eyes were turned with a sickening inquiry toward the burning pyre, when the horses shied suddenly from the road, prancing and plunging in their efforts to disobey the curb. After much coaxing the driver quieted them and again sprang from his box and stood speechless with horror when he discovered the cause of their excitement—a cradle, a sleeping child, and, beside her baby, the dead body of Ruth Palmer. She had drawn down the tall bushes with her dying hands and braided them into a sheltering canopy; had taken off her dress and wrapped it about the sleeping innocent, to protect it from the falling dew. With one arm thrown over her darling, she had met the pale messenger! How? Ah, none shall ever know! They lifted her body into the stage. Mrs. McDougal took up the sleeping babe, and her experience soon divined its illness. She pressed it to her nourishing bosom and said:

"Sweet little one, thy mother and my child are not! God has made our coming together a mutual blessing. Thou shalt be my own, and I shall be to thee a mother."

They made rapid and fruitless search for Palmer, and then resumed the journey—the saddest funeral train, perhaps, the cold moon ever shone upon. In a short time, unchallenged, they passed under the sentinel trees, and thus returned to their home the master and mistress of The Maples. 'T was a ghastly company, ranged in silence down the long, dim-lighted dining-room, the dead they had found upon the way and those they found here!

Then Robert sought—wildly sought—Nellie; but

he sought in vain. He penetrated the lone recesses of the wood, whose dim aisles mockingly echoed her name as he called her, using all the old endearing terms, framed in loving childhood and in their loving lives never forgotten. His shadow fell on grassy, well-remembered mounds, where many a time he had read to her while she made leafy crowns for him, and they had played at King and Queen ; then out upon the broad prairie, threading his way through its deep and tangled growth. All possible, all impossible places were searched, in the hope that some trace of the fragile, beautiful girl might be found—a tress of her golden hair ; an impression, ever so faint, of her dainty foot ; but his heart grew every moment more sad, until it slowly settled into deepest anguish.

Morning came, and the search was prosecuted with vigor, though with little hope. At sunrise, as Robert led a horse, saddled, from the stable, his eyes (that in all directions watchfully roamed constantly, hoping to catch some trace of his sister) fell upon a horseman cantering hurriedly up the road toward the house; alighting at the gate, they soon clasped hands. It was Captain Ellis, on his way home. Silently Robert led him to the dining-room, where he had so often been a guest, and there he looked upon the still features of his whilom host and hostess, with keenest sorrow in his manly heart, then into the face of the bowed and stricken son.

"The Indians !" he ejaculated after a moment's silence.

"Yes ; no other hand could be found to work such butchery."

Captain Ellis' voice grew husky and his face grew white as that of the sleepers beside him, as he faintly articulated :

" They must have gone farther than this ; perhaps ere this have desolated my home. I saw their wicked work at Ben Palmer's and hurried on—"

" Great heaven ! " said Robert, " forgive my self-ish sorrow. I had forgotten the very existence of the defenseless families at the settlement. Let us hasten, Ellis. Come, and eat some breakfast, and I 'll put your tired horse in the stable and bring out a fresh one."

" Breakfast, Maynard! and *my* wife, *my* babies exposed to the hatchet of these miscreants ! Not a mouthful."

And mounting, the two men dashed away, the fresh horses, seeming to realize the need, putting forth unaccustomed speed. Silently they rode, rising in their stirrups, teeth firmly set, as through the trees they saw the straggling columns of smoke, of burning homes, and the evidences of inhuman slaughter. Wilson's house was only a whitened ash-heap. The gore of violated dead was scattered around. Sick and faint, they were turning away, when a boyish " halloo " arrested them. Down from the screening boughs of a giant oak slid Thad, the youngest of poor Wilson's eight children. His story was simply and soon told ; of the midnight attack and the murder of all save himself ; how he had climbed the tree unnoticed and watched them finish up their deadly work, wrapping it all in a red wind-ing-sheet of flame, and then silently stealing away

toward other residences. Telling the lone orphan boy
to go to the Maples and remain till his return, Robert and his companion pushed on. They passed many
a corpse stark by the roadside, whose features were
familiar ; passed silent ash-strewn places where had
been human habitations, until they came in full view
of the spot where lately was a rose-bowered cottage,
but now could be seen only thin wreaths of smoke and
blackened ruin.

Capt. Ellis spoke not, but his face was white and
distorted by the anguish of his soul. He went
through the yard, opening a gate that led toward the
barn and shelters for stock, and without seeming to
know what he did, closed it again. The click of the
latch, with its familiar home sound, so long unheard,
together with the reflection how useless the precaution
of closed gates now, completely unmanned him. He
fell with a groan upon the ground, repeating the
names of his wife and children. At that moment a
snow white lamb with a gay ribbon about its neck
came bleating from the bushes behind the barn, followed by a child who cried :

"Nanny, Nanny, come back. The Injuns 'll cut
your throat ! "

Rich brown hair strayed in neglected rings over
his forehead. His only garment was a night-dress.
He paused to gaze in bewilderment upon the prostrate
man, who, springing to his feet, caught him in his
arms, saying :

"Do n't you know papa, Herbert? Where is
mamma and little Phil ? "

"Oh, it ain't mamma, it 's grandma. There she

comes now," said the boy, as grandma Smith, with Phil in her arms, came toward them, her dear old white hair wet with morning dewdrops and her soiled night-dress bearing evidences of contact with brush and brier.

"For God's sake, Mrs. Smith, tell me if Kitty lives," said Capt. Ellis advancing, taking the child from her and pressing it to his heart.

"I can not tell you, for I do not know. She bade me say to you that she *would* live and return to you and her children, but when she knew not. She is a prisoner with the fiends who compelled her to destroy her home. For some reason I felt uneasy about her last night, and at sunset came over to see if all was well. She begged me to stay all night with her. I was in bed and asleep when she waked me and in a whisper told me the Indians were about the premises. By her directions I got up, and taking the baby, followed her as she carried Herbert into the cellar. Telling me to remain there till she opened the outside door, then to take the children to the bushes behind the barn and hide with them, but in no case to attempt to assist her. She could speak a little Indian and perhaps might turn that to account. I staid in the cellar perhaps twenty minutes when the house door was broken in with a loud crash, and amidst the savage yelling I could hear her voice talking to them. It grew quieter as she went about getting supper for them. After she had got them seated she ran round and opened the door of the cellar. With a swift pressure of the hand and a kiss upon the lips of her children, she returned to the room, where the noisy, riotous brutes were eating. I hastened to the retreat she had indicated, thinking of home and the many who were exposed to those wretches, for I believed them to be only a part of a larger band. The dear children were both wide awake, but obedient to the charge not to speak. Some time we lay there and then I was startled by a cautious tread and a hand upon my shoulder. Mrs. Ellis whispered in my ear, 'The strychnine with which I flavored their food has proven fatal to three of the Indians; a fourth is dying, only one is left and he too must soon succumb. To save you and my children I must go, perhaps, with the others who even now come yelling down the road, but do not have any anxiety for me. Tell my husband I *will return.*' A moment she lingered, with loving messages for you, and then returned to the house, that was then in flames. Soon the place was silent and I knew that she had gone. I am convinced she will return, for she is a thorough genius and will obtain a controlling influence with the Indians."

It was plain that grandma little guessed the gravity and extent of the outrages that had been perpetrated the night before, for her voice sounded almost cheerful as she spoke; but the two men who listened to her strange narrative thought of the frail woman who had periled her safety to save others, and of the possible fate that awaited her. The anguish of the husband's heart can never be portrayed, as he recalled the passions to which she was exposed. At that moment little Herbert cried out:

"Why, there is uncle Carco Smith!"

"Why, sure enough," said grandma.

The old man, depending a good deal upon his cane, came with puzzled, inquiring eyes toward them. He had staid alone the night before, having retired early and slept very sound, had heard no unusual noise. After milking the cows and eating his solitary break-fast, he had come "cross lots," to see after grandma. Robert now informed them of the terrible work from the results of which they had so singularly escaped. A counsel was held, and a search commenced. Grand-ma and the children were sent to The Maples, where it was thought best for safety to get together all that were left. In the course of the deliberations, several neighbors, some of them living quite distant, who had escaped the night's slaughter one way and another, had joined them. There were ten or twelve of them altogether who set about the burial of the dead, and the sad task occupied the greater part of the day. The last mournful lowering to rest of the victims of these outrages was at The Maples. No hollow sound of falling clod upon a coffin lid had pained the ear. Softly were filled with earth the graves of those who slept, wrapped in a simple winding sheet. There was no time to prepare coffins ; the exigencies of the hour demanded speed.

As the red, Sabbath sun went slowly down the blue incline of heaven, Mr. and Mrs. Maynard were laid gently, side by side, in one broad grave. Mr. McDougal read the beautiful burial service from the lady's own prayer-book. Twenty-four hours before, they had been looking cheerfully out upon this same spot, now their tomb !

By this time quite a large company had assembled. Settlers had dropped in through the day, in twos and threes, and often singly—survivors of the massacre, some of them fearfully mutilated. After the ceremony they all repaired to the house where a good, comfortable supper was prepared by Mrs. McDougal with grandma's assistance. They had found everything in perfect order, from the very garret to the cellar, showing the taste and method of the dear presiding genius who would superintend the generous and beautiful home no more. After supper Robert went into his mother's room. On a small table beside her favorite seat, across the window from her husband's, lay an unfinished garment, a basket containing her thimble, scissors and cotton. Mechanically, he took up a scrap of paper and read a verse cut from Mrs. Browning's great poem. Bitterly he repeated:

"Ah, yes ; even so will my days go on ! "

Upon the window-sill, just where he had lain it, was Mr. Maynard's bible ; upon its open page, his glasses, and a delicate hyacinth, now withered, marking in purple this part of the twenty-third psalm :

"The Lord is my shepherd ; I shall not want. He maketh me to lie down in green pastures. He leadeth me beside the still waters. He restoreth my soul. He leadeth me in the paths of righteousness, for his name's sake. Yea, though I walk through the valley of the shadow of death, I will fear no evil, for Thou art with me. Thy rod and Thy staff, they comfort me."

While Robert reads this holy book the aching breast is eased by tears that heretofore have refused to

flow. It seemed as if sorrow had dried the eyes; but
now he sits down in the vacant arm-chair, weeping
gently and sweetly over his father's bible. He had
neither the time or heart to enter Nellie's room since
the search there last night; but at twilight he felt the
yearning to be where she so lately had been. He
rose and went in. The fragrance of sweetbriar hung
heavy upon the air. The branches of a large bush
had been coaxed through the window and confined by
bits of ribbon to the sash and casement, repaying liberally this care and protection by their delicious per-
fume. He sat down by Nellie's workstand, covered
with bright colored wools, tatting shuttle and spool,
a fairy thimble and bodkin. He took up a half-finished
book-mark she had been making for him. Wrought
in perforated card was this sentiment: "We live
in deeds, not years." On the sofa by the pillow
that still bore the impress of her head, lay an
open volume of "Faust." The door of the handsome wardrobe was open; by her chair lay tiny
slippers that she had exchanged for boots when preparing for her walk. A coquettish apron, with curiously contrived pockets, full of shells and a piece of
petrified moss she had picked up in some of her ram-
bles, hung on a hook near the bed. The bed was
daintily made, with its unrivaled white linen and
counterpane, puffy pillows, with wide, neatly-crimped
ruffles, buttoned with housewifely exactness. All
things were just as she had placed them. This room,
the shrine of a pure, beautiful girl, seemed to call her
back almost to life. Robert started up with a momentary illusion of her presence. He almost saw the

sylph-like figure flitting about in the old sweet manner, stopping in some half-completed task, to whisper
"Dear brother," or throw a kiss to him and smile her
love. He sat there while the night deepened, and
then feeling the absolute need of repose, he went to
his own room which his mother and Cloe had put in
order for him. A large new trunk, full of the many
comforts it was supposed his new life would make
welcome, stood in the room—upon the lid a card, bearing in his father's old-fashioned hand his name, company and regiment. He opened it. Upon the nicely-
folded clothing were a prayer book and bible. On
the fly leaf of each, in his mother's beautiful writing,
were his own and her name. He kissed the latter,
while sobbing, he repeated it, and kneeling, poured
out his grieved spirit in prayer to Him who has promised to be "a present help in every time of need." He
realized that promise and rose from the attitude of
devotion with a calmer soul and more implicit trust.
The inmates of the house were quiet, and hearing no
more the familiar household sounds of shutting doors
and grating chairs that brought the lost ones mockingly to his memory, he laid himself upon the bed,
and courted rest.

Heavy slumber fell upon him ; his exhausted frame
was refreshed. Toward morning he awoke, got up
and dressed, took from his pocket Annette's picture, and pressed it to his lips. Placing it under
the vase he had brought home to Nellie, which now
stood upon his table, he passed out, quietly shutting
his door. He strove by walking to allay the grief
that had wakened with him ; but of what avail the

effort? Was it not written everywhere he turned?
In the bare hope of somewhere coming upon her, he
wandered about, and twice crossed the path of Captain Ellis who was also abroad in the starlight.
Neither spoke, for each felt the taciturnity a great
sorrow imposes, and went his way.

Robert returned to the house at daybreak, and
going to his own room was surprised to find the door
ajar. He thought again to look upon the features of
his betrothed ; but what was his astonishment, to find
her picture gone, and in its place a note, written
hastily, yet legibly. It read :

Robert, I know not her fate. I believe she is alive ; but living
or dead, I will find her, and bring you tidings of Nellie. Your
search would be fruitless. Have you faith to confide in your
mother's friend? Her grateful Miannetta.

CHAPTER XII.

THE SEPARATION.

" Aye, we must part, but do not ask me why—
Enough, my suffering must equal thine."

THE old adage, "A friend in need is a friend indeed," was mutually verified, both by Robert and
Mr. McDougal. While to him was given the charge
of things without, Mrs. McDougal cheerfully accepted
the care of things within, and administered them both
gracefully and practically, with the assistance of a
young German and his sister, sole survivors of a family that had recently removed to Maple Range, and
found shelter and employment at The Maples.

Robert found great comfort in Miannetta's letter,
having the greatest confidence in her zeal and skill.
She could and would, he felt sure, penetrate the most
obscure hiding places of the savages, and would
obtain knowledge inaccessible to any one else.

With Captain Ellis, he joined the soldiers under
Sibley sent in pursuit of the Indians, and both were
present when the captives, women and children, were
given up at Camp Release. Both turned away with
still sadder hearts when the faces had been scanned,
for neither "Kittie" nor "Nellie" was among them.
They returned with the melancholy knowledge that all
pursuit on their part was futile. Captain Ellis made

R 11*

arrangements with grandma Smith to take care of his little boys, and returned to the army. Robert also turned from his desolate home to the more active yet equally sorrowful fortunes of war. One pang more, he thought, as he drove over the prairie after bidding his new-found friends adieu, and my heart shall know the fullness of grief. I must bid Annette farewell.

He reached the city and repaired, after dinner at the hotel, to her father's house, recalling as he mounted the stairs and passed the fountain his own lightness of heart'and her happiness when last there. Only a few days—and what a change! An age of suffering was condensed in that short space.

He was shown into the parlor, and having sent his card waited the appearance of the girl whom he regarded with a love, intensified by the loss of all his kindred. Mrs. La Moore came in, stately and frigid, and, after a ceremonious greeting, said:

"My duty imposes on me the performance of a most unwelcome task, Mr. Maynard! but you will see the impropriety of continuing attentions after I have informed you that they are not acceptable. I beg you not to repeat your visits here during the absence of Mr. La Moore."

"Pardon me; I do not understand you, madam," he said.

"That need not prevent your compliance with my request," she said, and swept from the room just as Annette entered by an opposite door.

The face of the young girl, though beautiful as ever, was very pale, and her eyes filled with tears as she crossed the room swiftly to meet him.

"You know all my loss, all my sorrow, darling," he said as he drew her to his heart and felt her arms twine about his neck.

Her sobs of sympathy were mingled with his own which he could not suppress, as with faltering voice he told the sad story.

"But the loss of mother and father, terrible as it is, is nothing compared with my anxiety for Nellie's uncertain fate. It seems to almost overwhelm me, and I can scarcely command myself to endure the fearful suspense," he concluded, still holding her in his arms.

"I know your suffering, Robert! I pity you with my whole soul ; and yet I am doomed to inflict another pang upon your noble, suffering heart."

"What do you mean, Annette?" he said. "Your very presence comforts me to whom all comfort seemed impossible."

"But, Robert, my beloved," cried the weeping girl, "this must be our last interview, our last embrace. I will not, dare not, tell you why! I love you truly, devotedly, and ever shall ; but—O God! help me! I tell you truly *I can not be your wife.*"

He drew back, half loosened his clasp, looked full into her lovely eyes as though seeking to read in their liquid depths the reasons for this strange, this terrible decision, then convulsively clasping her once more to his bosom he pressed his lips to hers in a long kiss. Then disengaging her arms about his neck, he led her to the sofa, and, without another word or look, went out from her presence into the lone, dreary world.

Mrs. La Moore had been an unperceived witness of the painful interview and its surprising finale. The moment Robert left the room, she entered, to find Annette in a strange state, between stupor and convulsion. She, for once intent upon alleviating the distress of her uncomplaining child, had Annette taken to her own room by the frightened and loving servants, and there for many days she lay in a low condition of pain and fever. No word passed between them in all these days; yet it was plain to the attendants that the mother's presence was no comfort to the suffering girl; that, while Mrs. La Moore was ever at her side, securing the most skillful medical attendance, nursing and comforts; still it evidently was not a labor of love. Fear lest Annette should die and fling another shadow across her daily path, was the inspiration of Mrs. La Moore's efforts to save the girl's life. But death, though longed for, came not. Slowly Annette crept back to the cruel realism of health. Though to herself acknowledging her cowardice in breaking off so mysteriously her engagement with Robert, she derived some comfort from the fact of his not knowing why she did it. She felt that if she had told him the cause that suddenly intercepted their union, possibly his regard for her might have been quenched. She had not courage to brave such a contingency. While he remained ignorant of the cause of their parting, he might continue to love her still. Selfishly hugging this thought, she had spoken the words that separated them.

Her suffering was great, yet life is sweet to all, and she clung to it with youthful tenacity, rousing herself, after weeks of quiet misery, to find some wholesome task. She sought and found it, ministering to the comfort of the widowed and orphaned ones, whose support had been shattered by war's mighty en gine; sought and found, oh, so much wretchedness and need, that never for one hour could her helping hands hang idle. Annette La Moore willingly took upon herself the task of alleviating, as far as in her power lay, the wants of the poor, the sick and the needy. Many a fevered brow was cooled and refreshed by applications from her gentle hands, parched lips moistened with iced drinks those hands prepared. Children regarded her with something akin to reverence as one who had nursed "mother" back to life, and mothers thanked her for the children her tender care had rescued from death. She was an efficient member of the "Ladies' Aid Society," that monument of humane effort that sheds lustre upon the memory of American women.

With another lady she had one day visited several families in the outskirts of the city, making inquiries for a house where was said to be great suffering, a case both of illness and poverty. Their carriage, well known in the city, was a novelty in this out of the way street, well known to poor pedestrians, but seldom visited by a vehicle of any kind, much less by a handsome private carriage. An English family, consisting of a war widow and her children, themselves in very reduced circumstances, had opened their door to receive a poor old refugee from the frontier, who had fled in terror from the Indians. She had made the long journey on foot and without money.

She also was an English woman, and this fact had secured to her this hospitality. It was evident she was at death's door when Annette and her companion found her. On entering the house, a tall, slatternly, watery-eyed woman, with twin babies in her arms, conducted them to the low, miserable pallet whereon a wasted creature lay, gasping for breath. Her withered face was distorted with pain ; great drops of death dew stood upon her wrinkled brow, while her sunken eyes shone with a preternatural lustre. Her words came slowly and between long pauses, as she replied to their sympathetic inquiries. They gave her cordial, chafed her hands and applied artificial warmth to her extremities, while she mumbled piteously :

"Too late, I's frightened, I canna mend mair, I canna mend mair. I moost die, and me eyes be shut be strangers. But I 'ave a soon—Gerge is 'is naame —Gerge Langmere—mabbe ye ken'd 'im soomtime ? He roon t' army — he tuck t' whisky till t' Injuns— t' Injuns I roon fra—he bides safe enow wi' 'em—but I for thrampin' moost die ! Oh, 'ees feyther was a clever big boog, an' wadna fret if 'is young 'un starved—an' 'e 's a big boog, too—an' turned t' cold shoulther on 'is mother, when she cood no mair stoob roun'—an' 'arn siller for 'un—"

Completely exhausted, she lay very still a few minutes, then, opening her eyes again, she resumed,

"Larnin' doon 't—larnin' chook't me in t' mire— larnin' pickt me old bones—an' larnin' kickt me oot to die !—"

Raising herself with an almost superhuman effort,

and sitting bolt upright, her glassy eyes uplifted in a frightful stare and fixed in their sockets, she fiercely struck her bony fists together, and in unearthly accents shrieked :

" Coorses upon larnin'—coorses—coorses !—" and fell back upon the pillow dead.

They composed her stiff old limbs that would never ache more, folded the ill-shapen hands over the breast that had held such a true mother heart. Covering the wasted form with a decent sheet borrowed from a neighbor, they turned with sad faces from the silent dust, all that remained of poor Sally Hopkins.

After engaging women to prepare the grave-clothes they would provide, and to watch the corpse until the interment, which they would arrange, they turned to make inquiries into the needs of the household.

CHAPTER XIII.

A MOTHER'S STRATEGY.

Though all can not live on the piazza, every one may feel the sun.
                                        —*Tuscan Proverb.*

THE same night that 'Lizbeth Harkness was spending the first dark hours of her "forced elopement" with Langmere near the little rivulet, a captive of love, held by other than love's restraining fetters, Mrs. Ellis was threading the same wood, and later in the night, indeed, it was almost morning, encamped upon the same stream, a mile nearer its source. She had been taken from her burning home, after setting fire to it herself, to hide the bodies of the Indians who had died from the effects of her generously administered compound. I can not say she went voluntarily, nor yet was her going altogether compulsory, but she had felt that a moment's hesitation either to apply the brand or go with the Indians, might result in a search of the premises and the discovery of grandma and the children. She knew that the house would be burned, and she feared the barn and stacks as well, if there was any delay. So, when she heard the yells of the reinforcement of Indians, she had lighted the building, having piled hay and other combustibles within the doorway, and just as, with ferocious

gestures, they began to circle and yell around the
fire and peer into the gloom for more victims, she
made a feint to get away, rushing through the gate
and down the road, while the whole pack followed
like a long file of yelping hounds. They overtook
and bound her and led her on, but her ruse was ef-
fectual in averting their attention from the premises.
Though she scarcely hoped to escape their murderous
hatchets, she felt sure that her children were safe.

Half a mile from home they were joined by a
party of squaws, who had in custody a number of
white women and children. Some of those Mrs. Ellis
attempted to address, but was immediately and violently silenced. A retrograde movement was at once
made. and continued till near daylight, when they encamped in the woods, as I before stated, upon the
same stream on which Langmere's encampment lay.

At dawn they were joined by a large number of
Indians, Yanktons, who informed them that a council
was called of the chiefs of all the tribes that were
allied in this movement against the whites. Also that
a small band of Sioux lay at their left, while a larger
force of more northern Indians was encamped half a
mile to their right. Mrs. Ellis understood that while
the main portion would breakfast, the "fathers"
would meet in deliberation, which must be hurried in
consequence of their proximity to the white settlements. A speedy move of squaws and captives was
imperative, and these captives were to be distributed
among the different tribes who had captured them.

By some magnetic influence. some people attract
all who come within the circle of their influence, and

12

Mrs. Ellis was one of these. She made friends with everything, brute or human. The squaws, " ugly and venomous," as they were, seemed particularly attracted by her good nature and apparent fearlessness, and procured for her many privileges which the other prisoners were denied. They acceded to her request to take her to witness the meeting of the sachems. So creeping through the bushes with them, she reached the appointed spot. The dignitaries were seated around a fire, whose light paled before the growing light of day. On a rich beaver skin near the fire lay a gorgeous calumet or pipe of peace. A proud, handsome young chief sat at the head of a circle of lesser magnates on the ground. They had all evidently retouched their paint, the only morning toilet of an Indian. This grandest looking of the band made a signal. One of the ring arose, advanced, and filling the pipe lighted it by the fire, and handing it to the first chief, retired again to his seat on the ground. With a haughty look that must have been very impressive, for the whole band delivered a concerted " ugh," the sachem rose, and taking a whiff, emitted the smoke in a heavy cloud. Then taking the pipe from his mouth he pointed with the ornamented stem first to the sun just struggling through the leaves of the dense forest growth, then held it to the earth, then circling it gracefully round his head he handed it to the right hand sachem. He then introduced measures which they discussed while the pipe circulated, each chieftain in turn taking it from his left hand neighbor and passing it on. The council was conducted in low, monotonous guttural tones. Mrs. Ellis, of course, understood nothing, but she remarked that there was nothing emphatic save the oft-repeated " ughs."

When their future field was decided upon, the spoils of war, namely, the prisoners, divided satisfactorily ; a bright belt of wampum was produced and handed from one to the others of the circle, each member handling it as reverently as if it were some grave talisman. The successive touching of this ornament ratified the proceedings of the council, of which this was the final ceremony. They rose immediately, and without a parting word, all save the Yanktons departed, striding in the different directions towards their several camps. Mrs. Ellis felt an almost irrepressible desire to visit some of the encampments to ascertain the fate of her neighbors, and a deep regret that she was to be one of those allotted to the Yanktons, whose gross features and sleepy eyes compared unfavorably with many of the other tribes.

Many had sat in council whose appearance of greater intelligence she believed might be an index to more humane hearts. Ah ! humanity never had any part in the emotions of any of those monsters, whose hands had desolated Maple Range, and were destined to wipe out of existence other frontier towns. Mrs. Ellis was ignorant of the extent of their outrages, and sometimes felt almost a criminal when she reflected upon her own work of *murder* and arson.

The sun was still low in the eastern sky when the squaws, accompanied by a few Indians, started on the trail, taking great care to step in each other's footmarks for a long way, to deceive the whites whom they feared would soon be upon their track. Orders were also given not to break any bushes upon the wayside, or to displace any object lying near it. Great care was taken that the captives left no shred of clothing or any article that might be a clue to their route.

The rapid traveling, added to the mental excitement of the prisoners, told fearfully upon them, and great suffering was the consequence. Mrs. Ellis set herself at once to acquire the Yankton dialect, conning the lessons as she marched, and taking them from the living text. Her success furnished amusement to the squaws, who applauded with hideous grins whenever she mastered a word or sentence. She experienced less pain from the forced marches than a more delicate woman, a Mrs. Cummings, and her children, who were fellow-captives and plodded despondingly along. She always accepted her fate, if not cheerfully, at least with a determination to make the best of it. Difficulty was always an incentive to her, but she had wonderful health and strength and was spared the suffering her poor neighbor experienced—that of seeing her hungry, weary children hurried on by the goads of the heartless wretches. She felt deepest sympathy with that poor mother and the objects of her solicitude, and tried, in many ways, to alleviate their distress, which was the more difficult inasmuch as an expression of sympathy was sure to result in greater hardships imposed upon the recipient. After three or four days of constant travel by day, and sleeping on the hard, damp ground at night, the little creatures were completely worn out.

Toward night one little girl began to cry ; her

mother stooped to take her in her arms, when a squaw interfered and separated them, which increased the child's crying, in which the other children now joined, through sympathy and terror. Mrs. Ellis felt such pity for both mother and children, that she ventured to plead for them. What was her horror then, when, with the look of a demon, the squaw caught up a billet of wood and deliberately pounded the little child to death ; then severing the head from the body, she held it toward Mrs. Ellis, saying :

" Here ! take the part that cried ! "

Mrs. Ellis' blood curdled at this ghastly cruelty, and recalling the Indians whose death she had caused, she pronounced it, not murder, but demon-slaughter, exclaiming in the best Yankton she was mistress of :

" You can not be a woman ! God never gave a heart of stone to one who might be a mother ! "

The hag heard her with apparent indifference ; yet she was observed to show many favors to Mrs. Ellis after that ; not that she was in any degree impressed by her words, but simply because she admired her courage in speaking them. Such scenes of cruelty were rife throughout their journey. They penetrated forests that seemed interminable ; ascended long rivers in birch-bark canoes ; climbed rugged heights. Ere the journey was half completed, save Mrs. Ellis, every pale face had succumbed to exposure or ill-treatment, and the sorrow-laden hearts had found in death the peace they prayed for. Her physical endurance, wonderful though it was, was severely tried, and was daily the subject of her morning prayers, as of her evening thanksgiving. She, each

day, felt new faith in Him who, she believed, would
guard her wandering and at last open the way for her
return.   As night fell, on the twelfth day after leaving home, she noticed that the foremost of the long
train disappeared, one by one, and at last they, in
turn, came upon what seemed indeed "the jumping-
off place."   In the twilight before her lay a vast
" hole in the earth."   They were, in reality, winding
down the steep sides of a precipice that towered hundreds of feet above a little valley scarcely a quarter
of a mile in width, and less than a mile long.   At the
upper extremity was a clear lake whose outlet, a
beautiful little brook, ran along the base of the bluff,
the whole length of the valley.   This brook tumbled
noisily through the channel formed by the bluffs that
surrounded it.   From the prairie above, the trail
wound curiously down, from ledge to ledge.   Its
descent, nevertheless, was not without danger to inexperienced feet.   Mrs. Ellis' heart sank, as she undertook it, in the gathering darkness.   But the steady
pressure of the mass behind compelled her to keep close
to the gradually moving mass before her.   At last, all
had descended into this natural fortress.   They crossed
the stream on the one log that served as bridge, and
filed on in a darkness deepened by the lofty walls of
solid rock.   Fires soon lighted up the curious place.
Part of the squaws prepared supper, and the rest
drew blankets over the tepee poles, that showed
it to be an old camping ground ; in reality, it had
been for many generations.   This place a few determined warriors might hold against tremendous odds,
and so it had been held, time after time, in the wars

with adjacent tribes. The waters of the brook were full of speckled trout, while the lake abounded in fish. The great prairie above was alive with wild fowl, antelope and deer. The forest that crowned the opposite bluff was the home of elk, moose and bear.

Supper being over, the tired savages sought repose, with heads to the fire and "feet to the foe," each family lying in a circle on the ground. Mrs. Ellis had fallen to the ownership of the principal chief, old "Running Moose," who, like the animal from which he derived his name, could run *three days and nights* continuously.

(La Hontan relates that the Indians told him "The moose could trot three days and nights without intermission;" and there are incidents recorded of Indians trotting a hundred miles between sunrise and sunrise, without once breaking gait.)

The family of Running Moose consisted of one wife and two papooses, and these, with most of the other women and children, had been transported in advance, though overtaken on the previous day's journey.

Before midnight Mrs. Ellis could see by the firelight that she was alone in her wakefulness. She was too tired to sleep, though she courted the god of slumber, in the hope that dreams might relieve the homesick heaviness of her soul. She turned upon her couch, the hard earth, and tried one position and another, to find them equally painful, and sleep equally coy. A strange bird in a neighboring tree-top began to sing. As Mrs. Ellis listened to this minstrel of the morning, the thought came unbidden, and with it her tears:

"At this hour my children would waken and twine their arms about my neck, each boasting of the biggest love. How many heartaches must I know before I hear again those sweet childish voices."

Such thoughts made sleep impossible for her. She got up and went out of the wigwam. As the day dawn made objects more distinct, she for the moment forgot her sorrow in the interest wakened by the many curious things she saw. The trees were, many of them, covered with the hieroglyphics of departed generations. The bark, 't is true, was peeled off; but still the trees had grown so as to leave the uncouth records, deep indentures, gray with the mould of the ages. Close by were the mounds in which the writers of those strange books lay buried. Colden says:

"These trees are the annals of the five nations. I have seen many of them; and by them and their war songs, they preserve the history of their achievements."

So absorbed was she in the reflections awakened by these strange records of ancient history, that an Indian got, unperceived, to her side. She did not hear him, but that peculiar sense which tells us, even in the dark, that we are not alone, induced her to turn around. He stood with raised musket, intending to strike her. (He evidently thought her lonely position pointed to flight.) She quickly caught his weapon and, looking full in his face, said:

"You would not strike me till my book is read. Tell me about these pictures, these mounds," and she pointed to the trees and the mounds, and the pyramidal piles of rock.

" Records of the red man's deeds, older than the trees that bear them," he said, and then as she cast a glance of inquiry at the mounds, he shook his head mournfully as he went on, "Count the trees, and know the age in generations of our people, count the leaves and know how many red men sleep in these full graves." He turned his look to follow hers and continued, " With stones we tell our numbers, and every twelve moons pile as many stones as there are red men in our tribe. When the piles equal in number the years of one age, we make a record on the trees, and unbuild the piles."

Though he spoke but broken, imperfect English, and she but very imperfect Yankton, they learned the import of each other's words enough to conduct a very pleasant conversation considering their relative positions.

Mrs. Ellis was saved by her perfect coolness and self control. Had she attempted to fly from that uplifted gun she would have been lost, but so cleverly had she averted his immediate purpose. that at last forgetting it altogether, he walked away from her to shoot a pheasant his dog had treed, while she went leisurely back to the lodge in time to assist in the preparation of breakfast, after which she was assigned to some light task of needle work wherein she soon proved her usefulness. The next day she was sold for a pony to another chief, One-e-ah-tah, whose lodge lay at the lower end of the valley, while that of Running Moose occupied a position on the lake shore at the upper end. She went very reluctantly for her mistress had been an easy sort of a squaw, the children

S

gave her no trouble and Running Moose did not offend her by attentions of any kind. At the wigwam of her new owner she could see she was not very welcome. He was something of a Mormon, and his household had several divisions or compartments already, each dedicated to the use of one of his wives. For a day or two she got along very comfortably, for he was away on a hunt accompanied by some of his squaws whose task it always is to bring home the game. When One-e-ah-tah returned however she was given to understand that her place would be nearer him than was at all agreeable. His lascivious glances, and patronizing gallantries, were so revolting to her that she was continually revolving in her mind some plan to avoid him. Suddenly remembering that the wampum—touching which is the oath of an Indian—had not been used to ratify her transfer, and that a question might be raised as to his ownership of her, she bethought herself of a plan worth trying. (Any plan to elude old One-e-ah-tah's persecutions would be hailed eagerly by the apprehensive women.) Watching for a favorable opportunity she escaped to the lodge of Running Moose, who flattered by her apparent preference, and pleased with her acuteness in discovering the omission, took her immediately under his protection on the plea that the sale was invalid. He lost no time though in disposing of the pony to another Indian, this time taking care to *bind the bargain.*

CHAPTER XIV.

"I TOLD YOU SO."

ACCORDING to all writers of Indian history, both the calumet and wampum are held in universal reverence by the savages. Of the first Marquette says:

"I must here speak of the calumet, the most mysterious thing in the world. The sceptres of our kings are not so much respected, for the savages have such a deference for this pipe, that we may call it the God of Peace and War—the arbiter of life and death."

Hennepin describes it as follows:

"The head is finely polished, and the quill which is commonly two and a half feet long, is made of strong reed. They tie to it two wings of the most curious bird that flies."

La Honton says:

"The *red* calumets are the most esteemed. They are trimmed with white, yellow and green feathers, and have the same effect among the savage races that the flag of truce and friendship has with us; to violate the rights of this venerable pipe is with them a flaming crime."

The poet Street sang:

"Whilst high he lifted in his hand
    That sign of peace, the calumet,
So sacred to the Indian soul
    With its stem of reed, and its dark red bowl
Flaunting with feathers, white, yellow and green."

Without touching the wampum no contract is considered binding, as it is the sign of the completion and perpetuity of all transactions. sealing the validity of all their treaties.

"This belt preserves my words."

"This colier (belt of wampum) confirms my speech."

These expressions occur many times in the speeches of La Barre and Garangula, in their famous interviews described by La Honton.

"Without the intervention of these belts," says that writer, "there is no business transacted, no negotiation among the savages, for, being unacquainted with writing, they make use of them for contracts and obligations."

One-e-ah-tah submitted gravely to a loss of property that was the result of his own carelessness. Mrs. Ellis was put to work by the wife of Running Moose, fashioning and remaking garments. with such approach to the prevailing styles among the whites as the material furnished would allow.   Cosmopolitan "la mode" is as arbitrary in the woods as in the cities, and presides over the making of the squaw's one yearly garment of broadcloth as much as over that of the plain drab dress of the Quakeress, and the multitudinous articles that comprise the wardrobe of a city belle.   White women at that period wore enormous

hoops and many yards of material were required to give
sufficient length and fullness to the dress. The narrow broadcloth skirts of the squaw, haply all of blue,
were subjected to no end of piecing and supplement-
ing to bring them to suitable width to cover the huge
imitations in willow of the "skeleton" in vogue with
white ladies. The outer garment, or skirt, would, expanded to its full dimension, hang with never a relieving fold, and much abbreviated in length, dis-
played the nicely fitted moccasin, and often considerably more. The wife of Running Moose had command
of more material than the other squaws, and her
dress was more easily made to conform to Mrs. Ellis'
taste.

She made her appearance one day in a new, long
trailing dress of blue, tastefully expanded. Her
frilled and neatly buttoned sacque of brown merino
was confined at the waist with a belt to match her
exquisite bead necklace and wristbands, and elicited a
hum of admiration among the feminines. In comparison with her, the comet sank to a miserable ten cent
side show. The members of One-e-ah-tah's harem
were filled with burning envy, and he was forthwith
besieged and implored to "buy Mrs. Ellis back and
put a stop to the triumph of Mrs. Running Moose,"
that the victory might be secured to their end of the
valley.

He had sundry reasons for listening to their peti-
tions, of which his weaker halves (or quarters) were
ignorant, and resolved to get possession of Mrs.
Ellis once more. He was a cautious, wary old chief,
and reckoned upon his revenge for the loss of his

pony in her aversion to him. Knowing that Running
Moose was an inveterate jockey, he thought he would
only have to make the offer to buy and she would be
his forthwith. But he had for once "reckoned without his host." Though Miladi declared she had no
more use for Mrs. Ellis, no sewing to do for a whole
year, and no work in the lodge for her, and she was
not strong enough to fish and hunt; though white
women were not to his taste, and were not included in
the market quotations, still Running Moose absolutely
refused to part with her; at least, he *would not sell
her to One-e-ah-tah.*

The affair was dropped for a fortnight. One day
a miserable dog of an Indian, a dependent on village
charity, proposed buying her. He had no squaw to
cook his samp when it was given him, and he thought
he might make Mrs. Ellis catch fish, trap woodchuck
and decoy birds enough to keep his soul and body together. He offered for her an old arquebuse (a
clumsy gun, the pioneer of the musket), the only
property he had in the world, useless by reason of his
laziness, and the offer was accepted. Running Moose
took the old weapon, hung it up on a hook where half
a dozen more modern ones were hanging, and taking
down a belt of wampum, said to Mrs. Ellis :

" Do n't come back again. You are Six Toes' (by
some accident he had lost four toes, hence the soubri-
quet) *slave;* by this wampum he holds you."

Mechanically she gathered up her scissors and
thimble and put them in her pocket (she had brought
these with her from home). She took out a fish line
and reel to return them to Mrs. Running Moose, to

whom they belonged, but her sharp-eyed purchaser insisted they were his, they having been in her pocket when the wampum sealed the bargain. Running Moose assenting, she obeyed him and putting them back, followed her new owner through the village down the valley. His tepee lay below that of One-e-ah-tah, and as they passed, that chieftain, who sat smoking in his doorway on a handsome mat, saw them and at once comprehended the whole transaction. Calling to Six Toes.

"Me buy your white squaw," said One-e-ah-tah.

"How much you give?" asked Six Toes, halting at the prospect of a bargain.

"Peck of beans."

"No!"

"Two pecks."

"No!"

"Three pecks."

"No!"

"Bagful."

"Yes!"

An imaginary bean porridge was already cooling under Six Toes' olfactories. At this Mrs. Ellis determined to either win her liberty or lose her life.

One-e-ah-tah's harem had heard, and visions of gorgeous apparel danced in the near perspective. One-e-ah-tah heard, and his savage face was lit up with the flame of passion long repressed, of vengeance long deferred. He said to her,

"Take these beans to Six Toes' lodge."

"What! and for that paltry price become your slave? *No, sir!* I know I am worth more than a bag of beans, and I intend to march till I am quoted at par."

Her intention, apparently so wild and barren of all hope, was not realized by them until she had turned, and was flying at a desperate speed, death behind her, home before her, down the green slope to the stream, which, by recent rains, was swollen even with its banks. She bounded upon the spanning log. Her weight was just sufficient to loose it from the bank, and it swung round with her to the other side, where, by a lariat loop it was fastened to a stump. She slipped the noose off the stump, and swiftly winding it about the log and her limbs so as to make her hold secure, she laid prone upon the floating spar. Just as the whole yelling pack of squaws, Indians and dogs reached the stream, her rolling bark whirled into the seething current. Their arrows flew thick about her, yet harmless, for tumbling over and over, she was as often below the surface as above.

She rode those blinding waters as though a part of the log to which she grimly clung. She had no sensation of fear from drowning; that fate was infinitely preferable to recapture. She heard the unearthly yells of the chase, for they followed her down along the bank of the stream, hoping by some chance she might drift ashore, toward the narrow gorge above the rapids, which they, with her, believed to be the very gate of death. But now the rocks along the shore, and other impediments, hindered their advance, and glancing back at their baffled, hellish countenances, she felt a pleasure in the thought, " They can not see me. I shall die alone."

A sob for the children who would wait her so long, a prayer that her husband might be spared to take care of them—and with a resigned expression, "Father! to thy bosom," she entered the wild, narrow space through which the waters madly rushed, with a deafening tumult and blinding spray!

O helpless voyager! no human hand can guide thy bark; no human hand can stay thy course!

With closed eyes and gasping for breath, she had no definite thought, only a dim consciousness of shocks and dashes and plunges, so rapid that, but for the security of the lariat, she would have lost her hold a hundred times. How long ere her feet shall step in colder flood? Her bark is still! A moment of wonder, and clearing her eyes of the spray she looks up to see her long craft fast, diagonally across the stream just above the yawning, boiling cataract, a bridge, reaching from rock to rock. She could not clearly make out her position, for night here deepened early owing to the towering rocks, so she resigned herself to waiting to see what morning should reveal. The position left her feet and ankles in the water. Toward morning she found the water was falling. Her feet could not feel it.

"Better," she thought, "be dashed to death, than to die by the slow torture of starvation, or the arrows of savages who may reach me as the water recedes."

Filled with such apprehensions, she moved uneasily about, until she reached—without intending it—the lower end of the log, which, she found, was resting on a shelf or opening in the rock, and she thought,

12*

"Perhaps this friendly cleft is large enough to hold me."

She could, however, only wait for increasing light. But at last her expectant eyes discovered a friendly cavern, inviting her to enter and repose—an invitation she was not slow to accept, as her position on that narrow bridge was tiresome in the extreme, and to sleep upon it was impossible. She slept most of the day. Toward night, undoing her fish line, she caught some trout.

"I can not eat them raw, *yet!* Perhaps I may be glad to," she said, and wrapping them in her apron, prepared for a desperate venture. She tied her fish-line to the loop or noose of the lariat, and dropped one end down to the rocks below; then she put the lariat round the log, slipped it through the noose, and by this means descended to the rocks. It was dark, but she found the fish line, and with it drew down her friendly lariat. The stream, like all mountain streams, rose and fell quickly, and now it was a subdued and decorous brook, and she found it easy to creep along its margin.

"I will go boldly up and take my chances of getting on to the prairie, by the only way I know. 'T is bristling with dangers, not the least being the red men, who will show me no mercy if I fall into their hands now."

But indeed the red men were thrown off the scent altogether. They had searched for her body below the rapids all day, believing it a physical impossibility for her to live through the passage of that gorge and the rapids beyond. She had now crept up the stream so long, over the boulders, that her hands were bleeding from contact with their sharp edges, and her naked feet (she had worn out the moccasins that had been supplied her when her shoes were gone) were very weary; yet she went on, thinking,

" 'T is long, but why so still? I can not hear the murmur of the stream!"

Light began to break gradually, and she feared the day would dawn just as she had to pass through the village! What should she do then?

She stopped a moment to wipe her brow and get a breath, and rising up, to her amazement, she stood upon the prairie. She had followed a ravine that, yesterday, most likely was a torrent, for it contained rocks and stones similar to those along the stream she had descended. Her pulse beat quick with hope, and stretching out her arms she ran as gleeful as a child, in the direction of her home. She knew the route, for she had noted its every feature in coming, and besides, in her clear head she carried a natural compass. If only she could strike the trail, perhaps she would be miles upon her way ere morning. A fire across the prairie attracted her. It was trees burning in a ravine. She sat down by a smouldering fire, broiled her fish and ate them. The night was chilly —the fire so grateful that she was overcome by drowsiness, and dropping upon the grass, she fell asleep.

The sun was high in the sky when she awakened and looked with sudden fright about her. A few feet from her couch was a yawning chasm, down which it was wonderful she had not stumbled in the dark. A pony was grazing quietly out on the prairie and toward it she crept, in the Indian manner, through the grass. Now her practice of throwing a lariat with the squaws served her a good turn ; practice and her strait perhaps gave her accuracy, for she succeeded in throwing the lasso over the head of the pony, a success which had never before attended her attempts. She tied some dry grass in her apron and bound it on her shoulders in such a way that it looked like a papoose, and mounting her pony *a la* squaw, she bounded away toward the trail, and struck it just at sundown on the verge of the woods. All night she rode on. That pony was used to long trips at a round trot. In the morning by the uncertain light of early dawn she met three Indians. She passed by without seeming to notice them but saw by a side glance that one of them sharply scanned the pony. About ten o'clock her steed turned into a blind trail leading to a little meadow where were water and grass. Dismounting and remembering the Indian's scrutiny of her steed, she made a more critical examination of him than she had done before and then discovered that *she had stolen the very pony for which she had been sold.* Then she identified the curious Indian as its former owner. She turned the pony to grass while she searched the woods for elm bark and wild berries to appease her hunger, after which, selecting a secluded spot, she lay down to sleep. She was wakened two hours after by her pony neighing. Much alarmed, she hurried out and found him resting after his bait and having evidently been asleep. Near him a sharp-pointed stick had been driven into the ground, to the top of which, securely

tied, were a piece of her own ragged dress and a piece
torn from a dress she remembered having seen worn
by Miannetta.

What could this mean? She was not long left to
conjecture. She concealed herself in the long grass,
for well she knew that device was a warning that
Miannetta was near, but dared not openly communicate with her. Volumes might be filled with her
hopes, fears, and surmises during that pregnant half
hour which Mrs. Ellis measured by still pulse and
bated breath. The silence around was broken at last
by a low sweet voice speaking her own name; another
moment and Miannetta stood by her. Greetings were
fervent but hurried.

"You must mount your pony and ride for your
life," said Miannetta. "Avoid meeting a Yankton;
from other bands you have nothing to fear—they will
not molest the prisoner of another tribe. I was on
my way to the Yanktons in search of our dear little
Nellie. I heard a white woman was with them."

"Not now," said Mrs. Ellis.

"No, *she* is drowned, a Yankton told me," said
Miannetta with a meaning smile. "I was on the trail
traveling fast when your pony neighed. I turned in
here and found him and the piece torn from your
dress, and understood all. From that pony's neigh I
knew other horses must be near, so setting up the
warning to you I hurried back to protect your retreat,
and none too soon, for I encountered the owner of this
pony looking for him. To his inquiries I replied that
I had seen a pony three miles to the sunset of us. He
turned back, but seeing the track of this animal,

wheeled his horse and pointed to it. 'Yes,' said I, 'that is the track of my pony feeding now in the little meadow to the left. I came back here to get good water.' He was satisfied, and turning his horse's head galloped away. We have both many things to say, but to do so would be to risk your life; but you must not go without food, take this piece of dried venison. Turn, take this trail which you remember well. God help you, my friend! Away!"

She struck the pony with a stick in her hand and Mrs. Ellis was flying away with a thankful heart that God had thus raised up a "deliverer" from imminent peril.

She kept her pony at full speed. 'Twas well for her he had been primed by hard riding under heavy horsemen; now, her slight weight was no inconvenience. After the next noon's short rest and bait, when she mounted him, he seemed still quite fresh and soon settled down to the steady trot which, by the rapid recession of trees, Mrs. Ellis knew was telling. She smiled as she patted his shining brown shoulder which she had gratefully rubbed, as well as his black legs and dark flanks, and said:

"My noble fellow-chattel, you shall never depreciate in value as I have. I have two charming little boys whose proud care it will be to groom you."

Grass being more easy to obtain than food for herself, his strength never seemed to flag though the farther she got upon her way the more she favored him and let him rest, though rest to her was a torture because of dreams of satisfying repasts. She would waken chilled and sick, yet full of hope as she neared the settlements. Once she came to a nice log farm house where she found food in the cellar. A cow came to the bars with her calf. Mrs. Ellis milked her, and O! the delights of that supper. Here her pony also fared well with a nice feed of oats in the sheaf. This silent home had been deserted by the owner and his family through fear of the Indians. Mrs. Ellis spent the night there and when she mounted Besom in the morning she said:

"One more long ride and to-morrow night you shall have a permanent stable."

She had procured food there to last her through, but the quality scarcely gave her the strength she needed for the last stretch. She was terribly exhausted, so that even her sleep that night had not refreshed her and it was a painful weary journey the next day, the seventh since her last sale to One-o-ah-tah.

The shadows of the maple trees grew longer and longer; something troubled her throat, the great choking lumps threatened to suffocate her, her heart kept up an incessant pit-a-pat, and she could not suppress hysterical sobbings, which her face however showed were not sorrowful ones. The trail now lost its forest appearance and was nothing more than a well-trodden cow-path From either side came the pastoral sound of familiar cow-bells.

Anon her pony pricked up his ears and neighed, as he struck his hoofs into the soil of a well-traveled road. Around a curve a white lamb bounded, and from behind him two childish voices rang:

"Nanny, Nanny, Nanny!"

Mrs. Ellis sprang from her seat, and holding out her hand, it was instantly recognized and licked. The children came running into view, stopped in astonishment an instant, and then the woods pealed with their glad shouts :

"*Mamma! mamma!*"

Uncle Carce sat smoking on the doorstep. Grandma was getting supper. Both ran out at the cries, and saw the three twined in a long, close embrace. A mist was before their eyes, but grandma, true to her sex, first found speech—and that speech was another characteristic of women,

"*There now, Carce, I told you so!*"

CHAPTER XV.

TWO RECOGNITIONS.

IT was December, 1862. The weather was extremely cold, and constant rains kept the roads on the Peninsula bad; but the worst could be found at Falmouth and along the Rappahannock, where the Army of the Potomac, under command of Burnside (McClellan had been relieved in November), was encamped. The rebel batteries were frowning upon the heights beyond the city of Fredericksburg. Rebel sentinels, buttoned to their chins, paced briskly back and forth, puffing the smoke of their pipes over toward the Federal pickets, within speaking distance, in a way that was sometimes considered insolent; but such insolence was now disregarded. On the eleventh, the city was shelled by our troops, and pontoon bridges laid, amid the hot hail of the sharp-shooters safely hidden in the houses and church steeples opposite. Of the soldiers engaged in laying the bridges, three out of every five fell at their work; but another gallant trio in every instance took their places. The interruptions, however, were so frequent and fatal, that it was thought expedient to send a force to dislodge the concealed foe. Several companies volunteered (that of Captain Ellis among them) for that preliminary service, which was accomplished with little loss. The

T   13

bridge completed, the troops marched over and took possession of the city.

Two days afterward, a dreadful battle was in progress. Cannon rolled out their death sentence, and the musketry was deafening. A man, in soiled, tattered garments, erstwhile a handsome Federal uniform, was observed to step out from the ranks of the enemy toward Captain Ellis, evidently with the purpose of speaking to him, but fell, whether from the effect of a deadly missile or not was not evident to his only observer.

Long Dave Persons marked the spot with his clear, eagle eye, with all the precision possible amid that cloud of dust and smoke. A few minutes afterwards he bent over that ragged, prostrate form. Turning it over, he discovered features that caused the rough old woodsman to relieve himself of expressions of surprise and emotion, far more forcible than elegant. He raised the unconscious man as easily and tenderly as an infant, and carried him away, past the shrieking groups of wounded, past the silent dead. Dave hurried to the hospital, in a church, where he laid him down, and stood anxiously beside the surgeon while he examined him. He caught the words of the report with avidity.

"Not wounded? Good God! what ails him then?"

"Exhaustion, my good fellow! He's been starved and exposed to some terrible privations. Look at his cadaverous face and his poor, maimed feet! Oh, this is a cruel war indeed!"

"Why, must he die, doctor?" said Dave, while his white lip quivered.

"With good nursing, he might recover, I think," was the reply.

Tears rolled down the bronzed cheek of the soldier as he grasped both hands of the kind-hearted surgeon, and looking into his face, said :

"Doctor, save his life if possible. After the battle I will come and help you nurse him—yes, I will, in spite of captains, generals, or even the President of the United States."

He was gone. Ten minutes afterward, his regiment charged those stone walls, fortifications which, situated as they were, might defy the armies of the earth, and whence death had been dealt to thousands who had attempted the impossible task of carrying them by storm.

Half way up the heights, and half their number lay dead or dying ; still, undaunted, they pressed on through the smoke. Ah ! 'twas repulse again ! The disastrous field was strewn with the mangled, valiant dead, who had not questioned, had not hesitated, but obedient to the shrill "Charge !" had rushed on, to fall in the great rivers of blood where no living man could stand.

Among the devoted dead, none more worthy of a tear than brave, generous Dave Persons, who lay among the upper tier, nearest the "mouth of hell," where he had been arrested and detained by a stronger power than "captain or President," even that of the King of Kings. Nor mother, nor wife, nor child shall mourn him, for he had no kindred ties ; but a grateful people will hallow his memory, in that he died in the service of their mother country.

After this useless effusion of blood, a council of war was held, and it was decided that the enterprise of taking Fredericksburg should be for the present abandoned. The army recrossed the Rappahannock under the cover of darkness. The retreat was accomplished and the bridges partly removed, before the rebels discovered the movement.

The unnecessary slaughter on those dreadful slopes of Fredericksburg, had a very depressing effect upon the army as it took its old position on the muddy banks of the Rappahannock, where, depressed and chilled, it gazed on the renewed insolence of rebel sentinels, and *waited* yet again. The Northern press was very severe in its criminating tone, and of all positions, civil or military, the least enviable at that time was that of the General commanding.

The wounded were sent to Acquia Creek, where they suffered exceedingly in consequence of inadequate sanitary stores, poor buildings and the inclement weather.

One cold December morning following a night of great mortality in the hospital, an old gentleman and young lady moved slowly down between the long rows of cots, peering wistfully, though politely and with evident sympathy, into the faces of the sick and wounded. Save an occasional word of comfort to the poor fellows as they passed, they spoke but little. It was Mr. Meade and Alice, in search of their son and brother, " Walter," who was known to have been in the recent battle, but of whom no tidings had been obtained since. They had come down, hoping a search in the hospital might reward them. Many of the

men were sleeping, and their hearts sometimes beat
with quicker throbs, as the cast of a face in repose,
or the tone of some speaker, suggested the lineaments
and voice of him they sought, and yet, following the
momentary illusion they would stand face to face with
a stranger.   In all the forms of suffering.humanity,
there had been no recognition of their own flesh and
blood, and they were about passing out the door when
a nurse followed them hurriedly, saying :

"You seek some friend ?"

"My son." said Mr. Meade.

"Follow me, please ! I was attending a man who
has been very low, but is mending. As you passed,
he appeared to recognize you, but fainted directly
you went on."

While she spoke, they were rapidly retracing their
steps, and now stood beside the pallet of the wan-fea-
tured man, just recovering from a swoon. As he opened
his magnificent eyes, Alice threw herself beside the
cot.

"O George! my darling, whom I believed dead !
Father, this is he whom I have mourned, who was so
wickedly personated by another. It is George Langmere."

Almost beside herself, she put her arms about his
neck and embraced him.

Then he faintly spoke,

"There is some cruel mistake here. My name is
Herbert Gray, and you—are you not the *wife of
George Langmere ?*"

You have seen the electric flash athwart a leaden
sky light up the heavens for an instant, then all again

has been enveloped in midnight gloom. So the face of Alice, supremely radiant with sudden hope, as his feeble voice pronounced his own and her husband's name, grew still and pale till it looked like chiseled marble. Her father, with an apology, unlocked the hands that had grown rigid in their clasp about Herbert's neck, and taking her in his arms carried her to the carriage and drove to a hotel, where she was many days ill and delirious.

That meeting had been a peculiar awakening to the pure young girl, whose ship, freighted with gorgeous wealth, had sunk months before, thousands of fathoms deep, into the silent waters of fate, when at Dr. Bartholt's she had married an impostor. This was the man she meant to marry, the man she supposed was the veritable Langmere, with whom she had corresponded; and behold, now he announced his name, one she had never heard, and yet, *mystery of mysteries*, he seemed familiar with the fact of her marriage.

"Who shall ever unravel the skein?"

When she had explained all this to her father, he, unknown to her, visited Herbert again, and following the impulse of his honest old heart, made a "clean breast" of the whole matter. During the recital, Herbert saw the villainy of Langmere and was moved to great compassion for the peculiar position of Alice, whom he loved all the more deeply that she owed her terrible predicament to love of him. His proud, upright nature forbade his seeing her, but he sent her assurances of esteem, and words of hope for a brighter day.

Capt. Ellis was unremitting in his care. Gradually strength came to him, Mr. Meade generously supplying him with many comforts and aids to speedy restoration, alternately taking him and Alice out for air in an easy carriage. In one of these long rides he learned the incidents of Herbert's imprisonment and sojourn among the rebels.

He was captured by Johnson's black cavalry. Pinioned upon a horse behind a brutal fellow, who, regardless of his discomfort, had ridden with him "hither and yon," now in pursuit of flying, demoralized Federals, and now searching for stragglers. Once he saw Dave Persons and Gus Harkness lying prone upon their faces, beside a fallen tree, over which the horse was compelled to leap at the risk of neck and limb. He tried to release his hand to drop to them some trifling token of recognition, which might serve as a clue to his fate, but he was too tightly bound. Watching the spot as the urged horse tore madly on, he saw other rebels approach very near, thrusting their bayonets at random through tangled bushes and firing into clumps of brush and undergrowth. He believed it almost impossible for them to escape; death would have been certain had they moved.

Late in the evening he was carried into camp, and after being exposed to the rude jests of common soldiers till nearly midnight, he was contemptuously handed over to the custody of an old Arkansas sharpshooter, whose

"Long Polly could whisper a lullaby at three hundred yards or more."

Supperless and without cover, he slept on the hard, open ground, and before morning was drenched with rain. He broke his long fast the next afternoon twenty-four hours after his capture, when the train which carried him was well on the way toward the Confederate Inquisition, the tobacco warehouses of Richmond. Of the long months of torture endured there, his experience differed not materially from that of others.

The vile food was eaten when revolting nature could hold out no longer. The loathsome vermin infested his garments, hitherto the subject of fastidious care, and multiplied in the little sixteen-foot room occupied by *six men* and the *jailor's dog*. It is not easy to conceive of the emotions of one so situated, much less delineate them. Marmontal said, "How can I take portraits before I have seen faces?" and how can I presume to portray the wretchedness of such a prisoner, who have never known anything like it. It is so easy to console ourselves for the miseries of others or to say, if so situated, we would find means to avert or mitigate them. It is as impossible for those at ease to realize the pain of perpetual toil, as for those who toil to conceive of a life without task.

Passing over this period of monotonous durance, let us examine with Herbert Gray the forlorn chances of escape.

He has come to be a favorite of the rough but heartsome jailor, who is greatly indebted to him for the quiet and subordination of the mutinous, noisy fellows under his charge. Rebel conscription is very close; every man it is possible to spare from places of trust is in the army, and here one man relieves two or three in the twenty-four hours. It is not wonderful that the turnkey is sometimes drowsy and sleeps at his post, and Herbert has humanely served him many times while he has snatched repose, when, if discovered, reprimand would be very severe. Herbert has more than once stood guard outside the door with *his* garments on, while he slept just within, and as no good chance seemed to offer or his courage would fail him if escape seemed possible, he had never outraged this confidence so strangely reposed in him. But the hour came when courage and temptation coalesced.

One dark, rainy night, the jailor's wife, who had been very sick for many days, sent a message to him to hasten, for she was dying, and he once more confided the key to Herbert, with the promise to return in a short time. Whether he did or not we shall never know.

The prison door closed behind two parties of three men, who had resolved to risk a desperate fate. The leading party, consisting of Herbert Gray, Fred Steele, a Michigan artilleryman, and Sumner Burgess, a citizen of Buffalo, New York, whose curiosity had led him sight-seeing to Bull Run. They threw themselves upon the sentinel who challenged them three feet from the door, bound and gagged him, and laid him carefully inside the room they had just quitted forever. It was quick work, for those men "kept time by heart-throbs," and arm in arm now the three named (the others were already gone in the gloom)

went stealthily down the streets, Gray, the lay figure,
to be exhibited as required, the "spokesman," Burgess, and the "man of news," Steele.

They ran on, they knew not whither, but always
instinctively away from the warehouses and the street
lamps. The rain deadened their footsteps on the
pavement, save an unfortunate slipety-slap that regu-
larly accompanied Burgess, whose boot was so worn
that upper and sole parted company every time he
lifted his foot. They had gone some distance straight
on, having said "in turning there may be doom,"
when a sudden and authoritative "Halt!" arrested
them. Burgess blustered out in genuine Arkansas
tones :

"Make it halter, old hoss, and we are at your service in no time. We 've got another candidate for the
maggot-shop. We clapt hooks on him jest as he
crawled into the lines to-night, an' had orders to pull
him through on the double-quick, though we 'd ruther
stretch his neck than his legs this minit. But we
must get back for another skunk that we reckon will
try the same hole. So give us the watchword, comrade, and save delay next time a sentinel bites his
word off. Hurry up your cakes !"

And the countersign was given by the raw sentry
or patrol, and they went on rapidly, "slipety slap,
slipety slap," through dim-lighted ways, ever straight
on. Once a fierce-looking fellow turned the blaze of
his bull's-eye full into their faces, and aiming a revolver at Burgess' head, halted them in the "name of
the Confederate States and commonwealth of Virginia."

"The same name commissioned us to take this man, who is one of the reliables, to division head-quarters, where he will make valuable disclosures concerning the enemy. We are ordered to observe haste, and without multiplying words with those whose business it is to demand the countersign," said Burgess, respectfully emphasizing the word that implied reproach, which the guard noticed and recovered his lost ground by immediately and sternly saying,

"I demand the countersign!"

"Stonewall," said Burgess, coolly.

"All right. Turn to the left the next corner or you will be on the old bridge that is very unsafe now. A bad night, comrades, a bad night."

On they went straight to the "old bridge," avoided by other men, therefore offering safety to them. A brief council resulted in the tearing up of three planks, upon which they purposed to embark and glide with the current. The dark waters were not more cruel than the enemy in whose stronghold they were.

After a mute grasping of hands, more eloquent than speech in the hour of peril, they launched out into the darkness upon their frail planks and dropped silently down the stream, committing their souls to Him who walked upon the wave. Once fairly poised and in the current, their peril lay in change of position, and though chilled through and through, Herbert dared not risk the advantages of repose in one position. Aching and stiff, and wet below by the

river, above by the rain, he still feared the dawn and
its revelations, but it came at last.

Before, behind, on either side of him fog, and beside himself, as far as he could penetrate the mist,
not a solitary voyager. Guiding his raft to the shore,
he clambered up, pulling it after him, and hiding in a
clump of bushes under a shelving bank, he lay down.
with the idea of remaining there till darkness again
favored navigation. His eye fell upon a peculiar impression in the mushy soil. He recognized the track
of Burgess' broken boot and with something of his
old pleasantry he laughed at the grotesque mark, repeating audibly Longfellow's—

> "Some forlorn and shipwrecked brother
> Seeing shall take heart again!"

The darkness being so many hours away. he was
not afraid of oversleeping himself, and so with tantalizing dreams of food and fire, he spent many of these
hours, waking as the sun sent red slant rays over the
water into his chamber. "As night dropped her curtain down and pinned it with a star," he embarked
again upon the water, and floated on past many a
guarded spot and saw the sentry on his lonely beat.
Many times he was painfully near discovery but, favored by fortune, he still followed the merciful waters.

At break of day the second morning he heard
dogs barking and other sounds of plantation life.
Hunger impelled him strongly to follow them. He
felt that he must make some effort to obtain food.
Without it he would be too weak to hold on to his

plank; it was with difficulty even now he drew it up the bank. He lay down to rest a little after the effort of pulling it out of the water and almost immediately dozed off into slumber. How long he slept he could not tell, but on waking he heard a voice chanting in a low mournful wailing tone something like a hymn. Raising himself on his elbow, he discovered an old negro fishing, with his boat fastened to a pile of driftwood. Hunger could be restrained no longer, prudence was cast aside, and he called out:

"Sell me a fish, uncle?"

The old man looked up, his eyes rolling so that it was some seconds before he fixed them upon his interlocutor, when, with a good natured grin that extended to either ear, he answered:

"Laws no, but I'll *gib* ye one, sah; an' I have got some hoe cake an' sweet taters heah that you may hab, for de Lawd help me if ever I seed a crittah look so starved like, an' wid eyes that seem as if washed wid de glory of angels."

He at once came up the bank with the eatables and set himself to broil the fish while Herbert dispatched the hoe cake and potatoes. Never had food seemed so delicious. The old negro seemed very watchful while thus engaged and to Herbert's inquiry as to what he feared replied:

"Dey's looking for ye, honey, with dogs, all ober the country an' thru de woods, three poor fellahs dey tuk this morning, an' one with a sore foot, went past here down the river this time yesterday. I give him breakfast an' he tole me to look for ye, an' I did all day, wraslin' and prayin' for ye, an' 'pears like some spirit tuk them 'titions up to the New Jerusalem, for here ye are, eatin' what I provided for yer, ye pore persecuted friend of the colored race. Ye would break the yoke an' let the opprest go free, an' for that reason the oppressors hunt and will harm ye if they find ye. The retribution that is waitin' 'em shall come as a whirlwind, an' they shall not see the glory of God when he shall come in pillars of fire for his own."

He was not a common specimen of the negro race and to Herbert became at once a psychological study. Some of his scriptural applications were very sensible and others showed that in his head sound was made sometimes to answer all the purposes of sense. He borrowed without stint from the Bible, uttering the texts with the peculiarity of intonation character-istic of the religiously inclined of his race.

He remained some time with Herbert, giving ut-terance at intervals to strange expressions, which seemed a part of a continuous prayer, either for the weal of the oppressed or the woe of the oppressor.

When it was dark, he rose from the ground and shouldering the poke (bag) that contained the remnants of the feast, said:

"Come! follow me closely, if I drop on the ground as if dead, drop you also, but do n't speak or ask me why."

They went on rapidly as Herbert's condition would allow, and made good use of the darkness. Sev-eral miles had been made, when suddenly the deep hoarse baying of near hounds startled them and in-creased their gait. They ran across a cornfield to a wood, on the right, and plunging into a morass struggled through it to a sluggish stream where they settled up to their ears in water. Some time they lay, trembling at the barking and growling of dogs, foiled in their pursuit by losing their trail at the brink of this morass. Mingled with the furious barking were curses and brutal oaths, which, Herbert noticed with satisfaction, grew fainter and fainter as the baffled pursuers retired. They crawled out of the stream onto the opposite bank and went on, more fearlessly, as the chase was now evidently miles away though its echoes even then sounded all too real. From the quaint rambling speech of the negro, when not in his absent prophetic moods, Herbert learned the most feasible route to Fredericksburg—where the Federal army lay.

"I 's scratched de grabble on dat are route two times, wid de dogs arter me, honey, I orter know de safe way, an' de safest way ain't de plainest, shore."

"'T is 'a narrow way, and few there be that find it,' suggested Herbert, adding, "Twice you have been a fugitive by this route?"

"Yes, sah! an' I 's been wuth a heap more to myself than to massa, ever since; for, tho' I 's worked hard nuf, I 's tole more niggahs how to git off than he got back in the two t'ousan' dollahs he swoah I was wuth, at Fredericksburg."

"And did none others return to him?" said Herbert.

"Yes, oh, yes!" he said, and then took up the tone of prophecy, crying: "Oh, yes; dat was my own chile, my Lizzie. 'Behold the stone doth cry out from the wall, and the timber doth answer it.' Why dost thou delay, O thou avenger of the weak? Did she not lie three days speechless upon my breast in this jungle, after that awful scourging, and did I not make her grave in the wilderness?"

They traveled on till near morning—sometimes in the water, the more effectually to elude pursuit, and as often on the spongy, springy banks where footing, always insecure, was much more so in the darkness.

As the day began to glimmer through the fringy needles of the pines, at the risk of discovery, they made a fire and cooked a chicken the negro had captured in a midnight raid upon the negro quarters of a plantation they had passed in the night. After eating they settled down into the grass, out of sight, and fell asleep. They were upon a little island, not more than ten feet square, of solid ground, and which seemed, from the high land, eighty rods distant, to be a part and parcel of the swamp that surrounded it—a perfect jungle of cat briar and tangled vine. Its existence, except in dire extremity like this of Herbert's, would never be ascertained by a white man. But the negroes of the South became familiar with such spots, to their great advantage over their pursuers when attempting to realize their liberty by flight North. 'T was afternoon when Herbert awoke. His companion was up before him, preparing dinner, which he had evidently procured in some clandestine manner not entirely without human assistance. He had a nice loaf of white bread and some butter, and he was busy broiling a chicken over the coals. He did not notice at first that Herbert was awake, as he was stooping at his task. When he raised he began repeating with monotonous enunciation: "Who is this that cometh from Edom with dyed garment from Basrah?" then in a louder tone: "I that speak in righteousness, mighty to save, I will tread in my anger and trample them in my fury, and their blood shall be sprinkled on my garments."

These quotations were made in clear, good English, and yet when Herbert, who had risen, came forward to the fire, he was addressed in the most simple negro dialect:

"Ye see, I's cum to luck dis mornin', sah! De Lo'd jest opened my eyes, an' I seed dis loaf and dis pot o' steamin' coffee settin' on t' other bank over dar, an' I could n't 'fend de Lo'd *no how;* so I jes' went over an' tuck 'em—yes, sah! One ting is bery certain: If de Lo'd sent 'em, de black folks brought 'em dar. But de black critters will—some of 'em—provide for them that is hunted an' starvin' an' is ready to perish. Was n't de ravens dat fed 'Lijah an' brought him de hoe-cake in de wilde'ness, black? Yah, yah; jest as black as Massa Wheelock's Grundy that brought dis supper down to the bank while I was singin'," saying which, he sang again in his rich deep voice:

"'Our harps that, when with joy we sang,
 Were wont their tuneful parts to bear,
 With silent strings, neglected, hang
 On willow boughs in mute despair.'

"Dat, sah, is de 'spression of dem dat hide from de terrors of de yoke. It means dat some poor, bruised reed is hungry and faint; dat some Hagar
U   13*

sits in despair in de wilds, or some broder is in strem-
ity. Ye can go into de wust swamp in all dis swampy
land, sah, an' sing dat ar little ditto, an' de plantation
hands will pack der bandannas wid hominy an' chick-
en, an' when night comes dey will flock 'roun' ye like
blackbirds in a co'n-field. Can ye sing?"

"Yes; but not like you," was the reply.

"Well, now, ole Whiting will l'arn ye some of
his songs that he sings as he wades the Jordan, 'ca'se
it's borne in on my mind that ye will be in some
powerful straits afore ye git through, an' it may sarve
ye to 'member this."

He repeated it over, line by line, till Herbert had
learned it; then he joined with him in singing it.

It began to get dark again, and the negro repeated
his instructions, which, when followed, were a perfect
key to this peculiar route—infallible as an engineer's
map—and now they prepared to separate. Remnants
of the supper were put into the bag where, also, another loaf was found, and swinging it over his shoulder as he was bid, Herbert wrung the hand of his
sable guide and friend. Turning away, he left him
standing on the little isle in the cane-brake, while
he plunged into and struggled slowly through the mud.
Now and then the rich voice reached him as, in wrapt
thought, Whiting gave utterance to snatches of the
inspiring poetry of those men of old, who saw visions
and dreamed dreams.

"'Amen! amen! Behold we are in readiness, O
Lord! Thy people have seen the sign of Thy coming.'"

"Amen!" was the last sound Herbert caught, vehemently pronounced by that overwrought soul, absorbed in unceasing calculations of human abuses and Almighty justice.

All night long he toiled on, feeling more lonely for the recent companionship ; but as details of that journey of days of rests and nights of unremitting effort would occupy too much space here, I will pass over the various incidents wherein he proved the usefulness of musical signals, and was fed and put in safer ways.

Two weeks had been occupied in this journey ere the heights of Fredericksburg rose upon his vision. It was just as the whispering trees waved their branches in salutation of the early dawn. He had with great difficulty drawn his wet, weary legs out of the river along whose shallow margin he had waded some hundred yards. Putting forth all his remaining strength, he climbed up a large oak where he saw an opening large enough to hold and hide him from view—a very necessary thing, as the whole country was swarming with rebel soldiers.

For two days he had tasted no kind of food except some nourishing roots that grew upon the banks of the sluggish stream he followed. It was the very day of the Federal troops crossing the river and taking possession of the city of Fredericksburg, and the whole movement he witnessed from his hungry outlook in the tree. Below him were encamped men he knew to be thirsting for Federal blood.

The company had been detailed upon some duty,

and left their camp under the trees for many hours
that day. He dropped down and found some cold
coffee and bread which sickened rather than refreshed
him; he had grown too weak to digest anything. He
climbed again to his lonely eyrie to wait with impatient heart the favorable chance to creep under the
beloved banner that flaunted its significant hues over
the rebel city *so near*, and yet, considering the desperate chances, *so far*.

Involuntarily he borrowed the cadence of his late
colored guide, and stretching out his hands toward the
flag, cried pathetically :

.   "O, that I had wings like a dove, I would fly to
thee, my beloved, and be at rest."

His excitement was so intense that he had no sense
of suffering, during the interim between his last as-
cension into the tree and the hour when he found himself unrecognized among his own comrades on the
battle field. He thought he must be dying, his sufferings all returning, and he remembered thinking he
must speak to Capt. Ellis, come what might. At that
point his memory failed him, not knowing even who
saved him till, in the description the surgeon gave him
of the man who brought him to the hospital, he recognized his old friend, Long Dave Persons.

The wintry days wore on. Alice had recovered
from her illness, and to-morrow with her father would
return home. A long drive had occupied the hours
of the last day of their stay at Acquia Creek. About
two o'clock they drove along past the headquarters
of an Ohio regiment and were attracted by the preliminary ceremonies of a military execution.

A private with his cap drawn down over his face so as to very much hide his features, came out of a tent, attended by the chaplain, and entered an ambulance. Behind in another ambulance was a coffin, on every side guards with bristling bayonets. A half mile was traversed, and then the soldier left the ambulance his arm interlocked with the arm of the chaplain. They walked thus to the designated spot, while the whole division was drawn up on three sides of a hollow square, the prisoner, chaplain and guard occupying the open side, where a grave had been dug, and by the grave they placed the coffin. He sat down upon the coffin while fetters were placed upon his feet, and his eyes bandaged. In front of him a firing party was drawn up composed of two from each regiment. One face in that party is particularly familiar to us; Gus Harkness is one of the firing party.

A division General stood by while the Provost Marshal read the death sentence, and shook hands with the condemned. A prayer was offered while all heads were uncovered solemnly, yet the faces of the officers and soldiers betrayed no evidence of emotion or sorrow. Evidently the wretched man who was about to experience the extremity of military discipline, had no personal friends. The chaplain shook hands with him, speaking some last words of spiritual consolation, and then stepping away, the prisoner stood alone. The word of command was given, one volley and he fell upon his coffin dead. He was lifted up and placed within it. The troops all filed by to look upon his face. Alice and her father felt an irrepressible desire to look upon him also. They left their carriage and fell in behind the soldiers as they marched past the dishonored dead.

One look, and the shivering girl clung tightly to the arm of her father as he led her quickly away from the mortal remains of George Langmere.

CHAPTER XVI.

CHECKMATED.

WE left 'Lizbeth Harkness and George Langmere on the lofty precipitous bank of a river, one Summer night, months ago, the first impressed with the Arcadian beauty of the scene spread out before and below them. The other more particularly impressed with the apparent difficulties of their descent, turned to their guides and inquired (rather sharply for a captive gentleman):

"How in the name of your dead sachems are we going to get off?"

"Why, jump," said 'Lizbeth, recovering her spirits in the excitement of a novel situation, "and light upon that inviting carpet of green, or more delightful still, upon the sparkling waters below us."

The Indians preceding them, followed a circuitous route down to a ford. It was twilight before they entered the town and drove to the most respectable structure, a white birch bark wigwam of circular form and very comfortable dimensions. Judging from olfactory evidence, Langmere's whisky had already found its home there. A bright fire burned upon the hard beaten ground, in the center, the smoke seeking an outlet through an opening on the top. The game upon the green was suspended and the

players were gathered in knots along the bank and
near the door where the travelers stopped, an idle,
listless, uncouth set of young loafers, behind whose
apparently imperturbable indifference and stoicism
were burning fires of curiosity. They had no appearance of seeing the newcomers, and the staring loung-
ers about a country church door might have taken
profitable lessons of them. Their method of taking
observations was so unobtrusive and inoffensive that
the chances would seem favorable to maintaining an
incognito—a grand mistake. Every feature, every
article of dress, every peculiarity of gait or gesture
were as clearly daguerreotyped upon those young
savage minds as are the delineations of the masters
upon the speaking canvas. Twenty years thereafter,
if 'Lizbeth or Langmere were to meet one or all of
them, they would be recognized instantaneously.

Langmere sprang from the buggy and assisted
'Lizbeth to get out. They were within half a dozen
paces of the door and together walked toward it.
Beside it Langmere, with considerable extravagance
of manner, bowed *too* graciously to suit the grave
mood 'Lizbeth happened to be in, at the same time
stepping to one side to allow her to precede him.
This was only natural gallantry, but she was a backwoods girl, with few ideas of the fine points of eti-
quette, and she felt a sudden suspicion of this movement, accompanied, as it was, by his whispered,

"Enter thy palace, my beautiful queen."

She had crossed the threshold, but his word
struck her ear and roused the thought, "He designs
this as my infamous abode." That thought awakened

a madness that was lurking in her soul. Turning round she would have darted out, but he had anticipated this and swiftly closed the door behind her. With almost superhuman strength she pushed him away and tried to open the door, but it was fastened already from without as well as within.

"What does this mean?" she asked passionately. "Why am I thus imprisoned and why are you here with me? Speak, for it is your plan, and the Indians are only your infamous tools."

"Yes," he answered, "it is my plan. What I value I will keep, and you know I love you."

"You are a perfidious fool to make such a statement to a married woman," again pushing him back from her.

"Thanks, you are quite too complimentary, especially as it is my pleasure to consider that married woman my wife. I suppose such compliments are frequently exchanged by married folks, and as I am an apt imitator it will not be long before I shall be an adept in those little amenities that tend so much to connubial felicity."

"Let me go! I will not stay here another moment. We are out of the woods now, and I answer your question as to our friendship, George Langmere, a thousand times no!" she cried.

"It is to your advantage to yield gracefully to my solicitations," he said, "while they still are the solicitions of love."

"No, no!" she shrieked, "I shall never taste guilty love, I have been vain, have loved admiration, and oh, how I am atoning for it, but I am not the

14

dreadful thing, the impure creature, that will accept such unholy love."

"I have money, 'Lizbeth, and will have more."

"Pile it to the skies and my indignation at your offer shall set it on fire," she said.

"Your caprices shall govern me, your will shall be my law."

He said it almost humbly, as if he really meant it, but she answered :

"Prove it, then, if you are sincere, by setting me at liberty.   That is my present wish."

"And will you love me, come voluntarily to me ? "

"No, you loathsome fool, I will put the widest space between us, and leave nothing but hate behind."

"Now, my little spitfire, just cool down a minute, while I tell you *what*."

"I won't hear you.   Open this door.   I hate you ; you are a hypocrite and a villain."

"But you *shall* hear me, you *shall* accede to my wishes, sweetly if you will, and so much the better; but listen, if by coercion, steeped in very shame you shall grovel at my feet and I shall spurn you, as you now spurn my offered love," he said, pausing a little, and then throwing all the meaning possible into his deep voice.   "Whether through love or through force, 't is for you to choose, but I swear it by the God you pretend to worship, you shall be mine."

"*Never*, as that same being rules on high, *never!* " she cried in a voice irrecognizable as that of 'Lizbeth Harkness, so harsh and unnatural had it become, as she realized now to the full extent the horror of her situation.

Again she tried the fastenings of the door, but they were too much for her strength, though that strength now was wonderful. He stood with folded arms and a cold, heartless smile, watching her efforts —a smile that would never, no never, raise the signal of relenting, though she might stamp and shriek all night, and call for the help that never would come. Tired at last of remonstrance and entreaty, tired of calling in vain for help, and finding no way of escape, she sank down at last in a heap, hopeless, yet still determined, near the fire. Her attitude of utter dejection did not touch his flinty heart, yet he spoke not ungently:

"Here are the materials for our wedding supper. Come, I remember you can cook nicely. See now, how I defer to you, though you are so cross to me. Shall I put on the tea kettle, my dear Mrs. Langmere?"

A startling whoop from without, from a hundred hoarse throats, answered a similar whoop in the forest, the exchange of salutations with the returning band of murderous Indians, fresh from scenes of carnage.

Langmere hurried to the door, but 'Lizbeth was there too and, determined to get out, clung to him desperately. At last finding egress impossible without her, he caught her up and flung her on the bed, fastening her hands and then her feet with strong cords; while her screams rose high and higher. Then he left her to ascertain the cause of a commotion which momentarily increased without, till Bedlam seemed reproduced in that Indian village. A hurried council succeeded the warriors' arrival, and as flight seemed imperative to the safety of the tribe, flight was decided upon and preparations made at once so that before midnight they were in marching trim. Langmere drove to the door of the hut in his buggy for 'Lizbeth, and entering found her of course just as he had left her. He told her of the enforced exodus, which compelled a postponement of their happiness (?). She cried piteously,

"O, leave me here, even alone in this wilderness. Its terrors are as nothing compared to my abhorrence of the relation you propose. I never can be anything to you; I never will!"

"Leave you here, ha, ha! that's a good one. No, ma'am, you have a destiny to fulfil. I have been casting our horoscope, and separation nowhere appears. You must go with me!"

"Very well, sir! When the destiny you speak of is fulfilled, you will do well to remember you insisted upon my going."

"Why, do you imagine I intend to leave pussy the use of her claws? O, no," he said laughingly, releasing her hands but not her feet.

The food he then offered her she ate through motives of self-preservation, thinking she must keep up her strength to resist this villain. He lifted her into the buggy and took his seat beside her, waiting to witness the novel process of packing his wares for transportation. Indian emigrants have a very peculiar method of disposing of heavy articles in their removals. Two long poles (in this case) or shafts were fastened on either side of a pony to the neck-yoke, higher however than shafts of a buggy. The long supple ends are left to drag along on the ground behind. Just behind the pony the load is bound tightly to the shafts and seems to be borne with all confidence as to result. It was a curious caravan that marched away that night, the central body consisting of about fifty ponies laden with the paraphernalia of Indian travel and Langmere's stock of merchandise. Some of the ponies were very small and looked funny enough with the pole ends sticking above their heads, and the load jogging along after them. Women with papooses on their shoulders, and little nude wretches beside them clinging to their skirts, trotted along. Girls with loads that were too heavy for their slight forms came chattering along, the difficulty of weight obviated by a broad strap that was connected with the load and brought up across the forehead; so that without knowing a letter of the alphabet, those girls would do more head work than many a conceited Miss who boasted of having mastered the "three Rs." Boys walked along erect and proud, without a burden save their bow and arrows slung at their side. Hungry dogs prowled along at their heels, while some of them led or jerked a lazy pony along.

There are flanking parties of the line of march on either side of the loaded horses. How the squaws move on! They whoop and struggle through the bushes, laughing, chattering, scolding children and horses. Behind these are marched the prisoners and behind them again are armed warriors to protect and

defend if surprised and overtaken. Strange pano-
rama! Of prisoners there are three only (by which
it is safe to conclude that this party of Sioux warriors
saved few lives — theirs were impatient hatchets that
could not brook delay), a man, his wife and child,
strangers to Langmere and 'Lizbeth, who rode along
just before them.

The second day of the march they became foot-
sore and weary ; the man begged that his wife might
be allowed to ride, and for an answer was shot
through the heart, the ball breaking the arm of the
child he carried. Langmere stopped his horse,
demanding the reason for the shooting.

"Ugh! He's a fool with a squaw's tongue, only
fit to kick," said the Indian as he spurned the body
with his foot contemptuously.

The poor distracted woman had caught up the crying child and was trying to still its moans at her
breast, when a repulsive-looking squaw turned back,
snatched the baby, and raising it with both hands
above her head dashed it upon the hard ground, still-
ing its cries forever. The tearless mother gathered
the form of her dead, crushed baby again to her heart
and said :

"Only me to suffer now and not for long."

Langmere pointing to the squaw with his whip
said :

"'Lizbeth, such are the women," then pointing to
the chief, "such are the men—"

"Devils you mean," she interrupted.

"Yes, devils if you will, whose aid I have secured
to bring you to terms. Take warning and be wise."

She was silent. Indeed her conversation now was almost entirely confined to monosyllables. She desired to give her seat to the poor creature thus violently bereaved, but she knew it was useless to offer such a petition, and she had made up her mind that she never would open her lips to ask a favor of him.

The next day when they broke camp and resumed the march, no prisoners toiled along with weary feet. The night before, 'Lizbeth had held the cold hand of a woman who, with dying breath, said that it would "soon be over and the anguish of the earth forgotten in the glory of the skies."

After thirteen days' flight they finally encamped in a locality as picturesque as the one they had left, a locality moreover that with beauty combined more natural advantages.

The final encampment took place about noon, and the afternoon was spent in getting comfortably settled.

Habitations were erected in the most primitive style of architecture, and the business part of the community (that is the squaws) worked industriously till dark. The last task was that of eating their supper. The great camp kettles steamed with their mysterious compounds, and the squaws that stirred them with their long paddles, looked in the glare of the fire, not unlike the legendary witches stirring their famous broth.

'Lizbeth was served with broiled venison and mush, but she could not bring herself in any instance to taste of the soups, which were eaten from the kettle; a whole family gathering round and dipping in their wooden spoons.

There had been great preparations on the green that afternoon. A council house had been erected, and now a bonfire blazed high in front of it to light up the ceremonies of exultation over the success of the late raid, and to exhibit its trophies. The council house (a long, low tepee of poles, covered with birch bark), stood upon a triangular plat of green, formed by the confluence of two streams. Before the council house, a ring of painted braves was formed. A rude drum made of raw moose hide, was beaten by an old white-headed prophet; while a boy rattled the senseless gus-tah-weh-sah, a gourd filled half full of beans. Foremost of the ring was a chief, bearing on his head a waving plume of deep vermilion dye; a snake of the same color was tattooed upon his breast. Every spot upon his huge form, naked to the girdle, bore hieroglyphics telling of his battle-deeds. Behind him were ranged warriors in all the pomp of plume and ochre, porcupine quill and beads. The first chief, when all were in position, waved his hatchet and brought it circling round his head, while with heavy stamp he opened the scalp dance.

Forward all with rocking feet, and heavy zig-zag of the body, while from every throat poured a wild, deep guttural strain, weird and unearthly. The wooded hills reverberating, as the long column like a writhing serpent, wound around and around the frame in the center, upon which hung the gory scalps, evidence of their prowess in the late massacre.

This is the translation of their song, or part of it:

Ho-ah! dance again the dance,
Let our knives and hatchets glance.
Loud and louder peals the strain;
Lo! the pale face mourns the slain.
    Great spirit unto thee,
    Swells the song of victory.

Scarce a mark our war-path made,
Gliding from beneath the shade;
Near and nearer still we creep,
Lo! the pale face is asleep.
    Great spirit, etc.

Whoop! and down the doors we crash,
Then on the pale faces dash;
Our bloody hatchets fly.
See! they pray, they groan, they die!
    Great spirit, etc.

They lie like the leaves around,
Thickly cover they the ground.
See! their heads are lowly now,
And our feet are on their brow.
    Whoop! Whoop!
    Great spirit unto thee,
    Swells the song of victory.

A very efficient adjunct to this ceremony was Langmere's liquor stand. A mark of civilization, recognized with enthusiastic patronage, which inspired hope in the owner's breast, for the success of his commercial venture among these sworn enemies of his race. He sat there without a twinge of conscience, pouring out drink after drink, the liquid that he knew would intensify the flame of animosity; setting an example by freely imbibing himself. To

V

make the "sixpence nimble," Langmere was willing
to suffer any amount of inconvenience. He drank
often and deeply, attracting attention to the fact by
holding up the empty glass and giving utterance to a
prolonged "whoop!"

Night had dwindled to the "wee sma' hours"
before the cheap whisky had done its work, and the
painted revelers had taken to grassy couches, and all
was still.

'Lizbeth, who had refused to witness this revolting ceremony, had been left in the care of a young
squaw, in a wigwam covered with blankets, hastily
constructed, but made more than ordinarily comfortable by an apology for a bed, composed of straw laid
upon bark matting and covered with blankets, all
supported by a rude tamarack bedstead. Upon this
bed, across the foot of which her drowsy attendant
had fallen asleep, 'Lizbeth half sat, half reclined,
her mind in no enviable state, for she was tied
securely, hands and feet, thus making escape impossible. She had requested the squaw to pin back one
of the blankets forming the side of the house, so
that she could look out into the moonlight in a direction opposite to that whence the yells and whoops
proceeded. Langmere had visited her several times
the forepart of the night, each time saying with a
meaning leer :

"Shortly I will come to remain with you, so be
patient."

Soon after his last visit, she was startled by a
shadow across her low doorway, and filled with

wonder, when a tall white man entered, and, seating himself on a keg of rum, said:

"I am addressing 'Lizbeth Harkness, of Clipnockum Hollow."

"Yes; you are a stranger to me; but, oh, you have come to save me from a villain!"

"Do n't flatter yourself! Your husband did not so deliver me! I have sworn to hate all that he loves."

"But he does not love me; he has given his heart to another woman. Oh, help me if you can; I am so wretched!" she cried.

"Did he not outrage my manhood and place a lasting shame upon my name?" asked the stranger.

"How should I know, who never heard that name?" she replied.

"Is it possible I am so changed? Well, Gus Harkness caused the change, and I hate him!"

"Why dwell upon the faults and misdeeds of Gus? He is nothing to me!" she said, almost petulantly.

"If I were sure of that, I would help you; but you were always thought insincere," he replied.

"I know it—and perhaps deservedly; but, oh, to witness murder and fiendish cruelty! to be bound and menaced with worse than death, is more than I can bear!" she said vehemently.

"'Bound' do you say? Are not your relations to Langmere voluntary?" he inquired.

"Oh, indeed, they are not! I loathe him as I loathe a reptile! Come here!" she said earnestly.

He came to her side. She lifted her hands so that he could see the cords with which they were secured. With his knife he cut them, muttering anathemas against Langmere. She looked up to thank him, and exclaimed with astonishment,

"Charles Center ! "

His knife had just released her feet, when they heard heavy steps without. Each sprang, for conceal-ment, to a darker corner of the hut, when Langmere entered and, staggering to the bed, fell upon it, draw-ing the squaw with disgusting familiarity to his breast, saying :

"Come, 'Lizbeth—hic—give 's kiss, an' then git-up-an-get-a-bite—hic—my stomach cries—cupboard—come, get-me-bite, then come snooze—hic."

The squaw started from her slumber, struggled desperately—a struggle which finally resulted in his rolling off the bed. As he fell, his head struck one of the kegs underneath, producing a tremendous con-cussion, which, added to his inebriated condition, effectually overcame him. He became silent, and went off into the deep slumber of intoxication. 'Liz-beth put her shawl about her shoulders, and seated herself with Charles Center, on a log near the wigwam, and in answer to his questions concerning his wife and child, told him of the former's patient suffering and tranquil death, and that her father took little Carlos home to Chicago.

"I am glad the old man had to come down with some of his cash. He might have helped me more than he did, and my wife knew it, but she would not ask him. I expected she would write to him and get money to take her to Chicago, for I gave her a hint that I was going to stir up some kind of a mess that would make the neighborhood pretty hot, and I did too ; but then

I thought she and the boy were gone. I did not want them harmed ; but I tell you I spread it on about old man Maynard to the Indians. Like my wife, they all worshipped him ; but I told them what a two-faced old fellow he was, and in less than two weeks after I came up here, they had alternately scalped, slashed and burned the old man in effigy—Mock-ane-sah, his sworn friend, assisting in the little ceremonies."

After listening to much about himself and his grievances, 'Lizbeth said :

" Charles Center, will you not help me to get away ? "

" I will," he said, and they then proceeded to discuss various plans of escape ; but none seemed immediately feasible, and they finally concluded that safety lay only in her waiting and feigning to regard Langmere's proposals with less repugnance. Not assenting all at once—that would be suspicious—but yielding little by little, to throw dust in his eyes while their other plans ripened.

" How can I, when I hate him so ? " said 'Lizbeth, with a shudder.

"I hate him as much as you do!" (It was a necessity for Center to hate somebody.) "I was a very king among the Indians ; had become identified with them in many ways. I sent old Jim John down to buy Langmere's liquors for me, and behold Langmere comes up to sell them himself *by the drinks*. He has supplanted me, but his reign will only last while the drinks last, and I will have every Indian under my thumb again. If he wants to sell liquor, let him go amongst white folks and do it, or hunt up some other tribe of Indians. This is my field."

"He will never go among the whites again," said 'Lizbeth ; "at least, if he does, he knows very well he will get shot."

"What for?"

"Desertion and some other crime, known to military law, I don't exactly know what."

"I 'll fix him then," said Center, with a smile that looked almost like genuine happiness. It was daylight when they parted—'Lizbeth seeking out the squaw who had attended her the previous night, and by signs and gestures seeking to establish a friendship with her. Together they joined a knot of squaws on the green. She was naturally something of an actress, and managed by significant pantomime to converse with them, and to some extent be sociable. She sought to make them believe she had great regard for Langmere, hoping thus to satisfy them that she had no designs upon any of their lords or lovers. She asked for breakfast, and forthwith they produced a wooden bowl of steaming soup and a piece of broiled venison. As the morning advanced, the feminine side of life began to show itself in the village, but not one of "nature's noblemen" graced the circles round the breakfast camp kettles.

When Langmere awoke from his long lethargy, he found a good meal ready—biscuits, baked in an old-fashioned, shallow kettle, a broiled pheasant and fried mush. Among his stores 'Lizbeth had found a sack of coffee, and she had prepared some in a camp kettle. She was sitting out beside the fire when he got up, feeling considerably the worse for his dissipation. He came as near feeling ashamed of himself as such a man could, and as if he had lost ground with 'Lizbeth. He went out of the tent at the opposite side from the fire, down to the river, and bathed his head and face and hands. Beginning to feel a little fresher, his courage revived, and with something of his usual *bonhomie* he came back and sitting down by the side of 'Lizbeth, said:

"I was drunk then; can you overlook it?"

"That depends upon whether you behave yourself as well when sober."

She said it so pleasantly that he dropped the stick he whittled with astonishment, and looking at her as well as his squinting eyes would allow, uttered a long, low whistle. She laughed and said:

"You do owe the squaw an apology, but she'll wait. Your dinner is ready; you went to bed hungry last night."

"That's so, and bumped my head to boot," he said, rubbing the sore spot.

"Yes, that concussion broke my cords. 'Twas awful; your head must be a regular iron clad.

"Well, come; you must eat too. All this nice dinner is not mine."

"Yours! I am only a servant, and servants do not eat with their sovereigns; but I want to make a bargain with you. Tell me you positively will not bind me again."

"And you, what will you do; try to escape?"

"No, no. I dare not do that; no, but I will be better than if bound."

"And be my wife?"

"Possibly in time," she said, looking over his head.

"How long, a month?" he said, peering into her face earnestly.

She looked away from him and said nothing.

"Two months?" he said raising his hand as if administering an oath.

"*Yes*, if you treat me respectfully," she replied, looking frankly into his eyes.

"I'll do that; give me your hand." He extended his own in which she laid hers with all seeming confidence. He raised it to his lips, but she exclaimed:

"No, no; during these two months all such familiarity is tabooed. I will keep your wigwam, cook your food, and be your friend, but you shall not touch me, you shall not offer to kiss me. Can I depend upon you?"

"Yes, but it's darned hard!"

From that time she treated him with marked deference, often putting on an appearance of fear that completely disarmed his suspicions. A new building was made in which were two rooms, one of which she occupied, having as a companion the young squaw already referred to. To Center she said little, telling Langmere:

"That man I will not speak to, no matter how agreeable he may be to you. I hate him. He is only attracted here, I believe, by the strong odor of your liquor."

"When I bring up another stock I will not have

it in the house we live in. I'll have it placed as far away as you wish it, darling."

"Look out, sir! When are you going for it? pretty soon?

"When I get to the bottom barrel of the stock on hand."

" And will you bring me a dress suitable to be—"

" Married in?" he interrupted.

" Well, I suppose so," she replied with feigned confusion, which fairly transported him, so genuine did it seem.

" I'll bring you a dress, and two or three of them for that matter, but it is not customary among these people to have any ceremony. It's only

> "You love me and I love you,
> Now let us be no longer two."

"Well, ceremony or no ceremony, I won't be married in this old dress," she said.

" You need n't; you 've been a good girl and shall have a new one. 'Lizbeth, I want to kiss you the darndest."

" Well, you can't while I wear this dress, but I promise you may as soon as I get another one."

" All right, but you shall have a new one right off, by thunder!"

The emergency seemed to warrant this deception of 'Lizbeth's, and justify any extraordinary measure to extricate herself from her present situation, even to wasting Langmere's whisky to hasten the time of " going below for spirits." She procured a gimlet and made some small holes in the lower side of the

14*

barrels, which greatly assisted the leak at the tap. The sandy floor of the lodge quickly absorbed the tiny but continuous stream, and gave out liberally intoxicating odors, that were powerful to attract the Indians and to call out their furs and greenbacks, to the great satisfaction of Langmere, who continued to bait them by drinking himself. One day, six weeks after the compact with 'Lizbeth, when all were more convivial than usual, a storm of snow drove them all to cover. Langmere's spirits rose with the rest, and his glass was emptied oftenest if possible. Center dropped in and called for a drink, a thing he seldom did, for he was no hypocrite and took no pains to hide his hate of Langmere, and generally kept away from him. Langmere poured out a glass and handed it to him, at the same time filling his own.

"Give me a glass from the bottle you take yours from," said Center.

"Mine is medicated. Do you fear poison that you ask this?" he said coolly, setting his bottle back upon the shelf behind him.

"Never mind what I fear. I insist upon a glass from that bottle."

"And I say you can't have it. I run this institution *myself*. A nice time I should have if I was to humor the whims of every old swill-guzzler that comes in for his es-coo-ta-wah-bo (whisky)."

Apparently satisfied, Center drained his glass, but turning to the Indians present he addressed them in their own language, of which Langmere understood little, save the common expressions in daily use. 'Lizbeth, who knew what Center was about, beckoned

Langmere to her and detained him by her on some trivial pretext, while Center proceeded to the accomplishment of his object.

"Why do you hate most white men?" said he.

"Because they have lying tongues and black hearts," was the reply of old Jim John, who was the spokesman generally in that division of the tribe, as Mock-ane-sah was in another.

"Do you believe Langmere would deceive you for the sake of inducing you to patronize him?"

"No!" was repeated by a dozen throats in concert.

"Will you do my bidding if I tell you how to prove him?"

"Yes," was the reply, but with less energy than the first. Their faith in Langmere was entire, and it looked treacherous to test his fidelity, shown in so many ways. However, they all crowded close to Center, curious to know what he would say next, and he, reaching across the rude counter, took down the bottle, tasted its contents and passed it to Jim John, who, tasting also, passed it with a grimace to the others, and as it passed round that circle, Langmere went down commercially in their estimation as rapidly as the contents of his private bottle, which contained —*water*.

There was a flash of indignation in the looks exchanged by that half-drunken crowd, and Center knew it boded mischief unless controlled. Langmere's trade in that village was over, and he had timed this discovery just as the "bottom of the last barrel" was reached, as 'Lizbeth's watchful eye had already observed, and that day's conviviality would finish what was left in the bottles. The savages stood there now, just as ready to commit murder, if that was his wish, as they were to obey him in anything. But violence was not his game just yet.

"Wait; I know of a punishment worse than murder, and I will show you how to lead him to it. For the present he must not know that you consider this deception as more than a good joke. Let us compel him to go to the river and there drink with each one of us."

Langmere, entirely ignorant of what had taken place, answered very reluctantly when called from his attractive conversation in the next room.

"Come," said Jim John, "it's *our* treat now. We know the drink you prefer."

And laughing, they led him down to the river. Amidst shouts of derision that reached 'Lizbeth's ears, they compelled him to honor each treat until nature revolted. Then they desisted and allowed him to return to his shanty.

He was able to confer at length with the cautious, cunning woman, who proposed to assist him in his preparations for "going below for spirits," where he hoped to secure a supply for the Winter's use from Indian traders who always hang upon the frontier.

Poor fool! He cared less for the liquor, for the sale was getting to be dry business, than he did for the dry goods that were declared to be indispensable to the consummation of his compact with the woman he had come to love. Yes, he was really in love, and he resolved to risk everything to realize the affection that

he believed was in store for him, when the womanish
caprice regarding the new dress was gratified. True,
he had enjoyed none of the privileges usually accorded to an accepted lover, but his imagination was active,
and readily construed the flashes of 'Lizbeth's dark
eyes, which we know were not lighted by love's fire,
into rapturous gleams of a passion she could not entirely control. He was determined to lose no time
now in accomplishing the work that lay between the
present and the accomplishment of his wishes.

She carefully assisted him in dyeing his hair and
arranging the heavy false whiskers, and declared him
a "duck of a man" when the disguise (which she
carefully explained to Center) was completed. She
actually kissed him when he left—two days after.

To that Judas-like salutation he was indebted perhaps for the happiest moment of his life, and while
over and over again he felt the thrill of her ripe lips
on his own, he congratulated himself upon the discovery that after all she had an affectionate nature.
He started on snow shoes; for in that northern region
snow comes early, and it was now November—with
three or four trusty Indians (that is trusty from Center's point of view). He had made arrangements for
a larger party to follow with dogs and sledges to bring
up his supplies, when he and they would return together without delay.

He had no fears that 'Lizbeth would try to escape;
how could she? Old Jim John was to guard her going and coming, and the snow forbade any woman's
traveling far. Besides he flattered himself she loved
him now.

He had not been gone two days, when 'Lizbeth, Center and Jim John, her trusty guard, with the larger party that he had arranged should follow him, set out on sledges, following the trail he had broken, towards the settlements. The young squaw that had shared her bed, also shared her journey. They had each acquired enough of the other's language to make conversation very brisk.

"Let 'em talk," old Jim John said. "Let 'em talk, big, long, then go faster."

The monotonous journey was over at last. In the comparatively comfortable sitting room of a half-breed, who kept an Indian post, near the frontier, they were divesting themselves of blankets and bear skins. They had detoured from Langmere's route about ten miles above to avoid his encampment which they knew was about half that distance above the post. The Indians that composed Center's party encamped below it two or three miles, while he accompanied 'Lizbeth and her companion to this place. Though the sympathy of the half-breed that kept this station was believed to be with the whites, the fact that he held that position through the massacre, and still held it, was indisputable evidence that his friendship was on the side of the aborigines. He entered heartily into Center's plans, who proposed with him to control the stores Langmere had come to purchase as soon as he had paid for them. The half-breed approved this plan so warmly that Center had the satisfaction of seeing a messenger depart for a military station some miles below. To avoid Langmere, he withdrew to the encampment to wait the development of his plan.

Langmere, confiding in his disguise, lost no time in calling upon the half-breed and making the acquaintance of some traders who had the very commodities he desired. These, in obedience to a hint, caused negotiations to hang fire several days, but finally promised to complete the trade the following day and give him an order on the person who had the liquors in charge. Agreeable to appointment, Langmere discovered a large covered sleigh coming through the woods. It stopped about ten rods from the camp. Three gentlemen got out and advanced to the fire. Langmere recognized two of them as his business acquaintances. They proceeded at once to the completion of their bargain, even receiving payment of the money and writing the order, when one of the traders said:

"You can get into the sleigh if you like, and ride down with us, and see that you get the worth of your money."

"Thanks," was the reply; "I will do so, for I am anxious to get started back; the force that came down to transport the stuff have arrived, but by some mistake are camping, I understand, below the station. I will go down and start them out. We can get a good ways up country before night."

While he was speaking they had been advancing towards the sleigh, and pausing suddenly, as if a mortifying omission occurred to him, one of the traders said:

".I must apologize to you, sir; though really, I

am not acquainted with your name, but it may not be too late to announce to you that of our friend, Mr. Burke, an assistant provost marshal."

That gentleman laid his hand upon Langmere's shoulder, saying:

"You are my prisoner, George Langmere, — Regiment, Ohio Volunteers. I arrest you as a deserter. Be kind enough to accept these bracelets; they are a little inconvenient but very expressive of rank."

"All right," replied Langmere, whose coolness never deserted him. "I shall face the music, and of course, covet all the honors."

As he stepped into the sleigh, he gaily addressed the person on the back seat —

"How are you, Mr. Center? How plainly one can see through a grindstone when there is a hole in it."

They took dinner at the station. Langmere, imperturbable as ever, seated beside the officer, was proceeding to tell a funny story, when 'Lizbeth came in and took a seat opposite. He bowed to her saying:

"Excuse me, but this gentleman insists that I must wear jewelry, which obliges me to shake hands with my elbows, so I fear we shall have to forego the courtesy."

She made no reply. Somehow she felt dreadfully sorry for him; could almost have cried at the success of the plan she had been so long working for. Her spirits returned, however, when at the close of the meal he hissed in her ear—

My robin got tired of waiting for her new feathers and her mate."

"She had fulfilled her destiny," she replied.

"Well, she must look to her own natural mate for the reward," he sneered; but she unflinchingly retorted:

"O you're welcome, I'm sure. I do not crave reward for serving friends to whom I am so deeply indebted."

"When you meet the interesting family of Gus Harkness, remember me to the yellow girl, and kiss the child for me," he said, insolently.

"I never kiss now, save to betray. As I have no further interest in either the child or yourself, I shall not undertake your commissions," she replied quickly.

The same conveyance that took the marshal and his prisoner to the settlements, contained as a passenger, 'Lizbeth Harkness. She was sad now. The excitement of foiling Langmere was over; she had positive news of the desolation of the settlement at home; and her parents' fate, though uncertain, could hardly be doubted. Nor was her sadness dispelled by thoughts of her husband. She had ceased to think lovingly of Gus, indeed, her nearest approach to that passion had been too much a love of being loved.

She would ride silently for hours, watching the trees as they glided past like unsheeted ghosts on either side of them, and listen to the low dirge-like wail sobbing through their branches, as they tossed them despairingly toward the sky. She had ample time to reflect and decide upon her future course. She could not, and would not entertain a thought of Gus.

Henceforth he should be to her as one who had never been. If her father and mother were living, she would devote herself to them, gladly toiling that she might provide for them. But she determined from this time to crucify her vanity and love of admiration, to exorcise by prayer and fasting the last vestige of pride and ambition; and taking up the humble threads of life, if she should not realize the picture of a singing Bertha, she would, at all events, prove herself the useful Priscilla. Thus musing and resolving, she made the long, lonely journey

Langmere never addressed her on the way but once. They had reached a little bridge, which spanned a stream, at which the driver stopped to water his horses. 'Lizbeth remembered the place well. Here it was, when her adventure with Langmere had hardly begun, that he first bound and gagged her, lest she should attempt to escape or attract attention by crying out. It occurred to them both now, vividly; and she seemed to feel the very emotions she had experienced then. Her then situation returned to her with such force that she actually put her hand to her mouth as if to remove the bandage, and moved her feet to make sure they were free. Langmere was sitting behind her, and seeing her movements rightly surmised their cause. As if uttering her own thoughts, with a voice so nearly like triumph, that the counterfeit seemed to have the ring of genuine metal, he said :

"*Checkmate !*"

CHAPTER XVII.

RESTORATION.

In the cool, green shade of forests,
Where the dew is never dry,
A twitter of birds in the branches,
And little blue spots of sky.

'TIS a hazy "Indian Summer" day. The waters of Lake Itasca shimmer in the sun. The shore is thickly wooded, the pine and the stately hemlock, the sensitive poplar, the sturdy oak, the beech, whose clinging moss guides the bewildered traveler northward; the maple, also, with its beautiful leaves, and the sweet birch, the "incense-bearer of the woods," all contribute their quota to provide that forest fringe around Lake Itasca's shores.

A narrow vista through the roof of interlacing branch and richly tinted leaf lets down the light upon a little bay where a canoe is moored. A dark-eyed, sad featured, but beautiful woman sits in the canoe. At her feet, her head inclined as if listening, sits a white girl, whose pearly complexion seems transparent in contrast with the dark skin of her companion.

The lovely sylvan scene is one to make the bosom thrill with emotions akin to higher life, lifted by their refined agency to heaven. Something of this silent worship seemed to hold this woman spell-bound, for she held in her hand an irresolute oar and gazed now with moistening eye upon the fair, pale face in her lap, now at the dimpling wavelets that musically lapped the shore, and then above, upon the Summer foliage, and the pure blue sky beyond. Love was written upon her features, love shone in her dewy eyes—love not all material, nor yet all spiritual.

A sound that the quick ear of an Indian only would catch, an infinitesimal echo of dipping oars, roused Miannetta, for she it was, and by a single stroke, that showed her mistress of the dainty shaft, the canoe was gliding noiselessly as a fairy craft out of its leafy hiding place. Now on the bosom of the lake she rowed rapidly toward an island, a half mile from the shore, nor was her tiny shallop all alone. A hundred others of similar construction accompanied it. Each moment, from some point on the leafy shore, there glided a re-inforcement, till it really seemed as if, from out the sky, a fairy fleet had suddenly dropped down, all heading towards the emerald isle in midlake. Then silently is moored to its bank that nestles down to the wave the fleet, whose crew have in a moment disappeared. Now, in the center of the isle, are warriors in fantastic garb. No war-paint disfigures the stolid yet fine-looking features, the fusee is left in the lodge, the hatchet is buried. The frontier settler never knows the hour of its resurrection.

At the apex of this little island mound a rude post has been set, and on this post, rudely traced, is

the coat of arms of a "Northern League"—a circle
of braves with a heart in their midst. These were
the small remnant of a once powerful tribe of Cana-
dian Indians, that belonged to that wonderful confed-
eration known as the "League of the Five Nations."

Around the post the silent band were seated on
the ground, smoking the calumet successively. Nearest the post, upon rich mats, were Miannetta and her
charge, evidently objects of particular deference, for
they were the only women within the charmed circle.
Other women were near, but remained outside, the
delighted witnesses of the several ceremonies.

On the other side of the post sat the musicians of
the tribe—an old withered medicine-man with his
drum, a sharp-eyed boy with his rattle, the latter
keeping slow time to the drumming and historic chant
of the bowed old minstrel, from whose lips dropped
the musical legends of the tribe.

An hour they listened to the monotonous recapit-
ulations. Then "Springing Panther," the chief of
the league, arose, and all in an instant were on their
feet. With low obeisance to the minstrel, the stately
chieftain opened the swinging dance, and every throat
droned out a deep, guttural strain, in time with the
beating of the drum. One after another fell into the
dance, a long, chanting, zigzag line, winding round
and round the post, a dusky, curious file. The sun
pours down its warm rays upon their hirsute limbs,
and their terpsichorean enthusiasm seems to gather
strength as they wind. Shorter and heavier grow the
beats upon the drum, the eyes of the boy are aflame

as he holds higher his vibrating rattle. The stamps of the dancers are more expressive now, and as if their voices were one, a deafening shout rolls out upon the air — echoed from the opposite shores. The whole band sinks to the earth in silence while the eldest sachem speaks.

"Brothers, this is our anniversary of the 'league.' The sun smiles; we have not offended him. Our rice and corn are plentiful; we have done well. Birds darken the sky, fishes flash in the water, game abounds in the forest ; we shall not starve. We have no fevers, we have no war ; let us thank the Great Spirit."

Waving his arm aloft, again rang out the shrill whoop, and then each dusky warrior sought in silence his canoe. Again, from the island across the lake, glided the fleet—men and women using the oars with equal dexterity

Upon the shore of the lake, two Indians raised upon their shoulders a litter, upon which reclined the form of the white girl ; and now to their village, miles up the lake, in single file they march—their trail like a deep furrow cut through the wood. A long row of tepees, curved like an Indian bow, nestled against a similarly curved forest, is reflected in the clear, still waters of the crescent-shaped bay. Here in this rude village, Miannetta, after long and indefatigable search, had found Nellie—but not the Nellie of the old "Maples" memory—merry, gentle and soulful. Of these, gentleness only remained, and that was of a kind that inspires pity. No word ever passed her lips, even to Miannetta, who loved her well,

and with whom she had been so familiar at home.
She seemed ever to be listening for something she
never heard. In other respects she retained her physical faculties, though her eyes had a vacant look, or
if any, an expression like that of some gentle animal.
She ate and walked like a somnambulist. She had
been picked up by the admiring chieftain, "Springing Panther," who found her where she fell, beside
the spring. Believing the blow she had received
would not be fatal, and obeying the attraction we
often notice of natures extremely opposite, he bore
her into the woods and gave her into the care of
squaws, who had treated her very tenderly, according
to his instructions.

During the long march to this northern locality,
she had been carried on the shoulders of the Indians,
growing apparently stronger, but never speaking.
Miannetta now claimed the right of an old friend, to
care for her; but she was first put under oath by the
intervention of the wampum, that she would never
take Nellie back without the entire knowledge and
consent of him who brought her away. Miannetta
had a sacred regard for that belt as well as he, and
she was bound. No harm would ever come to Nellie
if she attempted to take her away, but she had said
"I will not," and though she wished much to take
her to Robert, without the canceling of that promise
she never would. Alone she would thread the forest
path, go back and tell him all, if so it seemed best;
but she would keep her Indian vow. She was provided with all the comforts and luxuries available.
The elegant wigwam, assigned and fitted up for her

use and Nellie's, was a circular tent, made very warm
and neat by being lined throughout with the inside
bark of the birch, beautifully mottled and very sweet
to the smell. The hard-beaten, earth floor was car-
peted with wolf skins, sewed together with the sinews
of elk so cunningly as to look like a pack of the animals in chase. In the center of the room was a
hollow tree, at the foot of which was a stone fire-place,
so built that the former served as a chimney to carry
off the smoke. A low bedstead, with rich mattings,
blankets and seal-skin spread, occupied one side of
the room ; a table and cupboard, the other. The
latter was so covered with rare and valuable ornaments as to completely conceal the puncheons of
which it was composed. Rude ottomans, covered
with beaver or other handsome fur, lay carelessly
scattered about ; but Nellie's couch, near the fire, was
the crowning piece of furniture. Luxurious and soft,
its lavish profusion of magnificent furs, its ornaments
of beads and mother-of-pearl, would, in more civilized
circles, have indicated its owner as the scion of some
royal house, or the favorite of some Eastern harem,
and its beautiful occupant would in no wise have dispelled the illusion. The stuffed birds that were suspended from the tent's sloping walls, seemed to hang
poised on their waiting wing. A beautiful tame
mocking-bird, of dark red plumage, had the freedom
of the wigwam, and made music all the day for Miannetta, who watched her fair charge, not impatiently.
She was one who had learned that hardest of all
lessons, *to wait*.

Here the Winter was passed comfortably, and the

Spring came, bringing no change to Nellie, except that through the long Winter confinement she grew to look even more delicate and spiritual. She was always a sunshine flower, never seeming to flourish in the shade, and she looked very frail now. Miannetta would sigh as she held the little hand to the sunlight. It was clear as a beautiful carnelian, turning rosy in its rays.

Nothing of interest occurred during the Spring months, and in June the preparation for the festival, or, as the Indians term it, "the strawberry dance," was the first real appearance of gaiety.

It was a late season, and the very last of the month saw the best of the berries. The week's preparation completed, they all repaired, as before, to the island, where, on the ground around the post, was piled an immense bed of green strawberry leaves. The usual position was assumed, the chant commenced, and feet kept time to the weird music of the drum and rattle; but they did not *rotate* until some minutes, when each threw upon the leaves a basket full of delicious berries. Several times they went round, and then pausing, the foremost chief addressed them, recounting " the innumerable benefits and kindly offices of the Earth—the home of the living brotherhood and the cherishing tomb of the dead; the receptacle of the seed and producer of the strawberry. He bowed his head in reverential gaze upon the ground, and laying his hand upon his breast, cried:

" Earth, we thank thee!"

The whole band repeated his words in a wild chant, stamping and circling round, then paused.

The chief, turning his eyes to the Itasca's smooth
surface, proposed as the next sentiment :

"Water — bearing canoes safely, slaking thirst;
giving drink, and therefore perfection, to the strawberry—water, we thank thee !"

Again the march and chant around the post, then
the pause. The chief raised his head and waved his
hand to and fro, saying :

"For sweeping off all poison vapors, bringing
rain, cooling the weary frame and giving breath
while are gathered strawberries—air, we thank thee !
'On with the dance ! let voice be unconfined !'"

With chant and quickening feet, the sentiment is
enthusiastically received.

Nellie was dressed in the holiday attire of young
Indian women. Excepting her hair, there was nothing
unusual about her. Since her capture she had worn
it combed straight back and braided in two long plaits
hanging down behind, but to-day Miannetta had dressed it in the old style.

A shower of golden curls rippled down beside her
face and over her shoulders. She seemed as usual all
day, apathetic, unobservant—a beautiful statue of
some saint, an angel sent to earth on some divine
commission and frozen at her task. While the dance
was at its height, Miannetta, watching with jealous
care every movement of her charge, saw a quick,
burning flush upon the cheek that had so long been
colorless. For several minutes the unaccustomed carmine had lain there, while the wan hand, so long idle,
toyed with a curl that dangled against her forehead,
then fell helpless again in her lap, and the flush paled

out of her cheek.   When the dance ended Miannetta
arose, lifting her hand high above her head as betok-
ening a desire to be heard.   Every brave and every
maid sank silently to the ground while she spoke.

"Brothers, in the shade of yonder trees, when the
Autumn wind was blowing, I found this poor stricken
girl, and I gave you my word, with her to wait your
will.   You know with what faith my mother's line
bore the sacred flame through all the 'long house of
the League.'   That faith is mine.   Now by certain
signs I know the time draws nigh when light will
come again to these starry eyes, and sound to the long
silent lips.   But if she wakens here both light and
voice will last a moment only, for she will die!
Brothers, I have said?"

She sat down and the chieftain who had put her
under oath, arose and with the wampum in his hand
approached her, saying:

"Miannetta has spoken truly, her faith has been
proven hundreds of years by her unbroken lineage.
It shall be unquestioned now.   By this sacred token
she is absolved of her oath.   If she can save from
death the 'silent lily' she is free to take her to her
far off home and Springing Panther will die!"

He raised Nellie's hand to his lips, severed a curl
from her head and noiselessly departed.   The whole
band of dusky excursionists defiled to the water's
edge and "swift were the barks that bore them from
the lovely moss-grown isle."   Miannetta made rapid
preparations (assisted by Springing Panther, who however never ventured to look upon Nellie's face that he
had grown to love too well) for the long journey which

she knew must be accomplished by easy stages. Thirty stalwart Indians went with them, packing ponies bearing the provisions and camp equipage and canoes. Nellie, by the chief's orders, traveled as before, borne on the shoulders of Indians in a comfortable litter.

Two weary weeks they were on the march. They reached the boundary of the "The Maples" estate just at nightfall. Three trusty Indians remained with them. the rest had swiftly retraced their steps from the last encampment, for it was not safe for such a large force to be in the neighborhood of the whites. Miannetta took unusual care that quiet reigned about the camp and that her charge slept early. After Nellie was sound asleep, she left her and wended her way under the bright moonlight to the farm house. All was still in the kitchen, but a plaintive strain reached her ears from the side porch where Robert sat whistling. She approached, and, through the breezy lift of the vines, saw his noble face which bore the refining evidences of great sorrow. Gently she spoke :

"Robert, I have accomplished my mission."

"Miannetta! Where is Nellie?" he quickly asked.

"She lives ; come with me and you shall see her."

Together they walked toward the camp, Robert's eager step showing his impatience of her moderation.

"I can not keep pace with you, Miannetta ; pardon my impatience, but I long so to clasp my darling sister once more in my arms."

"And yet, Robert, you must promise me you will

not touch her, will not breathe a word in her ear, that you will be satisfied to look upon her sleeping face."

He looked wonderingly in her eyes. A terrible thought crossed his soul; a thought of the possible extremity to which his pure and beautiful sister might have been driven by savage passion. The thought was maddening. Laying his hand upon his companion's arm almost fiercely, and sending a look that explained his thought to her very heart. In a husky whisper he said:

"And is it worse than death! O, tell me not that, in God's name!"

"Robert, you do not comprehend me, poor boy! As unpolluted as the snow on the mountain top do I restore Nellie to you, but she now walks in darkness."

Then she told him all, of Nellie's long, long night, of which she seemed to have almost a premonition, the reader will remember, in that last good night exchanged with her father and mother a year ago.

Relieved of that one blighting suspicion regarding her, Robert listened almost calmly to the long story Miannetta told him, and acquiesced when she added: "To-morrow, as you know, is the anniversary of fearful events. Our prophets say, that certain influences prevail on certain days of the year, and recur in more or less force each anniversary: who knows what may befall Nellie to-morrow?"

"Yes, Miannetta, the idea is not new, nor entertained alone by your prophets. Our wisest, most philosophic minds believe that. But what do you propose doing? I know you have a plan, or you would have brought Nellie home to-night."

"I can not tell you all my plans, but this part is for you. Wait to-morrow till she comes to you and whatever whim she may have, do not thwart her, or enlighten her in the least; she must not know of your parents' death; she must not see the new faces at the farm house. To her questioning your answers must accord as far as possible with the answer evidently expected by her; there must be no shock. She must seem to take up her life just as she laid it down one year ago. Do you comprehend me?"

"Yes, and I am impressed with the cleverness of your plan. Now let me look at her."

He followed, stooping to enter the little bedroom of blankets, which was lighted by the bright camp fire before it. She lay like an exquisite piece of sculptured marble. One fair hand was beneath her head, crowned with its halo of sunset hair. Her slumber was so deep and motionless that he felt an icy chill gather about his heart. Miannetta read his fear in his face, and whispered:

"Do not fear; so she has slept each night for months."

His tears fell fast, as he bent yearningly over her, but those were not all tears of sadness. He went outside, and, seated by the fire, watched the camp till morning. He went home, and with Mr. McDougal, brought them breakfast, which, however, the three Indians did not share; they had left the night before, and were now far on their way toward Lake Itasca.

The warm Summer sun had passed the meridian, when Miannetta took from a bag the dress of dark

print, which Nellie had worn on that sad day, one
year ago, long preserved for this very purpose, this
very hour. It required some ripping of seams and
re-sewing to fit the form, which in the year had
rounded into more perfect womanliness. While thus
engaged, her hand trembled with excitement and fear,
lest, after all, she had not found the key to this poor
child's thralldom ; but there is an intuition in woman,
superior to all the science of professions and schools.

Nellie sat, unmoved as ever, under the hair dress-
ing and robing process. She took no notice when
Mr. McDougal and a farm hand lifted the litter,
hitherto borne by Indians, and carried her through
the woods. The sun was getting low ; Miannetta
looked anxiously upon its rapid decline, and then,
noticing Nellie's hand move to her head and take
hold of a curl, pulling it out straight and winding it
again about her finger, while a flush lay upon her
face, she whispered to the bearers :

"Increase your speed. In Heaven's name
hurry."

They did so, and set her down as Miannetta
directed, by the spring, then hurried away. She
made an effort to get upon her feet, but fell heavily,
Miannetta assisted her to rise, and then drew back
out of sight.

For a moment, Nellie stood as usual. A cow was
lowing in the lane that led from the clover field to
the dairy house; from a calf she had been Nellie's. The
spring gurgled, as its waters sought the channel under
the dairy wall over the smooth stone floor, and to
that sound she suddenly inclined her ear, that ever

seemed to be listening. The sun has gone, a flush
warms up her either cheek ; a light of intelligence
steals into her eyes ; she turns and looks upon the
familiar sights of her childhood's years, and womanhood's dawn—house, trees, and prairie—with almost
a smile on her glowing lips. She bends over the
spring, dips her hand in the cool water, and scatter-
ing the drops upon the grass at her feet, lays it
moist upon her forehead, while she gathers up the
threads of broken melody (dropped at the close of
the first line of her song, commenced a year ago this
very moment), and the air thrills to her sweet voice.
Hark !

> "From every cum'bring care,
> And spend the hour of closing day,
> In humble, grateful prayer."

While she sings she is following the path that led
out upon the prairie. She gathers a generous bouquet
of the rich purple flowers, and returns with them to
the spring. She takes out the vase so long concealed
and dipping it full of water, walks up the path
while arranging her flowers ; holding it up and
smiling with satisfaction at the perfection of her
work. She seems oblivious of all else, till, stepping
into the kitchen door, she meets Robert. She set
her flowers in a chair and threw her arms about
his neck, crying :

"O, brother Robbie, how glad I am to see you ;
you came sooner than I expected. See our flowers,
how perfect they are ; I was going to put them in
your room."

"I brought you a present; another vase, the twin I think, of this. Shall we go up to my room and see it?"

"Have you already been there?"

"Yes, and inadvertently left the vase."

"Why, what child is this?" she asked, as Ruth Palmer's boy, escaping from restraint, came in and ran to Robert, who explained—

"A little orphan child I brought you to take care of."

"What's his name?"

"Freddie Palmer," laughed the child, whom she kissed and said:

"Two little Freddie Palmers for me to love. Did you meet father and mother, Robert?"

"Yes."

Ah! how deep the wound opened by the recollection of that meeting.

"And tell them of this beautiful little fellow I am to care for."

He avoided an answer by saying:

"Come I want to compare the vases."

"Yes, in a minute, when I introduce Freddie to old Hector."

"No, no, I shall be jealous of both of them, if you don't come now."

He took her arm and led her away up-stairs, lest some change below should attract her. On the stair she stopped and called:

"Cloe! Cloe! She does not answer me, I must go and find her, and tell her to give Freddie some bread and milk, and when he goes to sleep to put him in my bed."

"Never mind now. She knows well enough what you will expect her to do. Come, I never like to wait when I wish particularly to do anything," he said, impatiently.

They entered the room, she advanced with her vase of flowers to the table, singing :

"Bring flowers to strew in the conqueror's path,
He has shaken a world with his stormy wrath.

"Forgive me, Robbie, I did mean to cry all the time when you came home."

"So sorry, eh ? "

"No," she said with a peal of laughter, " not sorry you came, but sorry that you must go again. But instead of being sad I am so joyous."

"Go where ? " he said, forgetting himself.

"Why, into the army, where you belong, Rob."

"But if I do not go ? "

"Robert ! " She looked at him very gravely, then continued, " Will your staying bring a blush to your brow, or grief to mother's heart ? Is there no shame in it, since, having enlisted, it will seem strange that you remain at home ? "

" No, Nellie, I shall not blush ; there is no grief, no shame ; it is not strange."

"Then I will laugh and you *shall* not be sad."

Miannetta came in with a lighted lamp and said,

" Why, Nellie, you are wildly joyous to-night."

" Behold my inspiration. My brother 's come to go no more." She sat down on his knee and putting her arms about his neck gave way to uncontrollable laughter, greatly to Robert's alarm, for he feared her mind would never entirely recover its equilibrium. She was so excited that he looked to Miannetta to stay the tide of tumultuous joy. But oh, who could speak the word to that lovely, joyous creature, that would shadow her spirit, just burst so radiantly from long continued gloom. Miannetta came close to her and said :

" I put a light in your room, Nellie, thinking you would be there. Shall I extinguish it ? "

" No ; I am going down now. Will you go with me, Robbie ? "

They all went down together. Robert had taken care everything should be as she left it, and she entered with his arm about her. She drew him along to the wardrobe and laughingly said as she shut the door,

" I do n't want that thing gaping at me."

" What do you read these days ? " he asked, taking up the book that she had lain down a year ago.

" Nothing to-night. I promised mother not to read."

" Well, let us sit down and talk then, instead."

" Yes, when I get my glass of milk. Cloe has forgotten to bring it; or no, she must be rocking Freddie to sleep."

" I will go for it," said Robert, " and prove my love by willing service."

She took the milk from him when he returned and drank it, saying :

" If that glass of milk were to be given to me at

the North Pole, I should know it was Zephyr's milk, it is so sweet."

A long talk followed. She told him all the little home gossip in which her mother figured extensively, and his tears were many times nearly discovered when the conversation dwelt upon events of a year ago.

"I am tired, Robbie. Will you excuse me to-night from visiting any more ? To-morrow morning I want to go out with you and sit on our old favorite tree-chair (the very spot where her mother was buried) and tell you some of my wonderful thoughts while reading that book. I dare not tell mother, she would put the book away."

" Well, you put the thoughts away, little sister, to-night, and to-morrow we will compare our thinking on your book. Good night."

He kissed her and left the room, but not to go to bed. When all was quiet, he, with Miannetta and Mrs. McDougal, went in to look upon the precious, fair face. A warm, healthy tinge was on her cheek, and in her slumber, blessed with pleasant dreams, she moved naturally, and threw a white, round, dimpled arm above her head. Smiling in her sleep, she mur-mured coaxingly,

"Mother, do n't tell Robbie. He 'll laugh at me."

When the women raised their moist eyes, Robert had left the room, unable to control his deep emotion. Endowed with strength of mind rare in one so young, Robert had still a heart sensitive to smallest wounds. Against that heart of late had been directed shafts steeped in sorrow, but though it quivered and bled, it had never grown bitter. As one who walks in dark-

ness, amid dangers, clings to the guide he feels but
can not see, there had been a clinging in all his sorrow
to Him who whispered, "Fear not, for I am with
thee." He drank in the soothing influences of the
moon's rays as he walked up and down the graveled
drive under the trees, where after a while Miannetta
joined him.

"Are you not very weary?" he asked.

"No," she answered absently; "at least, I am not
ready to retire. I have something to say to you.
May I say it now?"

"Certainly," he said, and offered her his arm.
"Has not the service you have rendered me given
you the right to command, rather than to beg attention?"

"I just came from Nellie's room; her sleep is as
natural as an infant's. You will tell her all to-morrow?"

"Yes, if you think best. I came out to think
how best to do it, I am so fearful she may relapse."

"I have no fears now," said Miannetta. "One
night of natural rest, I think, was essential to thoroughly restore her and call into healthy activity long
suspended faculties. These fragile women often bear
sorrow very composedly. Her late disability was
physical, the result of a blow she never realized. I
have known women that she resembles, who, with
the appearance of extreme delicacy, possessed powers
of almost marvelous endurance. I believe she will
bear this better, perhaps, than you have done."

"I hope she may," he said fervently. "But,
Miannetta, aside from the death of father and mother,

aside from the anxiety I have felt for Nellie, I have
waded through waves of sorrow that would easily
overwhelm stronger men than I."

Miannetta took Annette's picture from her pocket
and laying it in his hand, said:

"Tell me truly, I do not ask through idle curiosity,
do you love the original of this?"

"Truly, devotedly, as God is my witness."

"She is your affianced wife?"

"She was."

"Who broke the engagement?"

"She did."

"When?"

"Shortly after the massacre. Why, she never
told me."

"Have you a suspicion?"

"I believe her mother lies at the bottom of it.
She is a cold, haughty woman, and from my first acquaintance with the family has made me feel a want
of cordiality on her part, which has apparently deep⸗
ened almost into dislike. Her unladylike treatment of
and objections to me, I can not understand. Before
addressing Annette, I obtained her father's sanction
and consent. I believe in her affection—that it is in-
alienably mine."

"Ah, Robert, you do not know her mother. Believe me, she is the cause of your misunderstanding
with Annette, but not in the way you think, and if
you could know all, you would love the poor girl none
the less. It is a mysterious barrier—mysterious to
you, but clear as noonday to me, who, knowing her
well, can guess her secret."

" Yet the barrier seems eternal. No word gave me any hope of its removal."

" That depends upon *you*, strange as it may seem. The hour will come when you shall have to decide if the barrier shall be eternal."

" You know what it is, and that it rests with me to remove it, and yet do not enlighten me. Miannetta, is this kind ? "

" Robert, I dare not take the responsibility. Wait! Farther than to express my belief that the clouds will ultimately disappear, I have no words to comfort you."

" I am so little used to comfort, perhaps it is as well to administer it sparingly," he said, smiling sadly. " My heart is sore for all the sorrow that has been laid upon it. Life became suddenly a weary blank. For awhile I lost all interest, even in my military duties. I was callous to fear, for what physical suffering could be more poignant than the grief that was consuming me ! I was reckless of danger ; what was there in life that made it worth preserving ? It is all a dream, the scenes I passed through, the battles, the charge, the carnage. Once, I remember, I saw a face —that of a dead drummer-boy—as we charged a redoubt—fair and slight, with a mass of hair like Nellie's, but dappled with blood. The thought pierced me, ' So Nellie may have lain.' I recall our exposure now, but it was not terrible to me then. I was still in my dream. I felt that in all the world I had no one left to sorrow if I fell, to rejoice if I survived. I went on with others less desperate, but more nobly courageous. A color-bearer fell where four others lay dead. I caught the quivering staff from his hand, and firmly planted it where he had intended to, and still my dream went on in a whirling, melancholy maze. A ball struck my right arm and the pain brought me to a realizing sense of my position, the only upright man on the parapet which that flag now proclaimed as ours. To-day that banner hangs in the State House, a tattered memento of tremendous slaughter."

"And that banner cost you your right arm?" said Miannetta.

"Amputation seemed unavoidable and barely saved my life. Since the 20th of last May my coat-sleeve has been useless except to better set off the epaulet that since then has decorated my shoulder."

"I noticed with what care you avoided a disclosure to poor Nellie of the false arm; but of your wound, was it long in healing?"

"On the contrary, it healed too soon. I came home immediately. My health made service impossible and care imperative. Under Mrs. McDougal's nursing I got well rapidly, and thinking myself sufficiently strong, I went back to the field of action again the last of June, in time for the surrender of that Rebel Sebastopol, Vicksburg. But the exposure and exertion, together with the warm weather, proved too much for my strength, which I had believed greater, and the wound broke out again, resulting in a fever which lasted only a few days, but was very severe. They brought me home when I was too ill to know it, and again Mr. and Mrs. McDougal nursed me back to life, which to-night begins to seem more worth having. Miannetta, my more than friend, how shall I ever liquidate my obligations to you for bringing Nellie back to my desolate home?"

She whispered something in his ear. It must have been something agreeable, for he looked into her face with sudden animation and surprise, and a new hope, that, somehow through her, the mystery that enveloped his love would unfold, cheered his sad heart.

That night, when he besought God's favor, it was not without hope he pronounced the names of Nellie and Annette.

Early rising was the rule at The Maples. At six o'clock, Nellie, attired in snowy lawn, entered the breakfast room, where Robert and Miannetta were waiting for her. Coming forward, she reached out both hands to take her brother's, as of old. He advanced to meet her, and took her left hand, swinging her round somewhat suddenly, but successfully averting for that time her notice of his lifeless arm. Then leading her to the breakfast table, he said:

"You and I must preside this morning, with Miannetta for our guest."

Nellie bowed very gravely and began to pour the coffee, playfully laying great stress upon her importance and dignity, yet with all her playfulness showing how gracefully she might fill the chair, from which her mother had dispensed her noble hospitality.

Breakfast over, they went (Nellie and Robert) arm in arm into the parlor and stood by the window, Nellie tapping on the window-pane and singing,

" A steed came at morning; no rider was there,
But the bridle was wet with the sign of despair."

A gate had been carelessly left open. Old
Deacon had walked into the yard, round the house,
and right to the window where they stood—she still
wondering why her mother did not come. With a
little scream, she pointed to the old horse, and grasping Robert's arm, exclaimed :

"Something must have happened, Robbie! Where
can mother be ? "

"Come with me, darling, I will show you," he
said, and led her out to the graves and told her all.
Her grief was uncontrollable. She fell upon the
graves, kissing the earth that lay upon her mother's
breast, and calling upon her piteously; then she rose,
only to fling herself again upon the mound that hid
them from her view, to weep, pray and mourn,
calling them touchingly.

After a time she grew calm, and Robert, lifting
her up, led her away to their mother's room, where
for hours they sat, recalling her noble words and acts.
Then after another visit to the graves, they returned to
the parlor. Miannetta brought in Mr and Mrs. McDougal, and Nellie was made acquainted with all the sad
change in their home—the new faces there. Robert,
who noted the expression of her face, saw that she
already loved these people who had been so considerate
of him. Freddie Palmer was almost smothered
with her caresses, and she said, in a voice choked with
sobs :

"Don't you remember, Robbie, I said I would

care for Ruth's baby, if anything ever happened to Ruth herself?"

"Yes, sister; and I believe you are restored in part to fulfill that promise. But great duties require a proportionate fortitude and self denial. You must not indulge in the grief that will shadow his young life. We have, both of us, grave duties to perform, and eminent patterns to imitate, and must be careful that we may not fall short of the perfection they wished us to attain."

"Let us help one another, brother, that our walk upon the earth may be light as befitteth the children of saints, who must ever watch and rejoice over our progress."

So life was taken up again at The Maples—a life, 't is true, with a painful void, for the death angel had been unsparing, but there was yet a healthy cheerfulness pervading it. Robert was now altogether at home—his health utterly forbidding his return to the army, or as he expressed it, his "conscience forbidding the crippled service of a left-hand sword."

CHAPTER XVIII.

HEART'S-EASE.

TIME, ever on the wing, has brought us to Autumn again—that of 1864. Its signs are unmistakable. The trees are gorgeous with Autumnal tints. The grass is crisp and sere. The cricket's chirp is shrill, as if the early frosts had so disconcerted the piper's throat, that she sings perforce in the wrong key.

Herbert and Phil Ellis are busy as bees and more noisy, gathering cauliflowers and onions into heaps, and loading them onto their diminutive cart, which holds by actual count five large heads and ten small ones. To this cart is hitched the mettlesome little Besom, a manageable creature, between whom and the boys there is a perfect understanding. He stands gravely, with half-closed eyes save when roused by some louder burst of boyish glee, when he pricks up his ears, switches his long tail, and straightening himself up trim and firm, communicates by champing bit the assurance that he fully enters into the spirit of his loving little masters' frolic.

On the other side of the garden, digging potatoes, is the whole-souled boy, though a practical joker, Tad Wilson. He pauses in his work, now and then, to deliver himself of sundry odd speeches, only half understood by his limited audience, but received, nevertheless, with rounds of applause. The cheers and laughter strike Mrs. Ellis' ears, as she sews by the open window, and she smiles affectionately and says to herself, "Bless their young, joyous hearts!"

Captain Ellis smiles while he works, shingling the new barn, and wonders, between his hammer strokes, if there is no limit to boyish nonsense.

Tad stoops to examine his work close and longer than usual, and then calls drolly:

"I say, Herbert, did you ever practice much in 'Tithmeric?'"

"Not much; but I know the tables, and have ciphered as far as Long Division."

"Well, I never ciphered much by rule, but I've just now did a neat sum in Subtraction, with my hoe —took one toe from ten! Look 'e!"

"What is it, Tad"

Tad held up one of his great toes which he had mistaken for a potato, half concealed and half revealed as it was, by the dirt of the hill in which he was digging. He had struck at it with the sharp hoe, and nearly severed it from his foot, and with his usual impetuosity and fearlessness, had then completed the dismemberment with his knife. The sight of the blood and pain of his foot sickened him, and he sat down, while Herbert ran for his mother and Phil for his father. With many expressions of sympathy, he was carried to the house, where the wounded member was dressed carefully and laid on a pillow in a chair in front of him. He, regarding it with a comical face, said:

"I'm glad it's off! It was always bothering

me, one shape or 'nother, no matter what I went into."

While thus putting on a brave face, Gus and 'Lizbeth Harkness drove up in the bright, new lumber wagon. They entered the house unperceived, and in an adjoining room overheard Tad's short, comical speech, at the close of which they came forward, learned the nature of the accident, and expressed their sympathy. 'Lizbeth, laughing, said:

"Nobody will ever tread on that toe again! will they, Tad?"

"Not if I know myself," was the reply.

"Now, Tad," said Gus, "you just go in for a good time. Pass yourself round while you're sick. After you get tired staying here, let the boys bring you on their cart to our house. When that gets to be an old story, I will harness up the creams and take you wherever you say. Your home is everywhere now. I am glad you are in good spirits, for I have got a little news that might make you feel bad, but you mustn't let it, for you have got a plenty of friends, and—"

"What is the news?" interrupted the eager boy.

"Your father and Johnny have re-enlisted in a veteran regiment."

"What, won't pap be home this month with Mr. Porter and the others?" said Tad, with a quavering voice.

"No, my little major; Mr. Porter arrived at The Maples last night, and is there yet. I came from there here. Your father and Johnny sent love to you and some money, but will not come right away.

But do n't take it to heart so, Tad. I thought you was the bravest boy in all the world."

The boy that could cut off his toe and laugh over it, was sobbing now. Hope deferred had made his young heart sick. No word of compassion could ease the bosom that ached for want of a father's tender presence. Mr. Ellis took him up and laid him on the bed in the spare bedroom, and closing the door softly, thoughtfully left him alone with his disappointment and his tears. Homeless as he was, yet to every house in the neighborhood he was welcome, whenever and as long as he chose to abide there. Mrs. Ellis considered him a member of her family, alternating with uncle Caree Smith and the Maynards in giving him a home. Always lending the help of willing, cheerful hands in the hurry of planting, hoeing and harvesting at either place, he was a universal favorite; manners unpolished and rude of speech, but heart warm and true. The whole neighborhood, young and old, shared his sorrow and now sympathized in his disappointment. Cheerful, ready hands nursed him.

Capt. Ellis, with a few of the original volunteers, had been mustered out of Federal service the previous May. The history of the successes of the army in which they participated since we last saw them on the gloomy Rappahannock is so familiar to the reader that a repetition would be superfluous. Indeed, it was not my intention to follow them in all the incidents of the war in which they participated.

A handful of men, the remnant of some of the regiments that, three years ago, *saw* the Rebels at the first Bull Run, and were now *conquering* the Rebels in the Wilderness, were drawn up one morning to receive their discharge papers. They had stacked arms for the last time, within the sound of and not beyond the dangerous missiles of the deadly conflict then going on. Some apprehension had been felt the night before, that now their time was out they would not be allowed to go. At all events, the commanding general seemed determined they should work to the last. They had been under steady fire for many hours, and at last, in the evening, had been ordered to take respite in a trench, after an exhaustive and long continued struggle. They lay with their faces on their arms, without exchanging a word, but the half-suppressed sighs that would escape in spite of all effort, along the prostrate line, spoke, more than words could do, the hopelessness of the hour.

Suddenly a shell went screaming over them and struck the bank just above them, covering them with fragments of earth, announcing the frightful truth, that they were exposed to an enfilading fire, even while at rest. Still as they lay, speechless, what throbbing life was in that trench. If those guns should be lowered a trifle, what a furrow of death they would plow. Capt. Ellis spoke once :

"Keep up your hearts, boys. Unless those muzzles are put down, we shall be able to stand it."

"Arrah, yer honor, it's very aisy to say so, but thry it awhile. It's not aisy, at all, at all, to stand on yer belly when even the shmell of whishky is all gone from yer canteen, an' sin' daylight not a one of us has tipped the wink across the mess. The gineral has no right to hould us in sich exthremity, jist the last minit of our sarvice, begorra," grumbled Mike, without raising his head.

"Hush up, Mike, or the Rebs will get better range, and there will be corpses in this grave with never a b'iled shirt on," said a dashing young corporal, in a sonorous whisper.

"Och, bye, yer always thinkin' o' the decorations. Ye'd feel warse about the shot that peeled them sthripes off ye than the cannon charge that sint ye with niver a confession to judgment. Sure now, a good soldier is willing to die naked, an' he can be covered wid glory."

That poetic jest was Mike's last.

Just then a bomb, heralded by a deep hoarse cry, swung in its airy orbit, and coming swiftly down, plunged into that trench. Through that earthquake shock, Mike had passed to immortality. Those momentary lights, the wide-spreading glare of fearful discharges, flung back, as they were, by thousands of burnished gun-stocks, and the little pools of water here and there, revealed an awful sight. Dying and slain steeds in one gory tangle of trunk, harness, and half-severed limbs; officers in rich uniforms, and privates in plain coarse blue, side by side, were evidence how truly death obliterates distinctions. Men with stretchers, picking their way through the horrible debris, bear their bleeding burdens to burial or lingering pain, while on every side are the sharp crack and the incessant flash of musketry, and the grim, dirt-stained soldiery that press on, a living wall, toward the foe. All this beneath a cloudless Spring

Y

sky, bestrewed with glittering stars, and the May winds breathing cool and fragrant through the boughs of the wilderness wood, that are green and fresh and guileless, as if, instead of these grim horrors, they were the fairy haunt of innocence and love. But morning came at last to the sleepless men in the trench—a morning, chill and comfortless with rain and piercing wind. After a comfortless breakfast, they were ordered to headquarters and there received their discharge. Stiff and weary, their tread was heavy as they stepped in perfect time with the grand old "Hail Columbia," as they marched to the waiting train that was to bear them—Hark! that cheer shall tell you—"HOME."

Surely that train was drawn by a slow locomotive, for those eager men have made the journey home over and over again in fancy, while on their way.

Once again the train stopped at a beautiful little town in Ohio. Herbert Gray was observed to exchange a significant glance with Capt. Ellis. A few moments afterward he was seen on the platform of the depot, deeply engrossed in conversation with Walter Meade, the long-missing soldier. When again the conductor shouted, "all aboard," the young officer failed, for some reason, to hear it.

One by one the lumbering old stage dropped its passengers, pausing a moment, and then again its wheels hummed on over the smooth road. Conversation since nightfall had been very dull, each man was busy thinking, and his thoughts were such as could not be expressed, and, perhaps, would not be interesting to the others. Heavy sighs were exchanged as they passed the ruins of Ben Palmer's house, pleasant exclamations as they passed the Maples, and—

"Wonder who lives in Jehial Smith's house," as they drove by and perceived it lighted up.

A husky "good night, comrades," had been repeated at the door, until now, at last, only Gus Harkness and Capt. Ellis are left of the seven who entered the stage two days since. And yet the silence remains unbroken; a silence full of dismal forebodings for one, sweet, beautiful fancies for the other, in which he already enfolds in manly arms the blessed trio awaiting him within a half mile. A light twinkles through the trees from the window of his new home, built on the site of the old one. The vehicle stops, his baggage is thrown off, and, from an open door, two fine boys run out, shouting his welcome home. A short embrace must answer for them now, for in the shadow beside the gate, a bright little woman awaits his kiss, with speechless lips, but a heart throbbing warmest welcome. With his arm about her he went up the door steps, entered the house, forgetful in his great happiness of his lonely fellow-passenger and comrade, who was now recalled to him by a sight of that comrade's wife coming forward to greet him.

He ran out quickly to call Gus, but the coach was already gone, and Gus with it.

Much regret was felt for this, as Ellis termed it, "unpardonable forgetfulness and selfishness."

"I know how he feels, poor fellow, and how disappointed he will be to find no wife awaiting him. Why, I should have died, to-night, if mine had not been here," and he clasped his Kitty in his arms, and

kissed her again and again, till her round, full face
grew still rosier.

'Lizbeth replied to him coldly:

'Well, I do n't see how a man can expect to have
a wife at both ends of his journey. He should have
brought his yellow girl and her child along, if he did
not fancy being alone."

An angry crimson mantled her cheek as she
spoke, and she fairly trembled as with palsy, under
the astonished gaze of Capt. Ellis, as he exclaimed :

"What in the world do you mean, 'Lizbeth Harkness ? "

"Do n't call me by that name ; keep it for her
who has the *latest* claim," she said, spitefully.

Mrs. Ellis here interposed an explanation. She
had long known a coolness existed between 'Lizbeth
and Gus, but till that day had been ignorant of its
cause. 'Lizbeth wished to remain with her to avoid
meeting her husband, who she rightly supposed
would go on to his former home.

She did not mean to see him till armed with the
proofs of his guilt, which, strange to say, she had
not doubted. All this Mrs. Ellis told her husband,
while 'Lizbeth, sinking into a chair, sobbed bitterly;
her face buried in the folds of her dress. Capt. Ellis
listened patiently; and then said:

"'Lizbeth, pardon me if I seem severe. I
mean it for your good. You have made yourself
very unhappy by crediting the story of a man, who
not only disgraced his manhood, but sought to
involve womanhood as well. A person with whom
you had no business away from your mother's roof.

You have not only made yourself miserable without any cause, but have wounded the heart that was true to you as the needle to the pole. Gus has suffered untold agony by your mysterious silence of two years' duration. That story was a fabrication from beginning to end, and you woefully sinned against your husband, by listening to it for an instant. He has been under my eye almost constantly since he enlisted, and I do not believe that in that time he has had a thought, or a word, for any woman, save the wife whom he loved and trusted, as few men love and trust, but who has returned his confidence with cruel doubting and a silence that has grieved his noble heart to the very core."

When her husband began to speak, Mrs. Ellis, with a woman's quick instinct, divined what he would say, and knowing how it would end, had gone out, and putting Tad Wilson onto the back of fleet-footed Besom, she told him to "overtake the stage and send Gus Harkness back."

Entering the house, she delayed the supper, that was nearly ready when Captain Ellis came, in as many ways as possible. 'Lizbeth sat still in the chair, weeping and reproaching herself for the wrongs she could now see she had been guilty of against her faithful Gus. Mrs. Ellis at last placed the pot of fragrant tea upon the damask-covered table, with its tempting dishes. Just then her listening ear caught the ring of a firm, military step upon the walk, and motioning to her husband, he followed her from the room. The opposite door opened, and they caught a glimpse of the fine, manly face, radiant with expectation—heard

'Lizbeth's cry of surprise, ere it was smothered in the great black whiskers of Gus Harkness.

Gus never questioned his wife as to the motive of her ride with Langmere the night of her supposed capture by the Indians. There was a vague notion in his heart that she had accepted Langmere's invitation through the promptings of the lingering coquetry of her nature ; but he could not reproach her for that, for well he remembered that when most coquettish with himself, he had loved her the most madly.

Langmere was the villain who would have taken advantage of her innocence and love of admiration, and upon Langmere he vented the bitter reproaches of a man who, though not actually dishonored, had been saved from it only by the merest chance. He had no pity, no forgiveness, because the offender was in his grave. Often times when madly recollecting the unfortunate adventures of 'Lizbeth with Langmere in the woods, he would say to her :

"Fool, that I was, when I fired at him that day. Ignorant of the base wrong he had intended towards you, I prayed earnestly that my gun might not be loaded with the fatal bullet ; but now, to the latest day of my existence, I shall never cease to hope that it was loaded with ball and *my bullet killed him*."

A few weeks after the arrival of Captain Ellis, all theories regarding the strange failure of Herbert Gray to get "aboard" at that distant Ohio station, in response to the conductor's call, were set at rest by an announcement, contained in some newspapers received at Clipnockum post-office, to wit :

Married, on the evening of June 15, 1864, in ——, Ohio, at the residence of the bride's father, Captain Herbert Gray, late of the Federal volunteer service, and Miss Alice Meade."

A few days after reading this notice, the neighborhood was thrown into a "positive conniption," as 'Lizbeth said, by the arrival, in an elegant carriage, of Captain Herbert Gray and his lovely young bride. The happy pair were hospitably entertained many days at Captain Ellis'.

It was interesting to hear Herbert and his sister compare notes of their individual adventures "by field and flood;" to listen to the story of their captivity and escape from enemies, so different, and in regions so remote from each other and from the peaceful home where they were recounting them. Those adventures, similar in more ways than one, were particularly so in their deliverance from peril by the friends Providence had raised up from among the humble and despised colored races. As Mrs. Ellis would never forget how Miannetta had been chiefly instrumental in preventing her recapture, neither would Herbert ever forget old Whiting, the crazy boatman of the James river, who taught him how to sing for his dinner, and how to "trabble de hard, wat'ry roads ob Jordan."

Herbert and his young wife settled in St. P——, where the former entered upon the professional career for which he had fitted himself before the war, and to which he now applied himself with renewed vigor. His fidelity to justice whenever he represented a client, was almost severe, and many times he refused to defend a case which he believed was based upon ex-

tortion and wrong.   He carried this peculiarity to
such an extent that in a few months he established a
reputation as the "poor man's lawyer." Rich men,
as well, often sought his office when business of grave
importance had to be intrusted to legal hands.   Mr.
La Moore, who had failed to establish his claim among
the sharp Parisian lawyers, had returned to St. P——,
and placed his business in Herbert's hands ; but after
each consultation grew graver, until his gravity settled into a profound melancholy.   His two eldest children entered joyfully into a plan he proposed, for a
change of scene—a journey, in his own easy family
carriage, into the northern part of the State, accompanied only by them, as soon as the weather was cool
enough to make traveling agreeable.

We will now take a last look at some of the characters that have figured more or less conspicuously in
our long story, ere we pass to more interesting details.

The gloom that has hung over Maple Range since
the massacre, is gradually clearing off, and the settlement, ere another Spring, will no doubt show a profusion of roses.   Uncle Carce and grandma Smith, in
the blossom of good old age, "both still sixteen,"
occupy the cosy block house " across the lot," leading
to which are innumerable well-worn paths, attesting
the popularity of the dear white-headed pair.   Mr.
Porter boards with them.   He wears the appearance
of a second youth. Sometimes he seems rather absent
in conversation, and pauses as though listening for
the curious and inapt interruptions of his deaf spouse.
Gus Harkness noticing this once irreverently said
to 'Lizbeth :

" The only real mercy the Indians can be credited with was relieving Mr. Porter from the batteries of his wife, and at the same time affording her an opportunity to ascertain to a certainty the fate of ' Samantha's man.' "

Asa Birdsell, whose farm adjoins that of uncle Caree, and with his family escaped the notice of the Indians, is making handsome improvements with the money he has saved during the term of his service in the war.

Mr. Ellis has the finest, most commodious buildings; but then, his wife's good taste had draughted the plans, and who should know better than a farmer's wife, in what consists the convenience of a farm house and its appurtenances?

Mr. Center is supposed to be still with the Indians. His house and farm are taken by a stranger, with a large family of bright-looking boys and girls.

Gus has just completed his house in the Hollow, and taken as a boarder the dashing young tradesman who has built a new brick store opposite the old " Watkins stand," and is doing a smashing business, " *they say* " in the dry goods and grocery line.

Reader, are you thinking of the possible conquests in store for our impressible friend, 'Lizbeth. However, as she is now under the guardianship of a loving and forgiving husband, I must say that if she outrages his feelings again, she certainly will not be worthy of our regret, though we shall pity Gus. Mr. Cross, with his physical peculiarities intensified by the death of his sainted Polly Ann, resides with them, in a state of painful indecision on all matters of

16*

moment, as he can not know just "her sentiments," since her translation to the other world. Paddy O'Shannon, who was drafted, was wounded at Port Hudson, one burning July day, and died in the hospital that night. His wife and children were victims of the Indian outrage. His log hut has fallen into ruin.

A handsome new school-house is nearly finished in the Hollow, and the schoolmaster, who is "abroad," has promised to occupy the evenings of the coming Winter term profitably to old and young with lyceums, grammar and spelling schools. Mr. Sutton is about returning from the East, where, with his family, he has been the last three years, to occupy the new parsonage in Clipnockum, and perform the duties of his sacred office.

Measures are on *foot* to increase the gayety of the coming Winter, and Pomp (who, with Dinah, has brought up at last in Minnesota, and bought the house and eighty that Jehial Smith used to own), in consideration of a written promise of a good cow when the work is done, has agreed positively "to rosin the bow " on stated occasions, for the benefit of lads and lassies in the woods and Hollow.

Lincoln's proclamation of emancipation made a free nigger of Pomp, but it will require an amendment of the constitution and *his heart* before he can be a man. In his present neighborhood, the cultivation of self-respect will be greatly facilitated, and may, let us hope, lead to the practice of virtue.

Robert and Nellie Maynard are still at The Maples, quietly enjoying the many good things Providence and a productive estate of three hundred improved acres afford. The crops have been abundant; the herd sent to market in September netted a comfortable sum. A part of the elegant front just being finished is to be fitted up as a library, and some large boxes of books have lately arrived. By all appearances, The Maples will be a grand place to spend the Winter.

Mr. and Mrs. McDougal seem to be necessary fixtures, being as warmly established in the hearts of Nellie and her brother as they are firmly in their home. Miannetta also seems as much at home here as she did in the little village on the shore of the Itasca.

It is a warm November day, such a one as comes rarely so late in the season. The noisy blackbirds had their convention a month ago, and left *en masse* for Summer's climes. But the Winter birds, that sing loudest when it is coldest,—the blue jays, in dandy tuft and feathers, are shrieking and flitting from bough to bough of the maple trees under which Robert and Nellie are standing. They are discussing, with some difference of taste, the painting of the plain, heavy cornice of the new front. A call from the gate caused them to look around. A close carriage had, unnoticed by them, driven up, and the driver was making signals for assistance. In answer to his importunities, Robert ran down to the carriage, just as the door was opened and the form of a man, covered with blood, was revealed lying on the floor, with his head in the lap of a weeping lady. A gentleman was supporting his shoulders. One inquiring glance at the white face and Robert recognized the features of Mr. Pierre La Moore. In an instant his eyes had met the surprised look of Annette and Eugene, while the driver explained:

"Mr. La Moore had been shot in the breast by an Indian, half a mile from here. I hurried the horses to this, the nearest house."

The explanation had accompanied the rapid removal of the wounded man to the house. They laid him on a sofa, near a raised window, and tried to staunch the blood that flowed in bright jets whenever they lifted the compress. Robert applied camphor to his nostrils, but he seemed in a dead swoon. Suddenly Nellie said,

"I will call Miannetta; if it is a possible thing, she will save his life."

She left the room hurriedly, and in response to her repeated calls Miannetta opened the dining-room door and came into the hall. A hurried explanation was given of the arrival of strangers with a wounded and dying man, when the parlor door suddenly opened and the young lady stranger advanced towards them. Another second and with a low cry she was folded in the arms of Miannetta, while Nellie was thrilled by the exclamations:

"My mother!"

"My child!"

A moment after and the door opened again. The young gentleman, advancing with a bound, was in like manner embraced by Miannetta, who cried,

"My boy, my own Eugene!"

While he, disengaging her arms, cried,

"Mother, mother, come quickly. You can save him."

Hastily they all entered the parlor. Silently Miannetta glided to the couch, and gracefully she bent over La Moore. She kissed his marble brow, while she laid her finger on the wound and stopped the flow of the life-stream. With lips glued to his forehead, and drops of perspiration on her own that told her suffering, she seemed the silent impersonation of love. The man's lips moved at last and with difficulty he articulated, while feebly his arms drew her down to him.

"Miannetta, your kiss would almost bring me back to life—if I were dead—but it comes too late— save to make my exit more blessed. Forgive me, my wronged—my only wife. Kiss me again if you forgive—in God's name forgive."

The impressions of her lips were rapid and impassioned, but not life-giving. His clasp about her neck was relaxed. The change settled upon his features which we all instinctively recognize, and his disembodied spirit stood before the "Judge of the quick and the dead."

Then falling upon his motionless form, Miannetta uttered a wild cry. The cry was in the Iroquois tongue, and was followed by a shriek of agony so piercing, it made the hearts round her thrill. In compassion for her, they all left the room, and she was alone with her dead. After awhile, her children went back and knelt with her beside their father's still form.

What words they spoke. what tears they shed in this their hour of union, the imagination must supply.

An hour afterward, with a step stayed by the solemnity of the occasion, and yet with face radiant as with a new revelation, Robert entered the room. Gently raising Annette from her kneeling posture, he said :

"Pardon me for asking you the question at this painful hour, but is there still a reason why I may never call you my wife ? "

"Yes ; it still exists. *My mother's people murdered your parents.*"

"Ah, Annette ! Your mother is my truest, noblest friend. Will you not permit me to assume to her a nearer relation ? " he said, pleadingly.

" *Can* you, Robert ; knowing all ? "

For only answer, he laid her head upon his breast and drew her form to his heart, saying :

"Miannetta, mother, give us your blessing ! "

The weeping woman rose, and placing Annette's hand in Robert's, pronounced her blessing with faltering voice, and again knelt beside her husband's form.

Mr. La Moore was quietly buried near Mr. Maynard, and by his side Miannetta marked the spot where she too wished to be laid,

"When no more on life's rough billow—
All the storms of sorrow fled—
Death has found a quiet pillow,
For the faithful Christian's head "

CHAPTER XIX.

MIANNETTA'S STORY.

Her smiles are with man—her tears are with God.
Her heart may break, and who shall know it ?
—GRACE AGUILLAR.

THE forests of Canada have dropped their russet foliage full many an Autumn time, since by the red light of their hospitable fires, the dusky rulers of the Iroquois nation smoked the peaceful calumet with the simple-hearted Frenchman whose name and memory are revered among their rapidly diminishing numbers. Marquette, with soul aglow with religious fervor, wept with them when the missionaries recited the old, new story of Redeeming sacrifice ; bent, with king and sachem, an humble knee before the emblem of Infinite suffering and Love, as the cross was reared in the wigwam, and untaught hearts acknowledged Him, whose revealing is not alone to the learned. Adown the flowing tide of generations dropped the religion and sceptre of those forest kings, to Sam-o-so-nois—a religion as pure and sceptre as gracious as the heart of the monarch was gentle and great. His queen, Ros-qui-nah, was of the ancient line that min- istered to the Sacred Flame, an old and singular Indian rite. At a set time every year, I think, in November, when the nights were not moonlighted, a flame was kept burning—a flame of thanksgiving for the perpetuity of brotherly love, harmonious council, successful hunt and bounteous harvest. Some authorities insist that this flame was perpetual.

Sam-o-so-nois and Ros-qui-nah were blessed with one child, a daughter, the "star-eyed" and bird-voiced Lucille. She sang wild notes in the lodge, or by some murmuring stream, warbling in unison with songsters of the air that hovered around her feet, as fearless of her as of their mates.

One day, a scholarly adventurer, a young French gentleman of fortune was attracted by her wonderful voice; heard, saw and loved. It was the old story. He appropriated the sibyl, and her song, which in La Belle France softened by rarest culture, became irresistible, filling his stately home with its melody.

The marriage proved most harmonious, and one lovely child cemented this union. In her rich complexion, her raven hair and eyes, her clear-cut features, eloquently reflecting a noble soul ; in her form, exquisitely proportioned, she resembled her mother. The waving ripples on her hair, the mirthful flash of her eyes, the noble poise of her head and the high bred grace of her manner, bespoke the gentle French blood of her father.

Monsieur Montfort regarded his Indian wife and her child with a pure, doting worship, and their will was the lever of all his actions. While she was still a child, Miannetta was made to understand that only at her father's death could she administer the estates in France ; that she would inherit without question her father's fortune. She was petted and humored by both father and mother, who smiled at her childish caprices, and regarded with too much veneration by nurse and governess to ever receive a reprimand. What wonder, then, that the little Miannetta became slightly imperious?

When she was ten years old she expressed a strange desire to visit the woods of Canada where her mother was born, and, forthwith, that desire was gratified. Henceforth she was a bird of frequent passage between Canada and France, accompanied by her parents, but plainly their mistress. For their residence this side the ocean, a suitable mansion was purchased with Indian treasure, Madam Montfort's while living and Miannetta's in the event of her death. But this property, like the property in France, was so tied up by technicalities of entail, that only Miannetta, or her heirs, when they reached their majority could establish a claim to it.

It was M. Montfort's ambition that his daughter should excel in scholarship as well as in all feminine accomplishments, and of masters he provided for her . the best. He was doomed to disappointment. All the Indian in her nature rebelled against the restraint of books, and, beyond the common branches, she was, measured by her father's standard, lamentably ignorant. A child of nature, eager to read nature's books, and loving best the haunts where her favorite author had been least disturbed, music was the only accomplishment not contemned—music was her passion, and she possessed the same marvelous voice, which in her mother had so captivated her gentle-hearted sire.

When on the threshold of womanhood, she became acquainted with M. La Moore, whose proud family name, old as her own, was his only inheritance. To his protestations of undying regard her heart beat reciprocally. When her father cautioned her against a "possible interest in the fortuneless and rather profligate young La Moore," she declared passionately she "loved him better than life—had already exchanged with him vows of betrothal, and that positively she would wed no other."

In this, as in all things else, her will finally triumphed, and the doting father had only to acquiesce with what grace he could. He soothed his ambition for his only child somewhat, however, by bestowing on La Moore a gift, a sum sufficient to satisfy his fatherly pride, ere he consented to the young man's demand for his daughter in marriage.

M. La Moore had been more mercenary than loving in seeking the alliance with this heiress of a no'le house and race. He expected important social advancement as a result, whereas, at that time he held an obscure government position in Ottawa. There he took Miannetta, who loved him for himself alone.

A wife of seventeen can not easily leave father and mother, and they can not easily part with an only and adored child. It was arranged that M. Montfort and his wife should accompany the handsome young couple to Ottawa, where a residence was purchased that accorded with the elegant taste and generous purse of the old gentleman. They lived to hold the first born of that marriage in their arms —the grandfather's namesake, the passionate, but lov-

able little Eugene. When the child was a year and a
half old, Madam Montfort died. Lonely and sad her
husband's days dragged on, till a little pearl fluttered
down from the skies into the arms of Miannetta, and
he said, smiling,

"She is a messenger. I must go to my Lucille.
I long to hear her sing."

The baby's escort, when it returned heavenward,
bore his spirit to its seat among the ransomed.

Scarcely had he grown cold in death, when Pierre
La Moore instituted measures to secure a handsome
share of his possessions. He was unlike M. Montfort
in every respect, but while her father lived, Miannetta
had only casual glimpses of his real character, which
he found it wise to conceal, lest the wary old man
should take alarm and place her property beyond his
reach. Miannetta inherited Indian titles to some Canada lands, and these with much other property she willingly made over to him. She had solemnly promised
her father (who understood her husband better than
she did, and provided against his exactions) never to
give to anyone the power of attorney, but to hold in
her own hands the management of the French estates
and the Montreal property. These, he had told her,
must be held for her children. Now that he was
dead his wish to her was law, and La Moore became
cool, and even unkind, as she persisted in this determination. He was a handsome, haughty man, laying
great stress upon the conventionalities of society,
but careless of the small courtesies that spring from
the heart. He was never guilty of neglecting the
gentlemanly greeting and suave inquiry as to his

wife's health and happiness, yet he would utterly and designedly neglect to furnish the means to secure these blessings to her.

This proved a sad trial to the temper of the high-spirited woman, who in all her life had scarcely known rebuke—an angry one, *never*. Now, when the man who had vowed to love, honor, and cherish her, not only rebuked sternly, but even sneered at her relations and her resemblance to them, she grew wild with indignation, and gave him taunt for taunt. But when her passion cooled, she was filled with sorrow and contrition, and besought his forgiveness, as if she had been the sole offender. Her will was broken at last, and the imperious head bent before its master. Without reserve she gave up all her titles.

This very self-abnegation and humility inspired his scorn. Forgetting his French manners, he hurled her antecedents in her teeth, and, with the titles safe in his hands, pierced her heart with words that rankled like poisoned barbs. Upon the head bowed so lowly, he placed a cruel, crushing heel—was she not his wife, and an Indian ?

He made a trip to Montreal with the avowed intention of selling M. Montfort's family mansion ; and when, upon his return, she asked him what he proposed doing with the proceeds, he answered mockingly :

"I thought I would buy blankets and fit out an Indian expedition to the moon. You told me you were pining for a change of scene."

This was the only allusion she ever made to the sum she supposed he had realized from the sale of the

old home where she had been so happy. She was too
proud to brave another rejoinder. He, too haughty
to ask for the power of attorney, without which he
could not effect the sale, and the matter was dropped.
Sometimes she would take a long ride with her three
little children and their nurse, in the old Montfort
family coach, away through the green country to an Iroquois village. The two eldest would never forget the
unutterable delight of those days of unrestrained
freedom. These memories were clouded often by the
displeasure of La Moore, when he learned of these
visits, still he never forbade them until after the
birth of their fourth child; and the periods of his
long absences were now dull enough to Miannetta
One day she went into the nursery to find comfort
in the companionship of her children. She took little
Pierre, the baby, on her knee. He was the picture
of his father, and it was half for his father's sake
she applied tender adjectives to his name, as she
pressed him to her heart. She fell into loving muse
while singing him to sleep, recalling the time when her
husband was not so cold, when he was pleased to call
her "his warbler;" to sit beside her long evenings,
listening to and complimenting her music. Long,
she sat thinking over the past, recalling her beloved
parents and her early wedded happiness. She seemed
unconscious that Pierre had awakened, and with happy
little Josie, was pulling down her long black hair till
it lay in coils upon her shoulders. She was buried in
the past.

Her cheek was flushed with her recent abstraction,
her hair was all disordered by her children's playful-

ness; her eyes had a moisture that yet was not tears, when the door opened and her husband stood before her. With a joyous cry, her baby still in her arms, she sprang toward him, but there was no love in his glance to invite her tenderness, no response to the gladness of her voice. Seeking to hide her own embarrassment, she held up the child, gaily saying:

"See what a rich, rich man is Pierre. He has achieved a whole tooth in papa's absence."

He pushed his boy away and coldly said,

"Such nonsense is unworthy a woman, at least, a woman of *your age*, Miannetta. Your manner of spending your time will scarcely impress your children with your dignity, to say nothing of their improvement. Come, attend to your toilet; I have a matter to communicate that is full of importance to us all."

Dinner was partaken of in silence. She felt too heavy hearted to risk his displeasure by opening a conversation, and he was too much absorbed in his newspaper between the courses to make any remark. After dessert he sat long over his wine, forgetful of the wife who awaited his presence in the drawing-room, dreading something, she knew not what. At last he joined her and sat long in silence, smoking a cigar. She rose to ring for coffee, and he said,

"Sit down, Miannetta, and hear me. I have brought to Ottawa a very superior young lady, whom I have met several times in New York. She is a lady and will be just the person for our children and yourself to look up to. Of course I shall reward her for spending her time here and lending a little polish to our atmosphere, which I notice is getting strongly odorous of the woods. We need some civilization. But look you, Miannetta, no servile duties are to be required of Marian Ramsdell. She is to be in every respect, one of us."

That night she found among his treasures the picture of a young girl with fair hair, blue eyes and clear, beautiful complexion, such a face as she had ever admired, and contrasting it with her own dark, heavy beauty, she did not wonder that her husband had been attracted by it.

"But oh, could he not have admired this woman and still loved me? Now I know the meaning of those cruel words he spoke to-day: 'A woman of *your age!*' Am I growing old? Is it age that trembles in my limbs to-night and makes my weight almost insupportable?"

Next day he brought home the original of the picture. His eyes ever followed admiringly her graceful form. Miannetta saw the silent worship with which she was regarded, and resigned herself to a secondary place in her husband's heart and the home her father had provided for her. It was evident from the first she meant to entirely subdue Miannetta's spirit, to be her mistress, and the helpless woman, for her children's sake, submitted to it with aching heart.

Her eldest boy, Eugene, rebelled against the new "tyrant," as he called her, for she sought to subjugate children as well as mother.

Mr. La Moore had never undertaken the government of his children, and their mother's government was loving and serene. The combativeness of the two elder children, now, was a new feature which their father was soon called upon by Miss Ramsdell, to suppress by his own authority With many stripes and much wordy admonition, the beauty of civilization of which she was the embodiment, was impressed upon their young minds. Their obedience to her was enjoined in her own and in the presence of their mother, and particular stress was laid upon the fact that the latter was by nature incompetent to control or teach them, as she was an uneducated descendant of the Iroquois. From that hour, Miannetta was denied companionship with the children God had given her. A year of lonely suffering followed, with only stolen interviews with the little ones, who would have submitted to torture rather than betray her frequent embraces. At the end of the year, another little one was laid in her arms, but her strength was scarcely equal to the task of holding it. It was pitiful, her longing for one word of love and sympathy from her husband during her hour of trial. But he was too much in love with another, whose face was not distorted with pain. He preferred laughter to groans. His infatuation, indeed, had reached such a point that he disregarded her cry :

"Do not leave me, Pierre, I beg you. O my husband, stay till this is past !"

He sought the society of the haughty girl who now ruled his home and him.

Miannetta forgot in unconsciousness his indifference when the supreme moment came. For weeks she languished for the want of tenderness and air, which were both denied her. When the carriage rolled away, it was not her form that reclined against the crimson cushions, beside her animated and gentlemanly husband. She needed change of scene—had always been taken down for sea air after her confinement before this; but now it was not for her benefit that a seaside trip was planned, Montreal and other gay resorts visited. No, another and dearer was the invalid.

One morning shortly after the return from the seashore of Mr. La Moore and Miss Ramsdell, they were sitting together in the parlor near an open window. The young lady's head was bowed in her hand, and her whole attitude expressive of dejection. Mr. La Moore stooped and smoothed her hair, saying tenderly :

" You are not so well to-night, Marian ! I hoped our trip would give you better spirits."

" I shall never have better spirits here, while liable to encounter at any moment the only woman I ever really hated ! "

" Why do you hate her, Marian ? She dare not harm you ! she has not the spirit ! "

" She has the spirit to tell me my presence is loathsome to her ; that she and her children despise and defy me."

" Miannetta said that ? "

" Must I repeat my assertions, in order to be believed ? She did say so ! "

" Well, we will see ! "

He strode from the room in a towering passion, entered Miannetta's, and taking her roughly by the shoulder, turned her round toward the window.

Pointing to the distant forest where the Iroquois village lay, in a voice husky with anger, he said :

"Go to your own people! You can sympathize with the rudeness of their customs, but have no comprehension of the refinement of ours! Go, I say!"

"You do not surely mean this, Pierre? Their manner of life is as uncongenial to me as it would be to you! I have never known any, save a home like this, amid luxury and wealth. You do not mean that I shall leave *you, leave my blessed little children?*"

"Yes! I do mean it all! You only teach my children miserable Indian manners and resistance to all other authority. Give me that child!"

"No! Pierre, I will not! If you insist upon giving Marian all the rest of my children, you must leave me this one! I claim it by right of my most suffering motherhood."

"No, Miannetta, not one! not one shall you have! Here is money for all your needs."

"Perish your gold, as the love you feigned to obtain it, has perished!"

She rushed past him, with her child hugged closely to her bosom, ran up the long flight of stairs to the nursery, and sat down, breathless, in the midst of her wondering children. Then she told them with choking sobs, and amid their own tearful and indignant protests, that she "must go."

"I know all about it," said Eugene, setting his teeth, while his tears were interrupted by rising anger. "I heard them talking through the window. That woman told papa that you had been abusing her. I know it was a lie, and papa doubted it, for he made her say it again 'fore he'd believe her! See if I don't find ways enough to torment her! We can make her so unhappy, she will be glad to get away, and you sha'n't go a step, my precious pet mother!"

His arms were about her neck protectingly, and he looked toward the door, with boyish defiance on his beautiful young face. His poor, distracted mother thought:

"For this love and noble espousal of my cause, my boy must suffer."

Annette stationed herself on the other side of her mother, and with an arm about her neck, stood ready to re-echo whatever her brother said, to repeat his every gesture of protest and defiance. Little elfish Josie had climbed up on the back of her mother's chair, and was playing bopeep with Pierre who, upon his highly-prized seat, the maternal knee, was nestling his head beside the baby's, in the loved and loving bosom. So sweetly hemmed in, could harm fall to that trembling victim of a miserable woman's wiles? Could there be found a power so inhuman and relentless as to tear her from this childish love? Softly resigning herself to their affectionate demonstrations, Miannetta was almost happy till warned by the gathering gloom of night that she must break these chains; so calmly she sought to prepare for the long separation.

"Genie, my precious boy, you are the eldest and must set an example to be followed by Annette and the others. Your father has chosen to appoint another woman your mother in my stead, and you must remember, no matter what I may suffer, that he has a right to your obedience."

"I shall always mind papa," said Eugene, "but I won't mind old Purr daisy."

"Won't mind old Purr daisy," echoed Annette.

"But by making an enemy of her, you will make an enemy of your father, and your disobedience to her will bring upon you punishment that it chills me to think of. Your objection to my going will be fruitless as my own. Now for your own happiness and my peace, I want you *all* to promise to be gentle and good, to treat with marked politeness Miss Ramsdell, for coarseness and vulgar manners are the certain result of ugly thoughts. I do wish to think of you as preserving the old Montfort gentleness. But for this, my father's cherished trait, I might remain and try conclusions with this usurper. But," she added, as if speaking to herself, "though in my veins runs the purest blood of France, it is blended with that of a race that have no rights, whose women, when discarded by the caprice of husbands, have no refuge save in the forest; no redress save that from which my soul recoils. No, there is no way but to submit, all my claims upon my father's wealth are vested in him who drives me like a dog from my own door, who will tear from me the children that have lain on my heart."

"O, mother, do n't say so," cried Eugene, his big heart bursting at this outrage upon his adored mother, and ready to wage childish warfare upon its authors.

Miannetta again soothed him, and showed how love may lead the most fiery spirits.

"Genie stop! I know you love me well enough to defend me, but now I am going to make a request, and you must all remember it as mamma's *last wish*. It is that you will conduct yourselves as become the descendants of a man who was a gentleman by birth, and of a woman who was of royal blood, and detested untruth above all things. Do you promise me, my children?"

"I promise," said Eugene, and sank upon his knees sobbing, with his face in her lap.

"I promise," said Annette, striving to find a similar nestling place.

"I promise," said little Josie.

Thus La Moore found them, and passionately bade her hasten away. Upon each darling face she imprinted a kiss, the agony of which went up to heaven, then rising said:

"I am ready, Pierre."

He attempted to take the baby from her, but with the strength that comes of despair she clung to it, and O, could you have heard her plead with him, her own husband, the father of that child—

"Just this *one*, Pierre, to furnish sunshine for my dreary days."

But he was deaf to all appeal, his heart that must have been flint, was proof now against all importunities, and, taking the child from her clinging clasp, he dragged her down the stairs. At the bottom step Marian stood, the personification of sweetness and mercy, for she cried nervously to La Moore:

"Do n't hurry her so ; use as little severity as possible, dear Mr. La Moore, for *my sake*. Let me relieve you of the child."

That was the drop too much for poor Miannetta, when she found she was indebted for her husband's *gentleness* to another woman's prayer, when her baby, for which she so piteously plead, was given willingly into the arms of another—her successful rival in her husband's heart—shriek after shriek burst from her agonized soul, and she became helpless as the babe just forcibly taken from her. La Moore took her up and carried her to a door at the rear of the house, where a carriage was in waiting, which she was too unhappy to notice was not their own. A rough looking stranger opened the door, and she was thrust in, and it was shut again, fastened securely, and immediately she was driven rapidly away from all she loved.

For some time she seemed paralyzed, mind and body alike insensible, but gradually she roused herself, and at midnight, apprised by deepening shadow that they were entering a wood, she pulled the check string to communicate a desire to speak with the driver, and he, dismounting, opened the door, saying gruffly :

"What 's wanted?"

"Where do you intend to take me?"

"To the Iroquois village."

"Have you no fear?" she asked.

"No; the Indians are friendly and are Christians; they will hurt no one," he said, and she continued :

"You have undertaken a deed that will certainly

meet the reward of death. I can not save you.
Every fact of our coming will be known before we
reach them, no matter by what agency. Your blood
must be upon your own head if you neglect my
warning, and cross the boundary of the Indian reservation."

With an oath he slammed the door to, mounted
the box and drove on. The village was aroused by
their arrival just at dawn the following day.

Old Sam-o-so-nois received his grandchild cordially,
but he had expected this for a long time; faithful
agents had witnessed all, and preceded them with
the tidings. It was not the first woman of his people
who had come, driven from the arms of a false pale-
face, but this one was his own flesh and blood, and,
moreover, of that sacred line of women, whom every
Indian revered.

Not by his will, for he was a Christian though an
Indian, but through younger, more passionate agency,
the driver met the penalty of his service in bringing
Miannetta, a discarded wife, to the woods.

Before the sun had commenced its daily journey,
his scalp hung limp and gory by the hunting pouch
of a young brave. The third night saw that carriage
again upon its way city ward, driven by an Indian,
Miannetta within, and by her side the feeble hoary-
headed king of the Iroquois — Sam-o-so-nois. An
occasional remark broke the silence, but while they
rode, each told their beads devoutly. At the edge of
the wood the old man got out, and holding a crucifix
for her to kiss, said in good French :

" I will prevent La Moore from realizing anything

from the Indian titles. They shall be intact for the benefit of your children. Your father provided for such contingency in his will. The papers you gave La Moore are worthless to him so long as you live, since he has not been empowered legally to administer upon the French estates. I shall make rapid preparation now for removal west. The blood in the veins of my braves is boiling to revenge your wrong, and fatal collisions will occur with the whites if we do not go. Toward the sunset is a fairy lake, and a forest of wonderful richness in game. There I will go; come you too, when your heart will allow you. Command Indian currency as you need it."

. So saying, he disappeared. The coach was driven on into the lighted city, when the driver sprang down, opened the door with a guttural exclamation, and in a moment he, too, was gone.

Miannetta descended, hurrying to her late home, entered the rear grounds, and stood beneath the nursery window. She gazed with jealous eye upon the light, that unrebuked might fall upon the sleeping faces of her children, while she was shut out. She stood long in the shadow, comforted by her very nearness to them. Then she heard a feeble wail, then the petulant voice of the nurse, disturbed by the increasing cry of the baby. Her baby, crying for the nourishment with which her breast was bursting. The calmness that had supported her the few days past gave place to madness now, as through that cry she realized the bitterness of her relentless fate. A lifetime of frenzy seemed condensed in the minutes that followed. The doors, the windows, every possi-

ble and impossible entrance was attempted. No merciful hinge creaked a welcome ; no bar fell down to
let her through. She called wildly upon her husband,
begged of the servants to let her in to feed her child.
No response came, though the house was thrilled
through and through. The heads of Eugene and
Annette were seen a moment at the open window ; a
moment, and they were torn away, calling her name.

Her cries at last gave place to the silent agony of
a forced submission. When she would have fallen,
the arm of old Sam-o-so-nois, who, with another Indian, was waiting in the shadow of the shrubbery,
upheld and led her through several streets to the
comfortable but rude hut of an old Iroquois woman,
originally the owner of much real estate in Ottawa.
She willingly received Miannetta. They laid her,
senseless now, upon a bed where for weeks she lay in
a raging fever, only recovering through most skillful
attendance and care.

In Ottawa were warm hearts, who could not excuse La Moore for casting her off, even though she
had been entirely an Indian, since her Indian blood
was his plea. They remembered her in brighter days
when, the courted and brilliant belle of an aristocratic circle in Montreal, she gracefully accepted
homage that never questioned her antecedents. They
had loved her for her independent, vivacious, yet tender nature, never dreaming of the shadow of her
later years. A poor outcast, upon a mean bed in a
lowly hut, denied the wealth assuredly hers, denied
her own children.

White women have suffered the same way, but

with them redress is possible. Laws are enacted for their protection. But what law is there for a repudiated wife of mixed blood? What redress if her children are torn from her bosom?

In the weeks of her returning health, Miannetta was schooling herself to the renunciation she felt was inevitable. With wonderful trust in the love vouchsafed her daily from on high, she resolved through strength from the same source, to bear her afflictions. The day came when she could walk unassisted. Day by day she gained strength, though slowly, venturing each day a little further in her walks.

One night when darkness favored her (darkness now seemed her friend), she passed again into the inclosure of her children's home, and seating herself in the shrubbery where they had often played round her, she watched the light that came dimly from their room. The great, pitying eye looked down upon the tired, wandering mourner, alone in the dark. Suddenly the curtain of the nursery window was drawn aside, the sash was raised softly, and two heads peered cautiously out. Then a paper attached to a long cord was lowered. Dear little hearts! Thinking she would be there during the night, her children had determined to communicate with her. She sprang eagerly forward, detached the paper, and when the cord was drawn up, a lock of her long dark hair and a pure white rose were attached, which were laid carefully away under lock and key. Miannetta hurried away now with her treasure, repairing to the hut of an old Indian woman in the nearest wood. There she read her precious missive by the aid of the firelight, and we will be rude enough to look over her shoulder.

DEAREST MOTHER:

It's me, Eugene, that writes, but Annette thinks up some of the things to say. The poor little baby cried and cried till it died. The doctor said it was change of food, but we think it knew that you were drove off. Mariann, as we call her now, talks about the angels it has gone to live with, but we guess she'll never get near enuff to one to tell how it looks. We shall remember our promise to be polite to her, but we take turns making faces at her when her back is turned, Annette and me do. We are all sorry for you, and talk about you a great deal, so that Josie and Pierre won't forget. We will put letters out when we can get a chance, and if they are not gone in the morning we'll draw 'em up again. We expect you will go to the old king, our great-grandfather, and will have enough money to make you comfortable, but we know that you will miss us and be unhappy and lonely. Dear mother, this is full of love, for we have all kissed it, each just where their name is written. Josie, Pierre, Annette, and *me*,

EUGENE.

Strange! We have read this little letter two or three times, and yet, Miannetta seems to be long in making it out! Ah, she has fallen asleep over the childish scroll; and look at the blessed smile upon her wasted features! When she awoke it was in a delirium that lasted many weeks. She had taxed her strength too much. She came again very near death, but, at last, through the agency of powerful remedies administered by the medicine man of the Senecas, who visited the wigwam, she recovered. As soon as her strength would allow, she repaired once more to the Mecca of her hopes, her children's window. The light was gone; the house untenanted! She inquired among the neighbors, but no one could or would tell whither Mr. La Moore had taken his family. She returned to the deserted house and wildly sought for some word of farewell from her children, and found it at last skillfully concealed in the loose bark of the tree that was her own and their favorite resort. She read:

DEAR MOTHER : We have wrote lots of letters, but you didn't come for 'em, and we are awful afraid something has happened to you. Mariann has got a baby, and papa says we must call her mother now.

Papa sold the house for a pile of money, and we are going away—I don't know where, nor papa won't tell anybody; but I'm 'fraid it is a great way off, 'cause none of the servants but Lavergn and Casper are going with us, and we sha'n't see you again · but we shall try to let you know, and if there are any Indians 'round, it will be easy to do so. We won't forget you never—never. We will all be good, and love one another. You always said God would take care of us; and we ask Him many times a day to *never mind us*, but take care of poor mamma.

Good-by.   GENIE AND NETTIE.

This was the last she heard of them for twelve long, weary months, which she spent—part of the time in the woods, with different tribes that were of the League, at home and welcome always; but she had no heart for their wild life, that charmed her so in childhood. Once she visited Montreal, thinking it possible the beloved ones might be there; but she was almost maddened by the scenes that carried her back to happier days. She avoided all meetings with old acquaintances; but that was a great mistake. Miannetta Montfort was too well beloved by the noble French families in Montreal, to be dropped by them simply because her husband, who was not so favorably remembered, had dropped her. But she did not know this. Misfortune makes us sometimes suspicious and afraid of friends, especially when those we considered true as heaven have failed us. Many friends would have welcomed her, both in Montreal and Ottawa; but with a proud sensitiveness she avoided all who had known her in the days of her prosperity, not knowing to what extent her husband was censured for his cruelty and wickedness. With the Indians there was no question of her position. Sam-o-so-nois had carried out his avowed purpose to move west immediately; but Miannetta found homes in lodges belonging to other tribes, under the protection of other sovereigns. She remained near Ottawa, as there she was sure her children would address her whenever the opportunity should offer. After a year of patient waiting, she was rewarded by tidings. Two Indians had made the long journey on foot from Minnesota, in compliance with a request Eugene had made of them to find and tell his mother where they were. She returned with them, traveling on a pony. She reached St. P——, and gazed upon the roof that sheltered her dear little ones, but dared not approach it, and for days lingered lovingly near, without a sight of beloved face or form.

At last, one day, one of her escorts met Eugene in town, and communicated to him the fact that his mother waited in the long ravine at the foot of the bluff, to see him. Each afternoon she sat down there, to pick over the strawberries she sold in the city as an excuse for lingering near the residence of La

Moore. The noble little fellow desired to rush to her, but fearing the observation he might thus attract, he managed more prudently, as became his mother's son. With some other boys, he engaged in a game of ball, which had its disadvantages, to be sure, but which should serve his purpose, he determined. A good throw would do wonders for him now, and how his heart beat when the ball dropped almost into her lap.

"Run, Genie!" cried one. "The ball dropped down close to that old squaw, down there!"

Eugene had obeyed him, bounding down and laying his hand tenderly upon her shoulder, and looking with eyes overrunning with love into hers, as these words were quickly exchanged:

"Mother! my precious mother! we are dying to see you!"

"Genie, darling, I dare not kiss you; but I am so thirsty for your love!"

"I'll manage some way!" he said; but went whistling back up the bluff, saying:

"Let's find a better place than a side hill for this kind of a game, boys!"

His companions did not see that he was hiding a note away in his pocket, and had no suspicion that other than fatigue took him away from their sport shortly afterward. Going home, he sought Annette, and together they read:

MY PRECIOUS CHILDREN: I can hardly help rushing to you and braving all for one close, blessed embrace; but I know we must be cautious, or you will all be taken away again. Come, Genie, to-morrow afternoon, when I start to the city with my berries, and cross the slough bridge at the same time. We will talk; but don't look at me, nor appear to notice me. Oh, what love I have for you all !   YOUR MOTHER.

This letter, more precious than gold to them, was committed at once to flames; but in obedience to it, as Miannetta stepped upon the bridge, she heard a light footstep bound upon the plank, and knew that her boy was near. He appeared to be completely absorbed throwing stones into the water; but all the time they were conversing rapidly in French. It was a short walk for two who had so much to say ; but the language they used was eloquent and comprehensive, and no time was wasted.

"We are most crazy to see you," said Eugene. "Papa has promised me that we may go by ourselves in the carriage to-morrow, a nice ride. Lavergn will drive; he remembers you and would lose his arm for you, any day. So you be in the cooley yonder," (he threw a pebble to indicate the direction) "and we will pick you up. All the children shall be along— all but Mari-*ann's*—and you shall ride with us once more, mother."

He crossed over to the other railing in front of her, looking into her face, and their eyes met and spoke the depths of their love.

"Thank God for this," she whispered, as he commenced whistling noisily.

Just then a boyish acquaintance came along, and addressing Eugene, said:

"That's a Yankton squaw, and, they say, the handsomest woman in St. Paul. Let us follow and take a look at her."

Eugene, determined to keep his reckless play-
fellow by him until his mother should have left the
city, said:

"No do n't.   Let's go and take a ride ; I can get
the horses."

His friend readily acquiescing, they turned
towards the stables.   Winking significantly at the
old coachman, Eugene asked the privilege for himself
and his companion of riding.   His signal was
understood and the horses were put under the boys in
a hurry, Lavergn soliloquizing as they rode away,
thus:

"She's somewhere around, I know; that boy's
face is just like a book, and I can read his mother's
name all over it.   Let me see.   Yes, I have it now,
that's the reason the strawberries on the bluff side
are so much better.   Poor thing, to have to pick
berries for an excuse to be near the home she could
turn 'em all out of, by twisting a screw or two, but
she is made of better stuff than most women."

That night, with her blanket over her head, Miannetta lay wakeful in the silent thicket, to which she
had retired in alarm, having noticed that in spite of
her disguise, she had attracted attention and a certain
coarse admiration.   She felt that she was watched,
and determined to avoid the streets.   To visit her
children again might result in her being recognized
by La Moore, who, she felt sure, would hear of her,
if she were not more cautious.

While yet the dew lay in crystal globules in the
cups of the flowers, or hung like pearls on the quivering leaves, she crept cautiously from her leafy couch

to a place of concealment near the road that wound
down the long cooley, where she watched every
vehicle that passed. Not till late in the afternoon
was she rewarded.

La Moore's carriage came slowly down, the driver
— not Lavergn — holding the reins tightly. As
they reached a place where the carriage could be
brought to a stand without pressing upon them,
Miannetta stepped out of the bushes, and, by a word
of command. brought the horses to a full stop. regardless of the driver's imprecation. Quickly opening
the carriage door to greet her children, she encountered the cold, stern gaze of Marian Ramsdell, and
heard her command—

"*Jasper, get down and take this squaw away, and
then drive immediately home.*"

The driver sprang to execute her command ; Miannetta was partly in the carriage; he took hold of her
arm, but Eugene's determined fist was so skillfully
aimed between his eyes, that he was sent to the right
about in a hurry, while he was warned by Eugene not
to interfere with that woman again, as he valued his
place. but to—

"Get on to the box and attend to your business,
which is driving the horses."

The bewildered, half-witted fellow climbed back,
and taking up the reins, called out:

"Where shall I drive to ? "

"Home !" shrieked Marian, in a frightfully angry
tone.

"Drive on to the place you were told to before
starting." said Eugene.

18

"*No, Jasper, you dare not disobey me.   I will go home,*" said Marian.

" Well, you will walk then," said Eugene, opening the door for her.

She hurried out, crimson with rage, and in haste to inform La Moore of "Miannetta's daring and Eugene's insolence."

Those two offenders were all oblivious of her, of the past, or the to come, for now the tide of love was coming in, and all hateful things were lost sight of in the bewildering flood.   Miannetta was embracing her children wildly.   She would set Pierre down and take up Josie, put down Josie and take up Pierre, kiss Annette at her right, and turn quickly to her left to salute Eugene—all the time laughing and crying.

A stranger looking in at the window, would have thought an escaped lunatic was killing that load of children.   They were whirling away now rapidly behind unrestrained horses, into the solitary country, where, without remark, they might all laugh and shout and give vent to their joy at this re-union.

Stars danced in the sky when the carriage climbed the bluff again (for they had a picnic supper on the grass miles away), and still Miannetta rode with them.   The gate swung open, they passed through, the horses dashed up to the door, La Moore came and took the children out.   Miannetta, who was getting out the opposite door, heard him say to Eugene :

"Why did n't you bring your mother home ?"

" We did," was the reply, but when he looked

into the carriage for her she was gone, had disappeared in the shrubbery.

The next morning, the little crib of Marian Ramsdell's eldest child was empty. On the pillow where his pretty flaxen head had lain, a note was pinned, addressed to her. It read:

MARIAN:
By kindness and considerate treatment of my children, you may ensure the safety of your own.   MIANNETTA.

Marian read the note, and with it in her hand, rushed into the room where her child's father was reading the morning paper, and with frantic vehemence, shrieked:

"Miannetta has stolen my child!"

"You stole five of hers, and her husband," was the calm reply.

"Follow her, La Moore, bring back my boy—my darling baby boy. Why are you so indifferent? Will you not follow her?"

"No, indeed; my scalp feels better on my own head."

This was spoken lightly, but he knew well that a search for that child by him would certainly result in the loss of his scalp, as it also was certain to result fruitlessly. Miannetta would not wish to have him harmed, but she could not control the scalping knives, that had been dedicated to this service long since, and were only waiting a suitable opportunity to fly from their sheaths.

He knew her tender heart would not suffer a hair of its head to come to harm, that she had stolen it only to stay the vengeance of Marian, which might have fallen heavily upon the offenders of yesterday, but for this practical lesson. Though he knew that the child was as safe as in its own mother's arms, he would not tell Marian so. He did not care to comfort her now; that time was past, never more to return. She had no holy claim upon his love. Yesterday when she returned, all flushed and exasperated, from her unaccustomed walk up the bluff, and detailed to him the mortifying circumstances of Miannetta's appearance, how she had been "foiled by Miannetta—driven to an ignominious walk by the Indian," she paused, expecting La Moore would fly into a towering passion, but instead he straightened himself at full length on the sofa, and looking fondly at the end of his cigar, said:

"Well, Marian, Miannetta has let you ride in her carriage a long time. No one can wonder if she now plans to let you do a little pedestrianism."

"La Moore, would you insult me?"

"No, there would be too little satisfaction in that to warrant the outlay."

What could it mean? To coolly invite her to submit tamely to this outrage, inflicted by a woman—whom she had ousted from her home by her superior charms—that she hated, that La Moore had ceased to love long ago and forsaken for herself, she thought, forever. Ah! forever is a long word.

It was plain to her now, his infatuation for herself was over, and she feared he was returning to his old love.

'Twas true, the scales had fallen from his eyes,

the glamour which had blinded him had vanished, and deep in his heart he found her image was still tenderly enshrined. He heard a voice pleading for her—the voice of his own soul—and it should never, never more be silent. Had she even entered the house and asserted her rights, bidding the false woman begone, his heart would have admitted the righteousness of her act. He had not strength of himself to right the great wrong, but had Miannetta made the first move towards asserting herself, he would have supported her and rejoiced in the discomfiture of Marian. Though himself the greatest sinner, he would have felt a cowardly satisfaction in her punishment for their mutual crime.

Weeks ran on, months even, and Miannetta came not ; the children often heard from her ; letters were mysteriously brought from the forest, and the replies as mysteriously transmitted to her.

It was late Autumn. Snow already lay upon the ground and the weather was very cold. The family of La Moore were gathered in the sitting room one evening, La Moore reading, Marian busy with some fancy work, and the children variously occupied. Suddenly the door opened, and the child taken away months before was set into the room. The person who brought it as suddenly disappeared. The little fellow had forgotten every one of the family, even his own mother, and in his fright called piteously:

" Miannetta ! Miannetta ! "

His mother strove to win him back to some remembrance of her, but in vain. With tears and wailing he protested against being left, until both tears and voice were exhausted and he closed his eyes in sleep.

La Moore was now resolved to see Miannetta, and persuade her to return to his home. He knew she would not leave the city without an interview with the children, and by Eugene's connivance, he waited outside the door of Annette's room that opened into a charming little enclosure, filled with choice Winter shrubs and evergreens. As Miannetta stole out after a long conference with her dear ones, he caught her in his arms, called her his dear wife, kissed her fondly, and besought her to lay her head upon his breast—her shelter evermore ; but she responded not to his embrace.

"Miannetta, my beautiful wife," he pleaded, "do not look on me so coldly; do you love me no more, darling ? "

"Love you, Pierre ! Because of my love for you, my life is made wretched ; but my love is pure and will not mingle with that of an unholy passion. My love is beyond my control, as my person is beyond yours. Let me go."

With a vigorous effort she escaped from him, while he mournfully called upon her to return.

In his sleep that night, to the dismay of the woman who lay beside him, he called again and again the name she loathed and despised, the name of his true wife.

Eugene brought her a letter from her husband ; for a moment she held the unopened letter irresolutely in her hand, her woman's heart clamorous for him, her decision almost overcome, then snatching

a pen, she hastily wrote upon the envelope the words
"TOO LATE." With a deep sigh she turned the
key once for all upon her weakness and indecision,
and so the letter went back unopened and unread.

Miannetta bade her children a tender and long
adieu, and like Bunyan's Christian, with her fingers
in her ears, she fled from his contaminated love. Save
an occasional letter exchanged with her children, she
heard little from their home in St. P——.

Farther than to assure them of her well-being and
that she never ceased to think of them, she believed
it less cruel to remain entirely away. She had
adopted the dress of the Indians, and sought to dis
guise herself so that it should never be known that the
wanderer of the forest was the mother of the rich La
Moore's children. After her long absences and visits to old Sam-o-so-nois on Lake Itasca, who died at
last in her arms, full of grace and full of years, she
returned to the Sioux, with whom she had spent most
of the time since she came to Minnesota; not that she
preferred being with them—they were too wild and
savage for her gentle spirit—but gratitude largely
predominated in her nature, and the Indians who had
gone to Canada for her, at Eugene's request, were
Sioux. Through this tribe, also, she could oftener
communicate with her children in St. P——, and she
was among them when she first met Robert Maynard.

The next Spring she went to Maple Range and
spent the Summer, and we have seen how welcome
she was, especially at The Maples. The Spring that
La Moore went to France he also visited Ottawa, with
the intent of building up his finances sufficiently to

justify the immense expenses which he believed would
be necessary to unlock the legal barriers to French
bullion. But Sam-o-so-nois had placed similar barriers in the way of Pierre La Moore's realizing personally from the Indian treasure. Miannetta could
cancel the injunction, or her children when they
reached their majority, if she were dead; but he
might as well attempt to establish a claim to the ex-
chequer of the moon as to make a draft on the gold
that would pour from the treasury when demanded by
those to whom it was thus doubly secured. Though
his attempt had been unsuccessful, yet the knowledge
that he had again tried to feather his unhallowed
nest through the treasure of his discarded Indian
wife, had reached the ears of the little band of Iro
quois on Lake Itasca. The offense was designedly
exaggerated by the young orators, so that all the
white men, women and children of Minnesota were
regarded as guilty of the outrage against Miannetta. With wild, impassioned declamation, they
exhorted the Itascan braves to consolidate with the
other nations that were preparing to wipe out their
wrongs with blood.

La Moore, himself the author of the wrong they
proposed so madly to avenge, sat in security,
nor heard the first twang of the avenging bow, while
partly for his misdeeds the mangled forms of innocent
victims strewed the undefended frontier. Miannetta's
first intimation of the movement burst upon her
grieved sight in the flames that consumed Ben Palmer's dwelling, when returning after a search in the
woods for roots and medicine, she found the house on

fire and Ruth dead beside her baby's cradle. She was concealed near by when the stage with Robert arrived. She had seen the baby taken care of by Mrs. McDougal. She followed them to The Maples, still concealing herself, not through fear of Robert, but not knowing how far exasperation would carry the strange men who were with him, at sight of her Indian dress.

From her different hiding-places she had witnessed the search for Nellie. She knew the poor girl was not dead, or the Indians would not have carried her off. She stole into Robert's room to give him the comfort of a written promise to find her. When she raised the ornament to put her scroll under and saw the picture of her own child there, guessing that Robert and she were betrothed, such a flood of new feelings rushed over her who had known so many forms of suffering, that her head swam and her knees trembled. What if her relation to Annette, becoming known, should prevent their marriage and her daughter's life be overshadowed with gloom like her own.

She was not astonished when Robert told her that the engagement was broken by Annette's own hand. She knew the soul of the noble girl would revolt against a marriage with the man who was ignorant of her antecedents.

"Would Robert Maynard be likely to marry one whom he knew was even remotely connected with the murderers of his parents?"

Miannetta, however, had faith enough in him to believe in his constancy, and to give him the faint

2B

hope that it would rest with him to remove the barrier to their union, as he did when he called her " Miannetta, mother ! " the day of La Moore's death.

Reader, you have followed the wanderings of her weary feet, have heard the moaning of her broken heart, will you not now rejoice to turn a brighter page in the chequered life of this daughter of two races, each furnishing types of all that is noble and good, as well as of all that is ignoble and treacherous

If to the bloody authors of the Indian massacre the mind should revert to the prejudice of our noble Miannetta, let me ask : Does not our land give birth to the lowest types of human degradation, as well as to the transcendent charity which furnishes asylum for the degraded of all nations? If George Washington's name stands out resplendent upon history's page, is not Benedict Arnold's black with infamy? Were the faithful eleven less holy because of the treason of Judas ?

CHAPTER XX.

READING THE WILL.

"Her sceptre was a broken reed."

'TWAS the close of a gloomy December day— the snow pecking and pestering the faces of unfortunate wayfarers. Busy men rushed up and down the streets, with great coats buttoned up to their ears, and hats drawn over their eyes. Early lights gleamed from store and office windows. Carriages rattled noisily over the stones in the streets of St. P——. One, driven rapidly through the principal thoroughfares and up a roadway artificially cut in the bluff side, entered the gate and swept up the drive to the door of the residence of the late Mr. Pierre La Moore. Eugene sprang out and assisted Annette, who was waiting with hand outstretched at the open door for Miannetta, when Marian, in full dress, rushed down the steps, saying impatiently:

"So you have come at last! Where is La Moore?"

Annette, laying her hand restrainingly upon her arm, replied:

"Speak that name softly, Marian! He will never answer to it more."

"Why? Is he dead? Why do you call me 'Marian,' girl? Speak! explain yourself!"

Just then she was attracted by the lady clad in

deep widow's weeds, that Eugene was helping from
the carriage. The eyes of the two women met. The
usurper staggered to the steps of the home she felt
was even now no longer hers, and blinded, overcome
by conflicting emotions, sat down. Miannetta kindly
took her arm and said :

"Come in, Marian! It is very cold; " but she shook
her off, and recovering herself, replied defiantly :

"I know La Moore is dead, or you would not
dare to come here ; but the lawyers hold the papers
which will decide who shall say 'Come in' to this
house, madam! Summon them directly, Eugene,
for La Moore made his will years ago." Rising and
leading the way haughtily into the broad hall, she
threw open the door of the reception room at the left
hand, and bowing very graciously, said, as her eyes
again met Miannetta's :

"We receive transient visitors in this room."

Without heeding her, Miannetta passed on and
followed Annette, who opened the brilliantly lighted
parlor, and bowing her mother affectionately in, tall,
pretty Josie, now almost a woman, was once more
folded in her arms. Pierre soon came in, with
eager inquiry for supper. He was a ruddy-faced
little Frenchman, and rejoiced to see his mother,
whom he remembered dimly "as the big Injin woman
that hugged him in the carriage till he could n't
breath," the afternoon of their ride, long ago.

After supper, which Marian refused to partake of
with Miannetta, Eugene took Josie and Pierre into
Annette's room, and told them of the death of their
father ; and their sorrow was deep and true, for they

had loved him who, of late years, had been more affectionate and loving with them. Marian sent for Eugene, and again bade him summon the legal gentlemen who had custody of his father's papers.

"We had better wait till to-morrow, Marian. Mother is very tired, and poor Josie and Pierre are grieving bitterly," said Eugene.

"And am I nothing in this house? If your father were here, you would not dare call another woman 'mother,' or address me as *Marian*. I will not be set aside thus. I will show you my legal authority here, and, by the permission your father's will has given me, I will drive this intruder from beneath the roof that can not shelter us both, even for one night."

"As you insist, I will then summon the attorney; but you are the only one, Marian, who is anxious to hear father's will; the rest of us willingly would wait a decorous time," said Eugene.

"Talk of decorum, with Satan standing at your elbow disputing your rights, intercepting the commonest courtesies and even appropriating your title— decorum, indeed!"

An hour afterward, wheels were heard rumbling up to the house, and in a few minutes the parlor door was flung open. With some ceremony, the attorney, no other than Herbert Gray, was ushered in, followed by a handsome lad carrying a small box. He advanced and met Eugene's salutation cordially. A glance at Miannetta was followed by a few pleasant words of recognition. Her smiling greeting of the attorney's assistant induces us to look again. As he crosses the room to put his box upon a table, we notice a slight limp in his gait and a habit of putting the right foot, which he evidently regards as the best one, forward—a habit, by the way, which will stick to him through life, and eventually lead our old tree-climbing friend, Tad Wilson, to a seat in the halls of our national capitol.

After some short preliminaries, Herbert read, in a clear voice, La Moore's last will and testament. It read thus :

" ' Know all men, by these presents, that I, Pierre La Moore, being of sound mind, do hereby give and bequeath to my beloved wife, Miannetta, all right and title to the property hereinafter mentioned, the same being originally her lawful inheritance ; and I also recommend to her fostering care my seven children. ' "

Then followed the descriptions of property and the usual legal formulas, and Herbert was deliberately folding up the instrument, when, with a voice clear and cold as steel, Marian said :

" Read on, sir ! "

" There is nothing more to read, madam ! "

" What ! " she shrieked, " am I left at the mercy of this squaw ? my children delivered over to Indian tenderness ? Give me that instrument ! Let me see if I can not prove to you that Pierre La Moore was more just to me."

She snatched desperately at the hated paper, but Herbert was on his guard, and, drawing it back, placed it again under lock and key, while the room rang with the wretched woman's cries and hysterical laughter. Miannetta advanced and placed in

Herbert's hand to read, a document, which proved to be a deed to a farm on Lake Onondaga, which had been given her by Sam-o-so-nois after her separation from her family. Marian received the assurance from Herbert that to-morrow she should be in possession of a new instrument, by which the highly cultivated farm, with its stock and appurtenances, would be hers —Miannetta's gift. This seemed to rather subdue the ravings of the woman, who had only seen poverty and persecution in the future, and she quietly listened, as Miannetta addressed her—

"Marian Ramsdell, you are troubled about your children; now I hold that to every woman whom God permits to become a mother, there is given an unquestioned right, one which man's cruelty or adverse circumstances may thwart, but can not destroy—the right to nourish, educate and rear her child. I so far sympathise with you, as to think it a cruel act on the part of my husband to leave your children to my care. Rather than bear the weight of complicity in this act on my soul, I will place it in your power to generously care for your children yourself. I will not mock you with an offer of a home under this roof. As to our past relations, Marian, 'let the dead past bury its dead.'"

That night the same roof sheltered both—the noble woman who had so much cause to spurn from her restored threshold the creature who would have driven her forth in the inclement night, if their relations had been reversed; and the woman who shrank humiliated and cowed by the unexpected kindness, from Miannetta's glance.

The next day she received from Miannetta five hundred dollars. With her children she departed, unregretted, from the home on the bluff, where so long she had been undisputed mistress, save for the haunting shadow now quickened into life.

It was almost beyond Marian Ramsdell's comprehension that Miannetta should have thrown a veil over the dishonored brow, where most women would have placed the brand of harlot, compelling her in shame to seek the bread which the man who had ruined her had failed to provide. Alas! that such charity should be so rare. That for a woman, who yields weakly to the allurements of vice, and finds, too late, that men betray, *women* have the least compassion. That, too often, the hand that throws the first stone is the white hand of a sister, in whose soul is not the faintest stirring of that Spirit which prompted the Divine sentence:

"Neither do I condemn *thee;* sin no more."

"Let me abide in shade, I have followed the sequestered and lowly paths during the meridian of my life, and now, in its evening, it is not meet that I should sit upon the mountain top." Miannetta answered, when Eugene proposed her taking her place at the head of the table. This had settled the matter for the present. Later the question was again debated, when she replied:

"I have no ambition but to live with you; I do not wish to assume any responsible position."

"But, mother, we must have some one to pour coffee and do the honors. Since our year of mourning is expired, no doubt Robert will press his suit again;

indeed, he has been very considerate and patient in view of all his disappointments and crosses. For this reason I speak; Annette is as good as gone, you know."

" Well, my son, since you seem so impressed with the importance of a mistress to this house, which is unquestionably yours, I will leave you to settle the matter to your own satisfaction. I like to see you look about with such evident carefulness."

"You are making fun of me, I see ; well, you have had so few things to laugh at, dear mother, that I do not grudge you one smile at my expense. My only desire is to increase the number of your smiles—they become you, mother."

"Thank you, my son."

How bright the lining of a cloud may be, aye, almost dazzling to the eyes of the poor sufferer, who has been so long unconscious of brightness or gloom. Personal loveliness had come to be considered unimportant to Miannetta, but it must be admitted she was gratified at Eugene's affectionate compliment.

Eugene was a cultivated Frenchman, loved to have all his surroundings beautiful, and the face of his precious mother was no exception. His was a refined artistic eye that delighted in harmony, and he loved the beautiful in all the works of nature and her rival art. He admired his mother's dark regal beauty, but I shall show you how he sought to heighten the effect of that beauty by contrast.

Miannetta, though joyous, had still the pensive manner and calm look that long suffering will impart

18*

and indelibly impress upon spirit and brow. Though sometimes she would seem quite gay, yet it was chastened gladness ; she had been bruised upon the remorseless reefs of life's ocean, and though now healed, she was taking from her Father's loving hand, the hand that chastened, the convenient morsel in thankful humility. Her drafts were honored in Canada, cashed in France, but she valued money only as it furnished the means to be gracious and useful.

How much more truly has she earned the meed of lofty womanhood, in patiently accepting the cup of bitterness held to her quivering lips, and draining it without protesting word, than some of her fairer sisters, who, with less than half her sorrow, have haunted divorce courts, with importunate prayers for relief from conjugal infelicities, caused by grievous incompatibilities of temper, that patience and grace perchance might cure.

Many will say that Miannetta ought to have yielded to the mother's intense yearning for her children, and sought to *compel* their father to restore them to her ; that she *should* have sought redress, and not submitted tamely to such treatment. Well, reader, we will not say but what, in spite of the noble resignation and courage which enabled her to live under her sorrows, Miannetta might have yielded to the longing for her children ; but, you must remember, she was only an Indian in the eyes of the law, which provides no redress for such as she.

CHAPTER XXI.

THE WEDDINGS.

ROBERT led Annette to the altar in April, the second following Mr. La Moore's death, a quiet party attending. They were married according to the Roman Catholic ritual—Robert believing that Christian courtesy required so much of his leaning to the faith of Annette. Eugene and Nellie gave countenance to the union by supporting the principals during the solemn ceremony, and accompanying them on their bridal tour through Canada to the sea-board, and thence over the bosom of the Atlantic to New Orleans, and from there, after visiting the battle-field where Robert lost his good right arm, by steam up the Father of Waters, home. By Eugene's account, they, himself and Nellie, were the only ones of the party who reaped any benefit from the long journey.

"Robert and Nettie were so thoroughly absorbed in one another, that they might as well have been on the island of Juan Fernandez," he said.

In fact, the sight-seeing could have been all done by the bridesmaid and best man, and the result for the groom and bride been just the same. Whether it would have been all the same to them, without the tantalizing effects of a constant contemplation of the bliss of the newly wedded pair, is not so clear. Without discussing possible results, we will merely state the fact that Nellie, our pearly Nellie, was changed by that trip. She was not less pearly, but more exquisitely radiant, as if her cheek had been touched by the breezes from the promised land.

It was late in the evening of the balmy May-time when the bridal party disembarked from the steamer at St. P——, and were driven to the residence on the bluff. Before long they had exchanged their traveling dresses for comfortable home suits, and were seated at the sumptuous table awaiting them. It was an informal meal, though luxuries and dainties of every kind tempted their appetites. They were not so hungry as *glad to be home.* Annette declared it " a luxury to preside over a table where ceremony was tabooed and she could pick her own chicken bones."

The business which most interested Pierre being over, namely, the eating, and Josie having pocketed rather more than her share of the dessert, the two exchanged glances. Pierre said " *Oui,*" and they excused themselves. Miannetta, after a little time, begged leave to follow them. As she stood in the lighted hall, unperceived, watching her two youngest children through the open parlor door, Eugene joined her. She put her finger to her lip to enjoin silence, at the same time pointing to Pierre. Her youngest, her hopeful, was seated, or rather, was lying with the small of his back on the edge of a large upholstered arm-chair, in front of the grate, his toes making a desperate effort to cling to the edge of the ornamental mantel above, a large cigar between his second and third fingers, the big end of which was in his mouth. His footing, insecure, was ren-

dered all the more so that his faculties were all con-
centrated in the cigar.

Josie, who was sitting with her back toward him,
examining some fine drawings Eugene had brought
home, becoming impatient because he had not given
any sign of noticing her remark, several times
repeated, with a more·elevated tone of voice, said:

"I believe it is just as certain as 'communion
day' that Eugene and Nellie are going to be married;
don't you?"

No answer; but quite a respectable suggestion of
tobacco smoke.

"Pierre La Moore! are you deaf?"

"Whew! No."

"Well, why don't you answer me?"

"I *am* a shaking my head!"

A shout of laughter from Eugene and his mother
followed, while a pair of very short legs were observed
getting rapidly out of the front door, and a vision of
white ruffles at the same time fluttered up stairs at
such a rate that Eugene shouted:

"Less speed and more stairs, Josie!"

Miannetta, with a happy face, turned to Eugene,
and looking straight into his eyes, said:

"I agree with Josie, Eugene!"

"I agree with Josie, mother," added Eugene.

"I agree with Josie, mother," added Robert, who
came out to see "what was up," that made them
laugh so.

Robert's simple remark seemed to strike Eugene
as very witty, for he was taken again with uncontrollable laughter. Then turning, he said:

"Well, now, since the elder, the sterner, as well as the younger members of the family decide so unanimously upon the probability of my conduct, I should like to gratify them by an immediate fulfillment of their prophecies."

"What is to prevent?" said Miannetta.

"What, indeed?" said Robert, beaming at a possible reflection of his own happiness.

"Perhaps," said Miannetta, "it would be as well to discover the sentiments of another equally interested party."

"And I believe I shall be obliged to inquire what we are talking about," said Robert, who was not quite clear on the subject.

"Suppose we all seek enlightenment," said Eugene, leading the way to the room they recently left, without apparently disturbing the young ladies still sitting at the table from which, however, the cloth had been removed. They did not appear to notice the entrance of the trio; but Nellie's rising color was a true tell-tale, and induced Annette to look from her face up to that of Eugene, who was bending over her chair and whispering to her:

"Nellie, will you pity me?"

"Yes, what for?" she said, laughing.

"That sentiment proverbially leads to—," he stooped and whispered the last word into the pearly ear, and then as Nellie, blushing crimson, turned her tell-tale glances upwards, he said aloud:

"Yours is the task of refining a wayward Frenchman; will you attempt it? Will you be my wife?"

He put his hands each side of her head over the

delicate ears, and drew her face up toward his own. With an expression of unutterable fondness he gazed down into her pure heart through the beautiful azure of her eyes. But I just happen to think it is treason to my favorite Nellie, to tell what she said on that interesting occasion.

A few days afterward another wedding gladdens the heart of Miannetta.

Robert gives away the bride. It is the rich manly voice of Eugene, that says:

" With this ring I thee wed."

And 't is Nellie that lifts a calm and holy brow to the kiss of her adoring husband.

The bells clang out a wedding peal, the sunlight streams through the colored windows, and bathes with a flood of glory the happy twain, made one.

An hour later the same party are passing through the noble hall of the La Moore mansion, toward the large dining-room. Eugene, tall and elegant, with a grace that recalls olden times, leads Nellie to the breakfast table, and crowns her mistress of his magnificent board. All regard her with admiration as, with perfect composure, she performs this house-wifely duty, rather trying, you will admit, this first morning of her wifehood.

Later a carriage drove up to the door drawn by two superb white horses, whose bright coats, rosetted heads, and silver mounted harness, shone brightly in the morning sun. Eugene led the young bride forth, assisted and followed her into the carriage. On the porch, puffy and gracious, stood the old, but still dapper, French butler, Casper, whose services with

the family extended back to the old days, sacred to
the memory of Montfort, and gave him an importance and dignity which the other servants failed to
satisfactorily recognize.   He smiled in answer to the
coachman's saucy bow and wink.   The latter, drawing
himself up pompously on the box, swung his long
whiplash dexterously round, caused the horses to
rear and plunge, then go off with a bound.

Another equally elegant equipage drew up.
Robert and Annette, with more consideration for
other people (but they were old married people now),
paused on the porch talking with Mianetta, Josie and
Pierre.

Robert handed Annette in and took his seat
beside her just as the old family carriage, with trusty
Lavergn on the box, came to the door.   Miannetta
and her two younger children were soon seated, and
Lavergn, as Pierre insisted he should do—

"Gave the horses their heads!"

That young gentleman was delighted to see that
they held their own well with the "new spankers"
Eugene had just purchased, and were as often ahead
as behind in that week's journey.

It was night when the three carriages rolled up
the fine drive under the grand old maples, where we
have been so often, and so delight to be.   The house
is brilliantly lighted up and all is in perfect readiness
to receive them, even to proud little Freddie Palmer.
Uncle Carce and grandma, Mr. and Mrs. Ellis have
come over to welcome home the young people,
whom they love as their own.   Every eye is wet
when Robert leads his beautiful wife to the table, and

seats her where his mother sat. It is the law of life to forget the old loves in the new, but by the momentary pallor of his cheek, we know that his thoughts, even in this moment of supreme happiness, revert to his mother.

Later in the evening, Mr. McDougal led Nellie to the piano, and was rewarded with his favorite air, rendered with a sweetness and feeling which charmed the quiet Scotchman. His eyes glistened with a tender light as the gentle musician sang:

"It's hame, and it's hame, and it's hame I fane wad be;
O hame, hame, hame to my ain countrie;
There's an e'e that ever weeps, and a fair face will be fain,
As I pass through Annan water wi' my bonny band again.
When the flower is i' the bud, and the leaf upo' the tree,
The lark shall sing me hame in my ain countrie."

Afterwards Robert and she sang and played the dear old—

"Home again, home again from a distant shore."

Then Annette played some fine pieces, and sang with Eugene some beautiful French airs; and the house rang with the music of their fine voices.

After the music the two brides withdrew and returning in a few minutes, crossed the room gracefully together, each bearing in her hand a vase.

"York true to York, and Lancaster to Lancaster," said Mr. McDougal, as the two distinctly contrasting types of beauty advanced and presented to Mrs. McDougal the vases, that had been her mother's "Lang Syne."

After this the evening wore on pleasantly, en-
livened by the bright chit chat of the ladies (remember Mrs. Ellis and grandma Smith are of the party),
and apt retort follows sally briskly, while merry
laughter succeeds to both. Now the gentlemen of
the party seem to be drawing together, attracted by
the tendency to politics, which some one has infused
into their talk. As the gay voices of the ladies are
now subdued, that they may listen to the views which
they know will be well put and forcibly maintained;
we will listen too, and hear what our friends have to
say.

'T is our frank and impulsive Eugene that speaks,
evidently in reply to some remark of Robert's, which
we have failed to catch—

"I will agree to do all that work for you, Rob,
till your arm grows out again. I confess that empty
sleeve of yours is a perpetual reproach to me, remind-
ing me as often as I look upon it that I had no share
in the double glory attaching to the humblest soldier,
who has earned, not only the fame of well-fought
battles, on victorious fields, but the still nobler merit
of having aided to demolish the edifice of slavery
that so long shamed the Union."

"I believe I can fully appreciate your regret in
having had no share in the war," said Mr. McDougal.
"It must be a great satisfaction to feel that you have
participated in the perils and sacrifices of a struggle,
whose results are for all time. Lincoln died at a
moment most opportune for his fame. He had accomplished great things, and fell with his grandeur
undimmed by any commonplace statesmanship."

"It is a satisfaction to those who have lost their limbs in the war, that the sacrifice has not been in vain. Blood has been poured out and human life laid down upon the altar of our country, and great is the result," said Robert. "There is no merit in claiming to feel indifferent to the honor of having shared in the sacrifices entailed by the war. I lost my limb in a struggle that destroyed a monument of oppression, for slavery did not pass away by the slow process of inherent decay, but by a sublime stroke, which we must recognize as legitimately God's act."

"And Lincoln, as God's agent, for that stroke lies to-day in a martyr's grave," said Capt. Ellis. "I sometimes almost lose myself in contemplating the numerous results of the war. It is scarcely six years since we heard the first premonitory murmur of a gathering tempest. Men were doubtful if it would come, and read differently the handwriting on the wall. Time sped on, and though the heaven was angry with storms, yet in its lightning flashes we saw new ideas that dazzled us, in the thunder we felt old institutions crumbling. Through all we heard a mysterious moaning. It was the future, pregnant with the destiny of a race. Six years, and the cloud, no larger than a man's hand, has enveloped our sky with gloom, and again has rolled away. In this time a republic has proven to a doubting world that she is self-sustaining, that she is powerful to quiet her internal dissensions and subdue domestic strife."

"Lincoln died at an hour when his glory was brightest, for his public acts were graduated, the greatest, the emancipation of the negro," said Robert. "But if he could have lived to accomplish the work of reconstruction, before the expiration of his second term, our position would have been the grandest in the galaxy of nations."

"I agree with you," said uncle Carce, "that the emancipation was the greatest. Of his other public acts I generally approve, but *one* of them was unworthy. I did think of him as among men the most perfect, till he declined to punish the larger portion of the cruel murderers of my neighbors, until he exempted the Indians, fairly tried and condemned, of the doom their wicked deeds had incurred. In that act there was no justice. He seemed to say to the outraged people of Minnesota, Whatever the court-martial may have determined—though murder and other crimes may be laid by them at the red man's door ; though the frontiersman may tremble in fear, *I*, sitting secure in my high place, think it best to reverse the decision of the military commission, and give these Indians another chance. Even Lincoln was not superior to the conservatism that clings to power. He was unjust to Minnesota, and we shall have another deluge of blood to pay for the commutation of the death sentence at Mankato."

"I do not altogether agree with you, uncle Carce," returned Capt. Ellis. "Lincoln's course with the convicted Indians was in perfect accord with the humane policy with which he prosecuted the war. He followed the precedent of other nations in the execution of a percentage of the condemned, the thirty-six hanged at Mankato. He aimed to destroy the walls of prejudice against color and condition of the negro and the Indian. His efforts opened our eyes, as the eyes of the Egyptians were opened, to a recognition of universal brotherhood. But through the whirlwind of battle, amid the conflicting doubts of other statesmen, he walked stately and slow, with right for his guiding star, 'God for his judge, and history for his vindication.'"

· "Your figures are very nice, neighbor," said uncle Carce, "but how in the name of all that's sensible can brotherhood be established between the whites who have been so cruelly wronged and those savage wretches over the border, who committed those wrongs and are watching a chance to repeat them?"

"By brotherly integrity, by education and enlightenment," was the pleasant reply. "No doubt it was Lincoln's policy to revolutionize the whole Indian system; to impose laws and their wholesome restraints upon the savages, who, with all the national beneficences, have never realized that most desirable one of good government. You have expressed the sentiment that wickedness never goes backward, and it is true. The tendency of the unregenerate human heart, when left to itself, is toward evil. The Indians have gone down so low that goodness *per se* is a mere tradition. The age requires that they should be brought to a recognition of it."

"Now you are getting upon firm ground," said uncle Carce, approvingly. "We can cross palms on that sentiment. But we shall never bring them to practical goodness without holding them in fear of penalties when they outrage its principles. If, as often as they commit crime, they are turned loose upon the frontier without a reprimand, how are they to know good from evil? How shall they be brought to this recognition?"

"By the process of reason. The light of education and religion may be made to illume even the Indian system; to flood with its glory the recesses of the forest," said Capt. Ellis, earnestly.

"Would you apply such fine ideas to a race so low in the scale of being that they balance human life with a pair of stolen moccasins? whose deserts would be met if you loosed the hurricane and swept them them from the earth they cumber?" said the old gentleman, with a curling lip and eyes aflame, while his voice grew harsh with contempt.

"I would insist that enlightenment is possible where there is reason enough to weigh," replied Captain Ellis. "You must acknowledge it a grade above the brute, though the scales may be unfairly adjusted. Where tornadoes are most frequent, the shore is strewn with wreck. Hurricanes are not discriminating. They sweep away much more than rubbish; and if employed to purify the air *every* year, and to eradicate *every* evil, how soon would our land become a charnel-house of ruin! Reform is slow and tedious; as in agriculture, the soil must be prepared for the seed."

"Sometimes," said uncle Carce, smiling. "You remember that, by reason of deep dry sand, even agriculture is not triumphant; and if you find the intellect of the Indian very far below the surface— too far for the certain germination of your seed— *then* what would you do?"

"Excavate and unfetter it," was the reply.

"Your plan is too Quixotic!" said uncle Carce. "It entails an enormous expense of treasure and blood; besides, it has been tried."

. "Not thoroughly," continued Captain Ellis.

"Yes, so thoroughly as to have proved itself a failure," said uncle Carce.

"I do not agree with you," was the reply. "I could show you some marked success!"

"Not in Minnesota, captain! and I am too much of a home body to travel out of the State to see them; but I can cite you a *failure* within twenty-five miles," said uncle Carce. "I have seen the effort and the failure. 'I speak that I do know.' Civilization would have gathered the Indians under her wing long ago, but they would not. The government has made prodigious expenditure for their elevation, while paying them generously for their land. They have been offered every inducement to abandon their tribal relations, and to remain and participate in its cultivation and advantages. Churches have been built and schools established for their enlightenment. Thousands of acres of productive lands have been broken, fenced and seeded; farm houses and barns have been built and furnished with every comfort; teams and stock and agricultural implements abundantly furnished. With a fraction of these opportunities, the uneducated of our own race, both native and foreign-born, have by industry and thrift established themselves and added to our national greatness; while the Indians, with a few noble exceptions, have treated with contempt the effort made for them. They have

allowed their golden harvest to fall back into the
earth ; the soil, for want of culture, to run again to
foul waste. The comfortable homes have been abandoned for the smoky tepee. The advantages of society have been voluntarily exchanged for the wild life
of the wilderness. As the march of empire has
advanced, leveling forests, locating farms and building cities, they have slowly and sullenly retired from
the great good they were invited to share ; turning,
now and then, like some wild beast at bay, and raising
their red, dripping hands, have cried : 'No farther
shalt thou come, save through rivers of blood!'
Come, now, can you deny that they are radically
unworthy of further effort ? that all fraternal attempts
are simply a waste of pearls ? How, in the face of
these evidences of utter moral depravity and base-
ness, can you swing round to your ideas of final
enlightenment and elevation ? "

"Very easily !" was the reply ; " but, in the first
place, allow me to say that it is a false philosophy
that scoffs at the natural integrity of the human
heart. I deny that the Indians are *naturally* depraved
or worthless. (I must have the benefit of this position,
or decline the argument.) That they are so, practically, is wholly circumstantial, and largely owing to
the fact that they are capital imitators, and their
patterns are too often the most depraved and worthless of the Anglo-Saxon race. You can not deny the
fact that their first acquaintance with white men is
often with the basest of that race, unprincipled, ignorant traders, or refugees from justice, who, banished
from society, have crept into their wigwams and

wormed themselves into their confidence. Even their language is a reproach to ours, for they are obliged to resort to plagiarism to express disrespect of the the Great Spirit. Blasphemy in the Indian tongue is impossible. Missionaries are met with this question : 'Is this Jesus you preach about, the same Jesus that the white men talk to when they are angry or drunk?' Does not this, of itself, show that their impiety is a reflection of our own? You were frank enough to acknowledge some noble exceptions to the general worthlessness of the Indian character, and there can be no question as to their preponderance when such white men as Charles Center and George Langmere are placed in the scales with those noble aborigines— Wabashaw and Taopi.

" Go back in history, and in the gloom that envelops the overthrown columns of the Syrian desert, the monuments of Egypt, you will find among the monsters there, forms of majesty and worth. Through the darkness of crime and bloodshed may be seen gleams of the light of truth, that needed only cultivation. Though men were debased till they revelled in the false, the foul, the blasphemous—yet better instincts remained. Can you find among the North American Indians, a living picture that will compare with the imbruted sons of Rome, rioting in eternal orgies, consciously wallowing in foulest crime. History tells us they intoxicated themselves with human blood to drown despair. Yet even they were lifted out of their darkness, reeking with corruption, into the light of day. The Sun of Christianity rose, healing, purifying, and elevating. The tide of cor-

ruption was arrested.   Men abjured their heathen
gods, and knelt at the foot of the Cross.   The annals
of the world show the God-worshipping instinct of the
human race, that leads them to the true and the good,
when guided aright, and exposed to no contaminating
influence.   But they who presume to guide must
themselves be controlled by lofty integrity—an integrity which teaches faith in humanity and God.

"Now what influences are brought to bear most
powerfully upon the Indians?   Does the sale of ardent spirits teach them sobriety?   Do the licentious
practices of white men, traders and agents, teach
them virtue and fidelity?   Does the recklessness and
indifference to human life upon the frontier, teach
them its worth?   Does the system of extortion and
fraud practiced unblushingly, aye, even boastingly,
upon them, teach them honesty?   Does shameless
blasphemy and high-handed impiety teach them the
love of God?   Because, heretofore, success has been
the exception, failure the rule, we should not despair,
but calmly criticize the system.   We claim to be a
wise and magnanimous people; we contribute largely
to foreign missions, but are we taking the course that
will enable us to answer unembarrassed the great
question : 'Where is thy brother, thy wayward
brother, whom men called Ishmael?'   We have a
peculiar people upon our hands, for whose weal we
are responsible to God.   A race too noble to live in
slavery is certainly deserving of some consideration.
No doubt the Indian can dimly see that happiness
and prosperity are the result of a certain routine of
schools and toil.   That they are efficient as motives,

without being definitely understood by the white masses, but the character of that happiness and the routine necessary to its attainment, repels him. He can not bear the restraint of school, because he is Nature's out-door child. He despises books, because they imply restraint. Society and its laws are the modern schoolhouses and restraints on a larger scale, and he spurns them royally, as he would the slave-coffle and the lash. I have a conviction that the failure to Christianize and educate the Indians lies in part in the clock-work regularity and order of the system, that whatever would violate its uniformity would give it impetus. If this conviction is true, no doubt time will make it apparent to educators and reformers, and change will come. I believe that we shall see that this race, now so ignoble, is capable of much ; that they are able to think, to act, to rule, and above all to love ; that with the negro they may occupy equal ground with us on the great platform of humanity."

"Well I shall feel the less regret then when Gabriel blows his horn," said uncle Carce, shaking his head and laughing.

"Oh, this may not be in your time. It may be an hundred years," said Capt. Ellis, " before the rosy light just glimmering in the East, the fresh light of the new reformatory age, shall from noon-day heights illuminate the glens and forests of the West. But as certainly as the barbarians rose to the level of Christian manhood, so certainly must elevation of the Indian follow the *right effort* of a superior race, to fulfill the duties enjoined by a just and impartial God."

" Well, suppose we adjourn the argument till to-morrow, when I will agree to commence at you and talk till all is blue," said uncle Carce, rising and pointing to Eugene, who, it was observed, was con-sulting his watch.

" Late, is it?" said Capt. Ellis, observing for the first time, that the ladies had all retired.

" O no," said Eugene, " it is *early*, not quite one o'clock ; and Rob is actually fast asleep."

The gentlemen had soon followed the example of the ladies, and the house was so still that only the angels seemed to be guarding the Maples.

Miannetta, who, instead of going to her own room, had been sitting long beside her husband's grave, entered the moonlit parlor noiselessly. The piano was still open, and seating herself before it, wrapped in her own thoughts, she almost unconsciously exe-cuted a skillful prelude ; then evolving from the chords an impassioned accompaniment, her magnifi-cent soprano, that for years had been dumb, poured out upon the silent night, the anthem :

"Glory to God in the highest, and on earth peace, good will toward men."

THE END.

www.ingramcontent.com/pod-product-compliance
Lightning Source LLC
Chambersburg PA
CBHW030942110726
47900CB00004B/1094